**Praise for Melonie Johnson and *Getting
Hot with the Scot***

'A fun, sexy, and delightful read!"
  —*New York Times* bestselling author Julie James

'Unabashedly sexy and romantic, Melonie Johnson's debut is a fabulous read!"
  —*USA Today* bestselling author Kate Meader

"*Getting Hot with the Scot* is a wild romp, a ton of fun,
and a new addition to my favorites shelf!"
  —*New York Times* bestselling author
  Christina Lauren

Also by Melonie Johnson

Getting Hot with the Scot

SMITTEN BY THE BRIT

Melonie Johnson

St. Martin's Paperbacks

This is a work of fiction. All of the characters, organizations, and events portrayed in this novel are either products of the author's imagination or are used fictitiously.

SMITTEN BY THE BRIT

Copyright © 2019 by Melonie Johnson.

For information address St. Martin's Press, 175 Fifth Avenue, New York, NY 10010.

ISBN: 978-1-250-19305-6

Our books may be purchased in bulk for promotional, educational, or business use. Please contact the Macmillan Corporate and Premium Sales Department at 1-800-221-7945, ext. 5442, or by email at MacmillanSpecialMarkets@macmillan.com.

Printed in the United States of America

St. Martin's Paperbacks edition / May 2019

St. Martin's Paperbacks are published by St. Martin's Press, 175 Fifth Avenue, New York, NY 10010.

10 9 8 7 6 5 4 3 2 1

For my two redheads
I cherish being a part of your story and am so grateful
you are both a part of mine
I love you even more than I embarrass you, which we all
know is a lot
(I'm probably embarrassing you right now with this
dedication)
Always, Mom

CHAPTER 1

BONNIE BLYTHE HOVERED near the tall windows, nursing her cocktail and watching the lights from the Navy Pier Ferris wheel twinkle in the fading spring twilight. It was a romantic moment, one she should have been enjoying with Gabe, except her fiancé wasn't here. As was so often the case lately, her significant other was significantly absent.

Gabe had promised he'd accompany her tonight, but then begged off at the last minute. His PhD adviser had called and requested another meeting, and as Bonnie well knew, all things related to Gabe's dissertation came first. Thank God he was almost done with grad school, so they could focus on other things—like finally deciding on a wedding date.

The reminder of her prolonged engagement had Bonnie knocking back the rest of her drink. The bittersweet sting of alcohol burned her throat and warmed her belly, but did nothing to loosen the knot of frustration in her gut. She set her empty glass on the window ledge and adjusted her crown of flowers, fingers tingling. She never could hold her liquor. A source of eternal amusement for her Irish cousins, one drink was often enough to do her in.

Right now, she could go for a little bit of doing in. She was Ophelia without her Hamlet, so why not drown her sorrows in another cocktail? Bonnie turned away from the wall of windows and headed for the bar, attention focused on the trailing ends of her gauzy dress as she dodged Romeos and Juliets, Oberons and Titanias, Henrys and Falstaffs. The foyer of the Chicago Shakespeare Theater was stuffed with a menagerie of the namesake playwright's characters.

Each April, the company held a gala in honor of the bard's birthday, and this year's event was a costume ball. Bonnie had been looking forward to the gala for months, ever since her best friend, Cassie, invited her to attend. As a broadcast journalist covering stories for the local morning show, *ChiChat*, Cassie often scored tickets to the city's hottest events. Fresh drink in hand, Bonnie surveyed the room, looking for any sign of her friend. A flash of plaid caught her eye, and Bonnie grinned. *Of course*. She headed toward the couple lingering in a quiet corner.

"Bonnie!" Cassie exclaimed, pushing away from the man she'd been canoodling with. "I was wondering when you'd get here."

"Oh, I've been here awhile, but I think your attention was elsewhere." Bonnie nodded at the tall auburn-haired man standing next to Cassie. "Hello, Logan. Let me guess . . ." She pointed at the kilt he was wearing. "Macbeth?"

"And Lady Macbeth." Cassie held up her hands. "What do you think? Is it too much?"

Bonnie considered her friend's palms, dyed a grisly red. "I think you both look perfect."

"Aye. Well, I already had the kilt, you ken." Logan

winked. "And seeing as how the first time we met, I was accused of talking like a—what was it you called me, love?" he asked Cassie, a mischievous smile playing about his lips.

"A Macbeth reject." Cassie shook her head. "You're never going to let me forget about that, are you?"

Logan pulled Cassie close. "Neverrr," he growled against her neck, his Scottish burr a low purr that likely had every female in hearing distance perking up. Even Bonnie wasn't immune to the Scot, though she enjoyed his charm on a purely spectator level.

Not that it mattered. Logan only had eyes for Cassie.

Which was as it should be. Since he was engaged to her best friend, Bonnie would punch Logan in the sporran herself if she ever caught the Scot checking out another "lass." But Bonnie couldn't imagine such a thing happening. She knew how much Logan loved Cassie, had watched their romance blossom from the start—she'd even had a hand in bringing them together. Though, she hadn't expected their relationship to progress *quite* so quickly. Cassie and Logan had gotten engaged this past New Year's and had already set the date for their wedding in early August, on the one-year anniversary of the day they met.

Yep, Bonnie had been engaged for over a year to a guy she'd been with since middle school, and *still* didn't have a wedding date. Meanwhile, Cassie and Logan were getting married in less than four months.

Nope, she wasn't bitter. Or, at least, she was trying very hard not to be. Bonnie was truly happy for the couple and was genuinely excited to be Cassie's maid of honor. It's just when Cassie asked Bonnie her opinion on invitations or dresses or, well, anything wedding-related, Bonnie sometimes (okay, all the time) felt the sting of envy. They should be planning *her* wedding. But it was hard to send out invitations when you didn't know when or where to invite the guests.

Gabe said he wanted to get school over with, to have this final piece of his academic life wrapped up before starting the next stage. Bonnie understood. Mostly. But she and Gabe had been together for so long, she wanted to get on with the next step of her life. What was the big deal if they started planning the wedding before or after he finished the last leg of what had felt like a marathon?

She'd been by Gabe's side every step of the way, and though Bonnie may not have been the one running the race, she'd sacrificed much to help her runner reach his goals. She'd waited this long, she could wait a little longer. It was almost May. By this time next month, Gabe would be finished with his final semester of grad school.

Soon, she'd be applauding, bursting with pride as Gabe walked down the aisle and accepted his degree. She couldn't wait to call him Dr. Gabriel Shaughnessy. Couldn't wait to write it on their wedding invitations and finally, *finally*, walk down the aisle herself and become Mrs. Dr. Gabriel Shaughnessy.

"Where's Gabe?" Cassie asked, breaking into Bonnie's thoughts.

"He had a meeting with his adviser."

"Another one?" Her best friend frowned, brown eyes shadowed with concern. "On a Friday night?"

"The dissertation presentation is coming up soon, and they're working out the final kinks." Bonnie shrugged. "His adviser often calls on evenings and weekends."

"What a wanker," Logan said. Cassie slapped him on the arm but didn't correct him.

Bonnie wasn't sure if Logan meant Gabe or his adviser. Either way, she rather agreed with the Scot. She took a swig of her cocktail. Her glass was almost empty again.

The second one had gone down much smoother—and faster—than the first. Bonnie glanced toward the bar and considered seeing how a third would fare.

Following the line of her gaze, Logan flashed a grin. "Shall I fetch you a wee bevy to wash your cares away?"

"Sure. A Manhattan, please." She couldn't remember the last time she'd had three drinks in one night, but right now she didn't care.

"And for you, lass?" Logan turned to Cassie. "Dark and Stormy?"

"Perfect." Cassie went on tiptoe and kissed his cheek, fingers tugging on a lock of red hair as she whispered, "You know how I love ginger."

The Scot lowered his eyes, now hooded with lust. "Aye, I do." He bent toward Cassie, tilting his face so her lips trailed across his cheek and met his mouth. Sexual tension radiated between the two of them.

Bonnie flushed, looking away from the happy couple. Jealousy clawed at her insides, and she fought against the green-eyed monster. Of course, Cassie and Logan's relationship seemed fresh and exciting . . . they'd only met last summer. *But when's the last time Gabe looked at you like that? Or kissed you that way? With such raw hunger. Such need. Has he ever?* Bonnie swallowed the last of her drink and cleared her throat. "On second thought, maybe I should call it a night."

"No! You can't leave yet." Cassie slipped out of Logan's embrace and grabbed Bonnie's arm. "There's something I want to talk to you about."

Bonnie suppressed a groan; she was not up for discussing her friend's wedding plans tonight. "Can it wait?"

"I guess, but you may not get another chance to meet her."

"Meet who?"

"The lady from Cambridge."

"Explain," Bonnie ordered, pulse racing. What was Cassie up to?

"I'll see to those drinks, aye?" Logan excused himself, not at all subtle about being grateful for the opportunity to escape.

"Cassie," Bonnie warned, "spill."

"Well, one of the people I interviewed for the next segment of *Coming Out of the Book Closet* is a faculty member at Cambridge."

"Cambridge University, as in the UK?"

"Uh, yeah. And we got to talking and . . ." Cassie paused, attention drifting past Bonnie to scan the room.

"And?" Bonnie prompted.

"And she wants you to teach a seminar."

"What?"

"Six weeks." Cassie started to tap her chin but stopped, cringing at her bloody finger. "Or maybe eight, I can't remember."

"Here? In the city?"

Cassie shook her head. "In England. Some kind of Shakespeare intensive the university runs every summer. One of this year's guest instructors had to cancel, and they're on the hunt for a replacement. Of course, I thought of you. I told her about the adaptation you did of that fairy play a few years ago, and she loved it. Said she couldn't wait to meet you."

"She did?" Bonnie's head felt fuzzy. "What's the catch?"

"No catch." Cassie tugged on her arm. "There they are. Come on, just talk to her, okay?"

Before Bonnie could protest further, Cassie had dragged her across the room to where a short, stout Julius Caesar stood next to a statuesque Cleopatra, his crown of laurel leaves barely reaching her toga-clad bosom.

"Cassie Crow!" Cleopatra exclaimed in a throaty, cultured voice. "Please tell me your lovely companion is the talented lady I've heard so much about."

"Barbara." Cassie returned the hug, careful not to let her stained fingers mar the woman's white gown. "I'd like you to meet Bonnie Blythe."

"A pleasure." Cleopatra clasped Bonnie's hand. "Delighted to make your acquaintance, my dear."

Her smile was regal yet warm, and Bonnie relaxed, instantly drawn to the woman.

"Has Cassie mentioned the summer seminar to you?"

Bonnie's moment of calm collapsed. "Ah, briefly." *Very briefly.* She swallowed, wondering where Logan was with that third drink.

Cleopatra continued the introductions, turning toward the man at her side. "Philip, this is Cassie Crow, the young lady from the telly studio, and her friend Bonnie Blythe." Cleopatra—Barbara—paused for the man to greet them. As he bent forward to kiss Cassie's and Bonnie's hands, she told them, "Professor Newton is a fellow academic director."

"You'll be joining our merry little band this summer, eh?" the professor asked, adjusting his laurel wreath, which had slipped down his forehead, snagging on a pair of bushy brows.

"To be honest, sir," Bonnie hedged, checking to make sure her own floral crown was still in place as she tried not to stare at the man's eyebrows, which hovered above his sharp, bright eyes, quivering like a pair of restless ferrets.

"Please, call me Philip."

"Philip," Bonnie obliged before continuing, "I don't know if I'm qualified for Cambridge." She was only an associate professor who directed the occasional theatre production at a small liberal arts college. She had her master's, yes . . . but this was *Cambridge*.

"Oh, pish-posh." He waved his hand dismissively. "We have all the stodgy old scholars like myself we could possibly need."

"And if it makes you feel better," Barbara added, "this isn't the university precisely. It's Ice."

"Nice?" Bonnie repeated.

"ICE," Philip corrected. "Institute of Continuing Education. An international outreach program." His eyes widened with excitement, making the ferrets jump. "We want—we need—fresh blood."

"Please, Philip, you make us sound like a troupe of vampires." Barbara shook her head, black bob wig swinging, full ruby mouth pursed in repressed amusement. "What he means to say is, the summer program is a chance to explore new ideas." She laid a jeweled hand on Bonnie's arm. "We want people who've proven they can think outside the box."

"Oh, that's definitely Bonnie." Cassie beamed at her with pride.

Bonnie tried to return her friend's smile as her stomach rode the elevator down to her slippers. She knew Cassie was only trying to help, and at any other time, she'd be over the moon to have this opportunity. "I'm flattered," Bonnie said, "really, I am. But I don't think I could afford it right now." The European vacation she and Cassie had taken last summer with their best buds from college, the same vacation where Cassie met Logan, had drained what little savings Bonnie had. She'd scrimped and saved for five years to make that trip happen, there was no way she could go back to England so soon. Besides, she *hopefully* had a wedding to pay for in the near future.

"My dear, let me assure you on that score." Barbara

waved her arm, bangles jangling. "Room and board are provided."

"Yes, yes," Philip chimed in. "And in addition to your salary, a stipend to cover residuals such as travel expenses is provided as well."

"See?" Cassie grabbed her hand and squeezed it. "What do you think?"

"Uh . . ." Bonnie took in the three faces smiling at her expectantly, "I think I need to use the restroom," she said, struggling to keep her voice calm and polite as her heart hopped on the elevator to join her stomach. "If you'll excuse me."

Tucking herself into a stall, Bonnie took several deep breaths. The space was too tiny to allow for pacing, so she turned in a tight circle, careful not to let her dress fall in the toilet. *Why? Why did this have to happen now?*

At any other time in her life, she'd have jumped at the opportunity. Teaching Shakespeare, even only for a few weeks, at a school like Cambridge would be a dream come true. But this summer was supposed to be the summer another dream finally came true. She was supposed to be planning her wedding, not running off to England for two months.

"No offense, but how much longer you gonna be in there?" An irate South Side accent demanded from the other side of the stall.

Is forever an option? But when South Side began pounding on the door, Bonnie knew she needed to get out of there. She flushed the toilet for appearance's sake and opened the stall, coming face-to-face with an irritated-looking witch. Bonnie slipped past the girl, offering her an apologetic smile. Leaning against the wall, waiting in line, were two more witches, looking equally annoyed. "The Weird Sisters, huh?"

The girls glared at her. *Right*.

Before she found herself in double toil and trouble, Bonnie washed her hands and made a hasty exit. She hurried through the restroom door, careening straight into a solid wall of suit-covered muscle. "Oof!" she exhaled, stumbling as her floral crown flopped down over her eyes and icy liquid splashed across her chest.

"Sorry!" a smooth male voice apologized, his British accent slicing the *r*'s into a crisp *d* sound.

Bonnie froze. She recognized that voice, knew that polished British accent. Heart beating faster, Bonnie lifted her chin, trying to peek through the tangle of flowers currently blinding her. Warm fingers brushed her forehead, and a moment later she could see . . . straight into a pair of familiar blue eyes fringed with sinfully long, sooty lashes.

"Theo!" she sputtered. "What are you doing here?"

"At the moment?" He set his now-empty glass on a passing server's tray and reached up to adjust her crown, gently freeing a flower ensnarled in her mass of curls. "Assisting you." Theo grinned, twin dimples appearing in his cheeks.

A fluttering sensation tickled the backs of her knees, and she swayed.

"Are you quite all right?" he asked, holding her by the shoulders and steadying her.

"Me? I'm fine, totally fine," she babbled, wishing she'd gone home when she'd had the chance. Why hadn't Cassie mentioned Theo was coming tonight? She had to know he would be here; Logan was his best friend.

In fact, it was through Logan that Bonnie had met Theo in the first place while in London last summer, on a supper cruise along the Thames. It was a meeting she was unlikely to forget, even though she'd been trying very hard to do just that ever since. Tall, dark, and handsome, not to mention that accent, Theo embodied every Austen hero Bonnie had ever crushed on. And she'd crushed on several.

Meanwhile, her friend Ana, who'd also been on the supper cruise that night on the Thames, had christened Theo "Prince Eric." It was an apt moniker. With his cap of thick black hair, soulful blue eyes, and easy smile, the Brit did look like the cartoon prince come to life.

"Who are you supposed to be?" Bonnie took a closer look at the get-up Theo was presently sporting and smiled. Maybe he wasn't a prince, but he looked like someone noble . . . "A duke?"

He breathed in sharply. "Pardon?"

"Your costume." She gestured at the formal sash and medallion decorating his chest. "I'm guessing Orsino, maybe? From *Twelfth Night*?"

"Oh, right. Orsino. Exactly." He exhaled, shoulders visibly relaxing beneath the tailored cut of his coat. "If music be the food of love . . ."

"Play on." She finished the line, beaming up at him. Their eyes met, and just as she had last summer, Bonnie felt an irresistible pull. Well, not *literally* irresistible—she had managed to resist him, after all. Faithful to her fiancé, Bonnie might not be able to control how her body reacted to the dashing Brit, but she could control what she did about it. Which was nothing.

She pulled back, breaking their gaze and pushing another wayward curl out of her face. "Can you guess who I am?"

"Hmm," he murmured, "I'd wager on Ophelia." He looked her over slowly from floral-crowned head to slippered feet. "Going for the Millais version, I see."

"Very good." *He knew Millais? Impressive. Cute* and

smart. Oh, her willpower was going to get a workout to-night.

"You like Millais's work?" He pulled a handkerchief from his pocket and offered it to her.

"No, I *love* his work. And Waterhouse too." She sighed and accepted the handkerchief, dabbing at the alcohol soaking the bodice of her dress. A memory flashed through her. "I once tried to recreate his painting of *The Lady of Shallot.*"

"You paint?"

"No." She laughed. "Not well, anyway. I acted it out. I'd read about a girl doing that in a book and wanted to give it a try." It wasn't the first or the last time Bonnie tried to copy a scene from *Anne of Green Gables*. She believed Anne Shirley to be her literary doppelgänger and cast her best friend, Cassie, as Anne's bosom buddy, Diana Barry. Luckily, unlike the boat Anne borrows from Diana in the book, the inflatable raft Bonnie borrowed from Cassie hadn't sprung a leak.

Theo shook his head. "What is it with you and watery tarts?"

"Are you quoting Monty Python at me?"

He pulled a serious face. "I'm simply concerned about your apparent obsession with strange women lying in ponds."

She tittered. Oh God, she actually tittered. Bonnie winced. She dropped her gaze and dabbed harder at the dark stain spreading across the front of her dress. "The painting is so beautiful, so ethereal . . . even a copy of it in a book brings the magic of Tennyson's poem to life. I wanted to live that magic." She was rambling but couldn't seem to stop. Her brain went on sabbatical whenever the Brit was near. *That's it, Ophelia, time to get thee to a nunnery.*

"They *are* beautiful," he murmured.

She glanced up to find him staring at her chest.

"Excuse me?" Bonnie stopped dabbing. *Was he talking about her breasts?*

"Did you see them at the Tate?" His blue eyes met hers, coal black brows arched with polite curiosity. "When you were in London last summer?"

The paintings. Right. She shook her head. "We did the Victoria and Albert Museum instead."

"Shame." He sounded truly disappointed. "There's another Millais at the Tate, of a different Tennyson poem. Based on one of Shakespeare's comedies. Do you know the one I mean?"

"Please," she scoffed. "Is this a quiz? Mariana, from *Measure for Measure*." She handed him back his handkerchief, now a little worse for wear. "Though I could never think of that play as a comedy."

"The lady knows Shakespeare, poets, painters . . . and even Monty Python." He blew a soft whistle. "My, you are quite cultured for an American."

A hum of awareness threaded through her, and she tamped it down. "Are you complimenting me or insulting my country?"

He didn't reply, but the corners of his mouth curled with amusement, one dimple coming out to play.

The backs of her knees immediately began to prickle again. *Damn it.* Why couldn't the Brit have stayed on his side of the pond? "What brings you to Chicago? Aside from visiting your Scottish bestie, that is."

"Speaking of, where is the devil? He was supposed to meet me here." Theo glanced around the packed room.

Bonnie didn't miss how he'd avoided answering her question. The evasive maneuver reminded her she still had no idea what Theo did for a living. He'd been very secretive about his job when they'd first met him in London. At the time, Cassie had even teased Theo about being a spy. Bonnie narrowed her eyes, considering. The man did drive a car that looked like something straight out of an old James Bond film. She leaned closer and whispered, "Are you here on a mission?"

He stepped back, blue eyes going wide, in confusion or surprise, Bonnie wasn't sure. Her breath caught. She'd been kidding, but could he really be a secret agent?

"Bonnie! There you are!" Cassie glided through the crowd. "Where have you been?" She came to an abrupt halt. "And what the hell happened to your dress?"

"That was my fault," Theo confessed, adorable in his guilt. "Terribly sorry."

Cassie paused in her survey of the damage to Bonnie's bodice. "Theo?" she asked, doing a double take as she recognized the man standing behind Bonnie. "Hey!" She pulled him in for a quick hug, then added, "No offense, but what are you doing here?"

Exactly what I want to know. Bonnie joined her friend in staring up at the Brit.

Theo swallowed, clearly flustered and looking more adorable than ever.

Before he could muster an answer, Logan joined them, drinks in hand. "Theo! How's my best man?"

That's right. Bonnie should have made the connection before. As Logan's best friend, of course Theo would be the Scot's best man. But that still didn't explain why he was here in Chicago right now. While the two men exchanged greetings, Bonnie pulled Cassie aside. "Why didn't you tell me Theo was coming tonight?"

"Obviously because I didn't know." Cassie paused, dark eyes assessing. "Is there a problem?"

"Of course not." Bonnie glanced down, avoiding her

best friend's shrewd gaze. She couldn't hide anything from Cassie. She swiped at the stain on her bodice and muttered dramatically, "Out, damned spot! Out, I say!"

"Hey, that's my line." Cassie laughed, then stopped and looked to Bonnie for confirmation. "It is, right?"

"Yes, that's Lady Macbeth's line." Bonnie agreed, grateful her distraction had worked. "Look, I really should head home."

"What about your Manhattan?" Cassie gestured at the martini glass Logan was holding.

Bonnie shook her head. A third cocktail no longer seemed like such a good idea. "Since I'm wearing Theo's drink, let him have mine." She braced herself, expecting an argument.

But Cassie only sighed. "If you say so." She bent her head closer. "But don't think I don't know why you're escaping. And you're not off the hook. While he's in town, I'd like us all to get together. You know, chat about fun wedding prep stuff."

"Sure," Bonnie promised, but not even her theatre degree was enough to help dredge up a convincing smile at the mention of *fun wedding prep stuff*. Still. She loved her friend and she was happy for her. She hugged Cassie tight and said her goodbyes to the guys.

"You're not off so soon?" Theo asked, frowning. "Alone?"

"I'll be fine." She bristled, simultaneously annoyed and charmed by the Brit's masculine show of chivalric chauvinism. "I do manage to go about the city by myself on a regular basis."

"Of course. I didn't mean to imply—" He broke off, abashed. His palpable discomfort made the scales dip alarmingly toward the charming side.

"Yes, well. This Ophelia needs to get home to her

Hamlet." She emphasized the last bit, a reminder for herself as much as anyone else. "It was nice to see you again, Theo," she said, stiffly polite, praying he wouldn't smile at her again. She wasn't sure her knees could withstand another potent blast from those magic dimples.

CHAPTER 2

ON THE TRAIN home, Bonnie tucked herself into a corner seat and ignored the strange looks the other passengers shot her way. Nobody bothered her, though. This might not be LA or NYC, where girls in flowing gowns and floral headdresses riding public transportation likely wouldn't raise an eyebrow, but this was Chicago, where people minded their own damn business.

As Bonnie walked the block from the L station to her apartment in Printer's Row, the wind from the lake picked up. She shivered. The cloak she wore looked great with her costume but didn't offer much warmth.

Though it was spring, the nights could still get quite cold. Snow in April was unwelcome but not unusual. She decided she'd make hot cocoa when she got home. The good kind, with steamed milk, like Gabe liked it. Maybe she'd whip up a batch of gingerbread too. While it was in the oven, she could finish grading the papers she'd been procrastinating on all week. Bonnie smiled, warmed by the cozy scene. She'd curl up on the sofa, and when

Gabe got back from his meeting, he could join her for a snuggle, and things would be perfect.

The moment Bonnie entered her apartment, she knew things were not perfect. Not perfect at all. Her first hint something was wrong was the dress lying on her couch. Bonnie frowned; she didn't own anything in *that* color. She hated that color. A bright pink, it would clash horribly with her red hair. She set her cloak down. As she bent to pick up the curious article of clothing, a series of muffled noises echoed from down the hall.

Bonnie straightened. Numb fingers gripping the suspicious fabric, her mind seemed to separate from her body, floating above her as she shuffled, like a sleepwalker, in the direction of her bedroom. Pushing the door open, Bonnie caught sight of her fiancé's bare backside. She froze, transfixed in horrid fascination as she watched Gabe's pale behind move up and down while he thrust into a woman—a naked woman who looked vaguely familiar—not that Bonnie could tell much from this angle.

The woman was lying on the bed, moaning and gripping the quilted comforter. A strangled sound escaped Bonnie, and her hands went limp, the dress falling to the floor. Her *grandmother* had made that quilt. Bonnie closed her eyes, shutting out the awful scene.

Candlelight flickered against her eyelids, and her brain slammed back into her body, white-hot anger and burning shame fusing thought and feeling together. She'd bought those candles herself, had spent more than an hour in a little boutique on Belmont, agonizing over which scents were less likely to give Gabe a headache, as he complained her candles often did. It was why she'd gone to that damn boutique in the first place; she thought the pricy candles with fancier ingredients might bother him less.

Well, screw him. She hoped he got a monster of a headache.

Bonnie opened her eyes and forced herself to look back at the bed. *Her* bed, the one she had brought from home to avoid spending money on new furniture, since keeping pace with Gabe's education debt was already eating up so much of their budget.

The bonking couple still hadn't noticed her standing in the doorway. Obviously, more important things demanded their immediate attention.

Rage trembled in Bonnie's fingers and toes, raced up her legs, her arms, her spine, finally gathering in a red-hot ball of fury pounding at the base of her skull. She stepped across the threshold of her bedroom, and despite the trembling of her vocal cords, roared with the power of a former theatre major who could deliver skeins of iambic pentameter with scarcely a breath between stanzas.

"WHAT."

"THE."

"HELL?"

Her fiancé stuttered to a halt mid-thrust and looked over his shoulder, eyes widening, first in surprise and then unmistakable terror. He released the hips of the woman underneath him. As he stepped back, the details of the scene slammed into Bonnie, a sickening kaleidoscope of images that made her want to puke.

Swallowing bile, she looked away, attention snagging on the gleam of light bouncing off a silver nail file resting on the dresser. She crossed the room and curled her fingers around the cold metal, filled with a bone-deep understanding of what drove a woman to chop off her husband's dick with the nearest sharp object. And Gabe wasn't even her husband. Just her fiancé. Just her boyfriend for more than a decade.

Gabe instinctively placed his hands over his crotch. "Bonnie," he said, his tone cautious, eyes on the nail file. "Bonnie, you don't want to hurt anyone."

Her heart splintered, and his voice slipped between the cracks. She'd known that voice most of her life, been in love with the owner of it for more than half. Bonnie swiped a fist across her cheeks. "I think it's a little late to be talking about not hurting people, don't you?"

A sob escaped her, but as she took him in, standing there stark naked and stock still, with his hands hovering over his junk, the sob turned into a bubble of hysterical laughter. She set the would-be weapon down and twisted the sparkling band of gold on the fourth finger of her left hand.

Gabe stepped forward. "Bonnie, wait. We can talk about this."

The skin on her knuckle tore as she ripped the engagement ring off her finger. "You two can talk about whatever you want." She tossed the ring onto the bed, narrowly missing the woman who sat there, mutely staring at the two of them, clutching Grandma's quilt around her naked torso.

"But there is no *we*, Gabe." Bonnie stopped and swallowed back another sob as the weight of that statement settled on her shoulders. "Not anymore." Before she lost control of herself again, she kicked the offending pile of pink out of her way and exited the room.

Her cloak lay on the couch where she'd left it what felt like a lifetime ago. Low murmurs came from the bedroom. Her stomach churned. Hearing them talk to each other was somehow almost as bad as seeing them fuck. Bonnie quickly pulled her keys and phone from the cloak's pockets. Focused on escape, she grabbed a warmer coat from the hall closet, along with her purse, and fled the apartment.

Outside, the spring wind tore at the flowers in her hair. She yanked the floral crown off her head and started walking, with no plan or purpose other than to get as far away from her apartment as fast as possible. She passed under streetlamp after streetlamp, not thinking of where she was headed beyond the next circle of light.

As she walked, she began to tug at the flowers in her crown.

He loves me. He loves me not.

Petals floated on the wind behind her, leaving a delicate trail of dashed hopes and shattered dreams in her wake.

He loves me. He loves me not.

Reaching the end of another block, Bonnie paused. She held up the tattered stem of the last flower, examining the fragile beauty of the lone remaining petal. Fingers now stiff from the cold, she plucked it.

He loves me.

She dropped the naked stem, cradling the last petal in her palm. *He loves me?*

A sense of awareness crept over her, and with a start, she realized the wind had shifted, the air growing heavy with the promise of rain. As she glanced around the deserted street corner and gathered her bearings, fat icy drops began to fall, pinging off the concrete and stinging her skin.

She tilted her palm and let the wind catch the petal, watching as it rose higher in the night sky, dancing away from her, into the swirling eddies of the spring storm.

He . . . loved me.

CHAPTER 3

THEO TWIRLED THE cherry stem in his glass. Prissy cocktails weren't his preference, but shame to let good alcohol go to waste. And despite the syrupy sweetness, the drink had been made with high quality whisky and had a nice edge to it. Figures. Logan ordered it, and the Scot never skimped on the booze.

"Bonnie left in quite the hurry." *Blast.* He took a long pull on his drink. He'd promised himself he wouldn't dwell on the redhead, and not five minutes had passed since she'd vacated the premises before he couldn't resist mentioning her in conversation.

Logan shot him a knowing smirk over the rim of his pint.

Bugger off, mate, Theo silently shot back. He had better manners than to say it aloud, especially in the company of a lady. He turned to his best friend's lovely bride-to-be. "I hope she's not under the weather?"

"Bonnie?" Cassie frowned, delicate features creasing in concern. "I don't think so." Her face relaxed, and she shrugged. "She's just got a lot on her mind."

"Right," Theo agreed, ignoring the sudden sharp prickles in his gut. "The wedding."

"We really didn't have a chance to talk about my wedding tonight," Cassie said.

"I meant *her* wedding. Isn't Bonnie also engaged?" Theo bit down, trapping his tongue inside his mouth before he blurted out anything else.

Beside him, a very Gaelic snort escaped Logan.

Theo turned to his friend. "Pardon?"

The Scot shrugged. "Well, that's the problem. She hasna got a wedding to plan for yet."

The prickling in his gut intensified. "Sorry?"

Logan shook his head. "Her lad won't settle on a date." He leaned toward Theo. "If you ask me, the wanker's got a case o' cold feet."

"Nobody's asking you." Cassie poked her fiancé in the ribs. "I'm sure Theo didn't come all the way from England to gossip about Bonnie." Her dark eyes flashed as she glared up at Logan. "By the way, why didn't you mention he was going to be here tonight?"

"I only found out yesterday, lass." Logan held his palms up. "I swear."

Cassie looked to Theo for confirmation, and he nodded. "It's true. I sent him a text when I was boarding my flight."

"Aye. And when Theo asked if we were free this evening, I told him we already had plans, but I'd nip him a ticket."

"I see." She tapped her foot with feminine disapproval. "Yet somehow it slipped your mind to tell me?"

"It slipped my mind, lass," Logan purred, moving closer to Cassie, "because I was busy slipping something else inside your—"

"Point made." Cassie placed her hand on Logan's mouth, a pretty blush rising in her cheeks.

Theo chuckled, pleased—and relieved—to see them so happy, so content. His friend's relationship with Cassie had progressed so quickly, at first it was a bit of a shock. Last summer back in London, Theo had known there'd been something special between the two. He wouldn't say he believed in love at first sight or anything, but not too long ago, Theo recalled a much different Logan. One who swore he'd never get married. He wondered what, precisely, had changed his mate's mind. He'd have to remember to ask him.

The Scot prodded him with an elbow. "I'm that glad to see you. But I canna help wondering, what *are* you doing here?"

Theo sighed. "I'm in town to attend some bloody charity event tomorrow evening."

"Whatever for?" Logan cocked an eyebrow. "You don't have any quid to spare."

"Logan!" Cassie smacked her fiancé on the arm. To Theo, she said, "Don't mind him."

"Never do," Theo blithely assured her. "Though Lo has the right of it." His lips curled in a self-deprecating smirk. "Apparently, the pleasure of my company still holds some worth." He glanced at Logan. "I'm escorting an old family friend."

"Ah." The Scot's other ginger brow rose to join the first. "Is yer sainted mama still on her quest, then?"

"Does the sun still rise in the east and set in the west?" Theo raised his glass.

"Anyone I know?"

"Camille Fairfax. She's attending grad school here in the city. Her brother, Ethan, went to St. Andrews with us."

"That git we played rugby with?" Logan grunted. "Didn't we also play a few pranks on him?"

"Indeed, we did." Theo's mouth curved in a mischievous smile, mirroring his friend's.

"What pranks? Who? What's happening?" Cassie interrupted, glancing furtively around the room like she expected someone's hair to light on fire. Considering she was engaged to the host of a late-night talk show known for punking celebrities, her concern was not unfounded.

"Nobody here, hen," Logan assured her. "Just some prat we used to know."

She stared at her fiancé, hands on hips, lips still pinched with a hint of suspicion.

Theo didn't blame her. The first time Cassie had met Logan, he'd been filming a prank for his internet sketch show, *Shenanigans*, and she'd been adamant in her refusal to act as a punchline to one of the Scot's jokes. Who could have predicted that inopportune meeting would lead those two here? Theo shook his head. "Let's change the subject." He turned to Cassie. "How about you fill your best man in on some wedding details?"

"Really?" Cassie's face glowed with pleasure.

"Och," Logan groaned. "Now you've gone and done it, lad. It'll be nothing but guest lists and napkin colors and floral arrangements and all manner of matrimonial prattle."

"A tragedy, I'm sure," Theo scoffed. For all his bellyaching, the Scot appeared perfectly sanguine about the ordeal. Theo, however, dreaded the topic of marriage. He tipped his glass, swallowing the last of the fruity cocktail. The "quest" Logan had been asking after, was his "sainted mama's" determination to see Theo wed. Preferably to an attractive dowry. The appearance of the bride and his feelings for her were inconsequential. A lack of emotion didn't matter, so long as there wasn't a lack of funds.

"Emberton!" a distinctly British voice barked from somewhere behind him.

"Bloody hell." Theo stiffened at his official title. He wasn't expecting to run into anyone else who knew him this evening. He turned, gaze narrowing on the couple making their way toward him from across the room, frantically searching his mental database. "Ah, Professor Newton." Theo reached out a hand in greeting as his brain successfully produced a name to go with the face beaming up at him from beneath a crown of laurel. The effect wasn't nearly as fetching as it had been on a certain redhead.

"Fancy seeing you here, lad." The older man shook Theo's hand, chortling. He gestured at the medallion and sash. "A bit lazy with the costume, aren't we?"

"One works with what one has," Theo murmured.

"Fair enough. Who are you supposed to be then, eh?"

"Duke Orsino, as a charming young lady hazarded to guess." He turned toward the statuesque woman standing next to the professor. The Cleopatra get-up had thrown him for a moment, but on closer inspection, he recognized Barbara Hamilton, an acquaintance of his mother's. Though they did not run in the exact same circles, their social spheres often overlapped. He plastered a gallant smile on his face. "Had I known such an example of feminine perfection would be in attendance tonight, I would have put forth more effort. Perhaps donning my hotel bed linens and arriving dressed as Marc Antony."

"Flatterer." Cleopatra chortled and held out her hand for Theo to kiss, pinching him on the cheek as he rose. "Do you always have such a silver tongue?"

"Nay, madam, my mother taught me to speak the truth." *In the manner one saw fit, of course.*

"And how fares Her Grace?"

"Well. Thank you."

"And your sisters?"

"Also, well. All three of them." Theo didn't let his smile slip. He cleared his throat, wondering how quickly he could excuse himself.

Logan saved him, sidling up next to them, full of cocky Highland swagger. "Theo here's my best mate, and my best man, aye? We've got a wedding to plan." Logan tugged on Cassie's hand, pulling her into their circle. "I believe you know my fiancée?"

Cleopatra clapped her hands. "Oh, it truly is a small world. Cassie darling, my congratulations." She cast an eye back toward Theo. "Pleasant though it is to see you, dear boy, I admit I had approached with the hope to continue my conversation with the other young lady in your party."

"Sorry?" Theo frowned.

He was saved again, this time by Cassie. "Unfortunately, Bonnie has left for the evening."

"Oh my, that *is* unfortunate." Barbara tsked, and glanced at her companion. "Philip and I so wished to come to an agreement with her."

What's all this? Theo wondered, suddenly very interested in the conversation. How did these two old birds know Bonnie?

"I'm only in town for the weekend," the professor said, training his furry-browed gaze on Cassie. "Would it be possible to arrange a meeting tomorrow afternoon? Perhaps invite her to tea?"

"Oh, that will be delightful. You are a genius, Philip." Barbara beamed at Cassie. "Yes, please extend an invitation to your friend. We can meet at . . . what was the name of the hotel you were telling me about, dear? Where they serve such a lovely high tea?"

"The Drake." Cassie's eyes lit up. "That's actually

perfect. Bonnie adores that place. She'll never be able to refuse."

Theo followed the conversation, savoring each new crumb of information about Bonnie. He shouldn't be so interested, shouldn't care so much. The girl was engaged to be married, and he had enough to concern him. Rather than demand Cassie tell him what the bloody hell this was all about, Theo schooled his features and continued to listen politely as the conversation shifted toward a review of some posh hotel's elaborate afternoon tea menu.

His belly rumbled. All this talk of food reminded Theo he was starving for more than details about a lovely redhead. He hadn't had a bite since some quick takeaway at Heathrow. He shifted, discreetly scanning the crowded room for signs of nourishment. Blast. Didn't they feed people at these soirees? He could do serious damage to a plate of cheese on toast right about now.

"I'm off." Barbara leaned in and air-kissed Cassie, astutely avoiding contact with Lady MacBeth's bloody palms before turning to offer her hand to Theo once more.

"So soon?" Theo asked, repressing a sigh of relief as he briefly brushed his lips across the woman's knuckles.

"Yes, well, Philip here needs his beauty sleep. Isn't that right, Philip darling?"

"Quite so," her companion agreed, winking.

Or, at least, he thought the old gent was winking. Hard to tell. Theo smiled broadly, trying not to stare at the pelt of scraggly hair wriggling over the professor's left eye as they shook hands in farewell. "Good evening to you, then."

"Cassie, lass," Logan said, after the couple had walked on. "I've been a good lad, have I not?"

"You have . . ." She studied him, eyes narrowing. "Why?"

"We-ell," he drawled, his brogue stretching the word

into two syllables. "I was thinking we could make our own getaway, you ken?"

She glanced at Theo. "Is he up to something? Are the toilets going to start exploding?"

"Sorry?"

"Never mind," she grumbled. "I suppose you want to get out of here too?"

"Now that you mention it, I could do with a bite of supper," Theo admitted.

"See! It's settled." Logan stepped between Theo and Cassie. "We canna let the man starve, lass." He put an arm over their shoulders and steered them toward the exit. "Theo, mate. Have you ever tried deep-dish pizza?"

CHAPTER 4

BONNIE STOOD ON the street corner, waiting for the traffic light to change. Her right hand drifted to her left, massaging the abraded skin of the finger that felt colder, more naked, than the others. The walk sign lit up, and she started forward, fisting her hands inside her pockets and ducking her head against the rain. She was grateful she'd put on a warmer coat, but she hadn't thought to grab her umbrella, and no way in Hades was she going back to the apartment.

Fair is foul and foul is fair. The words drifted through her mind as she splashed through an icy puddle. She recalled the Weird sisters back in the bathroom at Navy Pier and shook her head, a wry smile tugging at her mouth. Too bad she hadn't asked them to read her fortune. Maybe they could've warned her how horribly this night would end.

At the next intersection, she headed east. As she got closer to the lake, the rain began to taper off. The air somehow felt warmer here, the city quieter. Everything was muted, the sharper edges of noise and cold insulated by a soft drifting mist.

Hover through the fog and filthy air. Dodging more puddles, Bonnie continued to silently recite lines from *Macbeth*, retreating to a well-worn groove in her brain. Comfortable and familiar. Safe.

That's what she thought Gabe had been.

That's what she thought her life had been.

In a rush, all that had transpired in the last few hours came flooding back, and her momentary sense of peace evaporated. Lost and disoriented, Bonnie glanced up and down the street, wiping her eyes and fighting a sniffle. She caught the warm glow of light spilling onto the sidewalk from the windows of a café, and instinctively began moving toward the entrance. A cup of tea was exactly what she needed to pull herself together.

After placing her order, Bonnie carried a steaming mug to a snug little booth. When she'd stormed out of the apartment, she'd just wanted to get away. That had been the extent of her plan. She'd had enough presence of mind to grab her phone and her purse, so at least she had credit cards. She could get a hotel room or something. Maybe call Cassie.

Wait. Cassie was out with Logan . . . and Theo was with them.

So that option was out.

The hotel room idea could work, though last minute on a Friday night in Chicago would be tough, not to mention expensive. Bonnie swiped through the contacts on her phone, considering possibilities while the tea steeped. Out of her close circle of friends, her best bet would be Ana, who owned a duplex on the northern outskirts of the city. Scooting deeper into the booth, she dialed.

"Ana's phone." A familiar voice, though not the one Bonnie had been expecting, giggled in her ear.

"Sadie?"

"At your service." Another giggle. "What can I do for you?"

"It's Bonnie. I thought you were still in New York."

"Flew in this morning for Passover. Since I'm not stuck filming the soap anymore, Daddy insisted on a family holiday this year. I think he's having an elemental crisis or something." Sadie hiccupped into the phone.

"Existential," Bonnie corrected automatically.

"What's essential?" Sadie slurred, *s* sounds sloshing together.

"Never mind. Can I talk to Ana please?"

"Oh, sure! Why didn't you say so before?"

Bonnie tipped the phone away from her ear as Sadie yelled for Ana.

"Hold on," Sadie said, her voice thankfully returning to a somewhat normal volume. "She's in the can."

"Excellent. I am sure Ana will be delighted to know you've shared this information with me."

Sadie dropped her voice to a dramatic stage whisper. "I think she's puking."

"Oh no!" Bonnie felt her own stomach drop. If Ana was sick, the last thing she wanted to do was impose.

"Yeah," Sadie continued, "we were supposed to be baking, but I decided to taste test some new Kosher-friendly wines. That stuff my nana always brings to Seder is shit. *Shit, I tell you!* And we have to drink four glasses of it!"

Once again, Bonnie tilted the phone away from her ear. As she'd learned firsthand from many a college party, along with diction, Sadie also lost volume control when she was hammered. "How many glasses have you had tonight?"

"Dunno. More than Ana. And she's had *a lot*."

Relieved Ana was only booze-sick and not real sick, and starting to wish she had a glass of wine herself, Bonnie tried one more time. "Do you think you can ask Ana to call me back, when she's done, you know . . ."

"Puking? Sure," Sadie jovially agreed. "Oh wait, here she is now. Bye-bye, Bon-neeeee!" Sadie dragged the end of Bonnie's name out in a long singsong before she was abruptly caught off.

"Hello?" Ana's voice was a tad scratchier than her natural husky tone, but otherwise seemed normal.

"Hey, Ana, it's Bonnie."

"What's wrong?"

Ana never was one to waste time on niceties, and her intuition was uncanny. Bonnie debated hedging, but experience had taught her that sooner or later Ana would drag the truth out of her, and besides, she was calling because she needed Ana's help, so sooner was better than later anyway. "Um . . . do you think I can crash at your place tonight?"

"You know you're always welcome here, Bon," Ana began, then hesitated.

"There's a 'but' in there somewhere, isn't there?" Bonnie asked, surprised at the surge of relief she felt. Tonight, she really wanted to be alone. If Ana was hesitating on inviting her over, then she could justify spending the money on a hotel room.

"What? No, no buts. It's just, I promised my mom I'd make a bunch of my matzah version of Mandel bread, and Sadie's here, and I don't think she's going home tonight . . ." Ana drifted off.

"Don't worry about it. It's cool." In the background, Bonnie could hear the tinkling of glasses.

"I *am* going to worry about it. Why are you looking for a place to stay?"

"Not a big deal." Bonnie shrugged, then recalled Ana couldn't see her over the phone. "I'll think of something, maybe book a hotel room."

"A hotel room?" Ana's voice rose with concern. "Bonnie, seriously, what's going on?"

"I just need some downtime." Bonnie decided to hedge after all. If she wasn't going to have to face Ana in person tonight, she could put off the explanations until later.

Before Ana could reply, Sadie grabbed the phone back. "Bonnie?"

"Yes?"

"Did I hear you say you're looking for a hotel room?"

"Um, yes?" Where was Sadie going with this?

"Well, why don't you take Daddy's?"

"Oh no, I can't. I couldn't."

"Why not?"

Bonnie really didn't have an answer. Not a good one, anyway. Why not indeed? Sadie's father worked for a major hotel chain. His job title had lots of acronyms and came with lots of perks, including a room at the Waldorf Chicago on permanent retainer, and not just any room—a suite. Sadie had hosted a slumber party in the luxurious space for her twenty-first birthday. A flurry of memories inundated Bonnie. She recalled high ceilings, tall, gleaming windows overlooking Lake Michigan and the Gold Coast, a bathroom outfitted like a spa, and a bed fit for royalty.

"Um, I don't want to impose."

Sadie giggled.

"Shut up."

"I'm not laughing at you. You should see the face Ana is making right now." Another snort of laughter escaped Sadie. "Oh, please," she protested, voice muffled, "it can't taste as bad as my nana's!" A moment later she addressed Bonnie, her tone serious. "Come on, Bon, take the room. It's just sitting there, waiting for someone to use it. I'll call Missy and tell her to alert the hotel staff."

Missy was Sadie's father's assistant. "Are you sure?"

"Of course, I'm sure. Just tell them who sent you and you'll be good to go."

Bonnie sipped her tea, imagining that enormous bathtub, picturing herself sinking below a froth of scented bubbles, and then climbing into that big soft bed—a bed her fiancé hadn't been screwing somebody else on. "Well, if it's not too much trouble."

"Are you kidding? It's, like, no trouble at all."

"All right, if you insist."

"I insist. Seriously, Bon. Go. You'll hurt my feelings if you don't."

"Okay, okay. You've convinced me."

"Good—*wait*!" Sadie yelled, "Don't dump that in the sink, I'll drink it!"

There was a moment of muffled shuffling, and then Ana was on the phone again. "So, you're all set?" she asked.

"I am, thanks." Bonnie glanced around the café, which had begun to empty while she'd been talking. A few other customers lingered while servers wiped down tables, flipping chairs and stacking them in a blatant hint. "Hey, I better get going."

"Yeah, me too. I need to get Miss Tipsy here sobered up before Seder starts tomorrow night. How about a late brunch on Sunday? I'm going to be dying for some carbs."

Bonnie grinned. There were few things Ana loved more in the world than brunch. It was comforting to know some things never changed. "Sounds like a plan." She was about to end the call when Ana spoke once more.

"And Bonnie?"

"Yes?" Her gut clenched, expecting Ana to demand she tell her what had happened, to give some explanation as to why she was looking for a place to stay when she should be snuggled up at home with her fiancé.

But, "Love you," was all Ana said.

Warmth lit inside Bonnie, a heating pad of affection easing the aching tension more than any cup of tea ever could. "Thanks." She may have made a bad choice in husband material, but her friends were top of the line. "Love you too. See you soon."

CHAPTER 5

THE RUMBLING WHINE of electric guitars burst from Theo's mobile as his alarm went off. He rolled toward the nightstand, blindly fumbling for his phone. Set to play Guns N' Roses, his favorite band was well into the opening verse of "Welcome to the Jungle" before Theo finally managed to grab hold of the bloody thing and cut off Axl mid-scream.

He rubbed his eyes, waiting for the numbers on his screen to come into focus. A quarter past eight in the morning. Which meant it was after one in the afternoon back home. He should be wide awake. He hadn't been out very late last night. After escaping the throng of Shakespeare characters, Lo and Cassie had treated him to supper and then dropped him at his hotel around ten. But ten p.m. in Chicago was three a.m. in London.

Jet lag aside, his arse would still be dragging this morning after the night he'd had. It would have been nice if Logan had warned him he'd feel like he was carrying around a bundle of soggy laundry in his gut after eating almost half a deep-dish pizza. Theo had been ravenous, and assumed his hearty British constitution could handle anything, but even the thickest steak-and-kidney pie had nothing on the famous Chicago slab of dough and cheese. He set the phone aside and rubbed his belly, knowing it wasn't indigestion that had kept him awake either.

No, the problem was lower down.

Last night, after he'd returned to his hotel, he'd still been preoccupied by his encounter with Bonnie. He could have sworn he saw her mane of wild red curls in the lobby, standing at the check-in desk. And even though he knew it was impossible for her to be there, he'd almost approached the woman, but changed his mind, deciding one, he'd had too much liquor and not enough sleep, and two, he needed to stop obsessing about the redhead.

But he couldn't stop the dreams.

Shifting beneath the covers, he let his head fall back on the pillows and palmed himself as he recalled the dreams that had kept waking him up—and kept him *up*—most of the night. The moment he closed his eyes, she was there. Laughing, bright blue gaze beaming up at him, twinkling with wit and humor. Delicate fingers dabbing at the stain on her dress, the front of the old-fashioned gown stretching tight across her breasts. His cock, already stiff, thickened, throbbing in his hand.

You're a randy lech, mate, Theo cursed himself. But he didn't stop. He stroked his length, up and down. *Not yours, you can't have her, she's not yours,* he chanted silently, eyes closed, mouth dry as his hand worked faster, hips lifting from the bed, back arching, head pressing deeper into the pillows.

Glorious red curls, pink cheeks kissed with freckles, sweet rosebud smile. He wanted to feel her soft full lower lip sliding across the tip of his cock as she wrapped her mouth around him . . . he gritted his teeth and pumped harder. *Notyoursnotyoursnotyours.* Theo groaned deep in the back of his throat, release whipping through him and wiping out coherent thought.

When the second alarm he'd programmed sounded, Theo threw his phone across the room. It landed on the plush carpet with a harmless thump, guitars still screeching. He kicked the covers off and growled, letting the music rage while he brushed his teeth. It matched his mood. And he wasn't worried about disturbing his neighbors. The Waldorf's suites were impressively soundproof. Even the noise of the bustling city beyond the wall of windows in his room barely registered.

By the time he'd showered, shaved, and finished buttoning up a crisply starched shirt, Theo was feeling better. More in control. He retrieved his phone from the floor and had just silenced it when the bloody thing blared to life again. This time with the chorus of Guns N' Roses's "Patience." Always a good reminder when dealing with his mum. He thumbed the answer key and steeled himself. "Good morning, Mama."

"Morning?" His mother paused. "Oh, my yes, quite right. But it's not dreadfully early. You were awake, of course."

"Of course." He managed to keep the snark from creeping into his voice.

"I hope you had a pleasant evening."

"Ah, yes." He cleared his throat. "Caught up with Logan."

"Your chum from St. Andrews? How nice. It seems everyone is visiting Chicago these days."

"Oh?" Blast. Had word already gotten back to his mother about his encounter with Dame Barbara Busybody and the professor? Barbara Hamilton was a notorious gossip, as was his mother, for that matter. Still. He could hardly see their little tête-à-tête last night causing a stir. He'd been exceedingly polite, their conversation—aside from the reference to Bonnie—exceedingly boring.

"Indeed. Did you know Prince Harry was there recently? Supporting the opening of a foundation or some such. It was in all the papers."

Even though his mother couldn't see him over the phone, Theo still smothered the instinctive grin creeping across his face at his mum's mention of "the papers." He knew it wasn't the *Times* she was referring to. A lover of gossip in all forms, she had a not-so-secret addiction to tattlers.

"And to think, *both* he and his brother are married and settled down now . . ." His mother paused pointedly. When Theo didn't take the bait, she continued, "You don't suppose either of them will be at the ball this evening?"

Theo snorted. "I'm afraid I'm not up-to-date on the royal family's social calendar, Mama, but I'd say it's doubtful."

"Hmm, I suppose you're right." Another pause. "Well, the reason I'm calling—"

"There's a reason for this call?" Theo couldn't resist goading his mum a tad. They both knew she wasn't calling for a chinwag. Theodora Wharton did *everything* for a reason.

Not taking the bait either, she continued, "I've just returned from lunching with Edith Fairfax. She's delighted you're escorting her daughter this evening. As am I. Lady Camille is such a pleasant young woman. And so pretty."

"Mmm," Theo replied. The girl he vaguely recalled from his childhood was neither of those things.

"Well, as I said, I was chatting with Edith, and we lighted upon the lovely idea that you and Camille should schedule a little reunion first, before the ball tonight."

"Oh?" *Bloody hell.* "Seeing as I barely know her, I'd hardly call it a reunion."

"Yes, well. That's precisely my point. We think it would be very nice of you to call on Camille this afternoon, allow the two of you time to get reacquainted."

"Mama . . ." he began, tamping down the exasperation rising in his chest. *Patience.*

"Edith is ringing up her daughter right now, so Camille will be expecting a call from you. My dear boy, you wouldn't leave the poor girl hanging, would you?"

"No, I don't suppose I would." He sighed, unable to completely conceal the irritation in his tone this time. His mother had always been relentless in her matchmaking campaign and Theo had always accepted the practicality of her machinations, in theory. But lately, she seemed to be dialing up the intensity of her efforts. In response, he found himself growing increasingly testy whenever the subject arose. The endgame was approaching faster than he'd thought. Granted, he tried not to think about it. Much.

"Then it's settled," his mother said. "I knew you wouldn't disappoint her."

Translation: I knew you wouldn't disappoint me.

"Perhaps you two could meet for tea? Do they do that sort of thing in Chicago?"

"I'm sure I can manage something."

"Well, make sure it is something nice. Not to mince words, but it's imperative you make a good impression."

"Mama, may I ask, what are you up to?" He knew exactly what she was up to, but he wanted her to come out and say it.

"Nothing!" she refuted. After a pause, she added, "Only, it would be wise, one should think, if we could strengthen our family connections at this crucial time. And the Fairfaxes are well-liked."

"Not to mention well-off," he added tartly.

"Quite."

And there it was. As she herself had said, his mother was not one to mince words.

"Very well," he capitulated.

"You'll arrange something for this afternoon, then?" she pressed.

"For this afternoon," he agreed. As if he had a choice.

His mother gave him Camille's number. "Are you writing that down?"

"I am." He scribbled the information on a hotel notepad, a sense of inevitability stealing over him. So much for feeling more in control. His darling, scheming mama had likely been planning this casual suggestion for a "chance to get reacquainted" all along. As in England, Theo was her pawn; she had simply moved him across the chess board.

"And I have her electronic mail address as well," she added.

"It's called an email, Mama."

"As you say," she huffed. "Where will you be taking her?"

Theo tapped his pen against the notepad, a wicked, rebellious thought occurring to him. "I hear the Drake hotel presents a fine tea service."

CHAPTER 6

SUNLIGHT BURNED THROUGH Bonnie's closed eye-lids. She rolled over, squeezing her eyes shut tighter, but the glaring light continued to sear her retinas. *Odd. There aren't any windows on this side of my bedroom . . .* Her lids popped open. Spring sunshine beamed in from the floor-to-ceiling windows, so bright she expected to hear trumpets blaring and angels singing.

She sat up and fisted her hands, rubbing her eyeballs. *Right.* She wasn't in her bedroom. She was in the posh suite of a Gold Coast hotel, the east-facing wall of windows offering a panoramic view of the sunrise over the city and Lake Michigan. And the bed she was ensconced in was not her own, but a king-sized confection of downy comforters and luxurious sheets. She pulled the ultra-soft, ultra-smooth covers over her head and lay back down, try-ing to blot out the image of what she'd seen happening on her own bed last night. But just as the morning sun broke through the darkness of her cocoon, the memory of last night broke through the haze of her thoughts.

Damn it, Gabe. Did you have to do that on Grandma Mary's quilt?

Bonnie rolled over, smashing her face into the plush pillows. The annoying sunlight couldn't get to her now, but neither could necessary air. Still, she lay there, face buried, until her lungs ached. Turning her head to the side, she inhaled, gulping oxygen. Something vibrated near her hip. *What the hell?*

She searched beneath the covers. The vibrating was her phone. She'd set it to silent last night after Gabe had tried calling twice. It rang again, buzzing against her palm, the screen lighting up with Gabe's number and picture. *Nope, not talking to you, jerkface.* She sat up and glared at her screen.

The photo was one she'd taken of Gabe last summer when they'd gone for ice cream at Navy Pier. Her stomach lurched violently. Had he been cheating on her even then? It was very possible the day she'd snapped this picture, the man grinning up at her with the goofy-sweet smile she thought she knew so well had been fucking somebody else.

Her phone went still, the screen dark. Either it had clicked to voice mail, or he'd given up. She dropped the phone and rocked back and forth on the mattress, arms wrapped tight around her middle. Everything hurt, like she'd been hit by a truck. In a way, she had. The realization Gabe had been cheating on her had run her over, pulled the rug of reality out from under her. Because what she'd believed to be real, had been a lie. The man she thought she'd been engaged to didn't exist, and neither did the future she thought they would have together.

Slowly, she stopped rocking and unclasped her middle. She stared at her fists, at the bare ring finger on her left hand. Maybe she could stay in bed all day. Wake up once the sun had retreated to the other side of the city. Bonnie knew what the mature thing to do was. The mature thing was to go back to her apartment and face Gabe.

And she would. Eventually. She needed clean clothes, after all. But she didn't want to be mature today. She wanted to hide out for the rest of the weekend in this sanctuary of a hotel suite and continue to reject Gabe's calls. As if conjuring the devil with a thought, her phone vibrated again. She reached for it and slid her thumb over the reject button.

A small wave of pleasure rippled through her. Yes, she rejected him. She rejected the cheating-asshole-scum-of-the-earth-excuse-for-a-man she'd almost married.

Well, not even almost. He'd done her that much of a favor. God, just imagine. If they *had* picked a date and she'd already sent out invitations to a hundred-plus people, had put a deposit on a venue, bought a dress . . . If she'd found out about his extracurricular activities *after* all that?

The thought of having to tell people the wedding was off made her wish she had a fainting couch handy.

Telling people the engagement was off was going to be bad enough.

Especially telling her mother.

Oh God, her mother.

Mom never had a wedding of her own, the day after turning eighteen, she and Dad had strolled into the county clerk's office and got married by a justice of the peace. No frills, no fuss. And while Bonnie's parents' marriage was strong, getting married and having a baby so young had been a struggle for the couple in other ways. They'd had to start out on their own with nothing.

When Bonnie was in middle school, her mom had decided it was time to finally venture into the workforce. She'd earned her certification to become a travel agent and enjoyed helping people plan all the fancy vacations she could never afford to take herself. Mom had been a big part of making Bonnie's dream vacation a reality last summer, helping plan the itinerary with such joy and excitement you'd think she had been going along too. But that's just how Connie Blythe was; she threw herself into everything she did 110 percent.

Which was one of the reasons why it was going to be so hard to tell her mom the wedding was off. Connie's latest pet project had been Gabe and Bonnie's wedding, and more importantly, their honeymoon. Her mother had spent hours perusing websites and stockpiling glossy brochures of smiling couples lounging on beachfront hammocks, traipsing through exotic city streets, and dining with a view of breathtaking landscapes. Mom had put together several honeymoon package options, and now Bonnie was going to have to tell her to forget all about it. There would be no wedding, and there would be no honeymoon.

Her phone buzzed. A text this time. But it wasn't Gabe, it was Cassie.

Did her best friend already know the wedding was off? Had Gabe called Cassie, looking for Bonnie, and explained what happened? She braced herself and opened the text.

Cassie: Are you free this afternoon?

Bonnie glanced around the hotel room. Studied the giant flat-screen TV and the big bed she'd planned to hide in all day.

Bonnie: I'm not sure.

Cassie: Come on, this is important.

Bonnie: What's important? She held her breath, waiting for the answer.

Her phone vibrated with an incoming call. Cassie.

Bonnie didn't pick up right away. Instead, she turned the volume on her ringer back up, listening to the song. A few months ago, Cassie had suggested they make special ringtones for each other. Bonnie had picked a Spice Girls song. It annoyed the hell out of Cassie, but as an unabashed fan of what her friends referred to as nineties chick-pop, Bonnie loved it. Once the chorus ended, she answered the phone.

"Bon? Is everything all right?" Cassie's voice was curious. Unsure, but not upset.

She didn't know.

"Yeah." Bonnie took a breath and fiddled with the ends of the hotel's bathrobe tie. Lying to Cassie was never easy. "What's so important, anyway?"

"Come on, Bon. The offer from last night. This is a once in a lifetime opportunity. Are you free this afternoon or not?" Cassie demanded.

The robe's tie slipped from her fingers. "Huh?"

"Cambridge? Shakespeare? Remember? Philip, Barbara's professor friend, flies home tomorrow, and they were hoping to meet with you today."

"Oh." With everything else that happened last night, she'd completely forgotten about the Cambridge offer. A clear sign of the current Dumpster fire status of her life—amazing dream job opportunity falls into her lap and proceeds to slip right out of her mind.

"You don't have to say yes, but at least get all the details, so you know what you are saying no to." Cassie continued, adding a seductive purr to her voice, "They want to meet for high tea at the Drake."

Oh, her friend was good. Cassie knew all her weaknesses. "Your idea, I'm guessing?"

"My suggestion." Cassie laughed. "Which they asked for. Well? Are you going?"

Cambridge. Shakespeare. England. One dream had just been shattered, why not make another come true? Could she do it? Could she really pack up everything and leave it all behind? It would only be for the summer. It wasn't like she was giving up her job—or her life—messy as it was. And what was she leaving behind, anyway?

"Fine." She glanced down at the hotel bathrobe again, and then at the discarded costume slung over a chair. If she was going to do this, she'd need some clean, twenty-first century clothes. "Tell them two o'clock."

CHAPTER 7

COWARD THAT SHE was, Bonnie did not go back home for a change of clothes. Instead, she donned her wrinkled Ophelia gown and hit Michigan Avenue with vindictive glee, giving her for-emergencies-only credit card a work-out at Water Tower Place. Discovering one's fiancé was sleeping around most certainly qualified as an emergency in dire need of retail therapy.

Besides, she could pay it off with savings from the suddenly superfluous wedding fund. She bought herself three whole new outfits from top to bottom, inside and out. Bra, panties, tights—the works. Shoes and jewelry too. All of it designer brands and none of it on sale. Bonnie couldn't remember the last time she'd purchased something for herself that wasn't off a clearance rack.

It felt good to splurge. *She* felt good. Bonnie smoothed the buttery folds of her new suede skirt over her hips and strode through the revolving glass doors of the Drake hotel, steps buoyed by the confidence only a great pair of shoes can give. Making her way through the hotel's elegant foyer to Palm Court, the Drake's tea room, she entered the dazzling space, glowing with plush ivory chairs and flow-ing white drapes, and was immediately greeted with a jovial shout.

It took her a moment to recognize the woman walk-ing toward her, arm raised in a wave, but as soon as she did, Bonnie smiled and returned the wave. Gone was the stylized wig and exotic eye makeup. In a collared silk blouse, graying hair piled in a bun high on her head, the woman she'd met last night had transformed from Cleopa-tra into Oscar Wilde's Lady Bracknell.

Back in college, Bonnie had played the role of Cecily in *The Importance of Being Earnest*. With a flash of bitter irony she was sure Oscar Wilde would appreciate, Bonnie recalled the infamous tea scene, in which Cecily believed the object of her affections had been unfaithful. Turns out, that had only been a misunderstanding of comic pro-portions. Unfortunately for Bonnie, there was no mistak-ing her fiancé's infidelity, and there was nothing funny about it.

"So nice to see you again, dear." She clasped Bonnie's hand. "Follow me, please. Philip is waiting for us. We'd best hurry, or the blasted man will eat all the scones."

They wove through the dining room, around snow-white tablecloths adorned with shining silver tea sets and elegant place settings. Waiters in waistcoats passed, carry-ing the Palm Court's trademark triple-tiered trays loaded with sweet and savory treats.

Memories of treasured afternoons spent here filled Bonnie with a warm glow. She loved this place. As an added bonus, she'd never once been here with Gabe. Men-tally shoving thoughts of her cheating dick-for-brains ex into a box and kicking it under a chair, she followed Bar-bara to a table near the antique water fountain. Festooned with beaming cherubs and bedecked with a grand floral arrangement, the Palm Court fountain was more than just aesthetically pleasing. The softly trickling water muted the clack and clatter of china cups and conversation filling the room, blending with the sound of the harpist strumming in the corner and making everything a touch more civilized.

"Ah! There you are." A gentleman in a tweed jacket stood as they approached, furtively brushing a linen napkin over his lapels.

"Caught in the act, you scoundrel." Barbara swooped down and poked him in his crumb-covered chest. "The evidence is all over you."

Biting her lip, Bonnie smothered a giggle. If the woman started making demands for cucumber sandwiches, she was going to lose it for sure.

The professor flushed and offered her an apologetic grin. "I'm afraid it's true. I have no control where scones are concerned. Especially if there's clotted cream on hand."

"Quite understandable," Bonnie agreed, taking a seat in the plush white chair offered her.

"Thank you," Barbara said to the waiter as he helped her settle into the chair between Bonnie and the professor. She placed a hand on his spotless jacket. "Young man, be a dear and bring another tray of scones." She gave the professor a haughty side-eye while she added, "And I believe we shall need another pot of clotted cream as well. I'd be much obliged."

He nodded and retreated with a bow.

"Now then," Barbara said, commandeering the teapot in front of her, "I've been dying to hear more about your work."

"Yes," Philip echoed, his eyes sharp and bright beneath his pair of bushy brows.

"What has Cassie told you so far?" Bonnie asked, trying

not to stare at the man's eyebrows, which hovered on his forehead, quivering like little caterpillars.

"Enough to make me curious. What was your inspiration for *A Midsummer Night's Dream*?" He narrowed his eyes at her, caterpillars wiggling. "I've seen my fair share of versions of this play. It's not often I hear of a production as unique as yours."

"Oh, well. Thank you?" Bonnie swallowed. *That was a compliment . . . right?* She reached for her teapot. High tea at the Drake included a private tea service for each guest. Pouring a measure of amber liquid into the china cup in front of her, she said, "I guess growing up in Chicago, on stories of mobsters and speakeasies, the idea of setting the play during the prohibition era just sort of came to me." She set the teapot down. "And once the idea got into my head, the pieces fell into place."

"Ah." The professor nodded, taking a thoughtful sip from his own cup. "Who did you model Duke Theseus after?"

"Al Capone. I mixed a bit of Dillinger's gang and *The Godfather* in there too." She added a dollop of honey to her tea. "Characters and tropes the audience would recognize."

The professor's face transformed, his voice taking on a raspy edge as he waved his hand and mumbled, "You come to me, on the day of my daughter's wedding . . ."

"Exactly." Bonnie chuckled, delighted by his rendition of Marlon Brando's famous character. Recognizing she was in the presence of a kindred spirit, her nervousness abated. She helped herself to a few pastries from the tiered tray. "I turned Bottom and his troupe into a gang of small-time bootleggers who needed to get into the mob boss's good graces."

"Brilliant!" Barbara interrupted, joining the conversation as she swatted the professor's hand away from the freshly replenished tray. "A stroke of genius." She broke open a scone. "Now, just as there's a proper order to dressing a scone," she said, spreading cream, then jam, on the golden halves, "there are some steps we must take if we are to proceed. That is"—she glanced up at Bonnie—"if we are to proceed?"

"Well . . ." Bonnie hesitated, nabbing a scone for herself and smearing it with a thick layer of clotted cream. She hadn't had scones like this since her final breakfast in England last summer. At the time, Bonnie had wondered if that trip would be her only chance to see the places she'd fantasized about for much of her life. But now, she was being offered another chance. A chance to go back, not only to visit, but to *live* in England. For a few months, at least. And to teach at Cambridge!

It would be a dream come true. And since so many of her other dreams had come crashing down last night, she had no reason to say no. And every reason to say yes. She cleared her throat. "Well," she said again, turning her attention from the scone on her plate to the two people politely waiting for a response. "Yes. I'd be honored to accept the position."

"Excellent!" Barbara raised her teacup in a toast, Philip and Bonnie following suit.

An hour later, both Bonnie's teacup and plate were empty, her belly full. So was her brain, bursting with details. Immediately following the celebratory toast, Barbara and Philip had gotten down to business, reviewing the specifics of the job with trademark British efficiency. As he rose from the table, the professor swiped the last lonely scone from the tray. He winked at her, one caterpillar wriggling with good-natured mischief while he popped the partially crumbled pastry in his mouth. She gave him an indulgent smile. His penchant for scones reminded Bonnie of her friend Delaney.

"Honestly, Philip," Barbara said, tsking. She turned to Bonnie. "It's been a pleasure, my dear."

"For me as well," Bonnie agreed, grabbing her purse. She began to follow them out of the tea room, when a flash of dark hair and broad shoulders snagged her attention. *No. Not possible.* A few steps later, her feet froze. Oh, it *was* possible. There, sitting at a table on the opposite side of the fountain, was Theo.

What are the odds? Bonnie wondered. Pretty good, obviously, since he was here. And maybe not so impossible. If, say, someone from England wanted to indulge in the comforts of home while in Chicago, the Drake's afternoon tea was a safe bet. Theo's perfectly coifed head tilted in her direction. She waved, thinking she'd caught his eye, but his gaze roamed right over her. *Was he purposely ignoring her?*

Annoyance flickered through Bonnie, but she brushed it aside and hurried to catch up with Philip and Barbara, who stood waiting for her at the Palm Court's entrance. She didn't have time to waste on the Brit anyway. There was much to do.

As they made their way through the Drake's foyer, Bonnie started a mental checklist. Pausing at the revolving doors, she said, "I'll be sure to have HR send over my records right away."

"No rush. Purely a formality, you understand." Barbara squeezed her hand, smiling warmly, and Bonnie returned the smile. For a moment, her smile faltered as she recalled how Theo's eyes had passed right over her, as if she didn't exist. As if she wasn't there at all.

"Something amiss?" the professor asked, caterpillars creeping up his forehead with concern.

"Ah, no." Bonnie shook her head, struck by an impulsive urge to march back into the tea room. "I think I left something at our table."

"Shall I fetch it for you?" he offered gallantly.

"Thanks, but I don't wish to keep you." She nodded toward the street and the line of cabs waiting. "You two go on your way." After another round of farewells and promises to talk soon, Bonnie waved one final time as they passed through the revolving doors. Turning on her heel, she retraced her steps to the tea room, arguing with herself all the way.

Inching around the fountain and telling herself she was *not* spying, Bonnie craned her neck to peer over the chubby shoulder of a marble cherub. A woman sat across from Theo. Young, pretty. Above the gurgle of bubbling water, she caught a masculine chuckle. He was laughing. Probably at something his companion—his young, pretty, *female* companion—had said.

Clotted cream curdled in her stomach, and Bonnie swallowed. Why should she care if Theo was having tea with some girl? Why did it matter if he found said girl amusing? And why did the thought he was turning that knee-tickling smile on anyone else bother her so much?

Not wanting to look too closely for answers to those questions, nor wishing to examine her motives for what she was about to do, Bonnie approached Theo's table, putting her Shakespeare voice to use again as she called his name, loud and clear. Let him try and ignore *that*.

At first, when Theo had entered the Drake's tea room and escorted his companion to their table, he'd been pleased to catch a glimpse of Bonnie on the other side of the fountain. But as he helped Camille into her seat, he'd caught sight of Bonnie's tablemates and blanched. *Blast*. He'd bloody forgotten about that part of the equation. Of course, those two would be here as well. It was the bloody reason Bonnie was there in the first place. What was it about the redhead that made his brain go foggier than a London morning?

He had a few ideas . . . Theo shifted on his overstuffed white chair and resisted the urge to steal another glance at Bonnie's table. He turned, determined to concentrate on his tablemate. His plan had been to do nothing more than engage in the standard polite teatime chatter that came as naturally to them both as breathing, but soon, Theo was pleasantly surprised to discover Camille wasn't such a bad egg after all.

As Theo sipped his tea, he became aware of a pair of familiar pale blue eyes watching him and knew without a doubt, Bonnie had spotted him. Every muscle in his body tensed, and he forced his gaze to wander aimlessly, passing right over the cap of red curls of the woman standing a few feet away, acting like he didn't see her wave. Pretending he didn't notice her face pucker in disappointment before she turned, hurrying toward the exit.

Out of the corner of his eye, he watched Bonnie go, remembering to breathe only when her tangle of red curls disappeared from view.

"Am I boring you?" Camille asked, the picture of politeness.

"Hmm?" Theo set his cup down, attention snapping back to his companion. "Sorry?"

"You seem distracted." She sipped her tea, watching him over the rim. "Well? Am I boring you?" she repeated, her tone more bemused than annoyed.

Shame heated Theo's cheeks. He was being less than a perfect gentleman. "Not at all."

Camille placed her cup back in its saucer. "I know our mums put you up to this little outing."

"No," he began, then paused before admitting, "well, yes, that's true, but I'm not bored. On the contrary, I've found your company surprisingly agreeable."

Her eyes widened. Theo smothered a groan. Where were his manners today? Attempting to salvage the situation, he hurried to add, "What I meant to say is, you're different than I remember. Perhaps I never gave you a fair shake. You know, because your brother was such a rotter." *Well done, mate. You've dug a hole now, haven't you?* Christ. His mother was going to kill him.

Theo shoved a tart into his mouth to prevent his foot from going in farther. Swallowing, he choked out an apology. "I beg your pardon."

Camille laughed. "No, you have the right of it. Ethan was a rotter. Still is."

He chuckled at her unexpected honesty. Relieved she didn't seem offended, he helped himself to another tart from the tray.

"And I *was* an awful child." Her eyes were warm, flashing with humor. "As bad as Ethan, no doubt. But it's nice to hear that may not be the case anymore." She gave him a conspiratorial smile.

Theo found himself smiling back.

"THEO!"

At the sound of his name, shouted loud enough to travel clearly over the din of the harp, fountain, and other diners, Theo dropped his fork. The lemon tart he'd been about to bite into slid sideways, landing back on his plate with a splat. He glanced up. Bonnie was stalking toward him, auburn curls bouncing. His gaze darted around the room, but he didn't see any sign of her two companions.

"Theo, it *is* you! How funny, running into you like this again."

Mechanically, Theo stood, but before he could unknot his tongue and form a coherent reply, she'd turned to Camille.

"Hi, I'm Bonnie," she said, wiggling her fingers in greeting. "Goodness, who knew what a small town Chicago could be, huh?"

Camille held her hand up, returning the wave. With a pleasant, albeit confused smile she glanced at Theo. "You two know each other, then?"

Beating him to the punch once more, Bonnie settled herself in the empty seat next to Camille and answered, "Oh my, yes. His best friend is going to marry my best friend this summer."

"How delightful!" Camille cooed. "I do so love summer weddings."

At the rate these two were nattering, he could keep his bloody mouth shut and let them carry on the conversation without him. Theo settled back into his chair and poked at the remnants of squashed lemon tart on his plate. He'd wanted to see Bonnie again, hadn't he? Well, here she was. *And what are you doing about it, mate? Playing with your food.*

"I say, Theo?" Camille asked.

He started guiltily and glanced up. "Sorry?"

"Aren't you going to offer your friend some tea?"

"That's very kind, but I couldn't possibly have another cup." Bonnie shook her head. "I've just finished having tea myself and was preparing to leave when I noticed Theo here and had to come say hello." She leveled her gaze at him for a moment. "It wouldn't do to ignore a friend, would it?"

Theo kept his smile frozen in place. She'd caught that, had she? *Blast.* He was making a right mess of things.

Camille laughed. "Funny you should say that." She slipped her phone out from under the table and tapped it. "I've been ignoring texts from a friend because I didn't want to be rude to dear Theo here." Camille nodded at Bonnie and stood. "But now I won't feel guilty, since I'll be leaving him in such excellent company."

Unable to resist years of habit, Theo stood as well. "You're leaving?"

"I'm afraid I must," Camille said. "You don't mind, do you?"

"Of course not." Theo paused, duty warring with desire. "Let me walk you out."

Camille brushed him off. "Nonsense. I can take care of myself." To Bonnie, she said, "So nice to meet you. Good luck with the wedding."

"The what?" The redhead's face blanched.

"Your friend's wedding this summer?"

"Oh." Bonnie exhaled, smiling weakly. "Right. That. Thanks."

"This was actually nice," Camille told Theo. With a polite peck on his cheek, she whispered in his ear, "And don't worry, I'll be sure to give both our mums a positive report. I'll see you this evening." She gave him a conspiratorial wink and was gone.

Theo's bum had barely landed back on his chair when Bonnie announced she needed to leave as well. "So soon?" A lump formed in Theo's throat. He'd been looking forward to having a few moments alone with her. "Is it the company?"

"No." She smiled, but it didn't reach her eyes.

Looking more closely, he noticed dark smudges beneath

her eyes, as if she hadn't slept well. Theo continued to study her. There was a tightness around her mouth, a hard set to her shoulders. Something was bothering her, and he'd give anything to know what it was. He stood and offered her his hand. "Shall I walk you out?"

"Didn't we cover this last night?" Bonnie stirred, shaking off the momentary ennui that had seemed to engulf her. She got to her feet, notching her chin up. "I'm a big girl. Like Camille said, I can take care of myself."

"What is it with you women?" Theo shook his head, signing off on the bill and handing it to a waiter.

"Excuse me?" She bristled.

"Beg pardon." Theo squirmed under her sharp gaze. "That, ah, didn't come out as I'd intended."

"Oh?" She fell into step with him as they exited the tea room. "And what were your intentions?"

"I was merely offering the pleasure of my company to escort you to"—he waved a hand toward the lobby doors —"wherever it is you are going."

"Why?" She crossed her arms over her chest.

"Because . . ." He faltered. "Because it's the polite thing to do," he finished weakly.

"How about this," Bonnie said, one corner of her mouth curling, the curve of her cheek ripe with mischief. "Since it's, as you say, the polite thing to do, and since we're in *my* city, how about *I* accompany *you*?"

"I suppose that would work." Theo nodded. He'd wanted to spend more time with her. This was his opportunity. He was going to seize it.

"It's settled, then." She relaxed, dropping her arms and passing through the hotel's revolving door.

"Yes," he agreed, following right behind her.

They stood on the street outside the Drake, staring at each other. He was at a loss for what to do next. Should he take her arm? Or would that set her off, launching her into another declaration of independence and self-sufficiency? Was he such a prig to assume it only proper to offer to escort a lady home? To pull out a chair for her? Hold the door? Take her arm when walking?

She solved the arm dilemma by taking his. Bonnie sidled up next to him, slipping her hand under his elbow and curling her fingers around his biceps. He stared at her hand, resting on his upper arm. A pleasant heat curled through him at the sight. He liked the way she looked next to him—liked the way she felt against him—entirely too much.

"Well?" she demanded.

"Sorry?" He glanced down at her, caught off guard by the startling blue of her eyes. She was so fair, her skin almost glowed, saved from being too pale by the delightful smattering of freckles dusting her cheeks and kissing the bridge of her nose.

The freckles bunched as her nose crinkled. "Um, Theo?"

"Yes?" he asked, distracted by her nose. It was adorable, sloping up slightly at the end and giving her a playful, elfish air. He wanted to kiss her there, bend forward and plant a peck on that cute little spot.

"You need to tell me where it is I am accompanying you to."

"Oh, right. The Waldorf." He turned with her, heading for the streetlight on the corner.

"The Waldorf between State and Rush?"

"Ah, I believe that's the one. Do you know it?"

"I do . . ." She tightened her hold on his arm, forcing him to a stop.

Pedestrians swarmed around them, jostling as they passed. He glanced down at her, concern rising in his chest.

She seemed paler than before, her freckles standing out in stark relief, her blue eyes wide. "Is something amiss?"

"Yeah," she said slowly, glancing up at him, a smirk curling in the corner of her mouth. "You were going the wrong way." Hand still wrapped around his arm, she turned around, tugging him in the opposite direction. As she moved forward again, she seemed to shake off whatever had been bothering her, and the color returned to her cheeks. Or maybe that was the blasted wind, blowing in off the lake, straight into his face, stinging his skin, making his eyes water and whipping her hair into a frenzy around them both.

He squeezed his burning eyes shut and let her guide him through the bustling throngs. Theo was out of his element here, literally. He was used to navigating blustery London weather and bustling London crowds, but Chicago was different. There was an aggressive energy to this city he'd never felt back home. To be honest, he was glad of her company. He cracked an eye open and cast a sideways glance at her, noting her quick, confident stride.

Unable to resist, his gaze strayed lower, relishing the glimpses of thigh revealed as each step tugged her hem above her knee for a tantalizingly brief moment. She was on the shorter side, the top of her head barely reaching his shoulders, and yet her legs ate up the sidewalk. Theo had to actively work to keep pace with her. Though lagging behind had its benefits too, he thought, ogling the lush curve of her bum beneath the smooth fabric of her skirt.

Forcing his gaze away, he quickened his step to match hers and took in his surroundings. Towering buildings lined the sidewalk to his right. Beyond the traffic-packed street to their left, the bold blue of the lake stretched all the way to the horizon. Above them, the late afternoon sun sank toward the line of buildings in the west. It was getting late.

Disappointment washed over him. He'd hoped to have more time with Bonnie, maybe invite her to the hotel lounge for a drink before he had to get ready for the event with Camille tonight.

"How much farther?" he asked as they waited for traffic to pass at a crosswalk.

She startled, as if she'd been lost in her own thoughts. "A few more minutes," she said, tugging on his arm and pulling him into the intersection.

He resisted, planting his feet at the edge of the curb. The signal had changed, giving them the right of way, but cars were still streaming past.

She tugged harder. "Come on, let's go." She moved forward, and he had no choice but to move with her. Around them, the crowd surged forward, crossing the street. Cars came to a reluctant halt, mere millimeters from striking pedestrians who seemed unfazed by the possibility of imminent death.

Safely on the other side, Theo stopped short. "Are you *all* insane?"

She released his arm, squeezing closer as the crowd continued to stream past them. "What are you talking about?"

He waved an arm toward the intersection.

She glanced back and then shrugged. "If you don't go, they'll never stop."

"There are traffic signals," he sputtered. "Rules!"

She snorted with laughter. "What, you think because the light changes, and drivers are supposed to stop, they will? Maybe even wave you through with a polite *cheerio*? Not happening. This is Chicago. The only way a car stuck in downtown gridlock is going to stop is if you go."

"But what if they don't stop?" he asked, still shaken at how the soft, sweet woman next to him had dragged them into the path of oncoming traffic without an ounce of hesitation. "What if they keep coming?"

Bonnie laughed again, reclaiming his arm. "Hopefully, you survive the impact."

"And then?"

"And then you make them pay."

"How?"

"As my uncle Donnie once explained it," she said, her voice taking on masculine swagger and an unfamiliar accent with a hint of something he recognized as Irish. "You got two choices."

"Which are?" Theo wasn't sure he wanted to know the answer.

She snorted and curled her lip. "You either sue their ass or kick it."

Theo shook his head but let her continue leading him down the sidewalk. "Bloody uncivilized Yanks."

"Don't let any of the Blythe boys hear you say that," Bonnie warned, sidestepping a street vendor with ease.

It was unlikely he'd ever meet this pugilistic Uncle Donnie, or any other members of Bonnie's extended family. Still, he found himself curious. "Why's that?"

"My cousins are diehard South Side Irish." She grinned. "Chicago first, Ireland second, America third."

"Duly noted." Theo matched her grin. "And for the record," he added, placing his hand over hers, still resting on his arm, "nobody says 'cheerio' anymore. It'd be like me saying 'howdy, pardner,' or some such nonsense."

"Duly noted," she echoed, her grin sliding into a teasing smirk, "pardner."

CHAPTER 8

AS THEY STEPPED off the sidewalk and entered the Waldorf's brick-paved courtyard, Bonnie plotted her escape. She didn't want Theo to know she was staying in the same hotel. First of all, she didn't want to have to explain *why* she was staying in a hotel. And second, she didn't think it was wise to reveal she was sleeping under the same roof as the too-charming Brit. As if letting him know she was also staying here would be akin to inviting him to her room or something.

The noise of the city was muted here, and their steps echoed on the brick cobblestones lining the courtyard. She cast a glance sideways, unable to resist admiring his profile. She could admit, from a purely objective standpoint of course, that Theo was a very handsome man. Tall and lean, but with wide shoulders filling out his suit jacket, his crisp Oxford shirt stretching snug across his broad chest.

Bonnie didn't have to imagine what that chest and shoulders looked like; she knew. She'd been standing in the hallway of a hotel in London when he'd opened the door to his room, dressed in nothing but a towel. The way she could recall the encounter in perfect detail, one would think she had a photographic memory. Still wet from a shower, his thick locks of hair dripped, the water beading on his chest, rolling down his abdomen, droplets following the trail of dark hair below his navel and disappearing beneath the white cotton wrapped around his waist . . .

She sucked in a lungful of bracing spring air and pulled up short a few steps from the hotel's entrance. "Well, then. Here we are." She smiled up at him, trying not to notice how the late afternoon sunshine slanted over the buildings at just such an angle to shine on his face, making his blue eyes sparkle.

"Fancy a drink?" he asked, nodding his head toward the hotel. "To thank you for accompanying me through the dangerous intersections." He grinned.

Heaven help her. "I shouldn't . . . I mean, I couldn't." She stumbled over her words.

He quirked a brow. "Which is it?" His grin widened, and a dimple appeared.

Immediately, the backs of her knees tickled, prickling with heat. "Can't," she said more firmly.

"I see." His face fell. "Forgive me, I'm sure you have other obligations to attend to." His gaze wandered to her left hand.

Bonnie flexed her fingers inside her gloves. No, she was not relieved he couldn't see she wasn't wearing her engagement ring. Fine, she was. But only because it saved her from having to explain anything. "I really should be going," she said, pasting a hasty smile on her face. "It was nice running into you. Again."

"The pleasure was all mine," he assured her.

Somehow, the line coming from him was endearing and not smarmy. Theo had a way of doing that. He reached for her hand, and she quickly thrust out her right. He took it, but rather than place a polite kiss on her gloved fingers, he turned her palm up and brushed his lips across the inside of her wrist, at the patch of bare skin between her glove and coat.

Oh. The prickling intensified, and her legs wobbled.

She yanked her hand back. "Well. I'm sure I'll see you around." She risked a glance up at him. "You know, with Cassie and Logan. For wedding stuff."

"Right," he agreed, watching her, "wedding stuff."

"Okay then . . . bye!" She turned on her heel, hoping she didn't look as awkward as she felt, and hurried out of the courtyard. *Don't look back. Don't look back. Don't look back.*

She kept up the mantra until she reached the sidewalk but couldn't resist one last glance over her shoulder as she eased into the crowd. Framed in a sliver of golden sunshine, Theo was still standing in the courtyard, the weight of his intense blue gaze landing unerringly on her.

Locking her knees, She forced her legs to keep moving and disappeared into the sea of pedestrians. Instead of stopping in the coffee shop as she'd originally planned, Bonnie kept walking, waiting for the tingling sensation to wear off. She rounded the corner and headed up State Street, knees still prickling.

The problem was, she couldn't stop thinking about Theo and his charming manners and his charming smile and his charming eyes. The man was a freaking British tea bag *steeped* in charm, and those darn dashing dimples of his turned her legs to jelly. She walked faster. Fifteen minutes later, cheeks cold and chapped from the brisk spring wind blowing in off the lake, Bonnie entered the Waldorf courtyard again, nodded to the bewildered doorman, and strode inside.

As she made her way through the lobby, she started

another mental to-do list. Focused on ticking off boxes in her head, she almost missed the tall dark-haired man standing at the bank of elevators, his broad back to her.

She knew that back, knew those shoulders and that perfectly combed head of hair. She'd waved goodbye to that head a quarter of an hour ago.

What the hell is he still doing downstairs? A squeak of frustration escaped her. Theo's head snapped up. Bonnie panicked. Before those dashing blue eyes turned in her direction, she backpedaled, scurrying into one of the many alcoves lining the lobby.

Huddled on the bench in the recessed space, she held her breath, listening intently for the ding of an elevator. Knowing her luck, he'd come investigate, if for no other reason than because she'd find it inconvenient. Any second now, his head would appear around the alcove, gorgeous blue eyes curious. He'd ask what she was doing there, and she'd say . . .

She'd say . . .

She'd say she had to use the restroom. All that tea at the Drake, you know? Then he'd smile that dimpled smile of his, and her knees would turn to water, and *oh, for heaven's sake, Bonnie, how do you get yourself into these situations?*

The elevator bell chimed, and Bonnie popped her head up. After the hushed whoosh of the doors sliding closed, she counted to ten, and then set her feet on the floor. She crept around the edge of the alcove. The coast was clear.

Phew. She hurried forward to catch the next elevator. As she waited, a new fear cropped up in her paranoid brain. What if he forgot something and came back down? What if the elevator returned to the main floor, and the doors opened to reveal Theo standing there? Deciding she was not willing to risk the possibility, Bonnie headed for the stairwell.

Three flights up, she was starting to regret her decision. She actually did need to pee, and her feet were killing her. She loved her new emergency credit card boots, adored them. But they were brand new, and walking to and from the Drake had barely begun to break them in. Now, each step she took was met with stinging pain as the cute ankle boots rubbed against the back of her heels.

When she reached the landing for the fifth floor, Bonnie decided she'd had enough. She didn't really plan to take the stairs *all* the way up to her floor anyway, did she? She was being an idiot; there was no way she'd run into Theo now.

She shoved the stairwell door open and hobbled down the hall toward the elevator. Moments later, she reached her floor and slipped into the empty hall. Relief flooded her. A few more steps and she'd be safely tucked away in Sadie's suite.

Barely twenty feet from where she stood, a door swung open. The tidal wave of relief froze, her blood turning to slush. Exiting his room, only a few doors down from her own suite, was Theo.

Of course.

Ice bucket in hand, he pulled his door shut and headed down the hall, away from her. She bit her lip and stared at his retreating figure. Fists clenched, aching feet poised to flee, she squeezed her eyes shut. *Don't look back. Don't look back. Please don't look back.*

"Miss Blythe?" a cultured English voice called out.

She scrunched up her face, closing her eyes even tighter.

"Bonnie?"

The voice was closer now. She risked a peek, opening one eye, and regretted the move instantly.

He'd reached the spot where she stood glued to the hall carpet.

"Theo!" She smiled wide, lips stretched across her teeth. "What a surprise."

"I could say the same." He looked down at her, mouth curving in a much more genuine, albeit curious smile. "Did I miss something?"

"What?" she asked, hating and loving how she had to tilt her chin to look up at him. Gabe was of average height, only a few inches above her own five-foot-four. Standing in front of her, Theo's chin cleared the top of her curls, and that was while she was in heels. It would be so easy to lean against him, to lay her cheek on his chest . . . "What's missing?" she asked, trying to focus on the conversation while her imagination continued to cuddle him.

"That's precisely what I'm trying to figure out." He chuckled, a low rumbling sound that did funny things to her insides. "Are you following me?"

Bonnie swallowed hard. "No."

He bent his head and leaned closer. "Are you sure?"

"Yes." She scooted away from him, but her hasty escape was impaired by a burst of fire in her right heel. Ignoring the excruciating sting of leather shredding her skin, she shuffled forward, gritting her teeth as pain lanced through her. Damn new shoes.

"Are you all right?" Theo called from behind her.

"Fine," she seethed, and kept moving.

"No, you're not." He caught up to her. "What is this, the Ministry of Silly Walks?"

She ignored his Monty Python reference. *Shuffle. Wince. Shuffle. Wince.*

"Bonnie, this is nonsense." He stepped in front of her, forcing her to stop. "I can see you are in pain." His blue eyes searched hers, brows furrowed in concern. "What happened?"

It was his concern that undid her.

"What happened?" Her voice was too high, too shrill. She paused and reined herself in. "You want to know what happened?"

"Yes."

She expected him to glance around, to check if they were alone in the hallway, worried about making a scene. But he didn't. He just stared at her, eyes intent, concern even more evident than before—concern for her. "Yes, I want to know. I asked, didn't I?"

"I bought new shoes."

"Oh." The abrupt shift from concern to confusion on his face was almost comical.

"Yeah, I bought new boots this morning, and they're killing me." She bent and yanked at the high-heeled boot, sucking in a breath as it rubbed against the blister, slicing into her skin while she pulled it off her foot.

"Christ, you're bleeding."

She glanced down. A bright red stain soaked the heel of her new tights. Bonnie stared at the blood, lip trembling. And then she just lost it. Dropping her boot, the floodgates opened, and she began to sob.

In an instant, Theo was there. He set the ice bucket down on the ground and wrapped his arms around her. She pressed her face into his broad chest, crying and sniffling and making a blubbery mess. But the tears wouldn't stop. They kept coming, waves of them, and all she could do was cling to him and ride out the storm.

Distantly, she was aware she was moving. Theo had picked her up and was carrying her, one arm tucked behind her knees and the other wrapped around her back.

Face still huddled against his chest, the sobs turned to hiccups.

Theo stopped walking. Leaning over her, his mouth close to her ear, he said, "I'm going to set you down now, all right?"

She nodded.

He lowered her to the ground, and she wobbled, unsteady with only one boot on. "My boot—"

"I have it, Cinderella." He held up the ice bucket, her new ankle boot sticking out of the top.

She giggled. Then hiccupped.

Tucking the bucket under his arm, he reached into his pocket and pulled out a key card. Swiping it in the slot, he held the door open and gestured for her to step inside.

Bonnie hesitated.

"Please," he said, "let me help you."

She eyed him. Theo's once crisp shirt was a disaster, a sodden, wrinkled mess, and she was pretty sure she'd gotten snot on him. "I ruined your shirt."

"I have others."

"You've done enough." She reached for her boot. "I'm fine, really."

He let her take it, swinging the ice bucket in one hand. "Don't you trust me?"

She stared down at her boot, fiddling with the decorative little buttons on the side. *He* wasn't the problem. She didn't trust herself.

"Come along." His starched accent brooked no arguments. "I'll get you patched up."

Before she knew it, she was propped on the chaise in Theo's suite, pulling off her other boot while he called the front desk and ordered a first aid kit sent up. Waiting for it to arrive, he busied himself with the room's tea and coffee service. "I'll make you some tea."

He smiled at her from across the room. Bonnie looked away before the dimples made an appearance. "We just had tea."

"Another spot of tea never hurt anyone," he said over the gurgle of hot water streaming from the coffeemaker. "In fact," he continued, popping a bag into the steaming paper cup, "I'd say it was just the thing."

A knock sounded at the door. He handed her the tea and went to answer it. She stared down at the amber liquid. As the heat slowly seeped into her palms, she realized she was still wearing her gloves, and still in her jacket as well.

Theo returned, carrying a small plastic box. "Now then, let's get you fixed up, shall we?"

He knelt at the end of the chaise and opened the kit. "Hmm," he muttered, inspecting her heel.

"What?"

He made an awkward little cough and glanced up. "Um . . ."

Bonnie looked at her foot and realized his dilemma. She was wearing tights. He could either cut them or . . . "Here." She passed him the cup. "Give me a minute." She scooted off the chaise and headed for the bathroom, half hopping, half hobbling on tiptoe to avoid possibly getting blood on the hotel's carpet. Closing the door, she tugged off her gloves and tucked them into a pocket, shrugging the jacket off. Then she reached under her skirt to shimmy her tights down her legs. She rinsed them in cold water, doing her best to get the bloodstain out of the heel.

She washed her hands and splashed her cheeks. Drying off, she glanced in the mirror, and immediately wished she hadn't. Her face was worse off than Theo's shirt. Beet-red nose, eyes puffy and smudged with streaks of mascara. Bonnie grabbed a couple of tissues and dabbed here and there, doing her best to minimize the damage. Or at least look less like a deranged raccoon. Whatever. She wasn't trying to impress anyone, right? She met her eyes in the mirror. *Right.*

A tap on the door had her wiping frantically at the remaining smudges. "Just a minute," she called over the running water.

"Is everything all right in there?"

"Yeah . . ." Bonnie rinsed her hands and shut off the faucet. She picked up her tights, squeezed out the excess water, and then hung them on the towel rack to dry. Taking a shaky breath, she opened the bathroom door.

Theo was standing on the threshold, his face inches from hers.

Unable to meet his gaze, she floundered for a distraction. "Your shirt!" She ordered, thrusting a hand out, "Give it to me."

"Pardon?"

"I'll rinse it out in the sink."

He made a face, looking as if he would argue further, but then sighed and began to undo the buttons. "If it will get you to hurry up, fine." He handed her the shirt.

Bonnie grabbed it from him and flipped the cold water back on. *No,* she told herself as she rubbed the little bar of hotel soap over the stains, *she was not disappointed he'd been wearing a T-shirt underneath. No,* she said, scrubbing harder, s*he'd not been hoping for another glimpse of his bare Brit bod.* She rinsed the shirt and flung it over the towel rack, next to her tights.

"Ready?"

She jumped. Theo was standing behind her. In the mirror's reflection, she watched him hold up the first aid kit and shake it.

"Um, sure." She met his gaze in the mirror. "It's not that bad, really." Her gaze dropped to his chest. *Not bad at all.* The soft cotton of his white T-shirt stretched snugly across his pecs and bunched tight around the thick swell of his biceps. He wasn't bulging with muscles, but what he had were well-made and . . . perfect.

"I can take care of myself, you know," she grumbled as he led her back to the chaise.

"Tut-tut." He brushed aside her protests and pressed down on both her shoulders, urging her to sit.

Lacking the energy to argue further, she sat. Theo knelt on the floor in front of her, rummaging through the kit. His shoulders bunched, and her belly quivered. She shifted her focus, studying the top of his dark head while he opened an alcohol wipe. A moment later his fingers wrapped around her ankle and lifted her leg. He swabbed the back of her heel.

She gasped.

He glanced up, and when his eyes met hers, she struggled for another breath, oxygen suddenly in short supply. She forced herself to continue to breathe, unable to look away, locked on his gaze. His eyes were a bright bold blue she'd found breathtaking enough from afar, but up close, she noticed a starburst of indigo encircling his pupils, creating a shift in color so slight as to be almost imperceptible. The discovery felt intimate, like a secret.

"Sorry." His face creased with concern. "Stings?"

Bonnie bit her lip and managed some sort of noise in response. It didn't sting, it tingled . . . everywhere. Awareness sparked from where his warm hand gripped her ankle, danced up her calf, tickled her thigh, and settled between her legs. She squirmed on the chaise.

"I'll do my best to be quick," he assured her, resting her leg on his knee and reaching for a bandage.

Honestly, the man could take as long as he wanted. The smooth linen of his dress pants brushed her bare calf, and she could feel his leg muscles bunching beneath her when he shifted his weight.

"There." His fingers were strong yet gentle as they smoothed the edges of the bandage over her heel. "All done." He patted her ankle and smiled up at her, twin dimples firing.

Good thing she was sitting down, because her knees would have completely failed her. Mouth dry, she licked her lips and croaked out a thank you.

"No problem at all," he said, his gaze shifting to her lips. He swallowed. She could see his Adam's apple bob above the cotton neckline of his tee.

"Sorry about your shirt," she said.

"Pardon?" He tore his gaze away from her mouth and met her eyes again.

"Your shirt." She tilted her head toward the suite's bathroom, then brushed a hand over the front of his T-shirt, indicating the faint stains where the residue of her crying fit had leaked through.

"It's no matter." He shrugged. "But, and forgive me for prying," he said, covering her hand with his own, "I sense there *is* something bothering you . . . beyond the, uh, injury." He cupped her fingers, pressing down gently, until her palm rested against his chest. "Care to talk about it?"

Bonnie shook her head. "I don't know where to start."

One corner of his mouth curled in the bud of a smile. "Perhaps you can begin with what you're doing in my hotel. Are you stalking me?"

"I already told you I'm not following you! And it's not *your* hotel."

"You know what I mean." The smile blossomed and, *oh God*, there were those damn dimples again.

She dropped her gaze and stared at their stacked hands. She shifted on the chaise, suddenly very aware of the fact he was crouched on one knee on the floor in front of her, her bare leg still propped on his thigh, her fingers still resting on his chest.

Beneath her hand, the subtle beat of his heart thumped against her palm, and Bonnie became aware of something else.

She was no longer wearing a ring on that hand.

She was no longer engaged.

"Bonnie?" Theo's soft voice prodded.

He wanted to know why she was here? Why she was in this hotel with him instead of home with her fiancé? Fine. She'd tell him.

"It's not just your hotel, it's mine too." She glanced up. "Remember my friend Sadie? Her dad works for this hotel chain and has a suite here." Bonnie pulled her leg off his knee. It might be easier to talk to him if they weren't touching so much. If nothing else, it would be easier to concentrate.

"Okay . . ." Theo said slowly, resting back on his heels.

She pulled her hand out from under his and waved her naked ring finger in his face. "My engagement is off."

His face went blank. Then his brows furrowed. "What happened?"

She patted the empty space on the chaise, inviting Theo to sit next to her.

"Last night," Bonnie began, and paused, emotion tightening her throat. *God, was it only just last night?* She took a slow, deep breath and started again. "Last night, after I left the Shakespeare gala, I went home and found Gabe . . ." She stopped, struggling to get the words out.

Why was this so hard? She hadn't been the one caught sleeping around, yet a sense of shame filled her.

"Let me guess." Theo's voice was mild but clipped. "He wasn't working on his paper."

"Uh, no." Bonnie tried to keep her tone light. "He was too busy working some blonde over."

"Fucking areshole!" Theo cursed, blue eyes flashing, growing dark as thunder clouds.

"You're right," Bonnie agreed, his temper igniting her own, replacing shame with cleansing self-righteous anger. "He *is* a fucking arsehole!"

"What did you do?" Theo asked. "Punch him in his cheating face?"

She shook her head. "No, but I, um, I did consider cutting it off."

"It?" His eyes rounded. "*It,* it?"

She nodded.

"With a knife?"

She shook her head.

"A scissors?"

Again, she shook her head.

"Well, what then?"

Bonnie blew out an embarrassed chuckle. "A nail file."

At the horrified look on his face, her nervous titter turned into an all-out belly laugh.

"What's so funny?" Theo demanded.

She wiped tears from her eyes. "Your face," she wheezed. Bonnie realized much of her humor was the release of pent-up stress, but still, he did look pretty funny.

"Forgive me," Theo said drily, "but you have to admit, that's a chilling prospect. I'd wager your fiancé made a few faces of his own."

"*Ex*-fiancé," Bonnie stressed, before bursting into another round of giggles as she recalled Gabe's pale face, hands crossed over his crotch. "And I didn't do it. I only thought about doing it. Briefly."

"Understandable," Theo agreed. "What *did* you do?"

Her laughter subsided. "Told him it was over. Tossed the ring onto the bed and walked out."

"Then it *was* you I saw in the lobby."

"Huh?"

"Last night, I thought I saw you standing at the front desk."

"Why didn't you say anything?"

"I wasn't sure it was you." He cleared his throat. "Sorry. You could have used a friend."

"Friendship is certainly the finest balm for the pangs of disappointed love." She sighed.

"Er, quite," he agreed, eyeing her with a confused half-smile.

"Jane Austen? *Northanger Abbey*?" His expression didn't change. Apparently, his Austen wasn't as up to snuff as his Shakespeare. "Never mind. It's probably a good thing you didn't talk to me then. I wasn't in the best mood."

What would have happened if he *had* approached her last night? Her emotions had been in such turmoil, anything was possible.

"What does Cassie have to say about all this?"

Bonnie studied her fingernails. "She doesn't know."

"You haven't told her yet?" His brow puckered.

"I haven't had time."

He didn't say anything, but those disapproving brows rose in doubt, and he pursed his lips.

"Stop it." She gave him a little shove. "You look like a judgmental schoolmarm."

His pursed lips quirked, and she could tell he was

struggling to maintain his dour expression. "I daresay no one has ever made such an observation regarding my appearance before."

"Well, I daresay I'm right," she teased. "All you need is a ruler and a pair of those horn-rimmed glasses."

He lost the battle with his mouth and burst into laughter. Bonnie's knees quivered. He really was too beautiful for his own good. Dashing when he smiled, absolutely devastating when he laughed. The tickling sensation moved from the backs of her knees, up her thighs, and higher still.

He waggled his finger at her, the picture of a priggish schoolmarm. "Enough trying to change the subject. Why haven't you told Cassie yet?"

She shrugged.

"She's your best friend."

"I know."

"Then, why?"

"I don't know."

He stared down at her, and this time, it wasn't disapproval she saw in his face, but pity.

"Don't feel bad for me."

"I don't." He scratched at the stubble on his chin. "Well, I do."

Her eyes widened, and he stumbled over the next few words, a string of nonsensical syllables stuttering out before he picked up a coherent line of thought again. "What I meant is, I feel bad you were treated so poorly,"

"You feel sorry for me."

"Not at all."

"Yes, you do," she insisted hotly, scooting away from him as she struggled to contain the bubble of anger and frustration rising inside her. "I don't want your pity. I don't want you to feel sorry for me."

He gripped her shoulders, voice gruff, his words coming out in a rush. "I'm sorry you were hurt, but I'm not sorry it happened."

The bubble popped. All the air in the room evaporated as they stared at each other, his confession hanging between them.

Bonnie's mouth opened, closed, and opened again. But nothing came out. She wet her lips and tried again. "Are you saying—"

"Yes."

"You mean you're interested in—"

"I am." His hands tightened on her shoulders.

"Would you mind letting me finish a sentence here?" She scowled and squirmed, trying to shake loose from his grip. "Besides, how do you know what I was going to say?"

"Shall I spell it out for you?" Theo's blue eyes bore into hers, cutting through her bullshit. "Yes, I'm saying I'm not sorry your engagement is broken. In fact, I'm bloody thrilled." He leaned closer, close enough she could smell the clean starchy scent of his cotton T-shirt mixed with something warm and spicy that made her think of delicious baked things.

"Because yes, I *am* interested in you. Very interested, indeed."

"Indeed?" she echoed, copying his accent, trying to diffuse the moment with humor.

"Indeed," Theo repeated, his gaze shifting to her mouth. The hungry look in his eyes completely nulled her attempt to lighten the mood.

"Oh. Well." Her voice sounded breathy and excited in her own ears. Heat crept up her neck and cheeks. She licked her lips, belatedly realizing he was still staring at her mouth. Again, his eyes flashed, and the temperature in the room shot up by at least ten degrees. *Tit for tat,* Bonnie decided, shifting her gaze to stare at his mouth too.

Fair is fair, right? What's good for the goose is good for the gander. What would be the harm in kissing him? Gabe had done a whole lot more than that. She continued to stare at Theo's mouth, a very nice mouth, really. Full and firm. If she were to nibble on it, would he taste as good as he smelled? All spicy and sweet?

"What are you thinking?"

She shook her head.

"Tell me." His soft command was laced with tension.

Sexual tension? "I was thinking," she began, pausing to take a breath before diving in, "about what it would be like to kiss you."

"Oh?"

She nodded.

"Is that all?"

He was giving her an out. *There it is, Bonnie. Take it and run.*

"Well, I was also thinking . . ." She shifted on the chaise, feeling silly and bashful, and about twelve years old. Which was probably, ironically, the last time she'd flirted. Was that what she was doing right now? Flirting? God, she was so bad at it, she didn't even know if she was doing it.

What she did know, however, was that she liked him. And he liked her too, he said so. *There you go again, sounding like a twelve-year-old.* "I was also thinking," she continued, "well, wondering actually . . ."

"About what?"

"About what you taste like." Her words tumbled over each other as she spit out the admission all at once. Then, before she could change her mind, she gripped the front of his T-shirt in her fist and tugged him toward her, pulling his mouth down to hers.

A second before their lips met, she hesitated. His mouth

hovered above hers. He didn't press forward, didn't complete the kiss. It would have been easier if he had. Would have taken the pressure off her, eased the responsibility of making a decision.

But he didn't do that. Holding himself back, Theo's action, or rather inaction, sent a clear message. If she was going to kiss him, it would be her choice. If she was going to put her mouth on his, it would be because she wanted to.

And, oh God, she wanted to.

Bonnie lifted her chin and met his eyes. *Screw your courage to the sticking place.* She brushed her mouth across Theo's. It could almost have been accidental, a momentary bumping of lips. But this was no accident. A mistake, maybe. But she'd think about that later.

Closing her eyes, she pressed her lips to his. And quickly realized she had no idea what she was doing. She'd never kissed anyone but Gabe before. Well, there'd been stage kisses with other actors, but those didn't count. Usually, when Gabe kissed her, there was a predictable pattern, a process she was familiar with. But now, kissing Theo, she was in completely new and unfamiliar territory.

She brushed her mouth across his again, back and forth, and each time a tingle of something electric vibrated along her nerve endings, making her skin feel more awake, more alive. The sensation encouraged her, emboldened her. She parted her lips, letting the tip of her tongue sweep against him.

Reaching out, a tentative explorer taking her first steps in the new world, Bonnie slid her tongue into Theo's mouth the tiniest bit, testing . . . tasting. Tart lemon bloomed on her tongue. She smiled against his mouth, tempted to go further, and thrust her tongue deeper.

Oh. More sparks.

She traced the shape of his mouth with her tongue,

licking the little dip in the center of his upper lip. Then she sunk her teeth into his full lower lip, nibbling.

He groaned. Or was that a growl?

Fascinated, Bonnie licked the spot she'd nibbled, then bit him again, harder, wanting to provoke the beast, hoping to rouse another growl from him. She got more than a growl. Animalistic sounds rumbled in his chest, vibrating beneath her hand, still fisted in his shirt.

He reached up and threaded his fingers through her hair. Bracing his palms on either side of her face, he pulled back and met her gaze, a question in his blue eyes. She answered him soundlessly, nodding. The movement caused his thumbs to brush against her earlobes and Bonnie shivered.

Permission granted, his eyes darkened to blue fire, icy hot and intense, the indigo flecks orbiting his pupils sparking. This time, when his mouth lowered to hers, he went all the way, closing the distance. This time, *he* kissed *her*, his mouth enveloping hers, all heat and hunger. He didn't taste, he devoured. With another growl, he thrust his tongue inside her mouth, invading, exploring—claiming.

Theo took Bonnie's mouth with his, kissing her hard and deep, the way he'd wanted to for so long. He'd waged an internal war against this desire, losing the battle every night when his guard was down and his subconscious took over, filling his dreams with kisses and so much more. But she'd belonged to someone else, forbidden fruit, and his dreams had remained just that, only fantasies.

Now she was free, and his fantasy had come to life. He knew her heart was raw, the wounds of her breakup fresh, and likely she wasn't thinking clearly or acting sensibly. But if, in this moment, she wanted this, if she needed this—needed him—if kissing him helped her heal, made her feel better, he was happy to be of service. To bandage her wounded heart the same way he'd bandaged her heel.

The ache in his groin reminded him, despite what noble stories he told himself, this was not a completely selfless act on his part. And likely it was selfish of him to take advantage of her while she was in this state, but bloody hell, he wasn't a damn saint. He'd given her an out, offered her a choice, made sure the decision to kiss him had been hers.

Theo traced the angles of her face, running his fingers along her jaw, across her collarbone, over her shoulders, and down her arms to rest at her waist. He shifted, pulling her closer, and she splayed her hand flat against his chest, the heat of her palm burning through the thin fabric of his undershirt. Her hand dropped lower, skimming his abdomen, until her fingers rested against the clasp of his belt buckle. His cock jerked, eager for attention. *Not yet, you little bugger.*

Breathing hard, Theo broke the kiss, and grappled with the tattered remains of his self-control. They were moving too fast. She hadn't had time to process what she'd been through, and there was a good chance she'd regret . . . whatever it is they might do if he allowed what was happening between them to continue. He let go of her waist, pulling back to look at her.

That was a mistake.

Her cheeks were flushed a rosy pink, lips swollen from their kisses, eyes bright with lust. His chest tightened, need and doubt and caution warring for space. That she wanted him, was obvious. *Why* she wanted him, wasn't so clear. Was he just a convenient distraction? A way to get back at the man who had cheated on her?

Do you care? That was the real question. Was he willing to let himself be used in such a way? Could he sleep with Bonnie, knowing he was a pawn, whether consciously or unconsciously, meant to level the playing field? He was fairly certain he knew the answer . . . and wasn't nearly as disturbed by it as he should be.

But he wasn't a complete git. For both their sakes, he'd give them a little space. A little time to decide if this was what they really wanted. He brushed a stray curl from her forehead. It twisted around his finger, soft and silky, clinging to him. "Well." Theo cleared his throat. "I hope that answered your question."

She stared at him blankly.

"About the kiss?" He gave her a light, teasing smile. "What I taste like?"

After a moment, understanding flickered in her eyes. "Oh, right." She followed his casual, lighthearted lead and returned the grin, smacking her lips. "I'm satisfied."

"Good." He wasn't satisfied—far from it—but he'd wrestle with that later. Likely while alone in bed tonight. Rising from the chaise, Theo busied himself with cleaning up the first aid supplies. He closed the kit and set it aside before returning to sit next to her, trying not to stare at her bare legs and the adorable sprinkling of freckles on her knees, or to think about how he wanted to kiss each one. He'd tasted her mouth . . . now he was dying to know what she tasted like everywhere.

He cleared his throat again. "Back to my original question. Why haven't you told Cassie about the breakup yet?"

She stared at her hands, resting in her lap. Her right hand fiddled with her left, twisting a phantom ring. "It's stupid," she finally said.

"I doubt that," he assured her.

"Well, it's juvenile." Bonnie raised her gaze to his. "I'm jealous of her."

"Of Cassie?" Theo straightened. Had he read her

wrong? Did Bonnie want Logan instead? Had she been attracted to his friend all this time?

"Yes, of Cassie. I've been engaged for over a year, to a man I've been with for freaking ever, and here she is, planning a wedding to a guy she hasn't even *known* for a year!"

"Ah," Theo said.

"What do you mean, 'Ah'?" She glared at him, her mouth twisting defiantly, petulantly.

"It's only, I understand now."

"You do?"

"Of course. Have I ever told you I'm the oldest of four children? And that all my siblings are sisters?"

"So?"

"Let's just say, I have a better understanding of the female psyche than most men."

"What a pigheaded, chauvinistic thing to say," she scoffed, voice rising.

"All three of my sisters would agree with you. And perhaps you're right, but chauvinistic or not, I'm right too."

She snorted. "Another chauvinistic response."

Theo ignored the jab. He'd been navigating the minefield of his sisters' emotional outbursts his entire life and had learned when to keep his trap shut. Even though now was very likely one of those times, he couldn't resist pressing the issue. "It's all right to be upset, to be jealous even. Your friend is getting the very thing you've been waiting a long time for. I agree, it's not fair. But that's not her fault. And it's not fair of you to treat her like it is."

"That's not what I'm doing!" she sputtered.

"Isn't it?" He held her gaze steadily, until she squirmed and looked away.

"You have your schoolmarm face on again," she grumbled.

He chuckled but resisted her attempt to change the subject once more. No, she was going to work through this. And he was going to help her, if she'd let him. Any way he could. And yes, Theo decided, that included if she wanted to use him as a rebound lover.

Perhaps that was for the best. It wasn't as if he could offer her more.

But part of him acknowledged he was interested in more.

Even as he accepted this truth, the same honest, no-nonsense part of him warned he couldn't pursue that interest. Aside from the fact he lived halfway around the world, as acting head of the Wharton family and heir to the Emberton title, he had duties to fulfill. Obligations. Expectations. People were counting on him. His mother, his sisters . . . every bloody soul who depended on the Embertons for their livelihood.

Unlike his failure of a father, Theo was determined not to let them down.

Land rich and coin poor, with many of their extensive properties mortgaged to the hilt, Theo's father had dug the family deeper into debt year after year, leaving the Wharton finances in dire straits upon his death. Theo had been raised knowing it would be his job to undo the damage. His duty to save the family from complete financial ruin.

Over the past several years, he'd thrown himself into the task. Through a series of wise investments and careful estate management, he'd been able to stave off the worst from happening and avoided bankruptcy. But keeping the Emberton holdings solvent was like bailing water off a sinking ship with a teaspoon.

Eventually, he would have to succumb to the inevitable and follow through on his mother's plan. Which meant marrying an heiress with pockets deep enough to buoy the

Wharton coffers. Which also meant he had no business contemplating a relationship, of any kind, with Bonnie.

And yet, he couldn't stop himself from reaching for her hands. "Look," he told her. "You said it yourself; friendship is the balm of broken hearts or whatnot. Cassie is your best friend. The two of you have been together even longer than you've known what's-his-name, right?"

"You mean Gabe?"

He nodded. He recalled the cad's name. He just didn't want to say it.

"Yeah, Cassie and I became friends when we were in first grade. How did you know?"

"You told me. In London, while we were on the Eye. Remember?"

Bonnie nodded, her smile turning shy. "I can't believe *you* remember."

Theo brushed it off. He remembered every detail about their encounter last summer, but she didn't need to know that. "Speaking of remembering, what's important here is that you need to remember how much your friendship with Cassie means to you. Don't let what that bugger— *Gabe*—did get between you two. Tell her what happened." He squeezed her fingers gently. "She'll be hurt if she thinks you hid it from her."

"Wow, that's really good advice."

"I told you." Theo leaned back, her compliment making him feel like a bloody king. "Three sisters."

"Okay, okay. Keep the ego in check, please." Bonnie made a show of rolling her eyes, slipping her hands out of his grip. "But you're right. I'll tell Cassie. She wants to get together and discuss"—she grimaced—"wedding stuff with us before you leave. When are you heading back to London?"

"Monday." Theo stood and offered her a hand up. "I

believe Lo mentioned something about supper tomorrow night?"

She headed for the bathroom. "That works." A second later, she returned, tights bunched in her hand. "We should take you somewhere special. A Chicago tradition."

"Sounds delightful." Theo fought to keep his smile in place and groaned inwardly, not sure his stomach could handle another round of gut-busting deep-dish. "Can I walk you to your room?"

She glanced up from grabbing her boot. "This again? I can get there by myself, thank you."

"Sorry. Habit."

"I know. You're just being polite." She sighed. "Truth be told, it's actually kind of nice."

The grin he flashed her faded when he noticed she'd begun to wobble a little. "Are you all right? You sure you want to walk back barefoot? I can carry—"

"I'm fine," she insisted, gritting her teeth as she gathered up her coat and bag, her movements jerky, almost brusque.

Theo decided it was best not to press. And carrying Bonnie to her room, soft bare thighs balanced on his arm, warm weight curled against his chest, was probably not wise. "Well then, until tomorrow night?" he asked, holding his hotel room door open for her.

"Yes." She paused in the doorway. "And thanks again, for . . . everything."

He held her gaze, unable to resist letting some of his pent-up feelings slip through. "My pleasure."

CHAPTER 9

BACK IN HER own suite, Bonnie dumped everything on the floor, checked to make sure the bandage was still secure on her heel and collapsed onto the chaise. *My pleasure.* Those two words had been loaded with double entendre . . . right? She was often accused of being too naïve, too innocent. And it was true, dirty jokes often went over her head, and she rarely caught on when innuendos were fired in her direction. Yet even she couldn't miss the sexual heat burning in Theo's reply. And if she had, there was no mistaking the fire sparking in those blue eyes. *He wanted her.*

The knowledge made her tingle all over, even more than his dimples.

But not as much as his kisses.

Bonnie leaned back, staring up at the hotel ceiling. She'd kissed him. Tasted him. And he *had* tasted sweet and spicy—tart. As good as she'd imagined. Better. Like the lemon icing Mom frosted gingerbread with at Christmas.

And then he'd kissed her back. Bonnie pressed her bare

thighs together, squeezing her legs tightly closed. What if he'd kept kissing her? Her hand had been on his belt buckle. What if they hadn't stopped, if he hadn't pulled away? Would she have let her hand drop lower? Her mouth went dry as she shut her eyes, imagining what she might have found if her fingers had continued to explore that particular piece of British territory.

A blast of Spice Girls interrupted her very specific and very inappropriate speculations. Bonnie rolled off the chaise and dug her phone out of her purse. "Hey, Cassie."

"So, how did it go?"

It took Bonnie a moment to realize Cassie was referring to her meeting with the Cambridge people. If what happened last night felt like forever ago, tea at the Drake this afternoon seemed to have happened years ago. Her life was taking so many twists and turns, she'd aged a decade in a day. "Fine. Great." She filled Cassie in on the details.

"You're taking it? Fantastic!" she squealed. "Oh, Bonnie, I'm so happy for you. I *knew* you were perfect for the job."

Joy and pride were reflected in Cassie's voice, and Bonnie felt a deep tug of affection for her best friend. And guilt too. Theo was right. She needed to tell Cassie about what happened.

As if reading her mind, Cassie asked, "And Gabe is totally cool with this?"

Again, Bonnie screwed her courage to the sticking place. Channeling Lady Macbeth was exhausting. "Gabe really doesn't have a say."

Cassie laughed. "Right. Okay. Very forward thinking of you, but you know what I meant, Bon. This was supposed to be a special summer for the two of you, right? Your time to reconnect and all that."

"We broke up," Bonnie burst out, unable to listen to any

more about what was *supposed* to happen this summer. *What's past hope is past care, right?* She realized now why Cassie hated that saying so much. It really didn't help at all. "Cassie? Are you still there?"

"Uh, yeah. I'm . . . just in shock. Did you say you and Gabe broke up?"

"Yes."

"As in you two are over? The engagement is off?"

"Yes."

"Oh, Bonnie. What happened?"

For the second time that day, Bonnie replayed the terrible details. "I caught Gabe cheating on me."

"Wait, what? When?"

"Last night."

"And you're just telling me now?" Cassie's voice rose. "Why didn't you say anything earlier?"

"I wasn't ready to talk about it."

"Um. Okay," Cassie said. "Did you kick him out?"

"No. I left."

"Where are you? Did you go home to your parents' place?" Cassie asked, then added, "You should have told me. That must have been a lot, to get back to the city in time for the meeting at the Drake."

"I'm still in the city." Bonnie took a breath. "Sadie hooked me up with her dad's suite at the Waldorf."

"Oh," Cassie said, hurt weighing the word down. But good friend that she was, she didn't say anything more. "Hey," she said instead, her voice brightening. "You know what's wild? Theo's staying at the Waldorf too."

"Yeah, I know," Bonnie admitted.

"You do?" Cassie asked, surprised. She paused, and then repeated the question, drawling suggestively, "Oh, you do, do you?"

"Knock it off. We just happened to run into each other."

"Uh-huh," Cassie mocked disbelievingly. "Is that what they're calling it now?"

"I'm serious. Actually, I ran into him at the Drake, and we walked back together." Bonnie tactfully left out the part about her pathetic attempt to evade him at the hotel. And the kiss.

Cassie laughed.

"What?"

"Nothing."

"What's so funny?" Bonnie demanded, knowing it would bother her incessantly if Cassie didn't elaborate.

"It's just . . . interesting, that's all."

"Don't give me your Minnesota 'interesting,'" Bonnie huffed. "I know what that means."

Cassie laughed again. "No, really. I'm serious. I find it very interesting the two of you *happened* to cross paths like that."

Bonnie rolled her eyes. An avid fan of romance novels, Cassie was always seeing meaning in things like this, the hand of destiny at work, blah blah blah. Not that Bonnie wasn't guilty of doing the same. But Gabe was supposed to be her destiny. She was Anne, and he was her Gilbert. This wasn't supposed to be how their story ended.

Only Anne hadn't caught Gilbert screwing some blonde on Marilla's quilt.

Her heart thudded in her chest as the reality of the situation gripped her. A sob ripped from her throat. Damn it, she was crying again.

"Bonnie?" Cassie's concern was clear through the phone. "Bon? Are you crying?"

"No," Bonnie lied.

"That's it, I'm coming over," Cassie said, her voice brooking no argument. "You're in Sadie's dad's suite, right? The one we stayed in for her birthday?"

"Uh-huh," Bonnie said, sniffling.

"Got it. See you soon. Should I call Sadie and Ana? Make it a girls' night?"

"They're busy doing family stuff. It's Passover."

"Oh, right. Okay, well just me and you, then. Still a girl's night. I'll bring chocolate."

"And ice cream too?"

"Already planning on it."

"Perfect." She rubbed at her tear-streaked cheeks. "Thanks, Diana."

"No problem, Anne."

Bonnie smiled through her tears. Gabe may no longer be her Gilbert, but Cassie would always be her Diana. When Bonnie Blythe had met Cassie Crow for the first time in first grade, she'd known they'd be the best of friends. With initials like *B.B.* and *C.C.*, how could they not? And when Bonnie had read L.M. Montgomery's books a few years later in third grade, she knew she was right, and that she, with her head of frizzy red hair, was Anne Shirley, and Cassie was the dark-haired, dark-eyed Diana Barry, Anne's best friend. Her bosom buddy. Sisters for life.

"You're the best. See you soon." Bonnie ended the call, her heart lighter.

Theo had been right. She was glad she'd told Cassie.

Much as he wanted to, after Bonnie left, Theo didn't step into the hall to watch her make her way to her suite. Instead, he closed his hotel room door and pressed his face against it, thumping his forehead a few times. Maybe that would rattle things around up there, get him to focus on the tasks at hand. Tasks which did not involve an adorable redhead with freckles sprinkled across her knees like cinnamon sugar. He pushed away from the door and checked his watch. He had about an hour before the car arrived to take him to meet Camille.

He stripped off the soiled T-shirt and tossed it on the chaise, then hit the loo for a quick onceover on his face with the electric razor, glad he'd remembered to pack the power adapter. He rinsed his face, now smooth again, and reached for a towel. His damp shirt still hung over the rail. Theo pulled it down and examined it, pleasantly surprised to note it was perfectly clean. Wrinkled and wet, but clean. She'd managed to get the stains out.

The memory of her tear-streaked face made his heart lurch. *That bloody friggin' tosser.* To make Bonnie cry like that. How could anyone hurt her so badly. Betray her? He wanted to kick the man's arse and thank him at the same time. But he would do neither. It wasn't his place.

Theo set the shirt aside, wishing he could set thoughts of Bonnie aside as easily. But unlike the stains she'd so tidily wiped away, the moment they'd shared couldn't be erased. As he began to pull on his formal wear, he acknowledged he didn't want to erase it. He didn't regret the kiss. Would do it again if given half the chance. If he was honest, he hoped he'd get that chance.

Was it wrong that he was preparing to spend the evening with one woman while wishing he could be with another? Did that make him no better than Bonnie's jackass fiancé?

Ex-fiancé. He rubbed a hand over his face. *Your point, mate?* She might be free, but he wasn't, not really. Right now, he had to focus. He was here on family business. Theo checked his watch. Thirty minutes.

Doing up his tie, the familiar sensation of being choked by his future began to creep in. But for once, the prospect didn't seem quite as suffocating. While he wasn't exactly looking forward to this evening, Theo realized he wasn't

dreading it. Camille was pleasant, well-spoken. Aside from
the awkwardness when he'd behaved like a buffoon once
he became aware of Bonnie's presence in the tea room,
he'd enjoyed their little "reunion" this afternoon. His
mother had been smart to arrange it, not that he'd ever tell
her so.

He could see the wisdom in her latest choice in quarry.
As far as chess moves go, this one was savvy indeed. The
Fairfax family did not have as high a standing in the peer-
age as the Whartons, nor did they own vast estates. But
they were well-respected, their holdings were secure, and
more to the point, profitable. Very profitable. Theo wasn't
sure how big a piece of the pie Camille was entitled to, but
he knew his mother well enough to be sure if she'd sent him
here to play escort, it was a generous slice.

Regardless of his personal feelings, on a purely objective level, Theo could see the advantages to this match.
Beyond the financial gain, Camille would make a fine
duchess. She understood the duties and responsibilities of
the role, had grown up navigating the same social circles.
And unlike many of the spoiled little heiresses his mother
had paired him up with in the past, Camille was, well,
nice. She'd seemed genuine. Easy to talk to. Smart, even.
And again, on an objective level, he could admit she was
attractive too, if in a pale British rose sort of fashion.

Yes, but are you attracted to her?

Refusing to dwell on that question, Theo straightened his
suit jacket, adjusted his sash and ducal crest, and manned
up. It was time to go.

CHAPTER 10

THE WARM BUTTERY scent of crêpes from a corner café greeted Bonnie as she exited off the Red Line at Harrison and crossed State Street. Her stomach twisted. Bonnie wished the pain was caused by hunger. Sunday morning. How many lazy Sunday mornings had she and Gabe made the short walk from their apartment to this café together? How many quiet weekends had they sat at one of those tables, people-watching or quibbling over the crossword in the *Tribune*? The ache in her middle expanded, compressing her lungs and stealing her breath. Bonnie stuttered to a halt.

Maybe it was best Ana had called to cancel brunch. With the way her insides were churning, Bonnie wasn't sure she'd be able to keep anything down. She wasn't sure she was ready for this meeting either, but after talking things out with Cassie last night, she knew it was best to get it over with and had arranged a meeting with Gabe.

Her apartment was less than a block away, but she couldn't go home. Not yet. She couldn't face him there. So, she'd chosen a location nearby, a place both familiar and safe. A place of comfort. She glanced back, toward the other end of Printer's Row, focusing on the giant redbrick clocktower of the old Dearborn Station rising in the distance.

Without making a conscious decision, her feet began moving again, carrying her forward. The moment she pushed through the doors of the Harold Washington Public Library, the ache receded, still there—a black hole of bitterness and pain—but more compact. Manageable. Riding the elevator up to the ninth floor, she took several slow, deep breaths.

The atrium on the library's top floor was one of her most favorite places in the city. It was a secret haven, a bastion of quiet. A refuge. Morning sunlight spilled across the tile floor from the wall of windows on the east side of the building. She walked toward the small nest of tables and chairs, her footsteps echoing in the open, airy space. Rarely crowded even on the busiest of days, on Sunday, Bonnie had the entire ninth floor to herself.

She settled into a chair and closed her eyes, soaking up the silence, the familiar scent of worn books and sunwarmed dust cradling her. The sound of the elevator chiming startled Bonnie, and she shifted, bracing herself.

"There you are." Gabe's voice broke the peace of her sanctuary. "I brought you some tea." He held out a ceramic travel mug. One of her own from home.

Bonnie imagined him in their apartment making this for her. The image shifted, and she saw *her*, standing naked in Bonnie's kitchen, wrapped in Grandma Mary's quilt, kissing Gabe while the tea brewed. Cassie's temper boiled, and she glared at her former fiancé.

He must have sensed the anger rolling off her because he abruptly drew his hand back, as if realizing offering her a cup of scalding hot liquid probably wasn't his best idea. *Smart man.* He set the cup on a nearby table.

Bonnie reached for it. He recoiled, and she smirked. "Calm down, I'm not going to throw this in your face"—she paused and glanced at his groin—"or anywhere else."

After a moment, Gabe relaxed and took the seat next to her. "I'm glad you agreed to talk."

Bonnie ignored him and sipped her tea. It was ginger cardamom, one of her favorites. With a bittersweet pang, she realized he'd even put a bit of honey in it, exactly the way she liked it. The problem with dating someone for most of your life was they tended to know everything about you. Or . . . almost everything.

She thought she'd known everything about Gabe.

Boy, had she been wrong.

"Who is she?" Bonnie asked without preamble, giving in to the overwhelming desire to fill in those blanks, to know the details.

"My adviser's assistant." Gabe's voice was low, the words almost mumbled.

"Well, that's not very original of you," Bonnie scoffed. "I thought she looked familiar." Her mouth twisted. "Though I admit, it was hard to tell at first, since she was wearing significantly less clothes than the last time I saw her. She was at your department Christmas party, wasn't she?"

Gabe nodded, not meeting her eyes.

"She must have known about me, then." Bonnie tried to take another sip of tea, but it tasted like bitter ash on her tongue. She set the cup down carefully. "She had to know about our engagement." Bonnie had shown her engagement ring to more than a dozen people at that party. Quite possibly to the very blonde her fiancé had been banging on the side.

Gabe shrugged. *Shrugged.* As if he couldn't muster the energy to form an actual reply.

A fresh wave of pain washed over her. "How long has this been going on?"

He didn't answer.

"Please, Gabe," she whispered, as a new thought struck her, "please tell me you haven't been sleeping with this girl since before . . ."

"Before I asked you to marry me?" Gabe asked, finally meeting her eyes. "No."

"Then when?" Bonnie pressed.

"Does it matter?" Gabe shot out of his chair, shoving his hands in his hair.

"Yes, it fucking matters!" Bonnie shouted. Her outburst bounced off the frosted glass ceiling, shocking them both. She didn't often resort to foul language. Thank God so few people bothered to come all the way up to this floor.

She stood and stared up at him, hating each of the few inches he had on her. "How long, Gabe?" She poked him in the chest. "I deserve to know." She did deserve to know. She wanted to know. She *needed* to know.

"Since last summer."

Last summer. When she'd been on her trip to Europe. Out of the country for six weeks. Away from Gabe for almost two months. "I see," she said. "You're telling me this started *after* I left for Europe?"

"Yeah."

Bonnie caught his second of hesitation. "Liar," she sneered. The truth of that word burned like acid in her throat. For a moment, she'd almost felt guilty. Like somehow her absence made her partially responsible for Gabe's infidelity. She knew that was illogical, and she'd unpack her own messed-up psyche later, but right now, she was going to get the truth.

"Care to try that again?" She stepped closer, no longer bothered by the fact that she had to tip her chin to meet his eyes. Fury made her feel six feet tall. "When did you start sleeping with her?"

Gabe swallowed, gaze darting around the room like a cornered rabbit. He retreated a step, and she advanced.

Why had she never noticed what a coward he was before? What else hadn't she noticed? She sifted through her memories. That he'd been cheating on her, for one thing. "Come on, Gabe. It's a simple question. *When?*"

"My birthday."

She stared at him. His birthday was June first. He'd been sleeping with another woman for almost an entire year. Bullets of pain and shame and fury ripped through her. "How?"

"My adviser held a little party for me, remember? You couldn't be there; you were chaperoning some event or something—"

"I wasn't asking you how it happened, jackass. I was asking myself how I could be so blind, so stupid . . ."

"You're not stupid, Bonnie."

"No? The man I was supposed to marry has been screwing around behind my back for months!" Her voice bounced off the high walls of the atrium, her anger reverberating, building. "Were you ever going to tell me?"

He turned away from her, walking toward the bank of windows.

She followed him. "Were you ever going to marry me?"

Gabe stopped, his back to her.

Bonnie stopped too, her breath harsh and fast in her ears. She forced herself to be calm, to take slow, deep breaths. To wait for him to respond.

Eventually, he pivoted and faced her. "I don't know. I wanted to marry you—I mean, I thought I wanted to, but then things started happening between Ali and me, and you were never around, and then you took off with your friends for that long vacation last summer . . ."

His voice held more than a touch of accusation, and it pissed her off. "Don't you dare. Don't you dare try to pin this on me! As if, what? You could have kept it in your pants if I'd been around more?"

"I didn't say that." His face flushed.

"It's not like you were there for me either," she snapped. Anger roiled, a snarling beast thrashing its tail inside her, wanting to lash out. "How often did you bail on me after I'd made plans for us? And I always made excuses for you, thinking you were working so hard . . ." Bonnie stopped, realization hitting her like a fastball to the sternum. "All those times you canceled our plans, or came home late, or missed a date. You were with *her*, weren't you?"

"Not *all* the time," he dodged.

Bonnie rubbed her thumbs against her temples, trying to release the tight knots of tension pounding against her skull. All the moments she'd thought something was off with him, when she'd wondered why he was being so distant and blamed school, their schedule, herself . . .

"Oh, well, pardon me." The razor-edge of her voice sliced through the air. "We can at least agree you were with her the other night, yes?"

He didn't reply. In the silence, she stared at Gabe, her gut twisting. She'd known him since she was barely old enough to ride a bike, a fact clear in her memory because it was the day she'd learned to ride her bike when she first met him. Mother's Day, when she was six years old. He'd moved into the house three doors down from hers and was standing on his driveway as she'd come barreling down the sidewalk, yelling at him to get out of the way because she didn't know how to stop yet.

By the time she'd turned eight, she had decided she was

going to marry him. How could someone she'd loved for more than twenty years suddenly turn into a stranger? But he was. The Gabe who stood before her now was not the man she knew, was not *her* Gabe. Her mind raced, and she was six years old again, careening down the hill, training wheels off, not sure where she was going or how to stop. She tried to compartmentalize her feelings, like she did when she was teaching or performing, so she could focus.

"What happens now?" he finally asked.

Her mind formed the answer to his question immediately. "I want you to move out," she said, without hesitation, her feelings crystalizing.

"What?"

"I want you out of the apartment."

"My name is on the lease too," he reminded her.

"Yeah, but who pays most of the rent?" She had him there. While he finished school, she covered most of their daily living expenses. She'd never minded. After all, he was working toward their future, and one day, when they decided to start a family, she'd take time off and he'd be the one picking up the slack. All part of her perfect, peachy plan.

All the plans she'd made for their future, the happiness she and Gabe would have, just like Anne and Gilbert, were gone. Erased. Not even. Hard to erase something that hadn't been written yet. She'd spent so much time focusing on what was going to happen next, so eager to start the next chapter, she'd forgotten to pay attention to what was happening on the current page.

Well, plans had changed. But lucky for her, she had a new plan. Would start a new chapter on a fresh page. And this time, she would focus on the now, and worry about the next, and all the rest, later. She turned her attention back to Gabe. "You know, you're right. Your name is on the lease too. Tell you what, you can have the place. I'll move out."

"Where will you go?"

"Not your problem." She wasn't about to tell him about the job in England. "Stay away from the apartment for an hour. I need to get a few things."

"Where have you been staying these last few nights, anyway?" he asked.

Oh, now he was concerned? "Also not your problem," Bonnie snapped. She wanted to ask if *Ali* had been sleeping over but restrained herself. The less she knew, the better. "I'll be back for the big stuff sometime next week, and see about having the landlord take my name off the lease."

"I can't cover the rent myself. I've still got another month of grad school!" Gabe whined.

"Now that," Bonnie said, gathering her things and preparing to leave, "*is* your problem."

Back on the street outside the library, Bonnie sucked in a lungful of air. Seeing Gabe had been both easier and harder than she'd expected. He'd been such a big part of her life for so long—no, that wasn't exactly right. A part can be removed, dissected from the rest. He wasn't one piece of her puzzle, but part of the whole picture. She had grown up with Gabe, and their lives had seeped into each other's, like colors bleeding into fabric, blending, leaving it forever changed.

She let herself into their apartment and forced herself to go straight to the bedroom. Rip off the bandage, so to speak. As much as Bonnie would like to bleach her eyeballs and wipe out the memory of what she'd walked in on Friday night, she knew she couldn't bleach the memory of all the years of Gabe away. Deep down, she didn't want to. Those memories made up the tapestry of who she was, like Grandma Mary's quilt . . . *Oh, bad analogy.*

She *did not* want to go there. But her mind went there anyway. And she had to admit, the metaphor worked in more ways than one. Made from pieces of old clothing from countless generations of Blythes, the quilt was a testament to all those lives. And while the last thing Bonnie wanted was a souvenir of *that night*, she also knew she'd never get rid of the quilt. She'd wash it. Several times. Maybe hide it in a closet, but she would never get rid of it. It was too precious.

Much as it hurt to even think about right now, she knew she didn't want to get rid of her memories of Gabe either. Or her time with him. If she was truly honest with herself, if she did the deep listening thing Sadie was always saying her acting coach made her do, Bonnie knew the truth. It wasn't the loss of Gabe she mourned so much, it was the loss of the idea of Gabe—the Gabe she'd created in her mind—the one she wanted him to be. The Gilbert to her Anne.

Beyond that, was the loss of the life she'd planned. Her friends teased her endlessly about how she had it all mapped out: marriage, kids, how many years apart each child would be, their names. She'd even mentally enrolled them in dance and art classes already. Daydreamed about watching her brood perform in the annual St. Patrick's Day parade. It was the loss of all that—all she thought had been meant to be—that she mourned the most.

Admitting that was hard. Admitting that hurt.

Leaving the quilt where it was, Bonnie pulled a suitcase out from under the bed and began packing. As she emptied out her drawers, her mind shifted, as it did too often these past few days, to a certain dark-haired, blue-eyed Brit with devastating dimples. Speaking of devastated, maybe Theo was part of the reason she wasn't as devastated over the breakup with Gabe as she should be. There was something there between them. Had been ever since she'd first met him back in London.

From the first smile he'd flashed her on a supper cruise on the Thames, she'd felt something. A lot of things, actually. But she'd ignored those thoughts and feelings, tried her best to smush them into a little ball, tuck them inside a box, lock it up tight, and drop it in a lake for good measure. But despite all her attempts to submerge those thoughts, they broke free, feelings rising to the surface again. And the kisses in his suite yesterday . . .

Knees weak, Bonnie sat on the edge of her bed for a minute. She needed to take some kind of Theo-conditioning class. Strengthen her muscles so she would stop going noodle-legged whenever his dimples appeared. She gripped one bed post, fingers curling around the glossy wood. She'd had this canopy bed since she was five, maybe six. She'd brought it to the apartment as another way to help save money, telling herself they could buy new furniture later, after Gabe finished school.

Now what? Should she bring the bed back to her parents' house? Put it back in her old room? Moving her bed back to Mom and Dad's posed another challenge—she'd have to tell them what happened with Gabe. Admit the engagement was off. There would be no wedding to plan, and even worse—in her mom's mind—no honeymoon trip to book.

Bed or no bed, Bonnie knew she had to tell her family. And she would. Later.

Stuffed with as much of her clothes and shoes as she could cram into it, Bonnie rolled the suitcase out of the bedroom. She grabbed the travel mug of tea Gabe had made for her and headed into the kitchen. Flipping on the faucet, she went to rinse out the mug, but froze when she noticed the dishes sitting in the bottom of the sink.

As the water continued to run, images flowed through her brain. Images of Gabe and that woman having an intimate dinner for two, eating off the plates Bonnie had bought when she and Gabe had first moved in together. Plates she'd washed hundreds of times after hundreds of meals they'd shared. She shut the faucet off, but the images kept coming.

They're just things. They shouldn't matter. But it did matter. And it hurt; it hurt so bad. Stomach cramping, Bonnie pulled a wineglass out of the sink, noticing the smudge of lipstick along the rim. Holding it by the stem, she smashed it against the countertop. It shattered.

Yesss. The sound the glass made as it broke, shards flying, felt good. Really good. She stared at the jagged stump that remained, touched her finger to the edge, watching as a thin line of blood beaded on her skin.

It was a fitting reminder. Broken things were sharp.

Setting the cracked stem aside, she reached into the sink again and took out a plate. Bonnie lifted it over her head, dropping it on the tile floor. *Smash.* She did the same with the other plate. Shards of crockery littered the kitchen and spattered her clothes.

Next, she grabbed the mug Gabe had given her this morning. Dumping the dregs of the now-cold tea into the sink, Bonnie turned, pulling her arm back and hurling the mug across the room. It exploded against the wall. She ducked, covering her face as fragments rained down.

Breathing hard, she straightened, admiring the carnage. Then she brushed off the pieces still clinging to her and inspected herself for damage. Aside from the cut on her finger, she had a few nicks on her arms. Nothing too serious. The wounds would heal quickly.

She wondered if the same could be said for her heart.

CHAPTER 11

AT HALF PAST six on Sunday evening, Theo left his hotel room and paused outside Bonnie's door. They'd agreed to meet in the lobby in fifteen minutes. He ordered his feet to keep walking down the hall toward the lift, but his body ignored him. Overruled, he knocked.

"Yes?" she called through the door.

"Ready?" he asked.

"Theo?" She opened the door.

He put a hand on the doorframe and leaned toward her. "You shouldn't open the door if you don't know who it is."

"I knew it was you." She crossed her arms over her chest and narrowed her eyes at him. "But how did you know this was my room?"

A guilty flush heated his skin. "I asked Cassie."

"Oh."

They were both silent a moment. Theo gestured toward the elevator. "Should I wait downstairs for you, then?"

"What?" Bonnie shook her head. "No. I'm ready." She stepped back and held the door open for him. "Just give me a minute to grab my things."

He followed her inside the suite. She scurried to pull her coat on, her arm tangling in a sleeve. "Here. Let me." Before she could argue, Theo gently tugged on the coat, holding it for her as she settled into it. A chunk of something fell from her hair and he caught it. "What on earth . . ." He held up a shard of broken pottery.

She glanced over her shoulder, blue eyes darkening as she stared at what he held pinched between his fingers. "Long story," she said, turning and holding out her palm.

Despite being desperately curious, he decided not to press. "I'm sure." He dropped it into her hand.

An embarrassed chuckle escaped her. She tossed the shard in the dustbin and grabbed her handbag. "All set." Beating him to the punch, Bonnie popped her elbow out, offering him her arm. "Shall we?"

His mouth twitched, but he nodded and accepted her invitation. "How's your heel?"

"Much better, thank you." She pulled the door to her room shut and made sure it locked.

Theo studied her covertly as they entered the lift. Her long red curls were mussed, and while he often gave his mate Logan shit for his head of unruly red hair, on Bonnie, disheveled was decidedly fetching.

"Long day?" he asked.

"Yes and no."

He frowned at her riddle of a response, but before he could ask her to elaborate, they'd stopped at another floor and several people joined them. Theo moved closer to her as they squeezed toward the back of the small space, making room. They rode the rest of the way to the lobby in silence, bodies pressed together.

Which was fine with him. He liked the way her lush little body curved against his. His hands itched to map the landscape of her shape. Learn each dip and slope. Were the curls between her legs the same shade as her hair? He ached to know. Mouth dry, he followed her into the courtyard of the hotel.

"Where to?" he asked, wincing at the hoarse rasp in his voice.

"You'll see," she said, not seeming to notice his distress as she led him to one of the cabs idling nearby.

Good. Hopefully she wouldn't notice what was happening in his trousers either. He followed her into the backseat of the cab, adjusting himself discreetly. What was his problem? He'd been indulging in too many fantasies about her, was what.

Last night, it had been late when he'd returned to the hotel after his evening with Camille, and yet he found himself restless and unable to sleep. He'd paced the suite, thinking of Bonnie, of how she had sat on the chaise in his room, remembering the gentle curve of her calf resting on his knee, the feel of his hand wrapped around her ankle. Then he'd collapsed onto the chaise, wondering what would have happened if he'd let his hand inch up her bare leg, let his fingers stroke the inside of her thigh. Imagining just that, he'd unzipped his pants and stroked his cock.

When was he going to stop? Stop thinking about her? Wanting her? Did he think he could jack his need for her out of his system?

Hardly.

If anything, it was making the situation worse. Schrödinger's cat or some bloody nonsense. He saw her, and *bam*, instant hard-on. What would happen later this summer, as preparations for Logan's wedding got well underway? Now that'd be a sight, the best man walking down the aisle, cock first, sporting a raging stiffy because he had the hots for the maid of honor. Theo shook his head.

"What's wrong?" she asked.

He jerked, realizing she was watching him, and wiped a hand over his face. "I'm, uh . . . frustrated is all."

She nodded in sympathy. "Long day for you too?"

He waved a hand dismissively. "We were going to talk about your day."

"We were?"

"In the lift," he prompted. "Remember?"

"Oh, right. Well," she began, leaning back against the cracked leather of the cab seat, "I talked to Gabe."

Rage bloomed in his chest, and again he had the urge to shove his fist into the worthless fuck who had hurt her. Head, gut, he didn't care, so long as it bloody hurt. He recalled the broken bit of pottery he'd found in her hair and frowned. His fingers curled, knuckles tight with tension. Had there been a fight? Had the arsehole hurt her? More than emotionally this time? Holding himself in check, Theo asked, "How did that go?"

"Not horribly." A chuff of laughter escaped her. "Not too horribly anyway."

"Oh." He studied her face, lit by the streetlamps passing overhead in rhythmic intervals. "How did you spend the rest of your afternoon?"

"I attacked a bunch of dishes."

"Pardon?"

"After meeting with Gabe, I went back to our place to pack up some of my things . . ." She paused, mouth working. "Anyway, I may have worked out some frustration in the kitchen."

"I see." That explained the pottery shard in her hair. "Feel better now?"

"I do, actually." She smiled sheepishly. "It was stupid, I know, but God, it felt good to break something."

"I understand." Hell, did he ever. He shifted on the seat

again and glanced out the cab window. "May I ask where we're going?"

"I told you, you'll see," she replied with a teasing lilt. "Trust me, you'll love it. Everyone does. It's a Chicago favorite."

Theo gave her his best polite smile and steeled his stomach. Much to his surprise, and gustatory relief, when the cab dropped them off a few minutes later, it was not at a pizza parlor.

He paid the fare and she pulled him through the revolving glass doors of a place called Portillo's. If the size of the crowd was any indication, the food must be good. People packed every booth and table, and the queue to order snaked through the restaurant. Over the murmur of dining room chatter, a woman wearing a black beret barked into a microphone, briskly calling out numbers.

Bonnie held his arm and stood on tiptoe, craning her neck to scan the room. He glanced around as well, easily zeroing in on his mate's wild thatch of red hair in a booth toward the back. He pointed. "Over there."

Logan stood and slapped Theo on the back while the girls greeted each other with a hug.

"We'll see to the food then, aye?" Logan asked.

"How about we handle ordering the meal?" Bonnie shrugged out of her coat and tossed it into the booth. "Since we know the menu."

"You two can take care of getting drinks." Cassie pointed to a corner of the restaurant, where a smaller line was queued at a bar counter. "I'll take a beer," she told Logan, then asked Bonnie. "Beer or wine?"

"A beer sounds good."

Cassie nodded, flashing a smile at her fiancé. "Two beers for the lassies."

The Scot laughed and brushed a quick kiss across

Cassie's cheek. "Come on, then," he said to Theo. "Let's see to procuring refreshments."

"Don't worry," Bonnie assured him. "I'll get you something good."

"That's an easy promise, because everything here is good." Cassie winked, and the girls headed off to join the masses waiting to order food.

Theo followed Logan to the beer counter.

"How's things?" Logan asked, his tone casual.

Theo didn't miss the curious gleam in his friend's eye. "Decent."

"Family 'business' wrapped up, then?"

He also didn't miss the quotation marks in his friend's voice. "For now. So mind your own bloody business."

Snorting, Logan moved to the counter and placed their order. Theo reached into his pocket for his wallet, but the Scot shook his head. "I got this." Before Theo could voice a protest, his friend continued, "Trust me, I owe you."

"You do?"

Logan handed Theo two heavy beer steins before grabbing the other two. "Aye. By the time my darling wife-to-be gets through explaining her plans for the wedding, you'll understand."

They returned to the booth and arranged the four glasses around the table. Cassie appeared, loaded down with napkins and assorted condiments. "Need any help?" Theo asked.

She waved him off. "You two sit. Drink your beer. Talk. We'll be back in a minute." She disappeared into the crowd again.

Theo frowned.

"You heard the lass," Logan said, easing into the booth. "Now stop hovering and have a seat."

"I'm not hovering," Theo protested. Though he was, indeed, hovering. It felt odd to sit here and relax while the women stood waiting. "Perhaps I'll just see if they need—"

"They're fine, Theo. Don't be a prig. Sit and drink your beer like you were told."

With what Lo would likely call a very priggish harrumph, Theo sat. This was not the way things were done. He eyed the beer in front of him. He wanted a sip, but his manners were so ingrained, his mind would not allow his body to pick up the glass, wouldn't process the desire and turn it into action.

"It wouldna kill you to wet your whistle while we wait." Logan lifted his heavy glass and took a long pull on his own beer, eyes taunting Theo over the rim. He set the glass down, smacking his lips and sighing with exaggerated pleasure. "Now," Logan began, the curious gleam in his eye growing downright fiendish, "what's going on between you and wee Bonnie?"

Willpower cracking, Theo took a sip of beer. He should wait for the ladies to return, but he needed something to fortify himself, especially if he was about to have this particular conversation. He knew his friend. Lo was like a dog with a bone, and wouldn't let up until he got to the meat of the story.

"You've heard, I take it, about Bonnie's engagement?" Theo began.

"Aye." Logan cracked his knuckles, ruddy color darkening his cheeks. "The goddamn bastard."

Theo smiled grimly, gratified at the banked violence in his friend's response. He'd like nothing better than to pay a visit to the bugger who'd caused Bonnie so much pain and have a word with him. Though he'd likely let his fists do most of the talking. He glanced up, checking on the girls. There was no sign of them, still lost in the crowd surrounding the pick-up counter. Another stab of guilt. He started to stand. "I really should go and help them . . ."

"Theo," Logan ordered. "Keep your arse right where it is. They can handle themselves, aye?"

"So I've been told," Theo grumbled.

Logan laughed. "Someone not appreciate your trademark British manners?"

"I was only being polite."

The Scot snorted into his glass.

"I fail to see the humor." Theo bit the inside of his cheek, gaze drifting to the pick-up counter again.

"Go on with you, then." Logan waved a dismissive hand. "See if they need your help." The Scot raised his eyes heavenward. "Save me from the stuffy, overbearing English."

Unfolding from the booth, Theo stood and stared down his nose at his friend. "We can't all be uncivilized heathens." He spun on his heel, the Scot's amused snort bringing a reluctant grin to his own lips. That *had* been a rather stuffy response on his part. Ah well, he was what he was.

Theo scanned the crowd again. Now that he was standing, the girls were easy to spot. Especially Bonnie. He moved toward her red curls. She was at the condiment station, filling little paper cups with a red sauce. "Can I be of assistance?" he asked over her shoulder.

She startled, squirting the sauce all over her wrist. "Ack!"

"Sorry." Theo fumbled with the napkin dispenser. "Sorry," he said again as he swiped a handful of napkins over the splotch of red covering her wrist. He'd made a bloody mess of things. Quite literally. He continued to dab awkwardly at her arm. "Um, er . . . I thought perhaps I could help?"

She looked from the wad of soiled napkins in his hand to his face. "Help, huh?" She shook her head, an exasperated grin curling one corner of her mouth.

"I know, I know. You don't need any help," he grumbled.

She tilted her head, mouth pursing in amusement as she considered him. "Actually, I could use your help." She stepped closer, making room for others waiting to use the condiments. "Here," she said, sliding the little paper cups she'd filled toward him. "Grab these and some more napkins." She raised an arm covered in goo. "I need to go wash up."

"Right. Sorry," Theo said for the third time, pulling more napkins from the dispenser and stuffing them into his pockets, pretending he wasn't wishing he could bury himself under a pile of them right now.

She laughed. "Don't worry about it."

"Order fifty-eight, don't be late," the loudspeaker crackled.

"That's us. Cassie can handle the food. I'll meet you back at the table in a minute." She slipped into the crowd.

Theo tucked a few more napkins into his pockets. Then he struggled to collect all the little paper cups she'd filled. How much sauce did they need, anyway? People were maneuvering around him, shooting him dirty looks for taking so long. Bloody Americans, always in a hurry.

Finally, he had everything balanced and turned slowly, shuffling carefully back to their booth. By the time he arrived, the girls were both seated, and Cassie was pulling containers out of red-and-white striped paper bags. He deposited his load of supplies on the table and slid into to the booth next to Bonnie.

She placed several items in front of him. "I wasn't

sure what you would like, so I ordered a couple different things." She popped open the lid of a sandwich box, releasing the succulent aroma of grilled meat. His mouth watered.

She opened another container, and the heavenly scent increased. His stomach rumbled with anticipation as he studied the contents of the boxes with avid interest and waited while she laid out a few other items, fussing with bags of crinkly chips and thick fried onions.

"You're not a vegetarian, are you?" she asked, brow furrowing with concern.

"Me? No." He swallowed and pulled his gaze from the food to meet her eyes. "Why?"

"You're not eating."

From across the table, Logan chuckled. "He's waiting for you, lass."

"What?" Bonnie glanced from Logan back to him. After a moment, understanding lit her face, and she smiled, shaking her head at Theo. "Here." She popped a chip into her mouth. "Better?"

He nodded, embarrassed but satisfied, and took a fried onion from the bag.

"Pass the ketchup, please."

He raised an eyebrow. "Pardon?"

She pointed at the little paper cups. "The ketchup."

"Oh, right." He pushed one toward her.

Cassie laughed. "She's going to need more than that."

Theo glanced at Bonnie, and she nodded. He passed her another cup.

"More," Cassie prodded.

Theo slid two more cups over. "More?" he asked.

Bonnie shook her head. "I think I'm good for now."

He watched as she dipped a chip into one of the cups, bathing it in red.

"Don't believe her," Cassie warned. "Most people eat their fries with a little ketchup. For Bon, it's the other way around."

"Whatever, pickle princess," Bonnie huffed, drowning another chip.

A bark of laugher escaped Logan. "She's got you there."

Theo stared at his friend across the table, eyebrows raised in question. "Pickle . . . princess?"

"Cassie always orders extra pickles." Logan slung an affectionate arm around her. "Extra, extra pickles."

"So what?" she protested. "I like a lot of pickle."

"Och," the Scot drawled, accent thickly exaggerated as he leaned down and whispered loudly in her ear, "I ken you do, lass."

Cassie punched her fiancé in the shoulder and rolled her eyes.

Theo hid his grin in his beer. Next to him, Bonnie giggled. The sound did funny things to his insides. Or maybe he was just hungry. He picked up the burger and took a bite, nearly groaning aloud with pleasure. It had been several years since he'd last had a burger stateside. He closed his eyes and chewed blissfully. God bless America.

"You like it?"

Theo opened his eyes to see Bonnie watching him. He swallowed and nodded.

"Oh, good." She gave him a shy smile. "I got you a hot dog and an Italian beef too. You don't have to eat it all," she quickly added. "I just figured you might want to try a few things."

"That was very thoughtful of you." He waved at his burger. "This is perfect."

Her face lit with pleasure.

Something quivered in his chest, too high to be passed off as hunger. He dropped his gaze back to the table.

"Don't worry," Logan interjected, breaking the moment. "Whatever he doesn't eat, I'm happy to take care of."

"Careful," Cassie teased, "you've got a wedding this summer, remember?" She poked him in the side. "You need to fit into your tuxedo."

"I'm wearing a tuxedo?" Logan asked, grabbing her finger.

Cassie shot him a warning look, eyes locked and loaded, but he grinned, walking right into the line of fire. "Tell you what," he teased, lifting her finger to his lips, "you can help me work it off, aye?"

The temperature in the booth shot up a few degrees. Theo squirmed uncomfortably. Next to him, Bonnie shifted on the bench as well. "Tuxedos?" he asked, forcing a note of jovial curiosity into his voice. "Will this be a black-tie event, then?"

"No," Logan said.

"Yes," Cassie countered.

"Yes," Logan echoed.

Theo smirked. He liked that Cassie held her own with Logan, his friend needed a woman who knew how to put him in his place. Still, he couldn't believe how close the two had become. He remembered when Logan had called him from Chicago last fall, eager to plan something special to celebrate the one-month anniversary of dating Cassie. And then, barely two months later, Logan had called again, with the news of their engagement. Theo took another swig of his beer. "Where will this formal event be taking place?"

Cassie fiddled with the corner of a paper bag. "That's one of the things we wanted to talk with you about tonight." She slid a glance at Logan.

"Right." Logan sat up straighter and cleared his throat. "Cassie and I've been discussing this. We've decided to have the wedding take place in Scotland. And we're think-ing Eilean Donan."

"The castle?" Theo paused, eyebrows raised, burger hovering by his mouth.

"I know," Bonnie said, "I thought it sounded outrageous too, but this whole thing is outrageous—no offense," she quickly added, glancing over at her friend. "It's a romantic kind of outrageous."

Theo bit back a grin. He agreed with Bonnie. This whole plan was bloody bonkers. He looked at Cassie. "What about your family? Won't an overseas wedding be difficult?"

Cassie shook her head. "We want to keep it small, only close friends and family. Like Logan, I don't have a big family, just my parents and an aunt in Minnesota."

"And Eilean Donan is close to Mam," Logan added. "She plans to bake the wedding cake." He rolled his eyes good-naturedly. "Even my sister is on board with the idea. If it makes the women I love most in my life happy, how can I refuse?" He raised Cassie's fingers to his lips, press-ing a kiss to the engagement ring on her left hand.

Theo chuckled, enjoying seeing his friend so smitten. It was obvious Logan would do anything to please Cassie. What must that be like? To be so in love you were willing to put the needs of someone else above your own? He thought he knew already. Hadn't he been doing that very thing all his life? He loved his family, and ever since he could remember, he placed their needs above his own. It was a heavy burden which often left him feeling trapped.

But somehow, he doubted Logan felt that way. If any-thing, Theo noted with a twinge of envy, his friend seemed lighter, happier, and freer than he'd ever seen him.

"It's getting late. We can talk about this another time," Cassie said abruptly, bundling some empty wrappers and

shoving them in one of the bags. She tilted her head mean-
ingfully toward Bonnie.

Theo followed her gaze. Bonnie was staring down at her
half-eaten burger, mouth pulled into a sad little bow. He
glanced at her bare ring finger. Blast, he was a git. A bum-
bling imbecile. Of course, wedding talk would be un-
pleasant for her right now.

As if sensing the weight of everyone's eyes on her, Bonnie looked up. She offered Cassie a weak little smile. "It's
fine, Cass. Really. I can do this."

Cassie shoved the paper cups out of the way and reached
across the table to clasp Bonnie's hand. "But you don't
have to. Not right now. I shouldn't have even brought it up
tonight after I found out—"

"That my fiancé was sleeping around on me? That the
guy I thought I'd known for over twenty years is a complete stranger to me?" With each sentence Bonnie's voice
rose, words warbling with tension and heartache.

Again, Theo's hands tightened into fists. Five minutes.
He just wanted five minutes with the bugger.

Across the table, Logan caught his eye, and Theo sensed
the same restrained violence, recognized the same urge for
retribution reflected in his mate's face. "I told you he was
a wanker."

"Shh," Cassie hushed Logan, focus still on Bonnie. She
squeezed her hand again. "You want to get out of here? Go
get a drink?"

Bonnie licked her lips. "If you don't mind, I'd rather just
go home—back to the hotel, I mean."

"Sure. Of course," Cassie agreed.

"I'm sorry I'm being such a bummer," Bonnie began,
but Cassie cut her off.

"Please. This is totally my fault. I wasn't thinking. Can
we drive you?"

"I'll take care of her," Theo said, his mouth moving before his brain could catch up. "I mean," he stuttered, turning to Bonnie, "if that's all right?"

"You don't have to—"

"That's great!" Cassie interjected, a little too brightly.

A staring match between the two women ensued.

Thanks to his sisters, Theo was well-versed in this game of ocular arguing. Steering clear, he shifted his attention to Logan. "Shall we clean up?"

Just as eager to escape, Logan helped Theo load the rubbish onto trays and followed him to the bins. "If you ask me," Logan began, dumping his tray, "the lass needs a distraction."

Theo stacked his empty tray on top of Logan's. "Nobody is asking you." He headed to the loo to wash his hands.

Logan trailed him. Over the roar of the air dryer, he tried again. "Come on, lad. She needs a bit of fun to take her mind off things. And I'm not blind, I know you're dying to shag her."

The dryer shut off mid-sentence, and the Scot's words echoed in the tiled space.

Theo pinched his lips together and glared at his friend in the mirror.

"Don't give me that hoity-toity face," Logan scoffed, staring back. "I know I'm right. And you two are staying at the same hotel, for Chrissakes. It's perfect. What could be easier?"

That's the problem, Theo thought. *It would be easy. Oh, so easy.* He replayed the short, sweet, but startlingly hot moment they'd shared yesterday in his hotel room. The details were still sharp—as he'd been recalling them over and over again ever since it had happened.

A stall door banged open, interrupting his thoughts.

"I'm not having this conversation with you." Theo escaped the loo, Logan on his heels.

"Fine," Logan agreed tartly. "Have it with her, then."

"What?" Theo growled under his breath, weaving through tables. "Ask her if she'd like to sleep with me? Just like that?"

"Why not? What's the worst that could happen? She says no?"

Theo ignored his friend, slapping a smile on his face as he approached the booth where Bonnie and Cassie stood waiting.

He hated to admit it, but Lo had a point. If she said no, it would be the end of this . . . whatever this thing between them was. If she said no, he could force himself to shut it down, move on.

But Theo wasn't worried about her saying no.

He feared what would happen if she said yes.

"Everything okay?" Bonnie asked while the cab idled at a red light.

"I should be asking you that." He turned toward her, but in the dark interior of the backseat, couldn't read her face. "How are you doing?"

"I'm fine," she said.

He felt more than saw her shrug. "I'm fine too." *Pathetic, mate. Very, very pathetic.* He thought again about what Logan had suggested at the restaurant. The persistent bastard had even sneaked a rubber into his hand when they'd said good night. Bloody Scot. Did he just carry those things around everywhere?

The light changed, and Theo shifted on the seat, tucking his hand in his pocket. He fingered the edge of the wrapper, wincing at the sound of crinkling foil, convinced she would hear it over the thrum of traffic. He folded his hands in his lap and proceeded to detail all the reasons he would *not* be asking Bonnie if she wanted to spend the night with him. The pain in his forehead returned, and Theo pinched his fingers against the bridge of his nose.

Suddenly, the touch of a feminine hand, smooth and soft, brushed over his brow.

"Headache?"

"It's nothing," he said, his voice rough pebbles skittering in the quiet darkness.

She slipped her thumb between his fingers, rubbing gently along the bridge of his nose.

A groan escaped him.

She hummed in sympathy. "Hurts?" she asked, pressing harder, her thumb making a soothing circle in the center of his brow.

You have no idea. He didn't want her to stop, wanted her hands all over him, her fingers stroking him everywhere. "I'll be all right," he said, tugging her hand away from his face. He pressed a kiss to her wrist and caught the faint, salty sweet tang of the sauce she liked so much lingering on her skin. He wanted to lick her. Nip and bite. Devour her. Lust heated and thickened his blood.

The cab made a sharp turn, and she rolled against him.

"Oh!" a sound of surprise escaped her. She cleared her throat and righted herself, gaze straying to his groin.

Theo bit his lip, releasing her hand. Their little encounter must have revealed the effect her nearness was having on his body. An awkward silence ensued. Luckily, the cab rumbled into the courtyard of the Waldorf a minute later. The car lurched to a stop, and Theo busied himself handling payment.

Rather than wait for him to exit the vehicle and come around to hold the door for her, Bonnie hopped out and stood by the entrance to the hotel.

For once, Theo was grateful for her reluctance to let him play the gentleman. By the time he drew up next to her, he had things, well, one *thing* in particular, under control.

The awkward silence followed them into the lift. He stole a few glances at her, but every time he looked her way, she was studying the floor, or the ceiling, or the panel of buttons, as if it were the most fascinating thing in the world.

He had the sense, though, whenever he looked away, she was stealing glances back at him.

Finally, they reached their floor.

"Well," she began, a forced cheerfulness to her voice as they walked down the hall. She bit her lip and continued, in a more normal tone this time, "You're going home tomorrow?"

He nodded, not ready to speak yet. Afraid if he opened his mouth, *that* question would slip out.

"Well." She paused outside the door to her room, dropping her gaze and staring at the floor. "I guess this is good night, then."

"I guess so," he managed to croak, joining her in contemplation of the hall floor, studying the diamond pattern on the plush carpet beneath their feet. He looked at her little black boots, noting how they hugged her trim ankles. He remembered how her ankle had fit in his hand, how his fingers had wrapped around the delicate bones. He imagined trailing his fingers up her leg, along her calf to her knee, then her thigh . . . his eyes traveled the path his mind was taking.

Mouth dry, he focused on the hem of her skirt, falling just above her knees, offering the barest glimpse of skin. He pictured the freckles on her knees and wondered where else she might be freckled. He decided he had to know.

Logan was right, what did he have to lose? It was one night.

"Unless . . ." Theo took a breath and stepped closer, filling her line of vision.

She looked up, eyes skimming over his body. He felt it, skin tingling every place her gaze touched him, as sure and real as if it were a physical caress.

"Unless what?" she asked, face tilted up to his, eyes wide.

Just go to your own room, lad. Say good night, turn around, and walk down the hall. Do not look back. Theo waited while she dug her key card out of her handbag and slid it through the lock.

She opened the door and began to step inside, pausing on the threshold to look over her shoulder at him. "Did you want to come in—?"

Yes.

"No." The word came out brusque, heavy and loud, landing with an awkward thump between them.

"Oh. Okay." Her cupid's bow of a mouth drooped, cheeks pinkening. "I guess this really is good night, then."

See? She made it easy for you. Say good night. Turn around. Walk away. Don't look back. He reiterated his instructions to himself, but his mouth didn't open, and his feet didn't move. He just stood there, staring down at her.

She propped the door open with her hip and fiddled with the handle. Over her shoulder, he could see a layout similar to his own suite, a desk and chair, sideboard with coffeemaker, a chaise . . . luckily the bed was hidden from view, in another room of the suite. Seeing the chaise was bad enough. He licked his lips. There was a long list of reasons he should do exactly what his brain was instructing him to do, and only one reason he should ignore his brain and listen to another part of his anatomy. But that one reason was reiterating its case very . . . pointedly.

Theo glanced down at Bonnie, from the top of her tousled red curls to the tip of her pert freckled nose to the glimpse of pale creamy breasts revealed in the deep *V* of her jumper. He itched to stretch the neckline open, hands spreading over her collarbones, thumbs sweeping up the sides of her throat, as he got a closer look at her pale perfect skin to see if she had any freckles there too. He hoped she did.

He swallowed hard and cleared his throat. The tension between them hummed at a low frequency, a constant subtle vibration that was likely the reason for his permanent state of semi-arousal around her.

Maybe he should take the Scot's advice and stop being such a prig. If she wanted him too, what was the harm? Before that meddlesome thing known as common sense could intrude with a neatly detailed list of all the reasons why this was a bad idea, Theo made a decision. Sort of. He'd let her decide.

Tugging at her hand, he kissed the knuckle over the bare skin on her ring finger. He wondered, if she'd been single when they'd first met back in London, what might have happened. Theo didn't consider himself a romantic, but he had to admit there had been something . . . magical about that evening. He remembered his first glimpse of Bonnie as she boarded the deck of the river cruise, auburn curls flying wild in the breeze off the Thames. Twilight dusted her profile in rose and gold, her cheeks glowing, eyes flashing. She'd turned those eyes on him, and he'd had to remind himself how to breathe.

He'd made a move to charm her, and been instantly rebuffed, the blue of her gaze turning as frosty as her tone as she addressed him with polite formality. Would she rebuff him now? Only one way to find out. He entwined their fingers before meeting her eyes, pleased to note the blue was much warmer, her expression much softer, than it had been that first night they met.

Rather than attempt to charm her now, Theo decided to be honest with Bonnie. He tightened his grip, squeezing her fingers with his. "Before I go, there is one thing I'd like to ask you."

"Oh?" She straightened, other hand still on the door handle. "What's that?"

Theo glanced around, he really didn't want to have this conversation in the hallway. But he knew if he stepped inside her room, all bets would be off, and he wanted to gamble. He wanted to play this game with her, put his cards on the table and see what she would do. Would she fold? Raise the stakes? Or would she call his bluff?

Only . . . he wasn't bluffing.

Hands still clasped together, he raised her arm over her head, pinning her wrist against the door. "Do you want to come to my room?"

She gaped up at him.

Maybe a little too blunt, mate. Well, he'd told himself he didn't want to try and charm her. Theo gave up on talking and bent his head, slanting his mouth across hers, thrusting his tongue between her parted lips. She made little noises in the back of her throat, and he paused, ready to withdraw, to pull away, but then she began to kiss him back, meeting each thrust of his tongue with her own.

"Do you want to spend the night with me?" he asked against her mouth.

"Hmm?" she mumbled.

He broke the kiss. "And here I thought I was being obvious," he teased, pushing his hips forward, the hard press of his erection sending a clear message. He bent his head and spoke low into her ear. "I'm going to say good night now. Then I'm going to turn around and walk down that hallway, and I'm not going to look back. If you want to come to my room, if you want *me*, you know where to find me. If not, then consider this a goodbye kiss."

He trailed his lips from her ear to her mouth, and she shuddered against him in a full body shiver. He didn't want this to be goodbye. Didn't want things to end here, with this kiss. But he'd said the choice was hers, and he wanted her to make that choice, to come to him, almost as much as he wanted her.

So, he broke the kiss again. Released her hands, peeled himself away from her.

"Good night." He turned around and walked down the hall to his room.

And not once, did he look back.

CHAPTER 12

WHAT WAS THAT? Oh, heavens. What had just happened? Bonnie stared after Theo as he strode down the hall, his dark head and broad shoulders lit by the soft glow of the hotel's tasteful wall sconces. He reached the door to his room and paused. Bonnie sucked in a breath and held it. He'd said he wasn't going to look back, but still, she waited for him to turn and look at her. See if she planned to take him up on his invitation. Maybe hold his door open for her.

But he didn't. As promised, he reached into his pocket, retrieved his key, and entered his room without a backward glance.

His door snicked shut, and she exhaled, all but melting into a puddle on the floor. Her right hand still gripped the door handle. With effort, she unwrapped her fingers and stumbled into her room. Dropping her purse on the desk, Bonnie began to pace. He wasn't serious, was he?

She replayed the press of his body against hers, the way he'd possessed her with his mouth, stealing her breath, her thoughts, and quite possibly her soul . . . but not her ability to choose. It was up to her, he'd said. Her choice. He wanted her. Did she want him?

God, yes. Ever since she first saw him standing next to Logan on that boat. He'd smiled at her, dimples turning her knees to water, and she'd debated jumping into the Thames. Instead, she'd armed herself with attitude, using cold aloofness as a life preserver, attempting to distance herself from the emotions swirling through her every time he caught her eye and made her have feelings she should *not* be having.

With each flicker of awareness that passed between them, Bonnie doubled her efforts to pretend the charming Brit didn't exist . . . or at least the things she was feeling for him didn't. She was determined to remain loyal to her fiancé back home, the man she thought was working hard on his doctorate, going to bed alone each night while she frolicked the summer away on vacation with her friends. Turned out, he'd been doing some frolicking of his own last summer, and he was hardly alone.

No. She pulled the plug on that thought. Not going there. She wasn't thinking about Gabe now. She'd turned the page, started a new chapter—a new story. And why couldn't Theo play a leading role, even for a little while, in this plot twist in her life?

Being around Theo put all her senses on high alert, waiting to absorb any bit of him she could get. Whether it was his voice, his scent, his touch . . . his taste. She licked her lips, the taste of his kiss still on her tongue. Yikes, she probably tasted like ketchup. She scurried to the bathroom and brushed her teeth. Her reflection stared back, curls wild, cheeks flushed, eyes wide and a little shell-shocked.

"Are you really going to do this?" she asked herself.

The question was only half-ludicrous. If her reflection answered back, then maybe she had a problem. But she did need an answer. Was she going to do this? He wanted her. She wanted him.

Could she let it be that simple?

Casual sex was not something Bonnie had ever considered. She didn't have a problem with the concept, she'd just never thought it was for her. For one, the only guy she'd ever been with was Gabe, and she'd planned on marrying him from the time she was eight, and even then, they hadn't officially "done it" until she was eighteen.

Also, Bonnie had a secret. Something she'd never told anyone, not even Cassie. Something she'd barely admitted to herself, even. But the truth was, as much as she loved Gabe, she'd never *wanted* him. Not that way. She wanted his attention, his kisses and cuddles . . . and when they'd had sex, she'd enjoyed it—mostly—it had been nice. But honestly, she could just as readily gone without it. She'd never felt this ache, this *need*.

If she *did* go to Theo's room, she had no idea what to do. Should she change? She'd packed up most of her clothes today, but didn't really have any sexy lingerie, just some comfy pajamas and her teacup robe. He'd seen the robe before, back in the hotel in London, and her teacup slippers too. Okay, even she knew those were *not* sexy. So no, she wouldn't change. Wait, did that mean she was going?

Bonnie ran her fingers through her hair, a useless attempt to tame the untamable. She needed to stop stalling. Was she going or not? Theo was leaving tomorrow. If things went terribly (translation: if she was terrible in bed), then at least she wouldn't have to face him—not for several months until they saw each other for the wedding stuff later this summer. And by then, it would be no big deal, right? Just this thing that happened one night.

Stop overthinking this. She looked in the mirror one more time, trying to channel Sadie or Ana, the two most

confident women she knew. She distinctly recalled how
Sadie had flirted with Theo when they'd all met that night
on the boat. Sadie wouldn't be having this silly little internal debate right now, she'd already be in Theo's room,
stripped down to one of her outrageously expensive bra
and panty sets. Bonnie still gagged a little at the memory
of how much money Cassie had spent on underwear during a pre-vacation shopping trip with Sadie.

Cassie had been determined to have a foreign fling during their trip, and the purchase had been part of the plan.
Considering what happened with Logan, it had worked,
though Bonnie couldn't say how much could be attributed
to expensive underthings.

Actually, the success of Cassie's endeavor was more
likely due to Bonnie. She'd been the one to encourage her
friend to spend more time with the "sexy Scot," after
Cassie had first met him under rather unusual circum-
stances inside Edinburgh Castle. And after what could
have been only a one-night stand, it was Bonnie who'd
given Cassie's cell number to Logan. It was even Bonnie
who'd suggested Logan meet them on that fateful supper
cruise on the Thames.

A one-night stand. That was what she was considering
with Theo, wasn't it? Maybe it wasn't such a bad idea.
After all, look what had happened for Cassie and . . .

Whoa. Bonnie disembarked from that boat before it
could head for trouble island. She'd only just officially broken off her engagement this morning. She was not ready
to jump into another relationship, and she certainly wasn't
going to contemplate marriage to someone else already.
Did she want to get married? Sure. But she was not so desperate for a husband she was going to start planning a
wedding with a man she hadn't even slept with. Yet.

One more time, Bon. Are you going to do this?

All Bonnie's stalling, all her mental games, were for naught. She'd known the answer all along; she'd just needed a little time to talk herself into it.

Of course she was going. She grabbed her key card, screwed her courage to the sticking place, and headed down the hall.

Minutes later, Bonnie stared out the window of Theo's suite, hiding her nervousness as she gazed upon the Chicago night. They both knew what her presence here meant. He'd spelled it out pretty clearly. Theo's room was on the same side of the hotel as hers and commanded an impressive view of the lake. The lights of the city twinkled all along the dark curve of the Gold Coast.

In the reflection of the window's glass, she saw Theo pull his sweater over his head and hang it on the desk chair. Her back to him, she continued to watch the ghost of his movements as he turned to approach her, rolling up the sleeves of the dress shirt he'd worn underneath. Bonnie's skin began to tingle, anticipating his touch well before he reached her side.

Finally, Theo stood next to her, the fingers of his right hand entwining with her left. "Lovely," he said, his crisp voice cutting through the silence of the room. He squeezed her fingers.

Bonnie smiled, glancing up at him. *Was he talking about her or the view?* "When I was little, I used to think Lake Michigan was an ocean."

"Well, I can understand that. It's bloody big." Theo chuckled. "One of the Great Lakes, correct?"

She nodded, the tingling intensifying as he lifted her hand to his mouth and brushed a featherlight kiss across her knuckles.

"How many Great Lakes are there?" he asked, his breath warm on her skin.

"Five," she croaked, watching as he held her hand out and spread her fingers apart.

"Lake Michigan is one," he said, wiggling her pinky. "Remind me what the others are?"

"Lake Ontario." That one was easy. Her grandfather owned a fishing cottage very near the Canadian side of the lake, and she'd spent many childhood summers visiting him there, pretending she was Anne on Prince Edward Island.

He pressed her thumb to his lips. "That's two," he said, his mouth moving beneath her thumb.

"Then there's Lake Erie," she continued, while he guided her thumb across the soft curve of his mouth.

"Three," he murmured, nibbling on her index finger.

"Uh . . ." Bonnie paused, swallowing hard as his teeth grazed her skin. "And Lake Huron."

"Four," Theo said before dipping his head to lick her middle finger.

The sensation tickled, but rather than make her laugh, it made her nipples tighten, and she groaned.

His smile was wicked. Confident. Pleased. "That leaves one more. What's it called?"

"Hmm?" she asked, her brain feeling like a balloon detached from her body and floating somewhere overhead.

"The last Great Lake," he reminded her, his voice a gentle tease as he raised her ring finger to his mouth, eyes on her face. His eyes were as blue as any lake, and just as beautiful, the swirl of indigo around his pupils expanding as he continued to stare down at her.

"Uh . . ." she stammered, her brain-balloon floating farther away, over the wide expanse of the night-shadowed lake beyond the window.

Theo parted his lips and took her finger into his mouth. He began to suck on the tip, his tongue stroking up and down.

This didn't tickle. Not at all. And if her brain was floating away, her body was grounded. Tied hard and fast to the point of contact between them. It was as if a wire had been strung from her fingertip to her core, creating a direct line of sensation. With each wet hot tug on her finger, an answering pulse came from deep inside her.

Bonnie squeezed her eyes shut. *Michigan,* she muttered silently, struggling to focus as he increased his tempo. *Ontario, Erie . . . Huron.* He sucked harder and the pulsing intensified within her. Suddenly, he bit down, and she gasped, "Superior!"

He laughed, a rich warm sound that dusted her skin with magic, made her whole body tingle. Again, with the tingling. She was a ball of nerves around this man, every sense heightened. And she loved it. She already knew by the way he'd kissed her last night that sleeping with Theo would be different from anything she'd ever experienced with Gabe.

At the thought of her ex-fiancé, Bonnie glanced at her finger, the one that had so recently worn an engagement ring—and even more recently been inside a hot British guy's mouth.

"Don't," Theo said, his voice quiet but commanding.

She tore her gaze away from her naked ring finger and met his eyes. She didn't pretend to misunderstand. Theo read her too well. How such a thing was possible, as they'd only spent a handful of days together, she didn't know, but he did, he knew her.

"Tonight is for you and me alone. No one else." He lifted her hand to his mouth and placed a kiss on the inside of her wrist.

His mouth hovered over her hand, breath warm on her skin. His eyes traveled up her body, as if mapping the route he intended to take. When his gaze landed on her face,

Theo paused. Everything inside Bonnie paused too. Her breath caught, her heart stalled, her mind went blank.

"Are you okay?" he asked. "With me? With this?"

"Uh . . ." She wet her lips, pulled air into her lungs, willed her heart to start pumping again. When her brain finally kicked back into gear, it was in full panic mode. *This is a mistake, I'm making a mistake. I can't do this. But I want to do this. Why shouldn't I do this?* The thoughts fired off lighting fast, circling around on themselves in nanoseconds.

Theo gently squeezed the hand he was still holding. "Perhaps this is a bad idea."

"No!" she exclaimed, the denial coming out in a desperate hiccup of sound.

He raised his eyebrows.

She dropped her gaze and stared at their joined hands. She wanted him to go back to what he'd been doing. Touching her, kissing her, licking and sucking and *not talking*.

She flexed her fingers and gripped his hand. "No," she repeated, more calmly this time. "I don't think we should stop, I don't *want* to stop." She rotated her wrist, flipping the position of their hands, so his was on top. "And no, I'm not one hundred percent okay with this, but not in the way that sounds . . . I'm not . . ." She paused, what she said next could ruin her chance with him, could end this night right now, but it needed to be said. "I'm not okay myself. Does that make sense?"

"I think so," he murmured, brow furrowing, "I don't wish to take advantage of the situation, of what you're going through right now. Which is why maybe we shouldn't—"

"No," she cut him off again. "You're not taking advantage of me. I'm afraid I'll be taking advantage of you. I just broke up with the man I've been dating since before I hit puberty, the man I was going to marry. And I can't be one hundred percent sure that this"—she waved her free hand between their bodies—"isn't my way of dealing with all that." She let her hand rest on top of his, sandwiching his palm between both her own. There. She said it. It was out there, between them now.

"Let me ask you one thing," Theo said, lashes dark against his cheeks as he stared down at their joined hands. "Are you one hundred percent sure you want this?" His lashes lifted, blue eyes meeting hers. "Are you sure you want me?"

"Yes," she said, instantly, breathlessly.

He pulled his hand from her grip and tucked a finger under her chin. He leaned in, eyes still intent on hers. She was unmoored, adrift in the penetrating ocean-blue depths.

"That's all that matters," he said, smiling.

Those dimples appeared, and Bonnie was a goner. Call in the Coast Guard, she was going under. She reached up, gripping his shoulders for support, and pulled him closer.

Smile still curving his lips, Theo bent his head and kissed her. He took his time, giving her mouth the same detailed attention he'd given her fingers. His hands came around her, roving up her back and threading through her hair as he deepened the kiss, tongue stroking over her lips. And then he was thrusting inside, delving deep into her mouth. He groaned, low in his throat, making that raspy, rumbling animal sound she felt as much as heard.

She shivered, and if she'd thought she was drowning before, it was nothing to the sensations battering her senses now. She was caught in a whirlpool, and he was the vortex, sucking her tongue into his mouth, pulling her down, down, down.

But he was the one going down. Releasing her mouth, he dropped to his knees in front of her.

Bonnie gasped, gulping air as she stared down at him.

Theo trailed his fingers along the backs of her legs, tickling her calves. He gripped the hem of her skirt and slid it up, palms grazing her thighs. The fabric bunched around her hips, and when he began to pull her tights down, Bonnie squeaked.

His hands froze. "Still okay?" he asked, glancing up at her.

She nodded mutely.

He snared his thumbs inside the elastic band of her panties, and then paused, eyebrows raised.

"I'm okay," she croaked, and attempted to offer him a reassuring smile.

"Okay," he repeated. "Good." He tugged her panties and tights all the way down, bending low to pull them off. "*Fuck*, you're gorgeous."

Oh, God. Oh, sweet baby Jesus. Bonnie struggled for balance. Had she ever heard Theo use the f-word? The crisp sophistication of his accent somehow made it sound dirtier. The way it slipped from his lips, raw and gritty, while he was face to face with her, well . . . *that*. She swallowed hard. Would he do those things he'd done to her fingers, to her mouth . . . down there?

"So pretty," he murmured, still staring at her. "Almost too pretty to eat."

Oh, please God, yes. Suddenly Bonnie understood why her friend Sadie got all religious sounding when she was horny. A giggle escaped her.

"Something funny?" He rested back on his heels, fingers stroking up her bare legs.

"I'm ticklish," she evaded, which wasn't a lie. She giggled again when he curved his hands around her bottom, the featherlight brush of his palms teasing her sensitive skin.

"Everywhere?" he asked, a wicked gleam lighting the depths of his ocean eyes.

"Maybe?" She licked her lips. "Only one way to find out."

Whoa, did that come out of her mouth?

It must have, because he was grinning, those dimples in full force. The backs of her knees prickled, and she bit her lip. *Don't fall, don't fall, don't fall.*

He kept his hands firmly planted on her bottom and pulled her toward him.

She flinched, but he didn't do what she'd expected. Instead, he rained little kisses over the soft curve of her stomach, then dipped his tongue into her belly button.

"Hey!" She burst into a spasm of giggles.

"Hmm," he mused, face a mask of analytic contemplation. "Definitely ticklish there."

"Let someone stick a tongue in *your* belly button and see if you don't laugh."

"Is that a challenge?"

Bonnie gulped, but didn't back down. "Maybe."

"Tell you what." He squeezed her bottom, and she realized his hands were still glued to her butt. "If I can make you laugh again, I win. If not, you win."

"What do I win?" she asked, feeling silly and playful and incredibly turned on all at the same time.

"Whatever you want," he countered, his confident tone telling her he fully believed she would lose.

"Does this mean, if you win, you get whatever *you* want?" she asked.

"Indeed." His hands shifted, drifting down over her hips, thumbs tracing the outline of curls at the juncture of her thighs. That move alone sent shivers pulsing through her, and she almost lost the game before it began.

She schooled her face and stared down at him. Tried to pretend she wasn't basically naked below the waist, and he had a bird's eye view of the landscape.

Speaking of landscape, when was the last time she'd trimmed things down there? *Why are you even thinking about that right now?*

Crouching lower, his lips followed the path of his thumbs. His breath tickled, and she clamped her lips together, determined not to laugh again. When his mouth moved lower, she resisted the urge to clamp her legs together too. She was shaking, her entire body tingling.

He paused, glancing up at her. "Was that a laugh?"

"Nope." Her throat worked.

He bent his head again, running his tongue along her center while his thumbs slid to the outside of her folds, stroking up and down. She moaned as a glimmer of pleasure flitted through her. Light and quick, like stones skipping across the glassy surface of a lake.

"That's right, love," he responded instantly, thumbs spreading her open as his tongue dipped inside. "Christ, you're sweet."

Oh God. *Oh God.* She bit down and breathed through her nose, slow and deep. In and out. In and out. The urge to laugh had completely abandoned her. What he was doing now wasn't tickling her, it was making her restless, achy. Needy. Her thighs trembled, and she widened her stance, opening herself to him even more.

A low growl erupted from his throat, and it was so unexpected, so masculine and feral and . . . hot, it made her instantly wet. He growled again, deeper in his chest this time, and Bonnie felt it vibrate all through her. Her knees buckled, and in a flash, she was flat on her back, bare ass scraping against the hotel carpet.

Theo was on her in a heartbeat, crouching over her on all fours. His hair was mussed, falling in his face, eyes dark as a midnight sea. Gone was the polite British gentleman who wouldn't start a meal before she did. In his place was this fierce and hungry animal.

He ducked his head, lapping at her. He devoured her, there was no other word for it. Sucking and biting and thrusting his tongue inside of her again and again until she was clenching her fingers in his hair, rocking her hips back and forth. Faster, harder, more, please more, more.

"Oh," she gasped as the ripples of pleasure became a tidal wave, sensation rolling through her.

He flipped her onto her stomach and pushed forward, pressing against her, hot and hard and. . . . *oh*. Beneath the thin fabric of his pants, the thick head of his erection rubbed between her legs. She could feel him. *There*.

She bucked backward. She wanted him to move again. Press against her like that again.

Theo lay on top of her, chest to her back, cock nestled between her spread thighs, hips cushioned by the lush pillow of her bum. He pressed himself against her, grinding against her backside. The friction was exquisite torture. He was wearing too many bloody clothes. He needed to get closer, deeper. He rested his hands on either side of her head, palms pressing into the hotel carpet and thrust harder, back and forth, back and forth.

She shuddered beneath him.

"Shit." He braced himself, taking his weight off her. "Sorry."

She tilted her head to the side, face in profile, cheek resting in the crook of her arms. "What are you sorry for?" Her words came out in breathy gasps.

"For crushing you." He pushed himself up to his knees. "You can barely breathe." He pulled her upright, so she was kneeling as well.

She shifted, leaning back against his chest and tucking her head under his chin. "That's not why I was out of breath," she said, voice still husky.

"Is that a fact?"

"That's a fact," she purred, rubbing against him like a cat.

"I see," he rasped, in desperate need of more oxygen himself. Her skirt was still bunched around her hips. He grasped the tangle of fabric in his hands and tugged it off, fingers trailing along her bare thighs.

She shivered.

"Cold?" He hesitated, hands on the hem of her sweater.

She shook her head, curls tickling his neck and chin.

He proceeded to lift her sweater, tugging it up. She raised her arms, helping him pull it off.

Theo tossed the garment aside, then rested on his heels, drinking her in from behind. She glowed in the soft light of the desk lamp, a galaxy of freckles sprinkled across her back and shoulders. "Beautiful," he murmured, his fingers tracing constellations on her skin before slipping beneath the delicate lace of her bra, "so beautiful."

He unhooked it, letting it fall off her shoulders and to the floor as he reached around to palm her breasts, thumbs flicking the pointed tips of her dusky pink nipples.

She moaned and leaned back, and he bent his head over her, capturing her mouth, stealing the sounds of her pleasure, taking them into himself. They needed to get off the floor. He needed to get out of these damn clothes. Theo broke the kiss. "Come on," he said, reluctantly releasing her breasts. He got to his feet and helped her stand.

She turned to face him, cheeks flushed, eyes hazed with lust. "Where are we going?"

"The balcony."

She frowned and covered her breasts.

"I'm teasing." He chuckled. "Where else would I take a gorgeous, naked woman?" He nodded his head toward the door of the suite's bedroom. "My bed."

"Oh," she said, still frowning, little rosebud mouth pursed. "You go first. I don't want you looking at my butt."

Another chuckle escaped him; he couldn't help it. But he turned without arguing and headed for the bedroom. "I like looking at your bum," he said over his shoulder. "It's a very nice bum."

She snorted.

He stepped inside the bedroom, then stopped, turning around to face her.

Unprepared for his abrupt change in course, she kept walking and slammed right into him.

Before she could back up, he reached his arms around her and pulled her closer. His hands snaked down her back.

"You're going to grab my butt, aren't you?"

He paused. "That was my plan, yes. Do you mind?"

"You are a strange man." She shook her head.

"Perhaps," he conceded.

"And this is a strange situation."

"Definitely." Theo drummed his fingers on the base of her spine. "Well? Can I grab your bum now?"

Bonnie laughed. An explosion of sound like a Christmas cracker, sprinkling the room in joyful surprises.

He smiled triumphantly. "You laughed. I win."

"No fair!" Bonnie wiggled out of his grasp. "I didn't know we were still playing that game!"

"Not fair, huh?"

She shook her head emphatically, curls . . . and other things . . . bouncing.

"You know what else isn't fair?" Bonnie narrowed her eyes, catching him in the act of ogling. "I'm standing here naked, and you still have all your clothes on."

"Well, I do want to win fair and square." He reached for the top button on his shirt. "Can I claim my prize if I get undressed?"

Her mouth curved. "Maybe." She tapped her chin in speculation. "Close your eyes."

"Why?"

"Still want to grab my bum?" she asked, imitating his accent.

He nodded.

"Then do it. Close your eyes."

"Fine." The moment he shut his eyes, a flurry of movement sounded around him. *What the bloody hell was she up to?* "Can I open them now?"

"Not yet." Her voice had shifted to across the room. "Now?"

"Almost . . ." More scurrying sounds. "Now."

He tentatively cracked one eye open, relaxing when he realized all she'd done was get into bed and crawl under the covers.

The sight of her in his bed, red curls spread out over her bare freckled shoulders, his sheets wrapped around her . . . Theo swallowed hard.

From her spot on the bed, she called out in a haughty voice, "You may disrobe now."

Theo grinned, he liked this new game. He bowed low. "Yes, m'lady."

She giggled as he undid the rest of the buttons on his shirt. She was nervous, he knew that. And if playacting helped her relax, he was up for it. He was bloody up for anything she wanted. He yanked off his belt, cursing under his breath as he tried to work the zipper over his swollen cock. Kicking off his trousers, he moved toward the bed.

"Ahem." She cleared her throat and eyed him pointedly. "The rest, if you please."

Well, mate, you wanted her to call your bluff. Theo put a hand on the waistband of his shorts and stepped closer to the bed. If she wanted to look, he would make sure she got a front row seat. He tugged the fabric down, expecting her to grow bashful and look away any second, but damn if she didn't keep staring at him the whole time.

Heat crept up Theo's face. Bloody hell, he was blushing. His cock suffered no such embarrassment however, springing forward with such enthusiasm it was almost obscene. He glanced down at himself. Correction. It was *definitely* obscene.

She didn't seem to think so, though. Her concentrated gaze took in every last detail. "For someone who didn't want her bum ogled, you're quite the ogler yourself," he observed drily.

"Oh." A flush crept up her cheeks, and she dropped her gaze. "Sorry."

Theo immediately regretted his words. He didn't want her to be sorry. He didn't want her to feel ashamed. He climbed into bed next to her. "No apologies, princess."

She smiled, the tension easing out of her. She rolled to her side, facing him across the pillow. "It's just, I've seen only one, um . . ." She paused. "One of *those* before. And I was curious."

"Ah." He tamped down the surge of jealousy at the thought of those gorgeous eyes resting on some other bloke's dick. "Well, no comparisons, all right?"

She giggled, then rolled again onto her stomach. "Go

ahead." The softly rounded curves of her bum wobbled temptingly beneath the white linen. "Grab a handful."

When he didn't move, she raised herself up on her elbows, propping her chin in her hands. "You weren't expecting me to hold up my end of the bargain, were you?"

"Uh, no. And now I feel all pervy about it."

She giggled again. "Come on, you know you want to." She teased in a singsong voice, scooting closer and wiggling her bum some more.

A moment later her bare bottom brushed against the head of his bare cock, and they both froze. The air became charged, all sense of playfulness vanishing.

"Should I get something?"

"What?"

They were naked. In bed. What did she think he should be getting? Usually she was quite quick-witted. Though admittedly, his own thought process was moving slower than normal. Theo shifted, easing back, putting space between their bodies. Giving them room to think. The condom Logan had forced on him earlier this evening was still in his pocket. He turned and stretched his arm out, grabbing his trousers off the floor and fishing for the foil packet. He held it up.

"Oh," she said, understanding dawning in her eyes. "Oh!" she said again, brow furrowing. "Do guys just carry those around with them everywhere?"

"Some do." Lucky for him, Logan was one of them.

"Do you all have sex on the brain twenty-four seven?"

His mouth quirked. "Let me ask you something." He set the condom on the bedside table. "Are you on the pill?"

Her eyes widened, but she answered him. "Yes."

Good to know. Not that it would prevent him from using a rubber, but still. "You take it every day, right?"

"You're supposed to."

"I know. Three sisters, remember?"

She rolled her eyes. "What's your point?"

"Do you have 'sex on the brain twenty-four seven' because you take the pill?"

She scowled at him. "Point made."

He smiled.

Bonnie sighed.

"What is it?" he asked.

"Your smile," she said, eyes bright and clear as a rare sunny day in London.

"Hey, no jokes about Brits with bad teeth allowed."

"It's not that. Your teeth are fine." She reached a hand out, running a finger first down one side of his face, then the other. "I'm talking about these."

"My cheeks?"

"Your dimples." She sighed again. "They're my kryptonite."

"What, like Superman?" His smile grew wider.

"You're doing that on purpose!" she accused.

"No, I'm not." He gave her the biggest grin yet. "Okay, maybe I am. A little." He scooted closer, until their noses almost touched. "Is it working?"

"I'm lying down, so it's not as bad right now."

"My dimples make you dizzy?"

She shook her head, and a lock of hair fell across her face. "It's my knees. When you smile at me . . . the backs of my knees get all prickly, and my legs turn to water."

"How extraordinary." He brushed the curl aside. "And how long have you been suffering from this affliction?"

"Since the first time I saw you," she confessed, eyes piercing his, pulling him into their endless blue depths.

Theo's breath caught in his chest, his lungs stalling. He felt—to borrow Bonnie's description—all prickly. When he was able to breathe again, he realized she was crying.

Tears crept from the corners of her eyes. He wiped a thumb across her cheek. "What's wrong?"

"Am I a bad person?"

"Sorry?"

"I was engaged when I met you."

"And?"

"And?" She sniffled. "And I couldn't stop thinking about you. I had . . ." She dropped her gaze, tear-thickened auburn lashes hiding her eyes. "Dreams about you."

"You did?" Now this was getting interesting. He wondered if her dreams about him were as vivid as his dreams about her.

She nodded. "I, um . . ." She rubbed her tear-stained cheek against the pillow. "I couldn't stop having thoughts about you."

"Indeed?" His heart began to pound.

"I kept thinking about you. And was so guilty and ashamed, here I was lusting after a stranger while my fiancé waited for me back home—"

"And we both know what *he* was doing," Theo growled.

"Yeah." A bitter laugh escaped her. "But that doesn't make it okay. My grandpa had a saying, 'two wrongs don't make a right.' And if I had followed through on my feelings for you last summer, if I had been unfaithful to Gabe, the fact he had been unfaithful to me wouldn't balance the scales. It wouldn't justify my own infidelity."

Theo tucked a finger under her chin, forcing her to meet his eyes. "But you're *not* with Gabe anymore, and you *were* faithful to him, even if the cheating arsehole didn't deserve it."

Bonnie shook her head. "I'm sorry for bringing this up. I don't even know why I did. I promised myself I wouldn't dwell in the past."

"It's okay." He brushed more curls away from her face. "Sometimes you need to work through feelings before you can let them go." He bent his head and said low in her ear, "If you don't mind, I'd like to hear a bit more about these lustful thoughts you were having."

She laughed, the tension in her easing, her body relaxing against him. She looked so guilty, so torn up, he decided not to press her. Instead, he brushed his lips across her forehead. "You are not a bad person. Attraction happens. I don't think you can control it. But you *can* control what you do about it, and you did."

Unlike that rat-bastard ex-fiancé of yours. The words lay unspoken between them, but by the storm clouds chasing across her face, he knew they'd both been thinking the same thing.

Theo kissed her on the forehead again, then urged her to roll to her other side. He curled his body around hers, and though his cock protested, it knew better than to argue. His chivalrous side had reared its head. She wasn't ready. Not yet. He thought he was willing to have her on any terms, take whatever she offered, even if it was just her body.

Now, he knew that wasn't true. Had likely never been true. Apparently, his moral fiber wasn't as paper-thin as he'd thought. She snuggled against him, the soft sound of her breath growing slow and deep.

Before he began to drift off himself, Theo slid his hand beneath the covers, fingers trailing over the lush curve of her hip. He reached between them and gave her bum a squeeze.

She shifted in his grip, a sleepy chuckle drifting over her shoulder. "Perv," she muttered.

He smiled into the soft curtain of her hair, wrapped his arm around her waist, and fell asleep.

CHAPTER 13

BONNIE STIRRED, SUNSHINE piercing her eyelids. This time, she remembered she was *not* in her own bed, but at the hotel. She pulled the thick comforter over her head and blocked out the spring sunrise. Dawn was breaking earlier and earlier. With a groggy sense of mild curiosity, she wondered what time it was. She pulled the covers back off her head and turned to squint at the bedside clock.

Several things caught her attention at once, and her brain went haywire, trying to simultaneously process the massive wave of incoming details. One: While she was in bed in a hotel room, it wasn't *her* hotel room. Two: On the bedside table lay a condom wrapper. Three: Next to the condom, the clock flashed 8:26 a.m. Oh, and four: She was naked.

Oh sweet, Jesus. Oh, no. This was *not* her hotel room, she was *no*t wearing any clothes and . . . she reached for the condom wrapper, relief flooding her when she realized it had *not* been opened.

The digital clock blinked. 8:28.

Fresh panic replaced her momentary calm. It was Monday. Which meant she had an Introduction to Shakespeare class starting in thirty-two minutes.

8:29.

Make that thirty-one minutes.

There was no way she'd make it across town to teach her nine a.m. class. Bonnie chewed her lower lip. Even if a hoard of fairies appeared and magically got her ready in seconds, she'd never get there in time. She was officially screwed.

Her attention shifted from the clock back to the condom. Details emerged slowly, shadowy memories crawling like strange beasts from the sludge of her consciousness. This was Theo's room. Theo's bed. Last night, she'd made the choice to go to his suite and they'd . . . heat suffused her body, from toes to ears, as memories of what they'd done—or more to the point, what he'd done to her—flashed through her.

She couldn't believe it. Part of her wanted to pretend the whole thing had been a dream, some bizarre fantasy brought on from too much beer and beef. Indigestion causing the mind to play tricks, or something. But she couldn't blame a cheeseburger for her memories of last night with Theo.

What happened may have felt like a fantasy, but it had been all too real. And it hadn't been in the bed. They'd done *that* on the hotel carpet. In here, they'd talked. Cuddled. She'd fallen asleep, cradled in his arms. And it had been wonderful.

A little too wonderful. She glanced at the clock one more time, hoping it would magically rewind. No such luck.

8:40. The little digital dots between the numbers winked saucily at her.

Apparently, it was going to be a day of firsts. First time

she'd woken in another man's bed. First time she'd ever called in sick to work. She wrestled with the nest of blankets. Tugging a sheet loose and wrapping it around her, she headed for her purse, which she'd left in the suite's living room.

As she passed through the short hallway of the suite, the steady thrum of shower jets sounded from behind the bathroom door. Theo must be in there. Up until that moment, she hadn't stopped to wonder where the Brit had gone—her brain was too busy playing catch-up on where *she* was.

Another memory slinked to the surface. An image of Theo, standing before her, bare-chested, bare-assed, bare-*everything*. She'd gotten into his bed and boldly ordered him to strip, watching with even more boldness as he'd crawled into bed next to her. Then he'd gotten out a condom, and the sight of that little foil packet had knocked the wind out of her sails.

What was a fun little game had suddenly become very real. Theo had sensed her hesitation. She'd felt his awareness of her change in mood—felt it in the shift of his touch, how his caresses began banking the fire instead of building it.

Bonnie swallowed and scuttled to the couch, retrieving her phone out of her purse. Plopping down, she tucked the sheet around herself and prepared to call her department's office line. It was nearing the end of her fourth year teaching at this college, and she'd never called in sick. Not once. Ignoring the nervous flutter in her belly, she dialed.

After assuring the department secretary she'd be in tomorrow, Bonnie ended the call, giddy with relief. *That wasn't so bad.* Turns out the process was much easier than she'd expected. She glanced down at her clothes strewn across the suite, then tilted an ear toward the bathroom.

The water was still running. This was her chance to escape. She could get dressed and slip out the door before he was done. But she didn't.

Feeling mildly wicked, she stayed on the couch, clutched the bedsheet with one hand, and scrolled through the messages on her phone with the other. A text from Cassie, asking her to check in later, let her know how she was doing. Two emails from Cambridge people, with links to paperwork she needed to fill out for the summer seminar. A dozen or so emails from various students making the usual excuses about why their weekend homework wasn't done—at least they'd be thrilled she was absent from class today.

Her phone dinged, and Bonnie opened the new message. A text from Ana apologizing for having to bail on brunch yesterday.

An idea occurred to Bonnie and she quickly texted back.

Bonnie: *No worries. How about today instead?*
Ana: *But it's Monday.*
Bonnie: *I know. So what?*

A second later, her phone erupted with another nineties girl-pop tune. TLC this time. Ana was calling. "Morning, Ana."

"Aren't you supposed to be at work?"

"I called in sick."

"Who is this and what have you done with the real Bonnie?" Ana demanded.

Bonnie laughed. "It's me, really."

"I don't believe you. When was Shakespeare born?"

"No one knows for sure, but he was baptized on April 26, therefore most scholars agree he was born on

April 23, the same date as his death. And come on, that's too easy."

"Okay, okay, I have no idea if that's bullshit or not, but only you would give that answer," Ana relented. "I can't believe you called in sick."

"The secretary couldn't either." Bonnie chuckled again, the flicker of wickedness returning. "So? Brunch?"

"Why not. Sadie is still in town, so she can come too. Does eleven work?"

"Perfect."

The pocket door to the suite's bathroom slid open and Theo stood there, wrapped in a fluffy hotel robe, dark hair dripping. "What's perfect?"

You. Her mouth went dry. Eyes glued to Theo, she croaked into the phone, "I gotta go."

"Why? What's going on? What's wrong with your voice?" Ana demanded.

"Nothing." Bonnie cleared her throat. "See you soon." Over the sounds of Ana's protests, Bonnie ended the call and switched her phone to silent mode.

"Who was that?" Theo asked, crossing the room toward her. Wet, his thick wavy hair had become a crown of ringlets. It was adorable. *He* was adorable.

"My friend Ana. You met her last summer. Remember?"

"Ana . . . right. Black hair. Tall. And, uh . . ." He floundered.

"And big boobs." She nodded. "Yep, that's her." She glanced down at the sheet wrapped around her significantly less impressive chest and sighed dramatically. "Some people are just blessed."

His gaze slid in the direction of her bottom. "You have your own assets."

"Nice choice of words there."

"Do you have to leave now?" He joined her on the couch and met her gaze, blue eyes intent and hopeful. *Stay,* they seemed to say.

"Not yet," she hedged, a wave of shyness rolling over her. She was wearing nothing but a bedsheet, and she didn't think he had anything on under that bathrobe. A bead of water dripped from a lock of hair curling by his ear, slipping down his cheek and into the line of dark scruff along his jaw. She reached a hand up and brushed at the droplet. His shadow beard scraped beneath the pads of her fingertips, making a delicious rasping sound.

"Sorry. I took a shower but didn't shave yet."

"Don't be sorry," Bonnie said, stroking her finger down his jaw, along his chin, and up to the other side of his face. "I like it."

"You do?"

"Mm-hmm." Touching him was easing her nerves. She brushed her thumb over his mouth, relishing the contrast between rough cheek and smooth lips.

"What else do you like?"

"Well, you know I like your dimples."

He smiled, and she closed her eyes, refusing to fall victim to his charms.

"Coward." He chuckled. "What else?"

She cracked one eye open. "Your accent."

He cocked his head at her. "Really? Logan says I sound pompous and stuffy."

"Maybe I like pompous and stuffy." She dropped her hands from his face and fiddled with the fuzzy neckline of his robe. "I like how smart you are. How loyal. How kind."

He was quiet then and didn't ask her for more. But in her head, she continued her list as she stroked his shoulders. *I like how you look at me, how it makes me feel. I like the way you touch me, soft and hard at the same time. I like it when you kiss me, fierce and hungry.* She slid her hands down his arms. *I like all the contrasts in you, especially the savage beast you hide under that calm polite exterior.* She fiddled with the belt on his robe. Only a little bit of cotton separated her from his body. His wet, naked body.

Theo placed his hand on top of hers. "Bonnie?"

She pulled her attention away from their hands to meet his eyes. "Hmm?"

"May I kiss you?" His focus shifted, dark sinful lashes lowering as he dropped his gaze to her mouth.

She nodded. "Yes."

The word had barely left her lips before his mouth was on hers. Hard and soft just as she remembered, taking what she was willing to give. Hot, fierce, and possessive, claiming what she offered. She parted her lips for him, inviting him in. His tongue thrust inside, and she welcomed the invasion, opening her mouth wider, sucking him deeper. He growled in response—a rough, husky vibration low in his throat.

He continued to kiss her, his hands drifting up and down her back before settling at her waist. He pulled her onto his lap, bringing her flush against him. The tip of his tongue traced the curve of her lips, and she knew he was asking for more than a kiss. He was so close, their bodies pressed so tightly together, she could feel *everything.* Was distinctly aware of every inch of the thick hard length of his erection as it rubbed between her thighs.

She relaxed, opening her legs, and he growled again, deeper, lower. The masculine sound undid her. She moaned, feeling him grow harder beneath her while everything inside her went soft, melting like butter on a hot scone.

Tugging the sheet off her, he shifted his hips, thrusting up. She gasped and gripped his shoulders, her nipples tightening, stiff and sensitive against the feathery tickle of his robe. Then his mouth was there, the scratch of his stubble against her breasts a sweet sting lighting her nerve endings on fire. She arched her back. Again, he took what she offered. Devouring her breasts with lips and teeth and tongue.

Bonnie shuddered. Liquid heat pulsed between her legs as he licked and sucked. He pulled her breast deep into his hot, wet mouth and her body went tight, muscles clenching. *Oh God, oh sweet God, I'm going to* . . . Her head fell back, and she clung to him, fingers digging into his shoulders as pleasure ripped through her. He held her, supporting her as spasms rocked her body.

The rough saw of Theo's breath filled her ears as she stilled, coming back to herself. His face was pressed into her neck, arms braced against her back. "Theo?" she whispered.

He didn't answer.

She shifted on his lap, and his breathing grew harsher. A thread of guilt wove through Bonnie as she realized what his problem was. "I'm in the lead," she said.

"Come again?" He growled against her neck.

She giggled. Had he managed the double entendre on purpose? "Not until you do." She slid backward off his lap, planting her knees on the floor. She reached for the belt of his bathrobe. "By my count, we're at two to zero."

"This isn't a competition," he mumbled, watching her hands. "You don't owe me anything."

"I know," she agreed, tugging the belt loose. "But you've given me two orgasms, and I've left you, um . . ." The robe fell open, his cock springing forward, making her point for her.

"You don't have to do this." He met her gaze, eyes steady, but his voice was low and reedy, chest rising and falling rapidly.

"I *want* to do this."

He began to protest again, but she wrapped her fingers around him, and his words abruptly ended on a groan.

She wrapped her other hand around him too, moving her fingers up and down his shaft, learning the feel of him. Theo groaned again. Bonnie glanced up, his eyes were closed, head lolling against the back of the couch. She returned her attention to his cock and wet her lips, considering. Her belly quivered nervously. She'd been having sex a long time, but oral was not something she'd done often. She and Gabe had tried it once or twice, but it hadn't really gone well, and they'd never tried again.

Maybe if you'd done a better job he wouldn't have needed to . . .

No. Bonnie silenced the insidious whisper. She wasn't going there. Especially not now. Lowering her head, she took a tentative lick. Theo moaned. Encouraged, she licked him again, circling her tongue around his tip. Then she opened her mouth and wrapped her lips around the head of his cock.

"That feels good." He threaded his fingers through her hair, urging her forward, guiding her mouth down his length. "So fucking good."

Eager to please him, to make him feel at least half as good as he'd made her feel, Bonnie followed his lead, taking more of him into her mouth, her hands dropping to the base of his cock. She gripped him tighter, and he jerked, hips thrusting, going deep. She gagged, tried to catch a breath, and then choked, sputtering as she fell backward.

"Bonnie?" Theo gasped, his voice rough and confused.

Stomach hurtling toward her throat, Bonnie scrambled to her feet, overcome with embarrassment as she vividly recalled *why* this particular activity hadn't worked for her in the past. Cheeks flaming, throat burning, she refused to glance Theo's way as she raced to the bathroom.

CHAPTER 14

"BONNIE?" THEO KNOCKED on the door to the loo. When she didn't reply, he knocked again. "Please, love, just tell me if you're all right."

Another few beats of silence passed before her voice finally sounded through the door. "I'm fine." The toilet flushed, immediately followed by the rush of water from the sink.

He waited for her to turn off the taps, then asked, "Do you need anything?"

"A few minutes alone would be good," she mumbled.

"Of course." A stone lodged in Theo's throat. With effort, he backed away from the door, swallowing hard. The stone dropped to his belly. *What the bloody hell happened?* He kicked the bedlinens out of the way and collapsed back onto the sofa, replaying the string of events leading up to her abrupt exodus. Had he scared her? Hurt her? Disgusted her? All of the above? He rubbed a hand over his face.

The bathroom door slid open, and Theo tensed, willing himself to stay seated.

Bonnie's head appeared around the side of the door, cheeks pink. "Could you, um . . ." she paused.

"Yes?"

"Could you bring me my clothes, please?"

"Oh. Right." He nodded and stood, gathering up the garments they'd left strewn across the suite last night. Adding her lacy knickers to the top of the pile, he crossed the room and handed them to her.

"Thanks," she said stiffly, sliding the door shut.

Christ, was it him or did it just get colder in here? "You're welcome," he said to the door. Theo stepped into the bedroom and tugged on his trousers, maneuvering them carefully over his aching hard-on. He glanced down at his crotch. "Sorry, lad." Mind whirring, he ditched the robe and pulled on a shirt. His cock wasn't what was really bothering him, though. The physical discomfort would ease, but honestly, what the hell?

He emerged from the bedroom just as she left the bathroom. Rather than meet his gaze, she turned and headed to the living room of the suite. He followed, bare feet padding silently on the carpet. "Bonnie?"

She jumped, evidently unaware he was right behind her.

"What's wrong?" he asked.

"Nothing," she snapped, rosebud mouth pinching in a tight little line as she gathered up her phone and purse.

"Are you sure?"

She nodded, a rosy stain creeping up her cheeks, so dark her freckles all but disappeared. She headed for the door of his suite, and he stepped in front of her, his longer legs giving him the advantage. Placing himself between her and the door, he faced her. Theo knew he should probably leave things alone but couldn't. "Talk to me. Please."

"I have to go."

"Now?"

She bit her lip, brow furrowing. "I'm meeting Ana and Sadie for brunch."

"Oh." He paused, struggling for what to say next. "I guess this is goodbye, then."

"I guess it is."

But he didn't move. Didn't open the door for her. The silence stretched between them. He didn't want to leave things like this. Strange. Awkward. Uncertain. But what could he do? She wanted to leave. He couldn't make her stay. And soon, he'd be on a flight back to England.

A flicker of hope staved off the panic rising in his chest. She would be in England soon too. And not far from him at all. Cambridge was an easy drive from his family's home. "When do you start your seminar?" he asked.

"End of June." She fiddled with her handbag, still not making eye contact.

Theo used every bit of self-control he had not to demand she tell him what the bloody hell was going on in that head of hers. Forcing himself to keep his tone light, he smiled and said, "Call me when you get to England. Perhaps we can meet up. Catch a meal or a drink once you're settled."

Finally, she lifted her chin and met his gaze. "Sure."

Her response didn't ring with the excitement he could have hoped for, but he'd take it. Opening the door, he stepped aside to let her pass. She started to leave, then stopped. Turning toward him, Bonnie went on tiptoe and pecked his cheek. The moment had a sense of déjà vu about it. She'd kissed him in a similar fashion, brief and grateful, back in London last summer, right before she'd left.

And now she was leaving again. Theo gripped the doorframe, aching with the need to pull her against him and press his mouth to hers, giving her a proper farewell kiss, full of passion and promise. Instead, he nodded his head.

"I'll wait for your call, then," he said, keeping his voice light. "Till June."

"June," she echoed, and walked out the door.

He watched her retreat down the hall, the distance between them growing exponentially with each step.

June couldn't get here soon enough.

As Bonnie crossed the street and headed toward the café, she glanced down the block to the old Dearborn Station. Exactly twenty-four hours ago, she'd stared at that clock, the hands in the same positions as they were now. So much had happened since then. With a shiver, she stepped out of the brisk April wind into the tiny elegant foyer of the hotel on the corner. Bonnie adored everything about this little boutique hotel and French café, from the vintage 1920s brass fixtures, to the feathery scroll patterns on the wallpaper, down to the black-and-white diamond pattern on the tiled floor.

Bracing herself, she pushed through the frosted glass doors leading to the café and inhaled. She'd been worried coming here would trigger painful memories. She'd spent so many lazy mornings in this café with Gabe, lingering over a second cup of tea while he worked on his thesis and she graded papers. But she wasn't going to give this to him. He'd taken enough from her; she wasn't giving up this place.

Bonnie scanned the dining room tables. Despite running late herself, she'd still beat Ana and Sadie. She shouldn't be surprised. As long as she'd known those two, they'd never been on time. Especially when they were together.

Settling into a booth by the windows, she ordered a tea while she waited for the dynamic duo to arrive. Café Nuage's gingerbread blend was a special treat, house-made and only available in the restaurant. Another reason

Bonnie wasn't ready to give up this place. She'd tried to replicate the flavor, but it was never quite right. She wondered if it was the water. Maybe the old pipes in this vintage building added a little something she couldn't copy, and even if she managed to get all the other ingredients to match exactly, it still wouldn't be the same.

As she sipped her tea, Bonnie considered that. The idea of trying to replicate an experience when its very uniqueness rendered it unrepeatable. Was that what her night with Theo had been? A unique experience never to be repeated? *Don't forget about this morning.* Her cheeks heated. She could add that to her list of firsts today . . . orgasm by breast play. What happened after . . . Well, she'd rather not think about that.

"Oh my, what are *you* thinking about?"

Bonnie glanced up, almost spilling her tea across the table. She set the delicate china cup back into its saucer. "Nothing."

"You're blushing," Ana pressed, sliding into the booth.

"The tea's really hot," Bonnie explained awkwardly, her cheeks rising another few degrees as she said it.

"I know that look." Sadie slid in next to Ana. "And that look is *not* nothing."

"Right?" Ana agreed. She paused when a server stopped by to take their drink order. As soon as they were alone again, Ana grabbed Bonnie's hand. "What happened?"

"This has something to do with Gabe, doesn't it?" Sadie demanded.

Ana held up Bonnie's hand. "Ring's gone."

Bonnie snatched her hand out of Ana's grip. "Yes, the ring is gone. And yes, it has something to do with Gabe." She waited while the girls' drinks were set down. "I broke up with him."

"What?" Ana gasped, blowing a puff of whip cream off

the top of her hot cocoa. It landed with a splat on the menus stacked on the table. Ana ignored the mess, leaning across the table to engulf Bonnie in a hug. "Oh my God, how are you? Are you okay? What happened?"

Squeezing Ana back for a moment, Bonnie finally said, words muffled by Ana's magnificent cleavage, "If you let go of me, I'll tell you."

"Release the poor girl before your boobs suffocate her," Sadie chided, wiping a napkin over the menus.

Bonnie sucked in a gulp of air as Ana let her go and settled back in the booth. "Thanks." She took the menu Sadie handed her and decided to get it all out in one breath. "Friday night, when I called you? I needed a place to stay because I walked out on Gabe after finding him in bed with someone else."

"That cheating dickhead!" Sadie growled. An elderly lady at the next table dropped her fork. Sadie bared her teeth in an unapologetic smile and then turned back to Bonnie. "What does the cheating dickhead have to say for himself?"

"Not much." Bonnie shrugged, fiddling with the handle on her teacup. "We met yesterday to talk about it."

"Did he apologize?" Ana asked.

"Please," Sadie snorted, voice rising as she poured a sliver of cream into her coffee. "What's he going to say? Oops, I stuck my man-meat into somebody else. Sorry. My bad."

"You're attracting an audience," Ana muttered under her breath as several heads swiveled their way.

Bonnie tugged the menu open and hid behind it.

"It pisses me off." Sadie stirred her coffee with brisk, cross strokes. "It's just, you guys were together for so long, I was starting to think maybe I was wrong. Maybe it *was* possible."

"Maybe what was possible?" Bonnie peeked over the top of her menu, curious at the change in Sadie's voice. She didn't seem so angry anymore, but rather . . . sad.

"It doesn't matter." Sadie set her spoon down. "Turns out, I was right after all."

Bonnie would have pressed for more details, but at that moment, the server returned to take their order and deliver a basket of pastries to the table. Another Café Nuage perk she was not willing to give up. She eyed the basket, wanting to eat everything in it, but knowing from experience she needed to pace herself and save room for the main event. As delicious as the pastries were, the breakfast was even better.

Even Ana held back, slicing a chocolate croissant down the middle and offering half to Sadie.

"No way." Sadie shook her head, crop of blond waves bouncing. An actress, Sadie tracked her calories religiously.

Ana ignored her and slid the pastry onto Sadie's plate. "You know you want it," she said, taking a bite of the other half and closing her eyes, groaning softly as she chewed.

"That good, huh?" Sadie poked at the croissant, considering. "Worth the extra cardio this is going to cost me?"

"Mm-hmm," Ana moaned in carnal pleasure, then swallowed and opened her eyes. "That reminds me." She licked a bit of chocolate from her bottom lip and raised one dark eyebrow at Bonnie. "What *were* you thinking about when we came in?"

"Yeah, Bon," Sadie added, thrusting her finger inside the croissant and scooping out a smidgen of chocolate. "I don't think it was Gabe the asshole who put that look on your face."

Bonnie shook her head and stared at Sadie's plate, heat creeping up her cheeks again.

"Bon?" Ana asked, concern creasing her brow. "Are you feeling okay?"

Sadie stuck her chocolate-covered finger in her mouth and began to suck.

Bonnie flushed deeper, watching Sadie slide her finger back and forth inside her mouth. An image of Theo before her, robe spread, popped into her mind. "So, uh, have you guys ever . . . ah . . ."

"Stop defiling your food," Ana ordered Sadie. To Bonnie, she said, "Spit it out, Bon."

That had kind of been her problem. She recalled the moment her morning went from delight to disaster. *Oh, God.* Her cheeks were on fire now. She licked her lips and dove in. "Have you ever given a blowjob?"

Silverware clattered against china. Bonnie froze in her seat as Sadie and Ana glanced over at the elderly woman next to them.

Sadie smiled at their neighbor again, adding a little wave this time. Then she eyed Bonnie. "Are you telling me you haven't?"

"You're twenty-eight years old," Ana added.

"Twenty-nine," Bonnie corrected. "My birthday was in February, remember?"

"Fine, twenty-nine, even better . . . or worse." Ana stared at her across the table. "I can't believe you're almost thirty freaking years old and have never given a blowjob!"

"I didn't say I've *never* given one," Bonnie whispered, glancing around, convinced every single person in the café could hear each word of this conversation. "I tried a few times." Bonnie squirmed in her seat. "Just not . . . successfully."

"Holy shit. Poor Gabe." Ana chuckled. "How many years were you two together?"

Their food arrived, saving Bonnie from dealing with

the direction that conversation was headed. *Poor Gabe.* "To hell with poor Gabe," she said, stabbing at a strawberry on top of her Cloud 9 crepes. "What about poor Bonnie?"

"Whoa, chill." Ana eyed the massacred strawberry. "It was a joke."

"Not a funny one," Sadie argued. "Gabe's still a cheating dickhead whether Bonnie sucked his dick or not."

Exactly. Bonnie swirled a fork through the mounds of melting whip cream on her plate. "I just want to know how to do it right," she admitted. "I don't think I'm very good at it."

"Oh, honey." Sadie reached across the table to pat her hand. "I think any attempt made in that department is appreciated. Besides"—she grinned—"you can always try again. Practice makes perfect, right?"

"What I want to know," Ana began, "is where this is coming from? Who are you planning to practice on?" She pinned Bonnie with a stare. "Is it the man I heard on the phone this morning?"

"Who now?" Sadie perked up, a wicked gleam of curiosity in her violet eyes. "Come on, Bon, spill."

Bonnie smiled weakly. "I think your eggs are getting cold."

Sadie ignored that and turned to Ana. "If she doesn't tell us, we can always ask Cassie."

"Hey!" Bonnie balked.

The Dynamic Duo stared at her from across the booth, Sadie's blond and Ana's black brows raised in mutual expectation. *More like Diabolical Duo.* They were tag teaming her. She didn't stand a chance. Accepting defeat, she decided to tell them everything.

"It's Theo," Bonnie mumbled, sinking low in her seat.

"Theo?" Sadie asked. "As in hot British Theo?"

"Mm-hmm." She sunk lower, wishing she could slide under the booth and slink right on out of the café.

"I *knew* it!" Ana crowed. "I shipped you two back in England."

"Nothing happened between us in England," Bonnie protested.

"Please." Ana snorted. "I've never seen two people eye-fuck each other so much."

Bonnie blinked. "Did you just say *eye-fuck*?"

"The attraction *was* pretty obvious, Bon," Sadie added.

"Whatever," Bonnie grumbled. "You're just saying that because you were flirty with him and he ignored you."

"Keep telling yourself that," Ana teased. "Now then, back to the matter at hand. Or *in* hand, I should say." Ana dropped her already husky voice to a seductive whisper. "Do you want some pointers?"

"Ana!" Sadie snickered.

"What? I'm trying to help. Good thing I ordered the Elvis French Toast." Ana smirked, dangling an obscenely long slice of fried banana off the end of her fork.

Bonnie eyed the banana, cheeks flaming. The idea of trying that again—with Theo—made her feel equal parts mortified and intrigued. She didn't even dare to glance around the dining room now. "Um, maybe later. He's headed back to London today."

"Too bad," Ana said, biting off the end of her banana. Gamely changing the subject, she asked, "This is, like, your first time playing hooky from work, right? Tell me, besides attempting a blowjob on a hot Brit and getting sex tips over brunch, what other mischief do you have planned today?"

Bonnie chugged her tea. "Since I'm already down this way, I thought I'd go over to the apartment, clear out some of my stuff."

"Ugh," Sadie groaned, "that's not fun."

"No," Bonnie agreed. "But necessary. And since it's Monday, Gabe will be gone all day."

"Are you sure?" Ana asked.

"Pretty sure." Bonnie paused. Ana had a point. Who knew how many hours of Gabe's busy schedule had actually been spent screwing his adviser's assistant?

"We'll come with you," Ana offered.

"No, I can't ask you to do that."

"You don't have to ask," Sadie said, rearranging the pile of scrambled eggs on her plate.

"Stop playing with your food." Ana snatched Sadie's fork away. "Why did you even order that? You hate eggs."

"I need the protein." Sadie snatched her fork back. "I told you, I have an important audition coming up. I've gotta get buff."

"Then shut up and eat so we can go." Ana nodded toward Bonnie. "We're coming with you." She hitched a thumb at Sadie. "This one can count it as strength training."

"Okay, thanks." Bonnie smiled, heart lifting a little. She wouldn't have to go to her apartment alone. She hadn't really thought about it, but the possibility Gabe could be there, might even be there with *her* . . . She recalled those dishes in the sink, the lipstick on the wineglass, and her fingers curled with fury once again.

Yes, it was definitely a good thing her friends were coming with. Not just for her sake, but for Gabe's too. Though if Sadie wanted to throw a few practice punches, Bonnie wouldn't object.

In the end, no punches were needed. The apartment was empty, Gabe was gone, and thankfully, there didn't seem to be any evidence anyone else had been staying here. Especially anyone female. She shouldn't care, but Bonnie still felt a pang of relief when she noticed there wasn't a new toothbrush in the holder next to his.

In the bedroom, Ana and Sadie stood side by side, double-teaming Bonnie again as they assessed the remaining clothes in her closet before handing them over. Items passing inspection were folded into a storage container while the rest went into a box for donation.

"Keep?" Sadie asked, holding up a dress. "Or donate?"

"Keep!" Bonnie snatched the hanger out of Sadie's hand. "I love this dress." She slipped it off the hanger and began folding it.

"It has pictures of birds all over the skirt," Sadie said, as if that were reason enough to get rid of it.

"It's cute," Bonnie argued. "It's quirky, like me." She placed the dress in the container.

"You say quirky, I say atrocious." Sadie shook her head. "Speaking of atrocious, where is that teacup robe of yours?"

"I already packed it."

"Too bad." Sadie grinned fiendishly. "We could have burned it along with those obnoxious teapot slippers."

"I love my teapot slippers!"

"Next!" Ana barked, breaking up their good-natured spat and holding up another dress. This one was green velvet, with long bell sleeves and ribbons on the bodice. "What about this one?"

Bonnie bit her lip.

Sadie eyed the dress. "It's weird, but it's pretty," she said, "like you."

"Gee, thanks." Bonnie took the dress from Ana and ran a hand over one soft, forest-green sleeve. She'd worn this dress two Christmases ago. The night Gabe had proposed.

Tears burned in the back of her throat, and she slumped on the edge of the bed, the dress still in her hands.

"Uh-oh." Ana dropped the hanger she was holding and hurried over.

Sadie glanced up from sorting sweaters. "You're not *that* weird, okay?" She hopped up on the bed and settled in next to Bonnie, legs dangling off the edge. At a hair under five foot four, Bonnie was shorter than average, but at barely five feet, Sadie was a little pixie of a thing. She'd always reminded Bonnie of Tinkerbell, or Titania, the fairy queen, tiny and delicate, but with a will of iron and a temper to rival the biggest Shakespeare villain.

"It's not that." Bonnie sniffled. "This was my proposal dress." Did she really have to start crying again? She swiped her knuckles across her cheeks, rubbing away tears she should not be shedding. Gabe didn't deserve her tears. Bonnie took a shuddering breath. "I was wearing this when Gabe asked me to marry him."

"Oh. Can we burn it, then?" Sadie asked, dead serious.

A puff of laughter escaped Bonnie. She hiccupped. "Tempting."

"You could donate it to your school's theatre department," Ana suggested. "It would make a great costume piece."

It was true. Bonnie gravitated toward clothes that looked like something from an Austen novel. "That's a great idea." She stood and tossed the dress in the donate box. It was time to stop being so sentimental. Instead of being Marianne, she needed to be Elinor. More sense and less sensibility.

"Thanks, Ana." Bonnie turned and glanced back at the bed. Sadie had sprawled across it and was now lying on *the quilt*. "Um . . . you might not want to lie on that."

"What?" Sadie stretched lazily. "Why?"

Bonnie explained.

Sadie scurried off the bed. When she was done gagging, she announced, "Okay, now *that*, we're burning."

"What's your obsession with burning stuff today?" Ana wondered. "I had no idea you were such a little pyro."

"Besides, we can't burn that," Bonnie added. "My grandma made that quilt."

Sadie's mouth twisted. "What are you going to do with it?"

"Dry clean it half a dozen times." Bonnie shrugged. "Box it up and store it with the rest of the things I'm taking back to my parents' house."

"I'd make it a dozen," Sadie said, eyeing the quilt like it was a snake waiting to bite her. "And maybe don't tell your parents about what happened on it."

"I haven't told my parents about any of this yet," Bonnie admitted, closing the lid on the storage container.

"What?" Sadie and Ana asked in unison.

"My mom is going to freak when she hears the engagement is off."

"Yeah, she is," Ana agreed.

"Not helping." Bonnie groaned and collapsed onto the top of the container. "I'll lose it if I think about it right now! I'll think about it tomorrow."

Sadie chortled with laughter.

"Glad you find this amusing," Bonnie snapped, feeling more than a little sorry for herself. It had been a long day. Hell, it had been a long weekend.

"Sorry," Sadie said, still chuckling. "It's just, you're acting exactly like Scarlett O'Hara."

"Please." Bonnie snorted. "I know I can be a bit dramatic, but—"

"I'll think about that tomorrow." Sadie cut her off with a saucy Southern drawl. Wrist pressed dramatically to her forehead, Sadie continued, "After all, tomorrow is another day."

Despite herself, a smile tugged at Bonnie's mouth. "That's a pretty good impression, but I've always thought Ana looked more like Scarlett. Or, what was that actress's name?"

"Vivien Leigh," Sadie replied instantly. A classic movie buff, Sadie knew as much about the Golden Age of Hollywood as Bonnie did about Shakespeare.

Ana turned her attention to Bonnie, green eyes glittering, one raven eyebrow arched in a very haughty Scarlett O'Hara manner. "Stop changing the subject. We were talking about you and your procrastination. Tell your mom. Get it over with. The longer you wait, the harder it will be."

"God, you sound just like Theo," Bonnie grumbled, pushing the container through the bedroom door.

"You talked to Theo about this?" Sadie asked, trailing behind Bonnie.

"I hope she did, considering our earlier conversation," Ana added, bringing up the rear.

"Ha. Yes, Theo knows about the breakup. He was giving me grief about not telling Cassie." Bonnie reached the living room and paused, catching her breath. How could a plastic container of clothes be so heavy?

"Whoa, whoa, whoa." Ana dropped the cardboard box onto the couch. "You haven't told Cassie about this yet?"

"Chill. I told her!" Bonnie kicked the container farther into the room. "But I told Theo first."

Sadie shook her head, short blond waves bobbing. "Doesn't that break the bro code?"

"What are you talking about?" Bonnie grumbled.

"You know what I mean," Sadie said, hands on hips. "You and Cassie are *best* friends. If something major like that happened with Ana, I'd want to be the first to know." She glanced past Bonnie to stare at Ana. "I *better* be the first to know."

"Calm down, small fry, I tell you everything first." Ana dug her keys out of her purse. "And Bonnie said she already told Cassie, right?" Ana glanced at Bonnie.

"Right," Bonnie agreed.

"Great. That's settled." Ana jangled her keys in the air. "Now, are you ready to go?"

Bonnie took one last look around the apartment. Most of the furniture was secondhand, and she didn't care about any of it except for the bed. As much as she loved this little apartment in Printer's Row, with the water fountain in the brick courtyard out front, the cafés, and the short walk to both the library and her job, she'd never planned for this to be her permanent home. Just the place she and Gabe would share until they got married.

Taking a deep breath, Bonnie nodded. "Ready." An unexpected thrill zinged through her. Moving out had been the right idea. It was time for a change. "If adventures will not befall a young lady in her own village, she must seek them abroad," she quoted, closing and locking the apartment door.

"What?" Ana huffed, pausing at the top of the hallway stairs.

"She's spouting Shakespeare. Keep moving," Sadie ordered, holding the other end of the box Ana carried.

"That's not Shakespeare," Bonnie corrected, following her friends down the stairs, "it's Austen." Reaching the bottom, she glanced back up. It wasn't the last time she'd be here, but still, it felt like goodbye. It was definitely the end of something.

With a final look, Bonnie realized by closing the book on her life with Gabe, embarking on a new beginning wasn't the start of a new chapter, but a whole new story.

CHAPTER 15

BONNIE SHIFTED THE duffel bag on her lap and looked out the window of the train car. She'd made it through the week without any more issues, showing up early to all her classes and powering through each lesson on autopilot.

As she watched the dreary spring landscape speed by, she wished there was a way she could avoid thinking about her personal life as neatly as she'd avoided talking about it. Not wanting to overstay her welcome at the hotel, at first she'd considered moving back in with her parents for a bit, but Ana had offered to let her have the spare room in her town house. It was only for a few months. Then she'd be off to England. After that . . . who knew.

Four more weeks until Memorial Day weekend. By then, finals would be over and she'd be done with the semester. It couldn't come soon enough. She hadn't planned to visit her parents until the holiday weekend, but Ana and Sadie were right—she needed to tell them about the breakup. That didn't mean she was looking forward to it.

It was Friday night, and she'd be spending the next thirty-six hours or so at her parents' house. The only promising thing about the weekend ahead was her plan to meet up with Delaney for dinner and drinks tomorrow. The fifth member of their merry little band of friends, Delaney had grown up in the same small suburban town as Bonnie and Cassie and ended up enrolling at the same Chicago university.

While Bonnie and Cassie had found work in the city after graduation, Delaney went back home and got a job teaching at the fancy-pants preschool that opened a few years ago in their town's most elite neighborhood. Honestly, Bonnie was pretty sure Delaney made more money showing four-year-olds how to create papier-mâché farm animals using organic non-GMO gluten-free paste than Bonnie did teaching nineteen-year-olds the three-act story structure.

Still, she loved hearing about Delaney's adventures in the classroom and couldn't wait to catch up. However, duty called, and Bonnie needed to spend her first night home with her folks. Besides, better to drop the engagement bomb right away than leave it hanging over her head, ticking away all weekend.

Rain started to splatter outside her train car window as the tightly spaced brick buildings of the city gave way to the mansions of the North Shore. By the time the scenery shifted to long stretches of muddy fields and early-budding trees, a full downpour was in progress. Torrents of rain streamed past. The soggy, gray scene made her think of London. And of course, thinking of London made her think of Theo.

She wondered what he was doing now. And was reminded again she had no idea what the man did for a living. They hadn't spoken since her abrupt departure from his hotel room Monday morning. Had it been only a week since she'd run into him at the Shakespeare event? A week since she'd gone home to find Gabe . . .

Squeezing her hands into fists, she resisted the urge to adjust a ring that wasn't there. She had to stop replaying that scene. More and more, though, she found herself replaying other moments from that weekend. Moments that had nothing to do with Gabe and everything to do with Theo.

Bonnie pressed her cheek against the damp, cold glass. What had happened with Theo was a one-time thing. A perfect storm of timing and emotion. As if on cue, lightning flashed. Bonnie closed her eyes, waiting for the crack of thunder to follow, counting seconds out of habit. It came almost immediately, loud enough to be heard above the rumble of the train. Her eyes snapped open. This was turning into a pretty serious storm.

But despite the uncanny metaphor unfolding, there was nothing serious between her and Theo. He'd walked back into her life at the exact right time. She thought of the scene in *Julius Caesar* when Marc Antony learns Caesar's nephew Octavius has arrived in Rome.

"He comes upon a wish." Bonnie recited Antony's line under her breath, finger tracing a pattern in the condensation on her window. "Fortune is merry, and in this mood will give us anything."

Had she subconsciously wished for Theo? He'd certainly been willing to give her anything she'd wanted that night in the hotel—even if it ended up being a pair of strong arms to hold her while she slept.

But what did she want now? How would she feel when she saw him again? He was Logan's best man, and she was Cassie's maid of honor. Sooner or later, they *would* be seeing each other again this summer.

She just didn't know which she wanted.

Sooner . . . or later?

The train rolled to a stop and Bonnie gathered her things. Hopping onto the platform, she held her jacket over her head and squinted through the raindrops, searching for her father's car among those waiting in the pick-up lot.

A pair of headlights shone on her, and a moment later, her dad pulled up alongside the curb. She scurried across the slick pavement and got in before he could get out to open her door.

She pulled the car door shut. "Thanks for picking me up."

"Glad to do it." Her dad pulled into the line of cars waiting to exit. "You should have let me help you with your bags."

"I didn't bring much," she said, biting back a smile. Like Theo, her father could be old-fashioned about certain things. "Besides," she added, tugging her jacket off her head and reaching across the seat to hug her father, "no need for both of us to get wet."

"A bit late for that," he grumbled, swiping at the droplets she'd left behind.

"Oops." She laughed and turned up the heater. "What's for dinner?"

"Your mother is making fish."

Bonnie wrinkled her nose. Fish Friday, right.

"Dessert?" she asked hopefully.

"Of course." He glanced over at her, corners of his eyes crinkling as he smiled. "Gingerbread."

"Yesss." Bonnie dropped back against the headrest, sighing. Her mother's gingerbread was heaven on a plate.

Sure enough, after her dad pulled into the garage, ignoring her protests and shouldering her bag as he led the way into the house, Bonnie was inundated with the smells of home. The less pleasant aroma of frying fish, most likely cod, mixed with the warm earthy scents of ginger and nutmeg and the sharp sweet tang of molasses.

She stepped into the kitchen, and it was like stepping back in time. Nothing had changed in this room in the nearly three decades Bonnie had been alive. Even the wooden high chair that had been hers as a baby was still tucked in one corner, pulled into service whenever members of the extensive Blythe clan popped in for a visit.

A fruitful brood, Bonnie was the only one in her extended family not to have any siblings. She was also the only female grandchild and the only one to inherit Grandma Mary's red hair. In short, she was the magical unicorn of the family.

"Bon-Bon!" Her mother wiped her hands on her apron and hurried across the kitchen to envelop Bonnie in a fragrant hug. Bonnie had long ago given up struggling against the ridiculous nickname. Though—after years of adolescent angst—she'd never admit to growing fond of it, but only from her mother. She let her besties get away with calling her "Bon," but no one else was allowed to call her Bon-Bon—ever. A lesson her cousin Ian had learned the hard way. To this day, Ian still sported a small scar on his chin after Bonnie threw a fork at him across the Thanksgiving dinner table one year when he'd asked "Bon-Bon" to pass the peas. Jerkface didn't even like peas.

Speaking of peas, she spied a pot of them bubbling on the stove. Fried fish and mashed peas. Mom was going full out with the traditional Friday night meal. Bonnie kissed her mom's cheek and stepped back, poking her head into the pantry to see if there was any soda bread. *Jackpot.* She

pulled out a round loaf and was headed to the fridge for
the butter when her mother stopped her with a click of her
tongue. "Don't spoil your supper."

"But—"

"No buts. Go wash up, then set the table."

Bonnie set the loaf of bread on the counter and stalked
toward the bathroom, passing her father, who was seated
in his usual spot in the den, stockinged feet propped on a
faded ottoman, watching a soccer match on TV. It was a
pattern as old as the peeling ivy wallpaper lining the bathroom walls.

Maybe she didn't want the married life after all, Bonnie thought as she dried her hands. Would that be what she
had to look forward to? She and Gabe had fallen into a
comfortable routine, but Bonnie never pictured her life
quite so . . . provincial. To be fair, her parents weren't that
bad. Yes, Dad had his little quirks, and Bonnie doubted
her mother had ever changed a tire or fixed anything
around the house, but her mom *did* have a job.

It had been her mother who made most of the travel arrangements for the dream vacation Bonnie and her best
friends had taken last summer. And hitting five European
countries in six weeks took a lot of planning. As did a honeymoon. Ever since her engagement to Gabe, Mom had
been working on plans for their trip. Now Bonnie was
going to have to tell her mother all that time and research
had been wasted. There would be no honeymoon.

Well, there was nothing for it. What is past hope should
be past care, right?

Easier said than done. Bonnie decided to wait to tell her
parents until after dinner.

Unfortunately, dinner was over all too soon. As the gingerbread cooled on the counter and the tea kettle heated
up, Bonnie stood at the sink, drying dishes while her

mother washed. "How's Gabe?" Mom asked, and Bonnie almost dropped the plate she was drying.

She caught it, gathering her courage as she set it on top of the stack in the cabinet. "We broke up."

There. Rip the bandage off.

"What?" her mother yelled over the rush of running water, glancing up from the pan she was rinsing.

Deciding this conversation would be tense enough without adding shouting to the mix, Bonnie reached over and turned off the faucet. "We broke up. Gabe and I. We're done."

Her mother stared at her, blue eyes wide. Looking in those eyes was like looking in the mirror. Aside from her pert ski-slope nose, Bonnie's eyes were the only trait she'd inherited from her mother. Everything else was a carbon copy of Grandma Mary.

Bonnie set the dish towel aside and held up her left hand, waggling her bare ring finger.

Understanding dawned in her mother's eyes. The pale blue of her irises deepened to a cobalt. Dad always joked that their eyes were mood rings, color shifting depending on what they were feeling. It wasn't so much a joke, as an astute observation. Their eyes *did* change color depending on mood. The problem was, Bonnie thought, unable to break away from her mom's stare, she couldn't decide if the darkening hue was due to anger or something else.

"What happened?" Mom finally asked.

The kettle whistled, and Bonnie turned away, grateful for the interruption. She busied herself making the tea while Mom bustled behind her, slicing the gingerbread.

Finally, when they were both seated at the table, thick slices of cake and steaming mugs of tea in front of them, Bonnie was ready to tell her mom the whole story. Everything. Even the most unsavory parts.

"On Grandma Mary's quilt?" her mother asked.

Bonnie nodded, poking at the crumbs on her plate.

Mom crossed herself. "Don't tell your father that part."

"Tell me what part?" Dad asked.

Bonnie and her mother both jumped, exchanging uneasy glances as her dad joined them at the table.

"Let me get you some cake, Bill." Mom sliced a generous slab.

He thanked her but kept his attention pinned on Bonnie. With a thatch of unruly black hair and piercing dark eyes beneath a slash of thick, black brows, like all the Blythe boys, Dad was what was often referred to as "Dark Irish."

Mom's coloring was more muted, a soft brown like that of a wren. She looked like a little bird now, hopping around Dad, clucking and fussing. Watching them, Bonnie recognized her parents were a good match—Mom's good-natured happy-go-lucky personality rounded the edges of her father's sharp trademark temper.

Despite growing up Protestant, Connie had been happy to embrace her husband's Irish Catholic heritage, learning how to cook his favorite foods and following the rituals of his faith, even raising her daughter in the traditions of her husband's family. But, easygoing as she was, Connie had insisted on doing a few things her way, such as letting Bonnie decide for herself if she wanted to take communion.

And after her college graduation, when Bonnie had announced she was planning to move in with Gabe, even though they had yet to be officially engaged, it had been Mom who convinced Dad it was okay, cajoling him into joining the twenty-first century. When Gabe had proposed two Christmases ago, Dad had finally stopped grumbling about how his daughter's virtue was in peril.

Now she was going to have to tell her father it was

over—that she would not, in fact, be marrying the man she had been "living in sin" with. Why? Because her fiancé had been busy committing a few other sins. Bonnie gulped the rest of her tea and tried to figure out the best way to broach the subject. This shouldn't be so hard. She was an English teacher; words were her world.

"Gabe cheated on her," Mom said.

Well, that was one way to say it.

"Is this true?" Dad's dark intense stare bored into her. "He told you that?"

"I, uh . . ." Bonnie broke eye contact and focused on the dregs in the bottom of her mug. "I caught him in the act."

"You mean you . . . oh." Her father cleared his throat. "I see."

"Be glad you didn't," Bonnie quipped, going for levity.

It didn't work. An awkward silence filled the kitchen. "I'm sorry, Mom."

"Whatever for?"

"I know you've been looking forward to planning the wedding with me. And then of course, the honeymoon . . ."

"Oh, Bon-Bon, don't worry about any of that," her mother said, reaching out to smooth a hand over Bonnie's curls. "None of that is important. Your happiness is what matters to me."

Bonnie nodded, eyes stinging.

"Do you want me to kill him?"

"William!" Mom gasped.

The ghost of a giggle escaped her. Bonnie couldn't be sure her father was joking. It was a good thing Gabe was over an hour away in the city. Come to think of it, maybe it was best if she kept news of her breakup under wraps from the rest of her family for a while—or at least the reason behind it. Too many uncles and cousins were in spitting distance of the apartment she'd shared with Gabe.

Even if Gabe deserved it, the last thing she needed was a Blythe Brigade showing up on his doorstep. Still, a small bloodthirsty corner of her soul would have liked to see what happened if they did. Her cousin Michael Jr. was an MMA fighter, and all the Blythe boys were born knowing how to throw a punch.

"That won't be necessary, Dad." She kept her voice light. "I'd prefer it if my next visit to see you wasn't in prison."

Later that night, Bonnie curled up under the pastel comforter in her old bedroom. Like the rest of the house, this room hadn't changed much over the years. Never really a fan of boy bands or television heartthrobs, her walls were covered in posters of Shakespeare and Oscar Wilde, interspersed with framed prints of some of her favorite paintings.

She rolled onto her side and studied the picture over her dresser. A poster-sized version of Millais's *Ophelia*. Again, her mind drifted to Theo. He'd been so easy to talk to. And fun. Constantly surprising her with his knowledge of artists and playwrights. Bonnie wrapped her arms around her pillow, wishing she could talk to him now. She squeezed the pillow and wished she could do a few other things with him too. Her skin tingled, pulse fluttering as she recalled the way he'd kissed her, the way he'd touched her . . . the way he'd made her feel.

Bonnie had been with Gabe a long time. Things in the bedroom had become routine, and, to be honest, rather dull. Over the last year or so, the number of times they'd had sex dwindled from a few nights a week, to weekly, to monthly—if that. She'd chalked it up to their hectic schedules, and in a way, she wasn't wrong. Gabe had been busy . . . getting busy with someone else.

That part hurt more than all the rest. The fact he'd cheated hurt, yes, but the fact he'd lied and been able to hide it from her for so long—that's what stung the most. Bonnie prided herself on her intelligence and insight. Yet she'd been completely oblivious.

From somewhere deep inside, the cold logical part of her stepped forward with an observation. If it was her pride that was hurt more than anything else, maybe it was best she wasn't marrying Gabe. If she regretted the past more than she mourned the future, if she was bothered by all the time she'd lost investing in their relationship more than she was upset about losing him . . . well.

Acknowledging this fact still didn't address the Theo issue. She realized she missed him. And that didn't make any sense. She barely knew him.

Done thinking about men but too wired to sleep—and not ready for any more sex-fueled dreams featuring a dimpled too-beautiful-for-his-own-good Brit—Bonnie got out of bed and crossed the room to sit at her old desk. She shuffled around in the drawers, searching for paper and something to write with.

It was an old habit, one she hadn't indulged in much lately. When she needed to work through stuff, she wrote. Not like a diary, where she wrote her thoughts and feelings down, but more like a story, where characters from other places and other times—even from other worlds— picked up the narrative of her life and acted it out.

As Bonnie began to scrawl sentences across the paper, she realized she missed this. Missed the escape writing provided. Sometime later, she put the pencil down and slowly uncurled her cramping fingers. Streaks of gray from the pencil lead were smudged across her palm.

She sat back, blinking at the little digital clock on her desk. It was after two in the morning. She glanced at the papers scattered across her desk. Gathering them together, she tapped the pages against the desk, forming a neat pile. It had felt good to let loose and just write. Really good.

Standing, Bonnie stretched, shoulders and spine popping. Writing was her first love. She'd been tinkering with novels since her early teens and had always hoped to finish at least one book while still in her twenties. But her teaching position had kept her busy, and the steady income from directing productions for the college had been too good to pass up, especially with Gabe working on his doctorate. She'd decided to set aside her writing and focus on teaching and directing, supporting him and saving money for their future.

The plan made sense. Once he was Dr. Gabriel Shaughnessy and they were married, she could take a year, maybe even two, off, go on sabbatical, and devote time to finishing a book. When he'd proposed, she thought it was all perfect, things were going exactly as planned, and soon she'd have everything she'd ever wanted.

Up until last week, she'd still believed that to be true.

Now, everything had changed.

Bonnie crawled back into the squeaky hideaway bed, pulling up the covers. She rolled onto her side. Eyes growing heavy with sleep, she stared at the neat stack of papers on her desk with a deep sense of satisfaction. Inspiration bloomed in her chest. With ten months to go before she turned thirty, it was not too late to accomplish at least one of her goals.

CHAPTER 16

THE NEXT MORNING, Bonnie pried her cramped body out of bed and fixed a pot of tea. She'd love nothing better than to sleep until noon, but she had papers to grade. She grabbed her laptop and settled into the big pink chair that had been in her room since she was a baby. She was pretty sure her mom had nursed her in this chair.

Procrastinating on the chore of grading, Bonnie pulled up the Cambridge University website and browsed the summer programs, getting a sense of the schedule and typical classes offered. She kept getting sidetracked with pictures of the gorgeous campus. Excitement bubbled up inside her. *She* was going to be spending her summer there, waking up in one of those lovely old brick dorm buildings, walking those garden paths, teaching some of those classes.

Argh, classes. She clicked on a saved file and began to sift through the analysis papers she needed to grade. She attempted to start in on one, but as she tried to focus on the words, her attention kept drifting, mind landing again and again on a certain pair of blue eyes matched with a set of dimples.

He hadn't called, but she hadn't expected him to. He'd told her to look him up when she arrived in England. She decided to look him up now. Opening a new browser tab, Bonnie typed Theo's name into the search box. She clicked, doing a double take as the results loaded. *That can't be right.*

Bonnie switched to image search. *Oh my God . . .* She clicked on another image. And another. *Oh. My. God.* There was no mistaking those eyes or those dimples. She skimmed article after article, soaking up tidbits on his family (there were those three sisters he'd mentioned), on his time playing rugby at St. Andrews (she remembered he'd mentioned going to school there, it's where he met Logan), and on his appearances at charity events (including, *holy shit*, a fundraising gala in Chicago last week).

For the rest of the morning Bonnie clicked and skimmed and skimmed and clicked some more until her eyes were dry and itchy. At last, brain on overload, she stopped.

Theo Wharton was a duke. An honest to God, living, breathing peer of the realm.

And she'd made out with him.

After several torturous hours grading papers, Bonnie was more than ready to meet Delaney for a drink. Cozied up to the bar at Finn's, the Irish pub across from Delaney's apartment in the little downtown area on Main Street, Bonnie shared her tale of woe once again.

"On the quilt . . . really?" Delaney asked, eyes wide with horror. "The one your grandma Mary made?"

Bonnie nodded, staring at the perfect line between the dark stout and golden lager of her Half and Half. Mick, the owner, was a master at pouring the drink. Just don't let him ever hear anyone call it a Black and Tan. "Yep."

"Did you burn it?"

"Nope." Bonnie shook her head and wiped a bit of foam from her mouth. "Sadie wanted to, but we decided multiple trips to the dry cleaners should sufficiently sanitize it."

"Too bad you can't dry clean your brain, right?" Delaney lifted her glass in a bottoms-up gesture.

"Right." Bonnie clinked glasses and swallowed a rueful chuckle. Yeah, she wouldn't be wiping away the awful memory of what she'd witnessed happening on that quilt anytime soon. Though having repeated the story to Theo, Cassie, Ana and Sadie, her mother, and now Delaney, the edge had worn off. Rather like the way her beer was taking the edge off the shock of this morning's discovery about Theo.

A band climbed the steps to a small stage set up in one corner of the pub and introduced themselves. Finn's often had live music on the weekends, and when the band began their set, Bonnie wasn't surprised to hear them playing an Irish tune. Mick liked to keep to his pub's theme.

For a few minutes, they relaxed, toes tapping against the rungs of their barstools in time to the fiddle as they sipped their beers.

"Have you talked to Gabe?" Delaney finally asked.

"Not since last Saturday." She set her glass down and rubbed the knuckle on her bare ring finger, thinking of their little chat in the library. "We said all we needed to say. There's nothing more to talk about."

"How'd your mom take it? When you told her the wedding is off?"

"Better than I expected, actually."

"And your dad?"

Bonnie shook her head, a reluctant grin breaking across her face as she recalled her father's answer. "He offered to kill Gabe."

"Good man." Delaney laughed, clanking her glass against Bonnie's again. "To Irish fathers."

"Sláinte," Bonnie toasted, the word falling off her tongue automatically. As she drank, she kept an eye trained on her friend. Delaney rarely mentioned her dad. Once the town's chief of police, Daniel Mason had been killed on duty almost a dozen years ago. Bonnie's heart squeezed when she realized the anniversary was coming up. "You okay?"

Delaney nodded, eyes on her nearly empty glass.

On stage, the band shifted to a new song, music rolling from a jaunty Celtic clip to a smoother, flowing melody. Delaney looked up, eyes meeting Bonnie's. "That was one of Dad's favorites."

"Laney . . ." Bonnie reached a hand out to her friend. Delaney had been a bit of a wild child in her teens. Forever getting into trouble, eventually she'd landed in a juvenile detention center for over a year. It was the summer after she came back, the same summer her father died, that Delaney turned over a new leaf and enrolled in college with Bonnie and Cassie.

Delaney tapped the counter by their empty glasses. "One more?"

Bonnie began to shake her head, then stopped and changed her mind. "Sure. Why not?"

"So," Delaney said as they watched Mick top off their pints with stout, "you're going to be spending the summer in England."

"Hard to believe, right?" Bonnie followed the change of subject without comment.

"It's cool. I'm jealous."

"Yeah." Bonnie grinned. "It *is* cool."

"The part I find hard to believe is how we're all going to be back in Europe together less than a year after our trip." Delaney shook her head. "I didn't see that one coming."

"I don't think any of us did. Least of all Cassie."

Delaney snorted into her beer. "I can't believe Cass is getting married. And in Scotland! In a castle!" She paused, glancing over at Bonnie.

"Stop doing that," Bonnie snapped, surprising them both. She took a sip of beer, smothering the burst of anger that had erupted out of nowhere. "You don't have to check in with me every time the word marriage comes up. I'm fine."

"Of course, you're fine," Delaney agreed serenely. "Do you want to talk about it?"

"No."

"Okay."

They sat in silence for a bit. Bonnie gave her friend the side-eye. She had the distinct impression Delaney was employing one of the tactics she used when dealing with her preschoolers. And it was working too. Because after a moment, Bonnie couldn't resist the urge to keep talking. "I should be fine with it. I *want* to be fine with it. But this was supposed to be the summer *I* got married. We were supposed to be planning *my* wedding. And now we're not, and I sound so selfish and—"

Delaney cut her off. "You're not selfish." She tossed her ponytail over her shoulder. "Well, maybe a little selfish."

"Gee, thanks."

"But there's nothing wrong with being a little selfish. You have every right to be. You've been with Gabe forever, and Cassie met Logan . . ." she paused and counted on her fingers, from August to April, ". . . what, eight or nine months ago? It's okay to be upset."

Bonnie kept her gaze trained on her glass. This was nothing she hadn't told herself already. "I'm not upset."

"Come on. I know how long you've been waiting to plan your wedding. Planning someone else's instead—even if it's your best friend's, *especially* if it's your best friend's— has to suck."

"Has anyone ever told you you need to learn some tact?"

"I work with four-year-olds all day."

"Uh-huh. And?"

"They are the most tactless creatures on earth." Delaney tossed back the rest of her beer. "Those sugar biscuits tell it like it is. The unvarnished truth."

Bonnie laughed. Knowing Delaney as she did, "sugar biscuits" was likely code for a variation of something crass and four-lettered. When Laney had become a preschool teacher, she'd learned to curb her perpetual potty mouth by substituting other words, and since she also had a perpetual sweet tooth, her preferences leaned toward the dessert aisle.

"Fine, you're right," Bonnie admitted. "It does suck."

"There." Delaney grinned impishly and waved at Mick for another round. "Doesn't that feel better?"

"A bit." Bonnie returned the grin and finished off the rest of her beer as Mick set the fresh drinks in front of them. She traded her empty glass for the full one, recalling how badly things went the last time she'd agreed to a third drink. "To all the things that suck."

One strawberry-blond brow rose. "You wanna toast things that suck?" Delaney asked.

"Why not," Cassie breathed, feeling giddy.

"Okay, but I think I'm driving you home, lightweight." Delaney lifted her beer. "To things that suck."

"Sláinte." Bonnie clinked her glass against Delaney's.

Maybe it was the release that came from admitting things sucked, or maybe it was the buzz from the two beers she'd already downed, but as the cool foam hit her lips, Bonnie decided that perhaps things didn't suck so bad after all.

CHAPTER 17

BACK AT HIS family's estate, Theo headed downstairs for breakfast. He'd flown into Heathrow late yesterday, and by some miracle everyone at the Abbey had been in bed by the time he arrived home. Which meant he could avoid having any uncomfortable conversations for a few hours. He'd hoped to get a good night's sleep—or some sleep anyway—before heading into battle the next morning.

Counter to his plans, too many of those hours had been filled thinking about a certain redhead. He still had no idea what he'd done to spook Bonnie into running off like she had. She'd promised she'd reach out when she was back on his side of the pond, and for the thousandth time, he told himself that would have to be good enough for now.

Besides, he had other, more immediate, problems to attend to. As Theo approached the breakfast room, he heard the low murmur of feminine voices. His mother and sister, no doubt. He paused outside the door and girded his loins for the interrogation session to come.

"Ah, Theodore, there you are." His mother waved him over the moment he entered the room.

He crossed to her chair and stopped, pressing a kiss to her offered hand. "Good morning, Mama." He glanced across the table to his sister. "Morning, Tabitha."

"How was your trip, Teddy?"

Theo grimaced at the hated childhood nickname but refrained from retaliating. For now. He made a mental note to call her by her own nickname next time their mother was out of earshot. Not quite a year younger than himself, Tabby was the oldest of his three sisters and the only other sibling finished with school.

Their sister Thalia was in her third year at university, and the youngest in the family, baby Tessa, who was not a baby anymore as she told anyone who would listen, would be graduating secondary school in a few weeks. Theo swallowed a groan. Come the end of June, all three of his sisters would be in residence and the house would be overrun with females.

But the end of June also meant the arrival of another female. Bonnie would be starting her teaching seminar at Cambridge around then. Appetite abruptly spiking, Theo took a seat and peeked under the covered serving dishes on the table.

"Shall I ring Marjorie to get you something else?"

"No need." Theo brushed aside his mother's offer and helped himself to a few fat sausages and a rasher of eggs.

"Tea?" his mother asked.

"Please." Theo nodded. His mother poured, and for a few minutes everyone focused on their meals. Theo knew his mother wouldn't jump right into the subject at hand immediately, she followed her own rules too carefully for such a breach of decorum. Sure enough, after finishing off a square of toast spread with the thinnest veneer of marmalade, his mother dabbed at her mouth with a napkin and casually remarked. "I gather your flight was comfortable?"

He nodded over a forkful of eggs.

"And your accommodations? They were acceptable?"

"Quite."

"Were you able to see Logan?" his sister asked. "Is it true he's getting married?"

"Yes," he grunted, answering both questions and sending his sister a baleful glare across the table. The last thing he wanted to do was float the topic of marriage.

Tabitha either missed his meaning or more likely ignored it. "When is the wedding?"

"August." He gulped down his tea.

"How does one go from being total strangers to getting married in less than a year?" Tabby shook her head. "I don't think I've ever dated someone for longer than a month, and I've certainly never considered marriage with anyone."

"That reminds me." Mama straightened in her chair, a gleam he recognized all too well lighting her eyes.

So much for steering this conversation in a different direction. He shot Tabitha a gaze full of daggers promising retribution before turning toward his mother, a polite look of interest plastered on his face. "Yes?"

"How was tea with Lady Camille?"

"Pleasant," he admitted.

"And the gala?" his mother continued.

"Very pleasant," Theo hedged. Ethan's little sister had been much more charming than he remembered. Again, Theo recognized Mama had played this hand well. He'd been surprised to find how much he enjoyed Camille's company. Several times during their evening together, he'd caught himself thinking he could see a marriage working with her.

But he didn't feel for Camille even a hint of what he felt for Bonnie. And the fact he was contemplating marriage to one woman while consumed with desire for another left him feeling like a cad.

Or worse, like his father.

"Delighted to hear it. Tabitha, dear, we should plan to invite the Fairfaxes to tea once Camille returns home."

"Of course, Mother." Tabitha's mouth pinched, and Theo smothered a laugh. Served her right. "There's nothing I'd like better in all the world than to make small talk over tea and cakes with the potential wife to your son and heir," his sister added.

"Tabitha!" Mama chided.

"What? Too on the nose?" Tabby split a crumpet down the middle. "It's no secret, Mama. Everyone knows you are on the hunt to find Theo a wife." She slathered both halves with butter. "Sounds like Lady Camille is a perfect candidate. The ideal partner for the Duke of Emberton." She picked up both pieces of crumpet, holding half in each hand. "A proper young lady, from a well-bred and well-off, if not as well-titled, family, and a dashing duke, the height of nobility, with a sprawling ancestral estate on the verge of bankruptcy." Tabitha smashed the halves of the crumpet together. "A match made in heaven."

"That's enough," Theo said quietly to his sister, eyes on his mother's pale pinched face.

"I'm just saying . . ." Tabitha began, but Theo cut his gaze to her, and she stopped, shoving a large bite of crumpet in her mouth and chewing angrily.

Tabby was right, of course. Her choice of words had been a little *too* on the nose. He wondered if his sister had been listening in to that early morning phone call the other day. The trip to Chicago had been a power play by his matchmaking mother. And he couldn't even hate her for it. He knew what Mama was doing, understood and even appreciated her motivation. He understood, too, that his sister was, in her own way, defending him. She was affronted at the idea that in this modern day and age, their mother expected him to marry not for love, but for the sake of the family. For duty.

Or, to put it more crudely, for money.

Luckily, it was his problem and not his sister's. Tabby may crack jokes about the ducal title, "following the next Wharton penis," but as the only male heir, Theo had been raised knowing his role. From the moment of his birth, the responsibility of preserving the family legacy fell to him. A responsibility that grew exponentially, the ledgers slipping further and further into debt the more his selfish spendthrift father pissed away that legacy with every foolish investment, greedy mistress, and drunken gambling loss.

These were details Theo had become all too familiar with since graduating university and taking the reins. He knew how easily one leaky roof or bad chimney flu could be the domino that brought the whole thing tumbling down.

Despite the uphill battle to undo the damage wrought by the last duke, Theo was determined to rebuild the Emberton fortune and make sure there was something left for the next generation of Whartons. Ensuring that his children, and his sisters and their children, wouldn't have to live under the threat of bankruptcy. Instead, they would be free to make their own choices, lead a life not dictated by duty to debt and decaying ducal properties.

The idea of children stopped him cold. Growing up, "the next generation" had been an ephemeral thing—something in the far-off future—not even really connected to him. But now, with his mother on the "wife hunt," as his sister had so crassly, yet accurately, called it, that far-off future was not so far away anymore.

Lately, Mama had been ramping up her efforts. Theo

wondered if it was the fact his thirtieth birthday was on the horizon that motivated her. Or was there some other development he was not yet aware of? Some impending disaster prompting her to prod him down the nuptial path with increased urgency? He poked at the remains of his breakfast, studying her. She seemed frailer than he remembered. Smaller. If he was getting older, so was she. Perhaps that's what had her doubling down.

Whatever the reason, maybe his mother was right. Maybe it was time. After all, his best friend was getting married soon. But unlike Logan, there would be no passionate one-night stands followed by a whirlwind courtship and a spontaneous engagement. Ultimately, the choice wouldn't even really be up to him. When Theo did get married, it would be planned with careful precision, and he highly doubted passion would play any part in the process—unless one counted his mother's passion to save their family's fortune.

Another reason he hadn't really cared much about his mother's marriage machinations was that he didn't much care for the whole business of marriage in the first place. If for no other reason than the very fact that's what marriage was—a business arrangement. His mother and father had shared a name and four children and very little else. They'd slept in separate beds, first in separate rooms, then in separate wings of the Abbey, and finally, in completely separate houses. Eventually, save for the occasional function requiring them to make a joint appearance, they lived separate lives.

In such an arrangement, love was not necessary. At the most, all that was required was a passing attraction, preferably enough to create an heir, and for that, the heart need not be involved. Theo always figured he could be satisfied with that kind of marriage—but now, he wasn't so sure.

He thought again about reaching out to Bonnie, even just emailing her. But he wouldn't. He'd stick to his word and leave it up to her to make the next move. In less than two months, she'd be on his side of the pond again. Hopefully, by then, he'd have gotten his feelings sorted out. His heart, which usually stayed out of his business, the bugger, decided to warn him there wasn't much chance of that happening.

"Theodore." His mother's voice broke through his musings. "I have a proposition."

"Ooh, this sounds serious," his sister said in a mocking, singsong voice.

"Finish your breakfast, Tabitha," Mama ordered. She eyed Theo appraisingly.

Dismissing his private thoughts, Theo returned his attention to his mother. "I'm listening."

"Do you recall the Rutherfords?"

Theo dipped into his mental filing system, searching through the scads of family names and faces he'd begun memorizing even before learning his letters and figures. His mother had been very keen that the Who's Who of English society played an important part of her offspring's education. "Lady Elaine is their daughter, correct?" Theo asked, wariness creeping into his voice.

"Mama, you can't be serious. She's younger than Tessa!" Tabitha interjected.

"Hush, girl," Mama said in that subtle yet piercing way British matrons had perfected, mouth pinched, a look of abject disapproval in her eyes.

"Don't give me your *Snooty Dame Monthly* face, Mama," Tabby protested.

"I beg your pardon?"

Theo smirked into his teacup, sharing a knowing look

with his sister over the rim. Tabby had come up with *Snooty Dame Monthly* years ago, when he and his sisters had all been home on holiday from school.

Even though Mum tried to hide it, they all knew about her obsession with British gossip rags. They also knew exactly where she hid her stash—in the old sewing basket by the fireplace wing chair. Their mother didn't sew; she fiddled with a pair of knitting needles, clacking away, a bundle of loose yarn in her lap conveniently obscuring from view whatever scandal magazine she was currently absorbed in.

On a wet and dreary afternoon a few days before Christmas, Tabby had been sprawled in Mum's chair, stockinged feet resting on the tipped-over sewing basket, toes warmed by the fire. Their youngest sister, Tessa, had been lying on her belly, one hand propping up her chin, the other turning the pages of the magazine she'd absconded from the hoard on Tabitha's lap. "Why do all these ladies have that face?" Tessa asked, turning another page.

"What face?" their middle sister Thalia asked.

Tessa rolled over and mimicked the dour expression of a proper English lady. She looked, quite eerily, exactly like their mother. All three of his sisters had burst into a fit of giggles and Tabby declared Tessa belonged on the cover of *Snooty Dame Monthly*.

The name had made even Theo chuckle from his seat across from Tabby, where he occupied the wing chair once reserved for their father, on the rare occasion he decided to grace them with an appearance. It was only later, after Papa's death, that Theo would come to the realization his mother was obsessed with reading the gossip rags because she was terrified she'd discover some scandal involving her husband printed in those lurid pages.

Theo turned to his mother. "I take it the proposition you mentioned is not an attempt to arrange my wedding with a teenager, then?"

"Heavens, no." His mother's mouth pinched so tight as to be almost invisible. "I mentioned the Rutherfords because Kitty has been remarkably successful with her recent endeavors, and I was wondering if we might attempt something similar here."

"Oh?" Theo sipped his tea. "Kitty" was the nickname for Her Grace, the Duchess of Rutherford. "What kind of endeavors?"

"Hunting parties."

Theo coughed, narrowly avoiding spraying the breakfast table. He swallowed and set his cup down carefully. "Hunting parties, Mama?"

"Yes. And shooting parties, perhaps."

"What would people be shooting?" Tabitha asked.

Good question.

"Pheasant, I suppose. Or partridge, perhaps?" His mother lifted one shoulder in a delicate shrug, unconcerned by the details. "Kitty tells me she had a group of gentlemen from Dubai stay for a month last season. She was able to repair the roof of the entire north wing with the profits from that one hunting party. It's quite the thing."

"I'm sure it is," he agreed. "But the Rutherford estate has long been known for its excellent game hunting, and the property is conducive to shooting. We can't say the same about the Abbey." Theo spared a glance in his sister's direction. His mother was usually sharper than this.

"Are you feeling all right, Mama?" Tabby asked.

"Quite well, thank you," she snapped, her voice like battery acid.

Tabitha's eyebrows rose, mirroring his own. Something was certainly amiss. Theo wanted to reach across the table, take his mother's hand, but restrained himself. Instead, he said, "I'll look into it, Mama. But I must say, I don't think the prospects are good."

"What about the Lakeland Cottage?" Tabitha suggested.

"What about it?" Theo glanced at his sister.

"That could work for shooting, couldn't it? And the fishing is excellent, as you know."

He did know. He'd caught his very first fish in the brook off the end of what his sister Tessa had christened Toadstool Bridge. The cottage was on a prime piece of land in the Lake District, modest in size, but very comfortable. Part of the inheritance his mother had brought to her marriage, the property had belonged to Theo's maternal grandparents, and he and his sisters had spent their summer holidays with them through most of their childhood.

Absolutely breathtaking at the height of summer, many of Theo's favorite memories took place there. Running over grassy hills with his sisters. Swimming in the creek. Fishing off Toadstool Bridge. It was the one place he'd truly felt able to breathe. Reluctance churned in his gut at the idea of turning the cottage into a trendy destination for the bored elite.

"We could rename it. Call it Lakeland Lodge instead," Tabby suggested.

"How original," Theo drawled, stomach tightening. But he had to admit, the idea had merit. Not long after taking charge of the estate, Theo had opened the family seat for public viewing. And while the money that tours of the Abbey brought in helped, it wasn't nearly enough.

"I think that has a fine ring to it," his mother said. "Do look into it, Theo. I expect a report within the month."

"Of course, Mama."

And that, Theo thought, staring down at a plate of food he no longer had any interest in eating, *is that.*

CHAPTER 18

WITH TERM PAPERS done and grades turned in, the semester was finally, blessedly over. Once again, Bonnie was on the train back to her hometown, only this time the sun was shining, and her best friend was along for the ride. Miraculously, Cassie had found an appointment that worked with all five of their schedules, and they were meeting up with Delaney, as well as Sadie and Ana, for bridesmaid dress shopping.

"Here we go . . . off to your first official bit of wedding stuff!" Bonnie squealed. She was determined to be upbeat and keep things happy and light for her best friend. "Are you excited?"

"I am," Cassie confessed, "and I should tell you, this isn't my *first* bit of wedding stuff. I picked out my dress already."

"You did?"

Cassie nodded, bouncing in her seat, a surge of anxious, happy energy bubbling over. "Special ordered it through a shop in London, so I don't have to ship it over from the States."

Realizing her friend had been holding back her feelings in deference to her own made Bonnie's heart shrivel and swell at the same time. She wanted to cry. But she wouldn't. She couldn't let Cassie's efforts go to waste. "That makes sense. I can't wait to see it." She smiled. "Now, tell me what you have in mind for the bridesmaid dresses."

"Well, I think I might go with bright pink."

"Oh, that's . . . nice." Bonnie struggled to keep her smile in place. Cassie knew she detested that color, always had. And she hated it more than ever now.

"I'm kidding, Bon!" Cassie shifted in her seat, leaning into her. "I'd never do that to you. And I appreciate your effort to put a good face on things today, but I still want you to be honest with me. Got it?"

"Got it." The tension fizzled out of Bonnie.

Cassie grinned. "Don't let me turn into Bridezilla."

"I'll do my best." Bonnie laughed.

A sly smile stole across Cassie's face. "I am, however, insisting all the groomsmen wear kilts."

"Seriously?" Bonnie blinked.

"You better believe it."

"I thought you said they'd be wearing tuxedos." Bonnie thought back to that night in Portillo's.

"They will, *with* the kilt." The slyness level of Cassie's grin reached Cheshire Cat proportions. "Business on the top, party below the belt."

Bonnie matched her friend's grin. "The best man too?"

"Of course." Cassie waggled her eyebrows. "You think he'll have a problem with it?"

"I've seen both Prince Harry and Prince William, as well as some other British nobles, in a kilt," Bonnie casually remarked, watching Cassie closely. "I know Theo's a duke, but I'm not sure if his family holds any Scottish titles."

"You know about Theo?" Cassie asked, surprise evident in her face and voice. "Did he tell you?"

"No, the internet did," Bonnie said.

"Oh." Cassie bit her lip.

"Yeah," Bonnie continued. "I know he's one of twenty-four non-royal dukes still in existence today in the UK."

Cassie's eyes widened, and Bonnie mumbled, "I may have done some research."

"Uh-huh." Cassie gave her some side-eye. "How long have you known?"

"About a month. How long have *you* known?" Bonnie countered, unable to keep the twinge of accusation from her voice

"Since London."

That long? "Why didn't you say anything?"

"Because it's not my place. And more importantly, Theo asked me not to. I only found out by accident. Logan let it slip when he had too much to drink." Cassie shook her head. "I actually didn't believe him at first. If you recall, I was pretty pissed at him about some other things at the time."

"I recall." Yet somehow, her best friend and the Scot had gotten past their rocky start and found their way to a happy ending. "Are you saying Theo doesn't want me to know?"

"I don't think he likes for anyone to know." Cassie shrugged. "I think he feels weird about it. But he did mention you specifically," she added.

"He did?"

"When I asked Theo if Logan had told the truth about him being a duke, he confirmed it, then demanded to know if I'd told anyone else, anyone like my *red-haired friend*," Cassie emphasized. "I told him I hadn't and promised I wouldn't. Simple as that." After a pause, she asked, brow furrowed, "Does it change anything? Theo, being a duke?"

Bonnie began to answer, then stopped herself. *Did it change anything?* "Not really," she finally said, hoping it was true.

"Good." Cassie flashed her a relieved smile. "Now, back to the kilts. It's my wedding. I don't care if he has a Scottish title or not, or whether he likes it or not," Cassie declared. "Theo is wearing a kilt. Let's hope he's got the legs for it."

"Whatever you say, Bridezilla," Bonnie teased, mind still occupied with the conundrum of Theo, not to mention the image of him in a kilt. She'd seen his legs, and yes. Yes, the Brit could pull off the look.

At the bridal boutique on Main Street, Cassie walked through the shop with the owner, musing over options while Bonnie lounged on a sofa with Delaney, waiting for Ana and Sadie, late as always, to arrive. Though Bonnie was still rooming with Ana, she had taken the train with Cassie while Ana drove to pick Sadie up from her new apartment in the Lakeview neighborhood. Since the movie Sadie hoped to win the lead role in was going to be filmed in Chicago, Sadie had decided she might as well move back to her hometown while she prepared for the audition.

"Did you hear that?" Delaney asked.

Bonnie glanced up from the tabloid she'd been skimming. "What?"

"It's my stomach growling."

"Tell your stomach to be patient, we're going to get lunch after this." Bonnie flipped the page.

"Why didn't we eat first?" Delaney pouted. "Finn's is open for lunch." She sat up and sniffed the air. "I think I can smell their corned beef on rye." She sniffed again and groaned, "Oh, and tater tots. I looove Finn's tater tots."

Cassie glanced over at them from across a rack of dresses, nose wrinkling. "I don't smell anything."

"Your senses aren't sharpened by hunger," Delaney whined. "I'm *starving*!"

"Listen, tater tot, you need to take a break from your preschoolers, you're starting to sound like them." Bonnie smirked, though to be honest, Delaney always tended to get juvenile when she was hangry. "Didn't you bring some snacks?" She'd never known Delaney to go anywhere without food.

Her face lit up. "I did!" Bounding up from the couch, she reached into her giant tote bag and pulled out a box of fruit roll-ups.

"I don't know if that's such a good idea," Bonnie warned, eyeing the growing pile of dresses Cassie had chosen for them to try on. Sticky fruit leather and expensive gowns were not the best combination. Luckily, Sadie and Ana chose that moment to arrive.

"We're here, we're here!" Sadie announced, busting through the door.

"And we brought champagne!" Ana raised a bottle in each hand. "Let's do this!"

An hour later, Bonnie posed in front of the three-way mirror, feeling pretty darn good. She looked pretty darn good too, though maybe that was the champagne talking. She was wearing her fourth dress and had polished off almost as many glasses of champagne. She wobbled, rotating so Cassie could inspect the dress.

"I love this one! It's perfect!" Cassie declared.

"You've said that about all of them," Bonnie reminded her.

"And I meant it. They're all beautiful. You're beautiful!"

She threw her arms out, wrapping Bonnie in a sloppy hug. Since Cassie would have her gown fitted in London and didn't have to try on any dresses today, she was in the lead on the amount of champagne consumed.

Bonnie did another little spin, looking over the dress. Of the various styles Cassie had pulled for them to try on, so far, this one was her favorite. Not hot pink, thank God, but a lovely shade of pale purplish-blue.

"Hey, Cass," Ana said, slipping out of a changing stall and tugging the bodice up over her ample bosom. "Isn't this the same color as that outfit you wore on your first date with Logan?"

"Good memory!" Cassie clapped. "Yep. The sweater dress you said made my ass look so good." Smiling angelically, she topped off her champagne. "Though according to Logan, my ass always looks good." She winked at Ana, then turned and looked at Cassie and Delaney. "I mean it, truly. You all look gorgeous." Cassie beamed. "Ladies, I think we've found the bridesmaid dress!"

"Thank Jujubes," Delaney groaned in relief.

Bonnie grinned at Cassie. "Have you told them what the groomsmen are wearing?"

"Will it make their asses look good?" Sadie asked from inside a dressing room stall.

"Possibly." Cassie giggled, glass empty again. "You'll have to check under their kilts to find out."

Sadie flung open the curtain. "Did you say the groomsmen will be wearing kilts?"

"Yep, all of 'em." Cassie nodded. "The best man too," she slurred, champagne sloshing. "My wish is their command!"

"Okay, I'm cutting you off." Bonnie grabbed the bottle away from Cassie before she spilled it on one of the dresses.

"Yeah, save some carousing for the bachelorette party."
Delaney laughed.

"Do you know in England, they call them chicken parties?" Cassie hiccupped. "Wait. Hen. I mean hen parties."

"Who's in charge of planning your *hen* party?" Delaney
wondered.

"Me." Bonnie held up the champagne bottle and wiggled her pinky finger. "As maid of honor, it's my job. Plus,
I'll already be over there for the Cambridge gig."

"I don't know," Sadie drawled, tapping her chin. "Planning a bachelorette party is serious business."

"Oh, Bonnie, if Theo's going to wear a kilt, it might
make it easier for you to *practice*," Ana teased, making a
crude gesture with the bottle.

"Practice what?" Delaney asked.

Sadie burst out laughing. "I'd almost forgotten about
that."

"What's so funny?" Cassie demanded.

"Bonnie here has never given a blowjob," Ana announced.

*Say it again, I don't think the lunch crowd down the
street at Finn's heard you.* Bonnie blushed, grateful they
were in the back of the store.

Delaney stared at Ana then turned to Bonnie. "Never?"

"Wait," Cassie protested. "Not neverrrr," she slurred
tipsily, *r* rolling like her future Scot husband's. "You
and Gabe—"

"No, not never," Bonnie agreed, cutting Cassie off. She
tipped the bottle back and swigged the rest of the champagne. She should have confiscated it sooner; there was
barely anything left. "I tried. Once or twice. It was a disaster."

"Did you puke on him?" Sadie asked.

"Not on him, no," Bonnie admitted. She'd made it to the bathroom.

"Then it wasn't a complete disaster." Sadie twirled in front of the mirror, checking the dress from every angle. "This is the one we're going with?"

"That's the one." Bonnie moved closer to Sadie. "Are you telling me you puked the first time you tried . . . that?" she whispered.

"Yep."

"You puked on Bo?" Ana glanced at Sadie, surprised. "You never told me!"

"Not something you bring up in normal conversation," Sadie said drily.

"Then why are we bringing it up now?" Delaney pointed out. "Look, if one of my students shows up for a flower girl fitting or something, ixnay on the blowjob talk, okay?"

"Yeah, I puked on Bo." Sadie shrugged. "I was young, and I don't know, I think I have a small mouth or an over-active gag reflex."

Ana bit her cheek. "No comment."

"Bo . . ." Bonnie sifted through her mental file box. "He was your first boyfriend, right?"

Sadie nodded, her expression pained. "Ancient history. We're talking about you right now."

"There's nothing to talk about," Bonnie shot back.

"I beg to differ," Sadie began. "Do you think there's a chance you and Theo might, you know . . . end up in a similar situation again?"

"Maybe." Bonnie glanced around the room, then looked deeper inside herself. "Yeah. I hope so."

"Good," Sadie said, "because that is a prime slab of British beefcake, and you are going to learn the proper way to handle it. I mean him."

"Oh!" Cassie perked up. "That brings up a good point. He's British, so he probably has his hat on."

They all stared at Cassie. She tapped her fingers together. "You know, his hat."

"You mean a hood?" Sadie asked, snorting.

Now Bonnie felt totally confused. "What?"

"For the love of—" Ana snapped. "Circumcised. He's probably not circumcised."

"Oh." The lightbulb popped on in Bonnie's brain, and her face got very hot. Glancing in the bridal shop mirror, she saw her flushed cheeks reflected back in triplicate.

Sadie shook her head. "If you can't even talk about what it looks like without turning red, how are we supposed to talk about what you should be doing with it?"

"Easy," Delaney said, clutching a fruit roll-up and waving her hand. "Let's not talk about any of it."

In the abrupt silence following Delaney's suggestion, the rusty off-key melody of an ice cream truck could be heard trolling down the street. The sound grew closer.

"I've got an idea." Ana grabbed her purse and raced out of the store.

"What do you think she's doing?" Bonnie asked Sadie.

"If I had to guess . . ." Sadie began.

Ana burst back inside, purse in one hand, a stack of popsicles in the other.

". . . I'd be right," she finished, smirking as Ana unwrapped a popsicle. "Way to go, Einstein, but what about the—"

Ana held up a hand, silencing Sadie. "Already got it covered. Watch." Grabbing a fruit roll-up from Delaney, Ana unwrapped the leathery candy and split it into strips. Then she handed a piece to each girl, along with a popsicle. "Watch." Ana opened her popsicle and held it up, wrapping her fruit strip around the top.

"Yay, craft time!" Cassie clapped her hands. "This is like art class."

"Totally." Sadie snickered, assembling hers the way Ana had instructed. Sadie held up her popsicle and admired her handiwork. "You know, that's not bad."

"I have my moments." Ana grinned.

"Everybody hold it right there," Cassie ordered, face turning fierce. "No eating popsicles in *my* bridesmaid dresses."

"But—" Bonnie began.

"Take them off!" Cassie demanded.

"Are you serious?" Delaney asked.

Cassie rounded on her, eyes narrowing to dangerous slits. "Strip."

Unwilling to argue with tipsy Bridezilla, everyone got to work removing their dresses.

"Now, are we ready to get down to business?" Ana barked, addressing them as if they were new recruits, not bridesmaids holding popsicles while huddled in the back of a dress shop in their underwear. "The first thing you need to know is despite the name, it's not about blowing."

"I feel like I should be taking notes," Sadie teased.

"Quiet, Pukey."

"Hey!"

Ana ignored Sadie and kept her attention on Bonnie. "It's okay to go slow at first. This isn't sushi—you don't have to put the whole thing in your mouth all at once." Ana took a lazy lick of her popsicle tip. "Take your time. Trust me, he won't mind."

Bonnie struggled to keep her piece of fruit roll-up from slipping off the melting popsicle. "But what about the . . ."

"The hood?" Sadie asked. "Pull it back, the head is more sensitive." Sadie peeled the fruit roll-up down and wrapped her mouth around the whole top.

"Do you bite it?" Bonnie asked, watching Sadie intently.

All the other girls spoke at once. "No!"

"God, no," Ana said. "Teeth are okay sometimes, but I wouldn't go there right away. Stick with the basics for now."

"Okay." Bonnie stared down at her own popsicle. "The basics."

"Play around with the licking," Ana suggested. "Delicate and fast." She flicked her tongue across the top. "Or long and slow." She stroked her tongue up and down both sides of the popsicle.

"You're really good at that." Cassie blinked. "You should make a how-to video."

"Great. I finally found my fallback career." Ana looked at Bonnie. "The point is to experiment. Find out what he likes."

"But how will I know?"

Cassie giggled. "Oh, you'll know. Honestly, though, I think guys like just about anything you do down there."

"Yeah," Delaney agreed. "If he's pitched his tent in your mouth, he's probably a happy camper."

"But if he *really* likes what you're doing, he's probably going to want to go deeper," Sadie warned. "Be prepared for some thrusting."

"Like . . . *all* the way in?" Bonnie asked.

Ana nodded, demonstrating by inhaling the popsicle, letting it slide into her mouth until her lips were wrapped around nothing but stick.

Bonnie's eyes bulged. "No way. I'll puke."

"I know it feels that way," Sadie said, "but it's easier than it looks. You just have to be ready for it."

"Mm-hmm." Ana popped the popsicle out of her mouth. "And you don't have to do anything you don't like. If you don't want him to go deep, don't let him."

"If he doesn't take the hint, then it's okay to bite him," Delaney suggested. "Sometimes when they start thinking with their dick, they forget their manners."

"And if you still feel like you're going to puke, you don't have to use your mouth," Sadie added. "When you sense things are moments from, uh, takeoff, you can switch to your hands." Sadie demonstrated by sticking her popsicle in the hole she made by touching her thumb and forefinger together, sliding it up and down. "Ugh, now my hands are all sticky."

Ana snorted with laughter. "And that brings us to the ending. When he's ready to launch, you need to decide—spit or swallow?"

"Again," Sadie said, "this is your choice. There's no right or wrong here."

"I don't know." Bonnie wrinkled her nose. "Is it gross? What does it taste like?"

"Not like grape candy, that's for sure," Ana said, finishing her popsicle.

They all giggled.

Ana stared at them. "What?"

Sadie drew a circle around her mouth with a finger. "You have purple all over your lips."

Turning to look in the dressing room mirror, Ana started to laugh too. "It looks like I've been blowing a unicorn."

"Unicorns don't have purple dicks," Delaney argued.

"Really?" Cassie stared at Delaney. "How do you know?"

Delaney waved a hand. "Bite me."

"I thought we weren't supposed to," Bonnie couldn't resist adding.

The dressing room erupted into giggles again.

"Hey, I just realized something."

Everyone turned their attention to Delaney.

"Cassie picked out the bridesmaid dresses, yet we're all still standing here in our underwear, and I'm still starving. Can we please put on some pants and go get some mocha frapping lunch?"

CHAPTER 19

TWO WEEKS LATER, Bonnie went back to the bridal shop one more time for a final fitting of her bridesmaid dress before making arrangements with Ana to pick it up with hers and bring it when she came over for the wedding. As so often happens in the early days of summer break, the hours flew by in a blur of books and naps . . . and packing. Staying with Ana had felt like a vacation, but before Bonnie knew it, June was half over, and she was on a plane headed for England.

Shouldering her laptop bag, she headed to the orientation meeting for summer instructors. She'd arrived in Cambridge a few days ago and had plenty of time to settle in, but still, as she walked through the Newnham gardens toward another of the old redbrick buildings, she had to fight the urge to pinch herself. She was really here—on her own in England. Really teaching Shakespeare at Cambridge University. Bonnie gave her fifteen-year-old self a high five. That girl would be so proud. Hell, current Bonnie was proud. She'd done it. She'd packed up her old life, closed the book, and was ready to start fresh. Who knew what adventures lay ahead?

She slipped into the meeting room and scurried to find a spot at the long wooden table. She was early, but several seats had already been taken. The room hummed with quiet conversation. Bonnie set her things down and looked around. A tea tray had been set up in one corner. *Oh yes, she was going to love it here.* Leaving her things by her seat, she made her way over to the tray. She filled a cup from the carafe of hot water and gleefully perused the tea selection. So much more variety than her office back home.

"Earl Grey would be my choice," a male voice suggested over her shoulder.

Bonnie startled, and the cup jerked in her hand, splashing steaming water on her wrist. "Ouch!" she yelped.

"Sorry," the voice said, doing that British thing she loved, rounding the middle of the word with a soft, crisp *d* sound. "I didn't mean to startle you."

"You didn't," Bonnie began. "Okay, well you did," she admitted, dabbing at her skin where an angry red welt was forming. For half a second, she'd thought it was Theo behind her.

"Oh dear." The man sucked in a breath through his teeth. "I'll wager that smarts."

"It looks worse than it is, really. Ginger problems." She glanced up to offer him a reassuring smile and almost spilled on herself again. The man was strikingly handsome, with tousled sandy-blond hair and soulful brown eyes.

What was up with her? For most of her life, she'd been immune to the male population, not noticing or caring what anyone who wasn't Gabe looked like. Now she seemed to drool over every guy she met. Well, not *every* guy, just those with nice hair and British accents. And she wasn't drooling, she was admiring. The man talking to her was very good-looking. This was a simple, objective fact.

He returned her smile, a sweet, crooked grin making him even more handsome. Despite this, aside from appreciation for the specimen of male beauty before her, Bonnie realized she didn't *feel* anything. She paused, mentally taking stock. Her pulse remained steady, and there was no prickling . . . anywhere. She wasn't sure if this made her feel better or worse.

"Are you going to take my advice?" he asked.

"Hmm?"

"The tea." His grin widened as he nodded toward the selection on the tray.

Nope, nothing. Not one flicker. "Oh, right. Earl Grey? Really?"

"Quite." He filled a cup for himself and popped a tea bag in. "I know it's not very continental of me, but I confess I prefer the old standby." He handed her a tea bag, brushing her hand with his fingers.

Was he flirting with her? Bonnie stared down at the tea bag. She wasn't a fan of Earl Grey. It was, in her opinion, boring. But not wanting to be rude, Bonnie accepted his offering and plopped the tea bag into her cup. "Thanks."

"Of course." He gazed at her over the rim of his steaming cup. His warm brown eyes reminded her of Cassie.

Her best friend's voice popped into her head. *Yes, he is totally flirting with you.*

A few others had clustered around the tea tray, and Bonnie stepped out of the way. Unsure what to do next, she headed back toward her seat. He followed her.

See? Cassie's voice sang between Bonnie's ears. *Told you.*

As luck would have it, though the table had begun to

fill up in earnest, the seat next to the one she'd left her things at was absent. She sat, and he settled into the chair beside her. Bonnie busied herself arranging her things, opening her notebook and digging a pen out of her laptop bag. She swore she could feel his eyes watching her every move as he sat back and sipped his tea.

Say something, Cassie whispered in her head.

Okay, Cassie really needed to stop doing that. Or, Bonnie needed to stop imagining her doing that. *Ugh.* Bonnie doodled on the corner of her notebook and stayed silent, willing her inner Cassie to do the same.

"First time teaching summer term?" he asked.

"That obvious?" She glanced up.

"I haven't seen you before." He tapped her notebook, his hand brushing against hers for a moment. "And you've come a bit more prepared than those of us who've been at this awhile."

"Ease off, Romeo," an older woman on Bonnie's other side ordered. She turned her attention to Bonnie, eyes flashing behind her spectacles. "Watch out for Ian, he's a charmer," she said, but her warning held more humor than heat.

"I'm only being friendly," he protested.

"I have a cousin named Ian," Bonnie blurted, unsure how to handle this conversation.

"There you go, Nan, we have something in common already."

The woman, Nan, shook her head, and huffed. "Whatever. It's not my business."

Ian snorted and leaned closer to Bonnie, whispering in her ear, "You'll find out soon enough, everything around here is Nan's business."

Despite herself, Bonnie giggled. She clapped a hand over her mouth and looked back at Nan, but the woman had turned away to chat with someone farther down the table.

"You leave me at a loss," Ian said.

"I do?" Bonnie returned her attention to the chatty Englishman.

"You know my name, yet all I know is you have a cousin named Ian, and I'm fairly certain you're American."

"American, yes." She nodded, cheeks heating. "And I'm Bonnie."

"Indeed you are." He reached for her hand. "A pleasure to meet you, Bonnie."

Really, that's what you're going with? Bonnie had to fight to keep from rolling her eyes at his play on her name. She didn't need Cassie's mentally voiced opinion to confirm this guy was *definitely* flirting with her. Thank God he didn't try to kiss her hand or anything.

Unlike another British charmer who had made her heart flip-flop when he'd pulled that move.

Though Bonnie wondered if the same gesture from someone other than Theo would affect her quite the same way. Again, she wasn't sure if she was relieved or bothered by the thought. For now, she decided to be relieved. She and Ian were going to be colleagues. The last thing she needed was to turn into a weak-kneed ninny around every guy with a cute smile and British accent.

But beneath that relief swirled fear. If only one man made her feel that way . . . if only *he* had that effect on her . . .

A woman approached the head of the table, and the room quieted. Bonnie silenced thoughts about Theo, tucking them away to worry about later. It had been three days since she'd arrived in England, and she hadn't worked up the nerve to call him yet. Hadn't even texted she was here.

You're hesitating. She pulled her notebook closer,

straightening in her seat. This time it wasn't the voice of her best friend invading her thoughts, but her uncle Donnie. Bonnie was waiting for a sign, when what she needed to do was just go for it. Theo had left the ball in her court. Told her to let him know when she was settled so they could meet up.

But would they be meeting as friends or . . . something more? Did he expect to pick up right where they'd left off? Hopefully not *right* there. They'd left things so awkwardly—*she'd* left things so awkwardly—and now the longer she waited to call, the more awkward it became.

She took a sip of tea, trying to focus on the schedule details the woman at the front of the room was reviewing, but her mind was a rubber band, snapping back to Theo. He'd wonder why she'd taken so long to let him know she was in town. And what could she say? That she wasn't sure what she wanted to do about her feelings for him?

Even saying that was an admission that she had feelings for him. Feelings she wasn't sure she understood. Feelings she wasn't sure she could trust. He'd said to call when she was settled. Well, her suitcases may be unpacked, but she still hadn't unpacked her feelings.

And she was far from settled.

After the meeting, Bonnie rose and discreetly dumped her tea in the trash. While the other staff members stood around and mingled, she made a beeline for the door. She was halfway across the garden courtyard when someone called her name, the newly familiar voice bouncing around the low brick walls. Ian. She paused and turned, waiting for him to catch up with her.

"Hey," he said, slightly out of breath, a thatch of hair falling over his brow.

"Hey," she replied.

"Let me guess, you're staying in one of the resident halls, right?" He pushed his hair back, looking like a wind-blown poet. He smiled, and something in her brain perked up and took note.

Hmm. Maybe she wasn't immune to him after all.

"Why do you want to know?" Bonnie narrowed her gaze at him. She wasn't a complete lackwit. She knew better than to hand out info about where she was living.

Picking up on her vibe, Ian stepped back. "I'm not planning to stalk you." He raised his hands, palms up. "God's truth."

She continued to stare at him.

"It's only"—he dropped his hands and shrugged—"if you haven't learned yet, the grub here is dodgy. I thought you might like to get off campus and have a bite with me sometime."

"Oh." She relaxed. He had a point. The resident banquet hall did leave much to be desired. Bonnie wasn't complaining; free food was free food, after all. But still, it would be nice to get out and have something other than cafeteria-style shepherd's pie. And she was curious about the city. Cambridge had a rich history, and she was aching to explore more. She'd been hoping to do that with Theo but . . .

"Why not." It would be good for her to get out.

A grin broke across Ian's face. No dimples, but still, a little tingle-worthy. "Are you free tonight?" His warm brown eyes sparkled in the late afternoon sun.

Maybe it was because his golden brown eyes reminded Bonnie of her best friend, or maybe it was because she was in a foreign country and was lonely . . . or maybe it was because she was mad at herself for not following up with a certain other Brit yet and this was a convenient distraction, but Bonnie decided yes, she did want to go out for dinner with Ian. "Sure," she said, committing before she could back out. "What time?"

"You're going on a date?" Cassie clapped her hands. "That was fast."

"It's not a date," Bonnie countered, sorting through her clothing options in the wardrobe of her dorm. She adored her little room, loved the tall oak wardrobe and matching dresser and desk, the narrow bed with the curling wrought-iron headboard. She especially loved the view of the garden from her window, and the glimpse of the other historic university buildings beyond.

"You know, this sounds very familiar," Cassie teased. "Isn't that what you all told me when I agreed to meet Logan for a drink last summer?"

Bonnie snorted. *And look how that turned out*. But this really wasn't a date. "It's not a date," she said again.

"If you say so."

Bonnie didn't need to look up and see her friend's face on the chat screen. She could hear Cassie's doubt loud and clear.

"What are you wearing for your non-date?" Cassie asked.

"Ha-ha," Bonnie said, but didn't rise to the bait. That was *exactly* what one of them, probably Ana, had asked Cassie last summer. "I'm thinking a sundress; it was pretty warm today."

"Just nothing with animals on it, please," Cassie admonished.

Bonnie stared at the outfit she'd been about to pull off a hanger. It was her bird dress, the one Sadie had wanted to burn. "Oh, come on. You too? What's wrong with it?"

"It makes you look like that wacky teacher who does all those wild experiments on a flying school bus."

She wondered if Cassie could see her glaring at the screen from across the room. "Just because we have the same red hair—"

"Please, Bonnie. Trust me. No animals. Or birds or insects or teacups, even."

"Fine." Bonnie tossed the bird dress onto the bed and tugged out another sundress. This one was basic black with an ivory swiss-dot pattern. She held it up to the laptop camera for Cassie's approval.

Cassie gave a thumbs-up, and Bonnie began to change. "No animals," she said, tugging the dress over her head. "Any other rules?"

"Are you going to be alone with this guy?"

"Nope." Bonnie pulled up the zipper and shook her head. "We're meeting in town. At a restaurant."

"What restaurant?"

Bonnie padded across the herringbone pattern of the honey-colored pine floorboards and sat down at the desk. She adjusted her laptop screen until her face popped up in the chat window. "It's walking distance from here. The Hawk, I think?" She grabbed her phone and double-checked the info Ian had given her. "The Eagle."

"Well, text me later so I know you got home safe," Cassie said.

"Yes, Mom," Bonnie teased. She was usually the one acting like a mother hen. "I'll bring a sweater too."

"Good. Summer evenings in England get cold." Cassie winked into the camera. "Hey, speaking of cold, why are you giving Theo the cold shoulder?"

"I'm not." Bonnie avoided facing the screen as she pulled on a sweater.

"You haven't called him yet."

Bonnie froze, meeting Cassie's gaze. "He told you that?"

"He told Logan, which is basically the same thing." Cassie peered at her. "Everything okay between you two?"

"Eveything's fine." Bonnie smoothed the sweater down over the pleats of her dress.

"I hope so," Cassie murmured. "I'd hate to see the best man and maid of honor at my wedding not getting along."

Ugh, another reason to avoid calling him. If she messed things up, if things got weird with Theo, or weirder than they already were, she could ruin her best friend's wedding. "When do we start planning wedding stuff over here?" Bonnie asked, taking advantage of the opportunity to change the subject.

"Soon. I fly in next week."

"Already?" She hadn't been expecting that. Next week marked the beginning of July. Cassie wasn't getting married until August. Bonnie had selfishly hoped she'd have a few more weeks to herself before all that started.

"Work, remember? I'm covering Wimbledon for my new segment on how the media portrays women in professional sports."

"Right. Sorry." Bonnie smiled apologetically into the web cam. "I've had a lot going on."

"That's an understatement." Cassie laughed. "Seriously, though, Bon, call Theo. And have fun on your date tonight."

"I will." Bonnie blew a kiss at the screen. "And it's not a date." Ensuring she got the last word, Bonnie quickly closed out the chat and logged off. She checked the time. She was supposed to meet Ian in about half an hour. According to her map app, it was only a ten-minute walk from her building to the pub.

She got up and hung her bird dress back in the wardrobe.

She knew she had quirky taste but couldn't help it. Besides, Gabe never seemed to mind.

Yeah, but maybe if you had dressed less silly and more sexy, you wouldn't have found your fiancé in bed with someone else. No. She shoved those negative thoughts back into whatever evil little dark cave in her brain they had crawled out from. What happened with Gabe was not her fault. She glanced in the mirror hanging over the dresser. *He* made that choice. How she looked or what she wore had nothing to do with it.

She scrunched up her face, considering. Like her literary counterpart, Anne Shirley, it had taken a long time for Bonnie to overcome her animosity toward her red hair and freckles. As she'd gotten older, she'd finally started to appreciate how her coloring set her apart. And now, as she neared thirty, she admitted it was nice to still get carded. At almost fifty, her mother often still got carded too. At least Bonnie had that to look forward to.

Before she could change her mind, she slipped on her shoes, grabbed her purse and phone, and headed out the door for her non-date. As Bonnie headed across campus, the sense of adventure returned, and a twinge of excitement blossomed. She was on her own in England, a professor (or summer instructor, at least) at Cambridge! And yes, she rather liked the fact that she was on her way to meet a handsome British professor for dinner. Once more, she high-fived her teenage self.

The Eagle was straight out of a dream. Historical places often turned Bonnie into an awestruck fangirl. She stared openmouthed, wanting to look everywhere—to touch everything—at once. Open since the 1500s, the former coach inn sported dark walnut panels and a curved antique corner bar.

Once she and Ian were seated, Bonnie stared up at the ceiling, where graffiti had been burned into the plaster. She squinted at the blackened maze of numbers and letters, trying to decipher their meaning.

"The Eagle is history personified," Ian said, following her gaze, "literally. Most of the graffiti was created in the early 1940s by pilots flying in World War II." He pointed to a big, bold *398* clearly visible on the ceiling near the entrance. "That's a squadron number."

Bonnie shivered, having removed her sweater, when one of the thin straps of her dress slipped off her shoulder. She tugged it back into place, thinking of the soldier who must have stood on a bar stool, or maybe a copilot's back, to make those marks, wanting to leave some proof of his existence behind, knowing any day his life could be cut short. "Amazing." She smiled at Ian, glad she'd agreed to meet him for dinner. This was just the kind of place she was hoping to experience.

He returned her smile. "Did you know the secret of life was discovered here?"

Bonnie had read the blue plaque on the wall outside describing how two Cambridge scientists who often lunched at the pub had announced their discovery of the double helix. So yes, she did know. But she was having a pleasant time listening to Ian talk, so she shook her head, encouraging him to continue.

Their food arrived, and Bonnie's stomach growled in anticipation. She'd ordered a savory tarte tatin, and the flaky puff pastry was perfection. She swirled her fork through the rarebit sauce, grinning.

"Care to share the humor?" Ian asked, sandy brows arching.

"I was just remembering how I used to think rarebit was

made from actual rabbit." Bonnie shook her head. "I was so relieved when I learned it was just cheese on toast."

"*Very* good cheese and toast," Ian amended, chuckling.

"Very good," she agreed.

By the time they'd both cleaned their plates, they'd decided to split an order of Cornish clotted cream ice cream, and Ian had moved on from discussing the pub's history to his own. He was midway through telling her about why he chose to become a professor when Bonnie spotted a set of broad shoulders ponying up to the bar. Her heart skittered, and she almost dropped her spoon. She struggled to keep her focus on Ian, but her gaze kept straying back to the bar and the perfectly combed head of dark hair topping those broad shoulders.

No. No way. It wasn't possible.

Ian coughed. "I'm afraid I'm boring you."

She flinched and turned her attention back to him. "Of course not."

"I am. I've been talking about myself for far too long." He smiled and dipped his spoon into the bowl of ice cream between them. "Tell me more about you."

"What would you like to know?" Bonnie hedged, setting her spoon down and staring into the bowl, clotted cream curdling in her stomach as she tried to get a grip. She refused to glance over at the bar again. It was not Theo. It *couldn't* be Theo. But the awareness prickling behind her knees argued otherwise. Unable to resist, she stole one more peek. On cue, as if he'd been waiting for her to look again, the dark head swiveled in her direction. Blue eyes met hers, dimples flashing.

The blood drained from her face. She swayed in the booth, lightheaded. This was ridiculous. *She* was being ridiculous. Bonnie gripped the edge of the table and channeled her energy into staring at Ian, pretending she hadn't seen Theo.

Under her intense gaze, Ian preened. He leaned across the table, heat sparking in his brown eyes.

Belatedly, Bonnie realized she might be sending the wrong signal. She licked her lips. Ian's gaze dropped to her mouth. He leaned closer.

Oops.

Why was it, when she tried to be sexy, she made a muck of it, but now she was suddenly Miss Alluring USA? She sucked in a deep breath and immediately caught her mistake when Ian's gaze dropped again, from her mouth to the neckline of her dress. He leaned closer still. Any farther and he'd end up on her side of the booth.

Bonnie froze, afraid to make another move in case it encouraged Ian to make another move too. Though really, what else could she do? The situation couldn't possibly get much worse.

"Ah, this looks cozy," a droll voice she knew all too well observed.

Bonnie squeezed her eyes shut.

She was wrong.

The situation could, indeed, get worse.

Theo stood at Bonnie's table, guts churning as he waited for her to look at him. All he'd been doing was waiting for her. Giving her space, waiting for her to be ready to move on, to decide if she wanted to pick up where they'd left off or leave things alone. That had been a mistake. Seems she *was* ready to move on.

But with someone else.

The rejection stung. When Logan called and mentioned he'd heard via Cassie that Bonnie was headed out on a date, something inside Theo snapped and he'd raced here, with no bloody idea what he'd do or say. He turned his attention to her *date*. "Theo Wharton." He thrust out his hand, forcing the words through lips that felt wooden, his face numb.

To the man's credit, he didn't curl up like a sniveling prawn, but held his ground and stood to shake Theo's hand. "Ian Hanson." His grip was firm, his eyes steady, his attitude confident.

Theo hated the bloke. Immediately and immensely.

He shifted his focus back to Bonnie. "I see you made it safely into the country, then."

"Yes," she mumbled, still not looking at him, her complexion fluctuating from pale to pink, a blush rising in her cheeks.

"You two know each other?" Ian asked.

Obviously. "We spent some time together last summer," Theo said. Let the git make what he will of that.

"Hmm. And now, here you are."

"Here I am."

"Extraordinary," Ian observed, lips pressed in a thin smile. "Please, join us." Ian slid back into the booth, moving down to make room for Theo to sit next to him.

"I don't want to interrupt," Theo began, "but if you insist." He ignored the open spot and nudged his way onto Bonnie's bench instead.

"Theo is my best friend's fiancé's best friend," Bonnie hurried to explain.

Ian's brow wrinkled, but after a moment, he chuckled. "I think I've got it worked out. When's the wedding?"

"This summer," he and Bonnie replied simultaneously. She scooted over, putting some distance between them.

Playing it that way, was she? He'd said he'd leave things be between them, but something impish drove him, and he leaned back, resting an arm along the top of the booth, his hand brushing her shoulder with familiarity as he smiled across the table at Ian. "We're a close bunch."

The other man's pleasant grin dropped a notch. *Take that, arsehole.*

"Ian is teaching in the same summer program I am," Bonnie offered. "But he's also a full-time professor at the university."

"I lecture on Shakespeare and all that, of course," Ian said. "But my passion is for the Old English works, *Beowulf*, *The Seafarer*, anything Anglo-Saxon, really."

Theo nodded, but kept his gaze trained on Bonnie. He did not like the way her eyes shone when she looked at the other man, like he was a bloody hero because he lectured about some mummified stories from a thousand years ago.

"And what do you do?" Professor Prick asked.

Theo cleared his throat, preparing to launch into his usual vague response, when next to him, Bonnie piped up, "Theo's a duke."

What the bloody hell?

"You don't say?" Ian straightened, his demeanor immediately changing. Features sharp with curiosity, like he'd caught sight of an interesting creature at the zoo and was moving in for a closer look.

"Non-royal, unimportant." Theo cut Bonnie a sideways look, but again, she was blatantly ignoring him.

"Do you serve in the House?" Ian asked.

"No, my family hasn't held a seat in decades." He brushed a hand through his hair.

They sat in awkward silence for a beat, until a barmaid stopped by with the bill. Bonnie reached for it, but Ian snatched it up. "Please, allow me."

"I couldn't," Bonnie began.

"I insist."

I bet you do. Theo glared.

Ian stood, meeting his glare with a weasel's grin.

Theo watched him head for the till, fists itching to pound a hole in the man's smug skull.

"What are you doing here?" Bonnie hissed.

He could play coy, pretend he'd just happened in for a pint. But it would be a waste of time. They both knew why he was here. "Logan told me about your date."

"Cassie." She ground her teeth then looked at him. "It's not a date."

Oh? Well, that was good news. The roiling heat in his belly settled to a simmer.

"And Logan had no business telling you," she added.

"He had no business telling you I was a duke," Theo muttered, watching for Bonnie's non-date to head back their way.

"He didn't, and neither did Cassie. I looked you up on the internet."

"You did?" He turned to face her.

She nodded, cheeks well past rosy to bright pink. "Theo Wharton. Sixteenth Duke of Emberton."

He grinned.

"Stop smiling."

"I'm not smiling," he said, mouth stretching wider. Her admission revealed she'd thought about him. Taken the time to research him. He paused, smile faltering. And now she knew the truth. Was that why she hadn't reached out? "Why are you avoiding me?"

"I'm not avoiding you." She scowled at him.

He scowled back.

"All set," Ian announced as he returned to the booth.

The man had terrible timing.

Bonnie was the first to break eye contact, her gaze shifting to the professor. "Thank you so much for dinner, Ian."

The prat beamed at her. "Anytime. Can I escort you back to your room?"

Hello? Was he invisible? Theo shifted in his seat, turning so his body filled the space between Bonnie and Ian. "No need, I'm happy to see her home."

Again, Ian ignored Theo and kept his focus trained on Bonnie. "Is that all right with you?"

He had to hand it to him, Professor Prick had some balls in those stuffy pants of his. And he couldn't blame the bloke, he'd have done the same thing. Theo turned, looking at Bonnie, awaiting her answer.

She glanced between them and blew out an exasperated breath. "I can see myself home."

He and Ian both started to protest. She cut them off. "But since Theo made the trip out here, he can come with me." Before he could feel too smug about his victory, she shot him a less than pleasant look. "We have a few things to talk about, anyway."

That didn't sound promising.

Ian must have come to the same conclusion, because he backed off, a sly smile slithering across his face. "Well, then." He bowed to Theo. "My lord." Theo narrowed his eyes at the cheeky, and blatantly incorrect, address, but Ian had already shifted his attention to Bonnie, mouth smoothing into a sappy, simpering smile. "It's been a pleasure. I look forward to seeing you again soon." He tipped his fingers to his forehead in a jaunty farewell and then spun on his heel.

The parting shot hadn't been lost on Theo. The little bugger had made sure to remind Theo he'd be spending time with Bonnie in the near future.

"Move," Bonnie said, poking him in the back.

He slid out of the booth, and she followed, scurrying ahead of him toward the exit.

Outside, he hitched a thumb over his shoulder. "My car's around this way," he began.

She shook her head. "Let's walk. We can cut through the campus." She turned and headed toward the university grounds, and he had no choice but to hurry up and follow her. It was late June, and the sun was just beginning to set, painting the old stone and brick buildings in shades of pink and gold, the sky awash in amber. He walked beside Bonnie, thinking of the long days of summer stretching ahead, and hoping he could spend many of them with her. But did she want to spend time with him? She'd been in England for several days, and yet she hadn't called, hadn't reached out.

Even now, after she'd said she wanted to talk, she continued to give him the silent treatment, walking next to him, spine stiff, steps eating up the pathway in brisk little chops. Unable to stand it any longer, he finally asked, "What did you want to talk about?"

Her pace faltered for a moment, but then she regained her stride. "Us."

"What about us?" he asked, chest constricting.

When she didn't reply, he stopped walking. Forcing air into his lungs, he asked the question that had been burning inside of him. "Is this about me being a duke?"

She spun around to face him. "What?"

"You heard me." He stared down at her. "Do you have a problem with the fact that I'm a duke?"

"I have a problem with the fact you *didn't tell me* you were a duke." She shook her head. "But no, I don't care you're a duke. Why should I?"

He shrugged, embarrassed he'd been the one to make an issue out of it in the first place, but it was a knee-jerk reaction, born from experience. "People tend to get dodgy when they find out."

"I can see that," she said, her tone thoughtful. "So, what

am I supposed to call you, anyway?" A small smile tugged at the corner of her mouth. "My lord?"

"Shut it."

"That's not very polite, *my lord*," she teased and began walking again. "What's it like? Being a duke?"

"First of all, as a duke, it's 'Your Grace,' and second, it sucks."

She laughed. A bright tinkling sound chiming all through him. He'd missed that laugh. Missed talking to her. "Delighted my misery amuses you. My family's estate is in dire straits," Theo admitted, surprising himself with his honesty, "and it's my job to keep the bloody ship from sinking."

"Ah, so that's what you meant last summer when you said you worked in finance."

He nodded. "You remembered."

"You're not the only one who remembers everything we've ever talked about," she said, her voice growing soft. Inside his chest, his heart went soft too. He took a step closer, but she held up her hand, placing her palm against him, right over the bloody aching spot. She sighed. "But it's too soon, I think. For me." She stared down at her hand. Her left hand. The hand that had sported an engagement ring not too long ago. "Maybe it would be better if we didn't see each other. I mean, aside from the wedding stuff."

"Oh." That was not what he'd been hoping she'd say. And not what he'd expected to hear either. "What if we're just friends?" He covered her hand with his, every nerve in his body zinging to life at the contact. *He didn't want to be just friends.*

As if hearing his thoughts, she glanced up at him, eyes doubtful. "Do you think that's possible?"

"I don't know," he answered honestly, brushing his thumb over her knuckles. She shivered, her gaze never leaving his face. The pale blue of her eyes shifted color, deepening to a sizzling blue that enflamed him, made him bolder. "Friends with benefits, perhaps?" he suggested.

"Tempting." She laughed, slipping her hand out from beneath his. "But I'm not sure I'm built that way."

"Only one way to find out." He stepped closer, missing her touch already. "I'd like to explore the possibility, but I'm not going to push you, Bonnie. If you're not comfortable with exploring . . . the physical side of our friendship, then that's that."

"If I decided I was comfortable, with some, um, exploring," Bonnie hesitated, licking her lips, "you're saying we would still be just friends?"

"Of course," Theo assured her. After all, they couldn't be more. *He* couldn't.

"That easy, huh?"

"Yes." *Christ no.* It would be hard. Very hard. But he was willing to try.

A chill breeze danced across the treetops lining the walkway. Bonnie started to tug on the sweater she carried.

He reached out to help her, but she pulled away. "I got it."

He dropped his hands. "Bloody hell, woman. What is your deal?"

"My deal?" She bristled.

"Yes. What do you have against accepting help?" All evening, he'd been fighting for control, and the grip on his temper was slipping. "There's nothing wrong with allowing me to hold the door for you, or letting me help you with your sweater, or bloody taking your bloody arm when we walk down the bloody street!"

"What the hell is *your* deal?" she shot back. "Showing up out of the blue at that pub tonight and acting all macho—"

"I wasn't acting macho." He crossed his arms over his chest, returning her glare.

She snorted and mirrored his stance.

Realizing how absurdly *macho* he looked, Theo relaxed his arms.

"I'm sorry," he began.

"No," Bonnie said. "You're right." She drifted off the gravel path and sat on a stone bench, pulling her sweater tighter around herself. "You said you have three sisters, right?"

He nodded, joining her on the bench.

"Well, I don't have any siblings, but I do have cousins. A lot of them. All boys. And every single one of them treats me like I'm a helpless kitten, a pet that needs protection." She swung her feet, sending a spray of pebbles skittering. "If you've got a chip on your shoulder about being a duke, I've got one about being—"

"A girl?"

She punched him in the arm. "Coddled."

"I'm not coddling you."

"It feels like coddling to me, okay?"

"Okay." He'd learned enough from his sisters not to argue. She had a right to her feelings, whether he agreed with them or not. They sat in silence for a few minutes, the gardens mostly quiet save for the muted shuffle of footsteps on the path, the voices of passersby mingling with the summer breeze.

"I'm sorry for crashing your date," he finally said, gut twisting.

"It wasn't a date," she quickly corrected.

"Well," Theo said, again struggling to contain his relief at that news, "I'm still sorry."

"I'll accept your apology," she began, scooting a little closer to him on the bench, "if you tell me why."

He stared at the space that remained between them, focusing on the pale cold stone. He wanted to scoot closer too, to close the distance, but he held back. "Why, what?"

"Why did you come here tonight?"

Because I missed you. Because the thought of you being with another man made me wild with jealousy. He reached for her hand, and she didn't pull away. "Because I couldn't wait anymore. To see you." He looked up, quickly adding, "To see my friend."

"Ah, Mr. Duke is impatient." She grinned, her voice teasing, but her eyes were solemn. She swallowed. "I owe you an apology as well, Theo. I should have called. I'm sorry."

The sound of his name on Bonnie's tongue burrowed a path through his heart, hollowing out a space and filling it with her voice. "I'll accept your apology," he said, indulging in a bit of tit for tat, "if you promise me one thing."

"Yes?"

"Never call me Mr. Duke again."

"Aw," Bonnie pouted melodramatically, "that's not one of those benefits you mentioned?"

"Certainly not." Theo's huff of indignation was equally melodramatic.

"Too bad."

"You weren't interested, anyway." Theo paused, afraid to press her too much. "Remember?"

"I said I wasn't sure," she corrected, adding, "lately, I'm not sure of anything." Bonnie studied his face, considering. "But I do like being your friend." She smiled, and this time it did reach her eyes, lighting her face with a warm, delicate glow. "And I admit, I'm curious."

"Oh?" Theo barely dared to breathe.

"What kind of benefits *are* you offering? Maybe we should make a list. I love lists."

Recognizing she was nervous and starting to babble, Theo squeezed her hand. Bonnie was putting herself out there, taking a risk, and it shredded him to see it. "How about," he said, his voice rough in his own ears. He cleared his throat. "How about," he began again, pulling his heart back together as he pulled her into his arms, "I show you."

CHAPTER 20

LATE MORNING SUNLIGHT slanted through her dorm room window, and Bonnie stretched luxuriously. *Ah, Saturday.* With her first week of classes over, she'd decided to indulge and sleep in. Her body had finally adjusted to the six-hour time difference but still, she welcomed any chance to nab extra sleep.

A night owl by nature, when left to her own devices, Bonnie preferred to stay up late and wake up late too. In college, she'd been able to tailor her schedule to her preferences, never signing up for a class starting before ten. But it was a habit she hadn't been able to indulge in much over the last several years. Mainly because Gabe hated staying up late, turning into a cranky pumpkin if he wasn't in bed long before midnight. And her teaching job didn't allow for sleeping in either.

Bonnie rolled onto her side and pulled her phone off the adaptable charger, noting with lazy satisfaction it was almost eleven. Her stomach growled, not as pleased with her delay in usual morning activities as the rest of her body was.

She'd missed the dining hall's breakfast hours but could easily grab a tea and scone from one of the many cafés dotting the campus. It's what she preferred to do anyway.

Pulling up a saved search on her phone, Bonnie spent a pleasant few minutes looking through her options. She'd made a list. By the end of her summer seminar, she planned to visit every café in reasonable walking distance, rating them from best to worst.

After she settled on a teahouse whose menu boasted hearty sandwiches as well as the usual tea and pastries, Bonnie set her phone aside and dropped back onto her pillow. When she'd first learned about this job opportunity, she thought it was a dream come true—and it was. This past week had been perfect. Better than a dream, even.

And it wasn't just the work. Bonnie never would have guessed how much she enjoyed being on her own. Even though she was an only child, she'd rarely been alone. There'd been her cousins, of course, and Cassie, as well as Gabe.

As always, the thought of Gabe caused her heart to squeeze, though this time the pain was muted, the ache brief. She was handling her breakup quite admirably, if she did say so herself. And she really did like being on her own. She'd begun to write again in earnest. Had even sketched out several plot ideas in a notebook she'd bought in an adorable stationary shop located next to the second café on her checklist.

Bonnie debated going back to that café instead, just so she could have an excuse to pop into that store again, but decided against it. She'd stick with her plan. Besides, she needed to stick to her budget. And that stationary shop was guaranteed to suck her savings dry if she let it.

In a burst of rebellious ecstasy, Bonnie decided she

would go back to that stationary shop today and buy whatever her heart desired. What did she have to lose? She was on her own and only had herself to please.

After placing her order at the tea shop's counter, Bonnie settled into one of the velvet-cushioned high-backed slipper chairs and opened her bag of treats. She even loved the bags the stationary store used, made of a thin cream-colored paper that crinkled deliciously. She pulled out the box with the pen and ink set and went to work assembling it. Blotting the freshly filled pen on a napkin, she set it aside and took out the new journal she'd selected.

Atrociously expensive, the journal was something she'd usually admire, maybe even carry around the store for a bit while perusing other items, but always put back on the shelf. Not this time. The rich leather binding was a bright bold blue. She rubbed a hand over the cover, finger tracing the words stamped on the front. A line from *Northanger Abbey*, one of her favorite Austen quotes. That story had crossed her thoughts often lately and felt like the perfect choice.

She was still petting the journal when a server dropped off her meal. After a bit of fussing to get the tea things to her liking, Bonnie opened to the first page. The lined paper was thick and smooth, the outer edges rimmed in gold leaf. She picked up her pen, and in between nibbles and sips, began to write.

As had happened back in her old bedroom a few months ago, her poor muse didn't seem to know what to do first. Ideas sprouted from her brain faster than her hand could keep up. Bonnie scribbled furiously, the fresh ink unfurling onto the page like a bolt of satin. Once again, she wanted to pinch herself. Here she was, lunching in a little English tea shop, writing with the most luxurious pen on the most delectable paper. A joy bordering on delirium filled her. She didn't think this day could get much better.

Her phone chimed, and Bonnie ignored it, continuing to write, not wanting to lose the narrative thread. Finally, muse spent, she set the pen aside and finished her tea. Her phone chimed again. Bonnie pulled it out of her purse. She'd missed a call, but there was a voice mail.

From Theo.

Her pulse quickened, fingers tingling as she clicked the replay option.

"Hi there, Bonnie. It's me. Uh, Theo. You probably already know that I suppose, with the caller identification or whatever it's bloody called . . ."

A grin crept across her face. She'd never have guessed the polished and perfect Theo could be so awkward on the phone.

"Anyhow, I've rung you because I was wondering if you would care to join me this evening. I've scored tickets to a show I think you'd enjoy. Well, um. Let me know. That's it, then. Okay. Bye."

There was a pause, and then the call clicked off.

Bonnie bit her lip, heart doing a jig inside her chest. She'd thought her day couldn't get any better, but with the promise of spending time with Theo tonight, she realized she'd been wrong. They hadn't seen each other since the kiss he'd given her on the bench. She'd thought she couldn't handle the friends-with-benefits thing, but maybe she'd been wrong about that too.

That night, they'd left it at a kiss. Just a kiss. A friendly kiss. Between friends.

And it had been perfect. Exactly what she needed. What she needed more of.

* * *

Theo waited on the platform of the Charing Cross train station. He'd offered to drive to Cambridge and give Bonnie a lift, but true to form, she'd refused, saying it made no sense for him to go out of his way. He glanced at his watch, she was due in soon. Piccadilly Circus was a scant five-minute walk, so they'd be at the Criterion in plenty of time for curtain. He checked his jacket pocket for the tickets.

This morning at breakfast, Tabitha had mentioned heading into London to catch a show with a friend, and Theo realized that was exactly the kind of "friendly" activity he could do with Bonnie. He'd been brainstorming ideas for where to take her all week, but nothing seemed right. They'd seen a show at the Globe last summer. They'd also ridden the London Eye together already. He could take her to a museum or a gallery, but that seemed too stuffy. Besides, he wasn't sure which ones she'd already visited. She mentioned she hadn't seen the Tate, but it closed too early for an evening outing.

Rationally, Theo knew he was nixing all his ideas because he was scared Bonnie would turn him down, but when he heard his sister mention the Criterion, he knew it was brilliant. Their shows were always lively and fun, and he'd use any excuse to hear Bonnie laugh. Plus, Piccadilly had a rousing night scene, and there'd be plenty of clubs and pubs to choose from to pop into after the show. He'd offered to buy the tickets off his sister, but all the nosy minx wanted was to know who he planned to take.

He checked his watch again, grinning to himself as he recalled this morning's conversation.

"At the Criterion? Is the show any good?"

Tabitha nodded. "It's my second time going. And I think Gwen's been at least twice already. It's a hoot. Why?"

He focused on his eggs. "Dunno. Maybe I'll go myself."

"Good luck, the show's booked out. Gwen thinks they might extend the run, but you never know."

"Oh." Theo set his fork down. So much for that idea.

"Well, don't look so glum about it. Since when are you interested in going to the theatre anyway?"

Theo cleared his throat. "I think someone I know would like it. The show, I mean." He drained his tea and reached for the pot. As he poured himself another cup, the weight of his sister's stare bore down on him.

"A female someone?" Tabitha asked.

Theo ignored her, holding up the pot. "Would you like more tea?"

"What I'd like is to hear more about this mysterious someone." Her eyes widened, brows raising. "Do you have a date?"

He lifted the pot higher. "Tea?"

Tabitha lifted an eyebrow higher. "Date?"

They held for a moment, locked in silent sibling challenge. Tabby pulled out an ace, employing one of Theo's favorite tactics. "Tell me who you want to bring to the show, and I'll give you my tickets."

"What about Gwen?"

"She won't care. I told you, we've already seen it. We'll skip the play and go to SoHo." His sister nudged her cup forward. "So? What do you say?"

Theo broke eye contact, glancing down to refill her cup. "I say my sister is a nosey parker."

"Part of the job description," Tabitha replied, unperturbed.

Theo set the teapot down and considered her. His sister was nosey, but she wasn't a gossip. He could trust Tabby not to say anything to their mother. It rankled him he was worried about that in the first place, but Theo didn't feel like stirring the hornet's nest.

Over the past few weeks, since he'd come back from Chicago, he'd been able to fly under his mother's marital radar, but word of him dating someone would be a blip on her screen that would have her zeroing in on her target, torpedoes at the ready.

"Fine. Yes, it's a date."

Tabby clapped her hands. "I knew it! It's someone you met in the States, isn't it?"

"Why do you say that?"

"I'm your sister, git. You've been acting dodgy ever since you came home from that trip."

"I have a lot on my mind."

Tabby gave him her best *oh please* look.

"Fine, yes," he said again. "It's someone I met in the States."

"And she's here in England now?"

"No, I was planning to have that Scottish bloke on the spaceship beam her up."

A crust of toast pegged him on the cheek.

"Tabitha!" his mother barked from the doorway, and they both started. "Are you throwing food at your brother?"

"Of course not, Mama." Tabby smiled demurely, winking at Theo. "Can I pour you some tea?"

While his sister went about preparing a cup for their mother, Theo stood and offered his arm, escorting Mama across the room before helping her into her seat at the head of the table. As he adjusted her chair, he wondered when his mother had begun to look so frail. She'd always seemed so strong, with a spine of steel, hard and unbending. Now she appeared brittle, ready to crack.

Neither mentioned their evening plans again, but after

breakfast, Tabby handed off the tickets, telling him she expected details later.

As the wait for Bonnie's train dragged on, Theo hoped he'd have something to tell. Not that he planned to share too many details with his sister. Though if he knew Tabby, she'd wheedle a few tidbits out of him. If any of the Whartons should have pursued a career in politics, it was Tabitha.

The shrill shout of the arriving train whistle scattered his thoughts, and the anxious ache in his belly was replaced with a nervous twitch in his chest. The doors slid open, and Theo sharpened his gaze, searching the mass of people departing the train cars for a tangle of curly red hair.

His chest began to tighten, heart slipping, as the number of people on the platform dwindled, and still no sign of Bonnie. Had she changed her mind? Decided she didn't want to try the friends-with-benefits thing after all? Christ, he didn't know if he could handle the roller coaster she put him on. Maybe it was for the best. If she decided not to come, he'd let it go.

He was supposed to be focused on other things anyway. Bonnie was a distraction he didn't need.

"Theo!"

His breath caught at the sound of Bonnie's voice. He turned, heart rocketing into his throat when he caught sight of her hurrying toward him. He crossed the platform, and before his brain could catch, up, he'd bent to kiss her, pressing his lips to hers.

"Hello to you too." She laughed.

"Sorry."

"Don't be." Her cheeks were pink, her face sunny, her eyes . . . happy. The joy he'd seen shyly peeking out earlier this week was now staring back at him in full force.

Good Lord, she was beautiful. Resisting the urge to kiss her again, he took her hand, leading her off the station platform and through the bustling crowds toward Piccadilly Circus. She didn't protest, a fact that pleased him more than it probably should have.

"It's like Times Square!" She gaped, spinning in a slow circle and gazing up at the giant flashing digital billboards. "A mini-version, anyway."

"You've been to New York City?" Theo asked, as always, eager to learn more about her. He found himself wanting to know everything about Bonnie, each new detail another piece to her puzzle.

"Once. Ten years ago or so. I got to see Patrick Stewart play Macbeth." Her face glowed with the memory.

"Would you have rather gone to the Globe? I didn't think so, since we were there last summer, and they can be tricky seats to nab last minute if you don't want to end up in the groundlings."

"Even for a duke?" she asked.

His mouth pinched.

"I'm kidding!" she said, jostling his ribs with her elbow. "Note to self, no duke humor."

"It's a sore spot," he admitted.

"You don't have to explain." She leaned against him. "And one cannot live on Shakespeare alone. I'm looking forward to the show."

"Then we'd best be off." He took her hand in his and tugged her across the square. "The show will be starting soon."

Exiting the theatre, Bonnie relished the blast of chill night air. A sold-out show, the seats had been packed. And while the play had been great fun, the full house quickly grew stuffy.

"What did you think?" Theo asked, strolling alongside her.

"I loved it." She grinned up at him. "Is it wrong to admit I appreciate British humor more than my native country's?"

"Not at all." He matched her grin. "Especially because you're right."

She laughed and paused at the fountain in the center of Piccadilly Square, soaking up the energy of the crowd bustling around them. "Thanks again for taking me."

"My pleasure."

As it had before in the hotel room in Chicago, the way Theo said those words made her pulse trip, tickling in the hollow of her throat. Her blood thickened, a slow throbbing heat spreading through her. Bonnie shifted, glancing around, searching for a distraction. Her gaze landed on the winged statue at the top of the fountain. "Where's Cupid's arrow?"

"That's not Cupid." Theo stepped closer, gazing up at the statue with her.

"Fine. Eros," she said, swapping out the Roman name for the original Greek version. And Bonnie thought she was a literary stickler.

"Not him either." Theo shook his head, blue eyes lighting with mischief. He was enjoying this.

Bonnie stared at the statue. Wings: check. Drapey Greek loincloth thing: check. Bow: check. The only thing missing was the arrow. Who else could it be? Bonnie scanned her mental files and came up blank. "Okay, enlighten me," she demanded begrudgingly. "If that's not the God of Love, then who is it?"

"Eros's brother, Anteros."

She wrinkled her nose. "Counter-love?" She tried to

decipher the root word. "So, he's the God of what, Anti-love?"

"Right translation, wrong interpretation." Theo smiled, leaning toward her, those dashing, devastating dimples getting up close and personal. "Think of it as counter-love, like love returned." He bent his head lower, eyes on hers. "Anteros is the God of Requited Love."

"Oh," she whispered, breath escaping in a little puff.

"Do you want to know how Plato describes requited love?"

"Impress me," she teased, already impressed.

"Counter-love is the mirror image of a lover's feelings. Love reflected."

"How interesting." Her gaze dropped to his mouth, which she found even more interesting. His lips were soft yet firm, a study in paradoxes. His kisses were a paradox too, smooth and rough, tender and ravishing. She very much wanted to kiss him. Glancing up, her heart stalled, then began beating faster, pulse zigzagging through her body. Reflected in his eyes, clear as a mirror, was his desire to kiss her.

Theo leaned closer. His mouth hovered a whisper from her own. If she puckered, they'd be kissing. *Then what are you waiting for? Pucker up already!*

"Theo!" A woman's voice rose above the crowd.

Theo's head shot up, gaze whipping over his shoulder. "Of course," he grumbled.

"What?" Bonnie asked, trying to see around him. Standing this close, the combination of her short legs and his broad shoulders created quite an obstruction. She went on her tiptoes, craning her neck. A woman around her age was hurrying toward them, long black hair flying behind her. "Who's that?"

The woman waved, blue eyes merry, dimples flashing as she smiled.

By the time Theo replied, Bonnie had already figured it out. She stepped around Theo and waved back, preparing to meet his sister.

"I was hoping I'd run into you." Theo's sister gave him a hug.

"I bet you were." Theo returned the hug, a little stiffly, Bonnie noticed. He turned to her. "Bonnie, I'd like you to meet my sister Tabitha."

"Hi." Bonnie offered her hand.

"Charmed." Theo's sister shook Bonnie's hand and nodded at the woman standing next to her. "This is my friend Gwen." Gwen nodded and smiled too. Tabitha kept her attention on Bonnie. "You're American."

"I am," Bonnie agreed.

"From Chicago?"

"You can tell?" Unlike her South Side cousins, Bonnie didn't think she'd ever developed an accent while growing up in the suburbs, but maybe she had.

"Not really." Tabitha shot her brother a grin spiced with sibling menace. "Theo's mentioned you."

"Oh." *Theo mentioned her to his sister?* Pleasure flickered through her.

"How long you here for?"

"I'm teaching some summer classes at Cambridge," Bonnie said, the words still giving her a little thrill. "Then will travel up to Scotland for my friend's wedding before heading home."

"Is that Logan's wedding?" Tabitha asked her brother.

Theo nodded. "Bonnie is best friends with Cassie, Logan's fiancée."

"Oooh, does that mean you get to be the maid of honor?" Tabitha asked.

Bonnie nodded.

"How fun!" Much less restrained than her brother in her display of emotion, Tabitha clasped her hands together. "I absolutely adore weddings."

"Is she having a hen do?" Tabitha's friend asked.

Thanks to a tipsy Cassie, Bonnie knew what Gwen was asking. "Yeah, I'm actually the one who is supposed to plan it." Bonnie had conveniently pushed that item to the back of her to-do list. "I'm not sure where to start."

"We can help you!" Tabitha squealed.

Theo cleared his throat. "I don't know if that's such a good—"

"Really?" Bonnie asked.

"Oh, yeah. We know all the best spots for that sort of thing. Right, Gwen?"

Gwen nodded, eyebrows wiggling. "You bet we do."

"See?" Tabitha reached for Bonnie's hands. "What do you say?"

"Cassie is in town next week," Bonnie mused. "She'll be busy with her work assignment most of the time, but we're planning to get together at least once while she's here."

"I don't want to intrude on catch-up time with your best friend," Theo's sister said. "Why don't you hit her up for some ideas, and then we can meet up later, hash out a plan." Tabitha squeezed Bonnie's hand. "Does that sound good?"

It would be nice to have other women to talk to, to hang out with, while she was here. Bonnie had yet to connect with any of her female coworkers, not that she'd tried very hard. "That sounds great." Bonnie squeezed Tabitha's hand in return, meeting the girl's infectious smile. "Thanks."

"Yes, Tabby," Theo said, giving his sister the kind of look one of Bonnie's cousins would shoot her whenever she cock-blocked them at a bar. "Thanks."

CHAPTER 21

LATER THAT NIGHT, Theo arrived home in a foul mood after seeing Bonnie off on the ten o'clock train. It had been a lovely evening, one he'd enjoyed. One he'd have enjoyed even more if his sister had gone on her merry way and left the two of them alone. *Bloody nosey parker.* He loped up the stairs and knocked on his sister's door.

"Enter."

"What the hell, Tabby-Cat?" Theo asked, opening the door and leaning against the frame.

"Come in or leave, *Teddy-Bear*, but don't hover." Lounging on the bed, his sister didn't glance up from her phone screen.

Groaning in agitation, Theo stepped inside.

"Shut the door unless you want Mum to hear our conversation."

"She's in bed."

Tabitha snorted. "Like that would stop her."

"Fair point." Theo closed the door. "Do you know what's going on with her?"

"I know, she's been odd, right?" Tabitha shrugged. "Menopause, maybe? Though I think late fifties is a little on the old side to be starting that."

Theo grimaced.

"Ugh, you're such a guy." Tabby rolled her eyes. "Lady part stuff, ew!"

"My mother's lady part stuff, yes, *ew*."

"Hey, you came out of that hoo-ha."

"You did too." Theo put up a hard block on that mental image. "Speaking of, as your mother's daughter, do you suppose your busybody tendencies are a product of nature or nurture?"

"Pardon?"

"Did you learn to be a meddler from our mother, or is it genetic?" He crossed to the swivel chair at his sister's desk and collapsed into it, swinging around to face her. "You just had to barge in on us tonight, huh?"

"Do you think your girlfriend wants to go more classy or sassy?" Tabitha asked, ignoring his question. She ran her finger down her phone screen. "Gwen knows tons of places right in the West End, and there's this saucy little show . . . it's in a club farther south than SoHo. Would she and her friends be up for it?"

"Sorry?" He was still stuck on the word "girlfriend."

Tabitha turned her phone toward Theo. He glanced down, doing a double take when a mostly naked man rolled across the screen in a giant hula hoop. "What the bloody hell is that?"

"A burlesque for ladies." She tilted the screen back her way. "Though I suppose gents can enjoy it too. Magic Mike meets Cirque de Soleil."

"Sounds like a train wreck to me," Theo muttered.

"Jealous?" Tabitha waved her phone, where a line of

men in tiny shorts now filled the screen, gyrating on their knees. "Afraid your girlfriend might see something she likes better?"

"Christ, get that out of my face." Theo pushed the phone away. "And she is *not* my girlfriend."

"Looked like it to me."

"We're just friends."

"Very good friends." His sister gave him a devilish smirk. "You were half a second from snogging her when we showed up."

"Thanks for that, by the way." Theo sat back in the chair and crossed his arms over his chest. "If you wanted to spy on me, fine. But you didn't have to interrupt my date."

"I wanted to meet her." Tabitha rolled onto her stomach and faced him. "She's pretty. And nice. I like her."

I like her too.

"When are you seeing her again?"

"None of your business."

"Oh, come on, Theo, don't be like that."

"I haven't asked her out again yet," he admitted.

"Why not?"

He shrugged and leaned back, resting his feet on his sister's bed. "I want to think of something special to do, something she'll really like."

"The Eye?"

"We did that last summer."

"You've known her since last summer?" Tabby punched him in the leg.

"Hey, what was that for?"

"Why haven't you told me about her?"

"I didn't realize I needed to discuss my love life with my sister."

"Well, you do. Read the sibling manual."

Theo chuckled and nudged Tabitha with his toes.

"Keep your stinky feet away from me." She shoved at him. "You really like this girl, don't you?"

"My feet are *not* stinky. And yes," he admitted. "I do."

"What kinds of things does *she* like?"

"Books. She loves Shakespeare." Theo scratched his chin.

"What else?"

He thought for a minute, reviewing his time with Bonnie. "Jane Austen."

"More books. Anything else?"

"Tea."

"Books and tea. I can work with that." Tabitha sat up and rubbed her hands together. "Oh! I've got it. The perfect place to take her." She grabbed her phone and started typing rapidly. A moment later, she handed it to Theo. "Beast, prepare to wow your Belle."

The following weekend when Theo called to see if she wanted to go out again, Bonnie agreed before he had a chance to tell her where he planned to take her, even agreed to letting him drive out and pick her up rather than take the train. She was becoming greedy for more time with him. Part of her warned she was getting too attached, that the feelings he stirred in her went beyond friends, but she conveniently decided to ignore those thoughts and focus on the wonderful time she had while in his company.

Easy enough to do, especially since the places he chose to take her were so wonderful. When Theo picked her up late that afternoon, rather than heading south toward London, he'd driven east. Arriving in a charming little town some thirty minutes or so later, Bonnie didn't know what to expect as he escorted her through a courtyard up to the door of a restaurant with tall white pillars bracketing the entrance. Neoclassical in style, the place resembled an

ancient Greek or Roman temple. But once inside, she had
to stop and catch her breath. It was a restaurant, yes, but it
was *inside a library*.

A real, actual library. Well, a former library. Called the
Library, the pub earned its namesake due to the fact it was
housed in what had once been the first public subscription
library in the UK. Bonnie turned in a circle, trying to absorb everything at once. The rows and rows of books
climbing up every wall, the little alcoves with tables and
chairs, diners surrounded by more shelves of books.
"Theo . . ." Bonnie's voice failed her.

"You like it?"

"*So* much." She rubbed a knuckle across the corner of
her eye, holding the prick of tears at bay. She loved it.
Warmth bloomed in her chest. He'd done this for her. A
simple thing maybe, but it made her feel special in a way
she hadn't in a very long time. Possibly ever.

"I'm glad." He smiled at her then, dimples winking, and
like clockwork her knees prickled with awareness. As if
knowing her legs were threatening to collapse beneath her,
he took her hand and led her to a table.

By the time their meal arrived, Bonnie finally managed
to stop skimming all the titles on the shelves closest to her
chair. She turned her attention to Theo. "How'd you find
this place?"

"The truth?" Theo asked, pouring her a glass of wine
from the bottle he'd ordered. "My sister suggested it."

"She has good taste," Bonnie said, smiling as she took
a sip. "I can't wait to see what she suggests for Cassie's
bachelorette party."

"Hmph," Theo grunted, refilling his own glass. "Cassie
is coming to London next week, right?"

Bonnie nodded, scooping up a spoonful of pumpkin
chestnut soup.

"I haven't talked to Logan recently. Is he coming with her?"

"I don't know," she admitted. "Probably not, though. Her schedule will be packed covering Wimbledon."

"She's venturing into sports journalism now?"

"Sort of." Bonnie grinned. "More about how the media focuses on what women players wear rather than how they play."

"Ah." Theo nodded. "How's the teaching going?"

"It's good." Bonnie took another sip of wine. "Surprisingly easier than my normal classes, actually. I'm enjoying it."

"See that Professor Ian often?" he asked, his tone casual, his gaze fixed on his plate.

Bonnie set her glass down, cheeks warm from both the wine and the company. *Was he jealous?* "Here and there," she said, equally casual. She'd run into Ian a few times on campus, and exchanged a few pleasant words, but when he'd asked her to go out to lunch again, she'd politely declined.

This was the second Saturday in a row she'd gone out with Theo, and though the night wasn't over yet, she was already hoping he'd ask her out again next Saturday. Was this urge to be with him a rebound thing? She didn't know. She didn't think so. Bonnie wasn't sure where things were going between them, or even where she wanted them to go, but she knew she wanted to find out. And she definitely wanted to enjoy the journey.

So far, their "friends with benefits" situation hadn't involved too many of the traditional benefits rumored to be associated with such a relationship. As she finished her wine, Bonnie wondered if they might explore a few of those benefits later tonight.

* * *

Theo pulled into a spot near the resident hall where Bonnie was staying. Putting the car in park, he undid his seat belt and glanced over at her. "Can I walk you up? Not to imply you're not entirely capable of seeing yourself to your door," he quickly added.

"I'd like that," she said, eyes sparkling with amusement.

Pressing his luck, he stepped around the car and held the door open for her. She allowed him to do so, and even took his arm when he offered. It was late, and the path was deserted. Though she'd likely be perfectly safe, he was bloody glad she'd agreed to let him walk her home.

They strolled through the campus garden in a companionable silence. The calendar had flipped to July, and the garden was bursting with color, a buffet of fragrances drifting on the evening breeze. Theo caught the sweet scent of English roses mixed with the sharper, almost smoky bite of night-blooming Jasmine.

All too soon, they'd arrived at her building. Theo took her hand, brushing his lips across her knuckles. "I suppose this is good night."

Her mouth curved in a soft smile. She lifted her face to his. "I suppose so."

"Well, then," Theo said, and bent his head, brushing his lips across hers the same way he had her hand. Soft. Gentle. She let out a sweet little moan, and he pressed his mouth harder against hers, deepening the kiss. His hands gripped her waist, and he leaned into her, craving contact.

She took a step back, and he felt the impact as her shoulders bumped against the brick wall of the building. Bonnie reached up, wrapping her arms around him, fingers threading through his hair. Her touch made little jolts of electricity spark across his scalp. Christ, he'd missed touching her, kissing her, tasting her. It had been too damn long since that night in his hotel room in Chicago. He hadn't stopped dreaming about it since. His body was at a constant slow burn; the brief kisses they'd shared since she'd arrived in England were bits of kindling tossed on the fire.

Dropping his hands from her waist, Theo traced the curve of her hips, reaching behind her to palm her bum. "You feel so good," he groaned against her mouth. He lifted her, sliding her up the wall, pressing closer to support her on his thighs. She wrapped her legs around his waist, arms anchored on his shoulders. He braced his hands on either side of her, the rough edges of old bricks scraping his palms as he kissed her again, tongue thrusting deep, taking her mouth the way he was dying to take all of her.

From somewhere in the distance, voices carried on the night air. Theo froze, and then released her, letting her slowly slide back to the ground.

"Maybe," she said, her voice raspy, breath coming in sexy little gasps, "we should take this upstairs."

His cock jumped, very on board with this plan. Struggling to collect himself, he dipped his chin, touching his forehead to hers. "Are men allowed in the girls' dormitory?"

"I don't know if there's an actual rule against it . . ." She paused, frowning.

"You're a teacher." He pulled back, glancing around. "I don't want you to get caught doing anything *improper*."

"I think," Bonnie said, lowering her voice to a dramatic stage whisper, "we may have already ventured beyond the boundaries of propriety."

He grinned, appreciating her ability to crack a joke in a moment like this. It eased some of the tension, took the bite out of the sting of needing her and knowing he couldn't have her. Not right now anyway. "Maybe a little," he agreed. "I'd better go," he added, gut twisting with regret.

"Before I allow you to sneak me upstairs for a night of debauchery."

She sighed but didn't argue. "Will I see you again next Saturday?"

"Count on it," Theo promised, touching his lips to her cheek in the most modest of kisses. He bid her good night, for real this time, waiting until she was safely inside. Then he retraced his steps to his car, wondering where he could take her that would give them some bloody blessed privacy.

Someplace where they could go as far beyond the boundaries of propriety as they bloody well pleased.

CHAPTER 22

THE FOLLOWING FRIDAY, Bonnie accompanied a group of her students on an excursion into London. The day's itinerary included a scavenger hunt of literary landmarks, starting at Highgate Cemetery, locating various monuments such as *A Conversation with Oscar Wilde*, eventually ending at 221B Baker Street, which unfortunately turned out to be a rather disappointing conclusion to an otherwise successful day. One young man in her group was quite put out to learn the address of London's most famous detective was fictional, and even more disgruntled to discover it "looked nothing like the show on the telly."

"The poor disillusioned boy." Cassie laughed after Bonnie relayed the story that evening over drinks. Cass had arrived in town on Monday, but this was the first time their schedules had allowed them to get together.

"How are your interviews going?" Bonnie asked.

"Great. I've even been able to sneak more 'Coming Out of the Book Closet' segments in, asking the athletes about their favorite authors and stories."

"You always were a multitasker."

"They're usually happy to talk books with me." Cassie grinned, but then her face grew serious. "You'd be amazed how often an interview with a female tennis player will center on crap like what makeup they prefer to wear on the court."

"Are you serious?"

"I wish I were joking." Cassie shook her head. "Can you imagine? As a journalist, you've been given the golden opportunity to talk to a world champion, an elite athlete, and the first question that comes to mind is what mascara does she like best?"

"Maybe you should interview some of the sports journalists too," Bonnie suggested. "Call them out on it directly, see if it motivates them to reconsider their talking points."

"Now that's some multitasking," Cassie said, clinking her glass against Bonnie's. She took a sip, and then leaned closer, giving Bonnie a wicked little grin. "Speaking of multitasking, I hear you've been keeping yourself busy on the weekends too."

Bonnie almost choked on her cocktail. She forced herself to swallow, alcohol stinging the back of her throat. "Theo's been talking to Logan, I gather?" she asked, setting her glass down carefully.

"Hey, at least Theo tells Logan stuff," Cassie said, a twinge of hurt reflected in her voice.

"There's nothing to tell." Bonnie fought off a reciprocal twinge of guilt. "We've been getting together on Saturdays. It's been nice."

"Nice?" Cassie's eyebrows rose.

"Fun." Bonnie shrugged.

"Fun, huh?"

Her best friend studied her, eyes shrewd. Bonnie stared at her drink, squirming under the assessing gaze. She might have a theatre degree, but she'd never been able to fool Cassie. Talking about this was a bad idea. Cassie would want to know how she felt about Theo. How could Bonnie discuss this with Cassie when she wasn't even ready to have that conversation with herself?

After a moment, Cassie leaned back, her gaze softening. "Well, good for you."

Bonnie held back the sigh of relief, trapping it in her lungs.

"You could do with a bit of fun," Cassie added. "Hell, we all could." She elbowed Bonnie playfully in the ribs. "I'm looking forward to having lots of fun at my bachelorette party."

Right. Bonnie exhaled. The bachelorette party. The plan was for Cassie and the other girls still stateside to fly in to Heathrow first, party in London, then keep the party going on a luxury overnight train to Inverness. They'd be renting a suite of apartments within walking distance of the castle where the wedding was to be held. Logan's mam had invited them to a special wedding party breakfast, and then there was the rehearsal dinner, and finally, the actual wedding. "Do you have any ideas of what you want? Any preferences?"

"I want it to be memorable." Cassie stirred the ice in her cocktail. "Magical." She waved her stir stick in the air and grinned. "No pressure." When Bonnie didn't smile in return, Cassie patted her hand. "Seriously, whatever you come up with is fine. You've got a lot on your plate, and I realize maybe it's not fair to ask you to plan something like this with, well . . . with everything you have going on."

"Like my fiancé cheating on me and my own wedding getting called off?" Bonnie held Cassie's gaze, a flicker of irritation flaring in her chest.

"Um, not just that, you're busy teaching and—"

"It's fine, Cass. I got it covered." At least, with the help of Theo's sister, Bonnie hoped she had it covered. They still had about a month to plan. Plenty of time. She made a mental note to ask Theo for Tabitha's number next time they got together.

Thinking of Theo reminded Bonnie of what they'd been doing the last time they were together, not that she'd ever really stopped thinking about it. She may not want to examine what being with Theo did to her heart too closely, but there was no question about what being with him did to her body. The kiss on her resident hall steps had been so freaking hot, she'd been burning up ever since. Bonnie added a few other things to her mental to-do list, things she'd like to do to Theo. Things she'd like him to do to her.

With any luck, she thought, her body growing warmer, he was good at multitasking too.

When Theo had asked her to meet earlier than usual for what was becoming their standing Saturday date, Bonnie had been curious, but he wouldn't tell her why. Her curiosity piqued even further when he wouldn't tell her where they were going, only what stop she should meet him at in London. The Blackfriars station was near all kinds of tempting possibilities, so many she couldn't begin to guess which it might be.

"You're lucky I like surprises," she said as they crossed Millennium Bridge. He didn't reply, just reached for her hand, and the brush of his skin against hers made a burst of light glow inside her, warmer than the sunshine gracing the sky above. It was a gorgeous summer Saturday in London, and the pedestrian bridge was packed with people out enjoying an afternoon of fun.

Bonnie was dying to ask Theo where they were going

but decided to keep quiet and play along. The anticipation heightened the experience, a little like Christmas. At
first, she'd wondered if he was planning to take her to the
Tate, but when they'd crossed to the south side of the
Thames, she'd crossed off that possibility.

"Now don't get too excited," Theo warned her as they
exited the bridge and turned toward the Globe.

"I'm not," she lied. Had he managed to score tickets?
She knew from planning the trip she took with her friends
last year, seats in the open-air theatre were hard to come
by—especially on a gorgeous day like this. She held her
breath as they got closer, scanning the playbills plastered
along the low wall surrounding the theatre. When she realized they'd passed the entrance, a little sigh escaped her.

"Hold on, we're almost there," he promised. A few steps
later, he pulled her through the door of the building right
next to the theatre.

"Welcome to the Swan," a young woman in a crisp
black pantsuit, her accent equally crisp, greeted them as
they entered.

While Theo confirmed his reservation, Bonnie absorbed the details of the space. She thought he'd outdone
himself last week when he'd taken her to the Library, but
this was even better. Antique bits of props and costumes
were featured in little nooks, and large vintage stage lights
were placed in various corners.

"This way, please." The woman led them down through
the restaurant, sunlight spilling in from the wall of windows, sparkling off the Thames and the dome of St. Paul's
Cathedral in the distance.

"What a view," Bonnie breathed, almost bumping into
Theo when the woman stopped at a table.

"We're quite fond of it." She smiled, waiting for them
to settle into the plush cornflower-blue sofas bracketing

the booth. "You'll be taking afternoon tea?" she asked Theo.

He nodded. "Make mine the gentleman's tea, please."

"Of course." She turned to Bonnie. "And for Miss? Bubbles or no bubbles?"

"Um . . ." Bonnie glanced at Theo.

"Bubbles," he replied for her. He winked. "It's champagne."

"Oh." She smiled. "Yes, bubbles, please." The woman nodded and headed off, and Bonnie leaned back, bouncing a little on the springy cushion, giddy with pleasure.

"You like it?" he asked, watching her with amusement.

"I love it," she gushed. "Tabitha's idea?"

Theo shook his head, a cocky grin tugging at the corner of his lips. "Actually, I came up with this one myself."

Again, her chest suffused with a warm, sunshiny glow. She was, quite simply, happy. Happy to be out on this gorgeous day, spending time with this gorgeous man, who seemed to have made it his mission to find ways to please her. She hoped to be able to return the favor. "I like spending time with you," she admitted.

"Good. I like spending time with you too." His smile widened, and oh, Lord help her, here came the dimples.

Thankfully, their tea arrived, and Bonnie distracted herself by watching as tiered trays, similar in style to the ones the Drake used, were placed on the table. She looked closer, studying the plates. She gasped, delighted when she realized each plate was painted with characters and quotes from *A Midsummer Night's Dream*. "These are beautiful."

"They were designed especially for our tea service," the server proudly informed them as she poured a measure of piping hot tea from a sterling silver teapot.

"What's this?" Bonnie asked the girl, holding up a tiny

stoppered bottle filled with a sparkly, mulberry-colored liquid.

"That's our special Love Potion cocktail." The server winked and finished arranging the tea service before moving on to her other tables.

"Do you think it works?" Theo asked.

Bonnie held the bottle up to the light, turning it from side to side. "Only one way to find out." She glanced at him. "In the play, Puck drops the potion in people's eyes."

"I think we should stick to drinking this one," Theo suggested.

"You're probably right." She unplugged the stopper and took a sniff. It was tart, but not with the sharp bite of lemon, more like something berry, and a little sweet, like honey. "Here goes nothing," she said, and took a sip.

"How is it?" Theo asked, brows raised.

"Not bad." She licked her lips. "It tastes like blackberries"—tiny bubbles fizzed on her tongue—"and booze." She handed him the bottle. "Your turn."

"Bottoms up." Theo took the bottle and downed the rest in one gulp. "Oh, that *is* boozy."

She giggled. "Do you think it's working?"

"You know"—he stared at her across the table, the secret shards of indigo surrounding his irises glinting in the afternoon sunlight— "I think it might be."

Swallowing, Bonnie dropped her gaze, eyeing the trays of food in front of Theo. "So why do they call that a 'gentleman's tea' anyway?"

"Because it's full of manly stuff," he teased, puffing out his chest and lowering his voice to a baritone. "Like beef and fish fingers."

She snorted. "Fish fingers don't sound very manly."

"What would you call them, then?"

"Well, in America, they're called fish sticks . . ." She

started giggling again as a thought occurred to her. Her head swam a little, warm and fuzzy. Maybe she shouldn't have ordered the bubbly, not on top of the boozy Love Potion.

"What's so funny?" he asked.

"I thought of a joke," she said, stifling another giggle and shaking her head, "but it's kind of crude."

"You don't say." He bent toward her. "How about you whisper it to me?"

Just tipsy enough to do it, Bonnie leaned across the table and told him the fish dicks joke.

"Hmm." Theo straightened, mouth quirking as he poked his fork into a Scotch egg.

"I know. It's not *that* funny," she said, resting her head back against the cushion of her seat, giggling some more.

"I do believe you're drunk." Theo chuckled, clearly finding that more amusing than her joke.

"Highly probably." She wrinkled her nose. "Probable," she corrected. "Low tolerance."

"Very low," he agreed. He pointed his fork at her tea tray. "Perhaps you should eat something to soak up some of the alcohol in your system."

"Perhaps I should." She popped a tiny sandwich in her mouth. Then tried a few of the mini quiches.

Moving from savory to sweet, Bonnie considered the plate piled high with adorable little cakes and macarons. "I can't decide," she said, finally choosing a miniature fruit tart. She examined the delicate pastry. "It's almost too pretty to eat."

"I know the feeling."

The rough edge of Theo's voice caught her off guard, and she glanced up. His eyes were on her mouth, hot and hungry. Then he lifted his gaze to hers, and there was no mistaking his meaning.

Liquid heat pooled low in her belly, tingling between her thighs as she recalled the words he'd whispered to her, remembered his mouth on her, there. Bonnie swallowed.

A charged moment passed, and then Theo shifted in the booth. "I don't know about you, but I could use some fresh air. Ready?"

She nodded, and he handled the bill before leading her back outside.

They strolled along Bankside path. A slight breeze blew in from the Thames, cooling the flush of alcohol from her cheeks, but doing nothing to ease the warm ache inside. Bonnie leaned into him, craving his touch.

"Have you ever been to the Lakelands before?" Theo asked.

"You mean the Lake District?" Bonnie sighed. "Only in books. And my dreams."

"My family has a cottage up there. I've been thinking of taking a little holiday." He wrapped an arm around her shoulders, pulling her even closer. She snuggled into him, enjoying the solid feel of his strong arm and broad chest against her. "Why don't you come with me?"

"I don't know." Her brain was still pleasantly fuzzy, but she was sober enough to recall the Lake District was all the way across the country. "How long would it take to get there?"

"About five hours," he admitted.

"Oh, that's not so bad." She forgot all the way across the country of England was only across a state or two in America. "When would you want to leave?"

"When does your last class end next week?"

"Before lunch." She shrugged. "The students have Friday afternoons off to go on day trips to museums and such. The teaching staff takes turns chaperoning."

"Is it your turn next week?"

"No." She paused to mentally make sure. "I've done the last two."

"Well, then. Spend the weekend with me." He pulled the hand she rested on his arm up to his mouth and pressed a kiss to her fingers. "I'll sweeten the deal with another surprise."

"That's not fair. You already know I can't resist surprises." She looked up at him, batting her eyelashes. "What kind of surprise is it?"

"Uh-uh." Theo wagged his finger, schoolmarm face on. "It's a secret. If I told you, it wouldn't be a surprise."

"I just want a hint."

"No."

"Please," she pouted. "Just a tiny one?"

He stared at her mouth, catching his lower lip between his teeth. Bonnie's breasts tingled, nipples tightening at the memory of his teeth on her, his lips and tongue making her come. She shivered, wondering if he had any idea what he was doing to her. She also wondered if he knew she would have said yes to spending a weekend with him regardless of the promise of surprises.

"Fine," he acquiesced. "One hint."

Perhaps it was wrong to be so pleased with herself, but she was. She loved that she could make this man cave. Or at least make his defenses crumble a bit.

"I'm ready." She made a gimme motion with her fingers. "What's my hint?"

"LMP."

"LMP?" she repeated. "What kind of hint is that?"

"A tiny one," he teased. "Never say I'm not a man who gives a lady what she asks for."

CHAPTER 23

THE WEEKEND COULDN'T get here fast enough. More than halfway through the summer semester, up until now the days had been flying by. But this week, the hours dragged as Bonnie counted each one until her trip with Theo. To keep herself occupied, she visited several more of the local tea shops on her checklist and spent most evenings writing in her journal. She'd had various story ideas flit in and out of focus, and she ran with them for as long as they held her interest. So far, nothing had stuck beyond a few pages. But that didn't matter; she was rediscovering her love of words. As long as the ideas kept coming, she'd keep writing.

At last, Friday afternoon arrived, and she hopped a train. Since the Lake District was in the opposite direction of Cambridge, Theo had suggested she take a train to the station closest to his home. Rather than waste time driving in a circle, he'd pick her up from there and they'd be off. He was waiting for her when she arrived and helped carry her things to the car. But it wasn't the classy aging James Bond–mobile he usually drove. "What happened to 007?"

"I love her, but I don't think she has many long road trips left in her," Theo admitted. "This is my sister's car."

"I will never understand why cars are referred to in the feminine," Bonnie mused as he held the door open for her. She realized she'd been letting him do little things like that more often. But somehow, she wasn't bothered by it. The gesture didn't feel patronizing. Maybe it was because of the way he did it or maybe it was that the chip on her shoulder had lifted. Or maybe it was both.

"I never really thought about it," he admitted, setting her overnight bag in the back.

Overnight bag. As in she was staying *overnight*. With Theo. They hadn't discussed sleeping arrangements, but she'd rather hoped things would figure themselves out. Bonnie buckled her seat belt. Beneath the strap, her belly quivered. She felt all nervous and giddy. Like she was headed to her first school dance or something.

"So, you live nearby?" she asked as he left the station and headed north.

He nodded. "The Abbey is about ten minutes from here."

"Abbey?" That sounded grand, and very Jane Austeny. Part of Bonnie wished they'd stop by his home on the way. She was dying with curiosity to see what it looked like, but also a little ashamed of her curiosity because it stemmed from her fascination with the fact that he was a duke. A fascination she couldn't completely deny.

For the most part, she forgot Theo held the highest rank in the aristocracy, save for a monarch. But sometimes, she'd remember, and a little thrill would shoot through her. She wasn't proud of it, but there it was. And it helped her understand why he might be wary of letting people know.

It was closing in on seven in the evening when Theo pulled up to a quaint gray stone building, long fingers of ivy stretching toward the cobbled roof. "Is this it?" Bonnie yawned. She'd nodded off somewhere around Darrington, where the endless stretches of highway surrounded by green pastures reminded her of driving through Wisconsin.

"No. The cottage is only a bit farther down the road, but I thought I'd stop here and we could have supper."

Bonnie's stomach grumbled loudly in response and Theo laughed. "Come on, let's get you something to eat."

The café was storybook quaint, with charming little wooden tables like spools of thread and a counter lined with glass jars full of old-fashioned sweets. Despite the noise from her empty belly, Bonnie didn't have much of an appetite. The twinge of nervousness she'd felt at the train station had abated over the long drive, but now that she knew they were almost at the cottage, that they were perhaps only minutes away from the place she'd be spending the night with Theo . . .

"Everything all right?" he asked, reading her mind as usual. Was she that transparent, or was he just that good at interpreting her thoughts?

"Yeah." She smiled at him and soaked a heel of bread in her soup, tomato basil, not very adventurous, but one of her favorites. "I think I'm just a little sleepy."

"I'll have you in bed soon enough," Theo said, then froze, sandwich halfway to his mouth. He set his sandwich back on his plate and cleared his throat. "That didn't come out right."

Was he blushing? Bonnie grinned. For some perverse reason, realizing he was nervous too made her less nervous. Appetite suddenly restored, she hurried to finish her soup.

Not long after, they drove past a wooden gate painted a bright bold purple. Theo maneuvered the car down the narrow gravel path slowly, and as they rounded a bend,

Bonnie sucked in a breath. He'd called it a cottage, but the structure was much larger than what she'd imagined. Three stories, the walls made of the same gray stone as the café they'd eaten at, the roof was slate, with a row of adorable dormer windows. And rising up behind the house was what seemed, in Bonnie's Midwestern imagination, the looming shadow of mountains.

The setting sun was slowly slipping past the tree-lined ridge, painting the sky in bold streaks of color. Orange and gold and rose, lavender and midnight blue.

Theo sat, quietly watching the sunset with her. Once the sun drifted below the craggy horizon, and the twilight sky began to fade, he asked, "What do you think?"

"It's perfect." The words fell from her lips with breathless sincerity. If she had closed her eyes and described her dream home to a sketch artist, this would be darn close to the end result.

Already half in love, Bonnie fell the rest of the way the moment Theo opened the front door. Simple, yet elegant, grand but somehow still cozy, she stepped over the threshold and her heart said *home*.

Theo dropped their bags by the stairs leading up to the second floor. "Mrs. Lindsey?" he called. "You about?"

"In the kitchen," an aged yet pleasant voice called from the back of the house.

Taking her hand, Theo led Bonnie down the hall.

The kitchen, Bonnie was surprised to discover, included modern appliances nestled within antique woodwork. A long wooden island stretched across the length of the room. An older woman stood at the counter, slicing a brick of cheese, silver hair a halo of tight curls.

Her eyes lit up when she caught sight of Theo, and she set down the knife, maneuvering her short but ample frame around the island. "Your Grace, so good to see you."

Theo smiled and wrapped the woman in a hug. "You too, Mrs. Lindsey." He gestured to Bonnie. "Please meet my guest, Miss Bonnie Blythe."

"Miss." The housekeeper nodded, bobbing a curtsy. "A pleasure."

Bonnie felt a little tongue-tied. The whole "Your Grace" thing still threw her. And what now? Was she supposed to nod, or maybe curtsy back? She settled for a smile. "Nice to meet you, Mrs. Lindsey."

"I'm sure you're peckish after that long drive. I was just about to set out a tin of biscuits." The housekeeper bustled over to a large pantry.

"Very thoughtful of you," Theo told the woman.

With a sweet tug of affection, Bonnie noted he didn't mention they'd already stopped for supper in town. "Yes, thank you," she added.

Theo moved to a glass-fronted cabinet and pulled two wineglasses off the shelf. "Please." He glanced over at her. "Make yourself at home."

"Where's the restroom?" she asked.

"Around the corner by the stairs, down the hall. Third door on your left." He pulled a corkscrew from a drawer. "Don't get lost."

She was tempted. If he only knew how hard she was fighting the urge to run up and down the stairs like a puppy exploring a new place, poking her head into each room.

Mrs. Lindsey wiped her hands on her apron. "I'll show you, dear."

Bonnie paused at the stairs to grab the overnight kit out of her bag before hurrying to catch up with the housekeeper. "This house is lovely," she said, taking in each detail, from the wainscoting in the hall to the detailed trim around each doorframe.

"I've always thought so," Mrs. Lindsey agreed.

"How long have you worked here?" Bonnie asked, hoping she wasn't breaking some rule of etiquette or something. Ah well, she could blame it on being a boorish American.

"Oh, since well before His Grace was born," Mrs. Lindsey answered. "My mister as well."

"Your husband works here too?"

"Mm." She nodded. "He's the groundskeeper."

"You both live here, then?"

"In the cottage up the hill." The housekeeper stopped near a window and pointed.

Bonnie followed the direction of her finger, to where a cozy building sat nestled beneath a large willow tree. Lights glowed in the windows and smoke curled from a chimney in the thatched roof. Like everything else in the Lakelands, it looked like something out of a fairy tale.

"And that's the loo," Mrs. Lindsey added, pointing to a door down the hall. "There's fresh soap and I've just laundered the linens, so you should be set. But if you need anything else, you know where to find me." The housekeeper nodded her chin toward the cottage.

"Thank you."

"I'll say good night to his grace and be on my way." She ducked a quick curtsy and was gone.

Even the bathroom in this house was a treasure. A little jewel box of a space, with lushly patterned wallpaper adorning the walls and a vintage pedestal sink, above which hung a large ornate beveled mirror. Bonnie rinsed her face and brushed her teeth, digging in her kit for floss. Then she took a good look at herself, running her fingers through her hair, only succeeding in making the curls messier than before. *Stop stalling and get out there.*

Exiting the bathroom, she slipped off her sandals, bare feet slapping quietly over the honey-colored pine floors as she retraced her steps. Bonnie recalled the mental check-list she'd made of all the things she wanted to do with Theo the next time they were together. To date, she hadn't made much progress on that list, and it was time to get busy.

Literally.

After he'd seen Mrs. Lindsey out with a promise to meet with her husband in the morning, Theo poured two glasses of wine and set them on the low table in the sitting room situated off the kitchen, then kicked off his shoes and tossed them by the doors leading out to the back patio. He'd missed this place. Why didn't he come out here more often? The moment he pulled past the gate and began the crawl up the winding path to the house, he felt lighter, more relaxed. More . . . himself. As if he was able to be some-one here he wasn't allowed to be anywhere else.

He heard the door to the downstairs loo open and called out, "In here."

She padded through the kitchen in her bare feet. Theo loved that—loved she already seemed so comfortable here. He'd watched her face carefully when he led her inside ear-lier and had caught the rush of emotion sweep across her features. It was then he knew she felt it too. This house spoke to her, the same way it did him. He was so glad he'd brought her here.

Once more, he wondered how he'd ever be able to give this place up, even for a few weeks at a time.

"What are you thinking about?" Bonnie asked.

Theo ran a hand through his hair. "I have a confession."

"Oh?" Her auburn brows drew together in concern. "Is something wrong?"

"No, not exactly." He took her hand and led her to the sofa. They sat, and he handed her a wineglass. "I wasn't entirely forthcoming about my reasons for coming here," he began, fiddling with the stem of his own glass. "It's not just to go on holiday. Remember when I mentioned my family's, uh, financial issues?"

"You said it's your job to keep the 'bloody ship from sinking.'"

"Quite." He couldn't help the grin at her mimicking of his accent. "Well, this cottage could be a life preserver. We're looking into renting out the property."

"Ah." Bonnie swallowed. "Is there a lot you have to do? Will I be in the way?"

"No." He shook his head. "No, of course not. I have a few things I need to go over, some items to review with the groundskeeper, but nothing too serious." He glanced up at her, feeling loads lighter after his admission and suddenly playful. "Still plenty of time for the surprise I promised you." He winked.

"That's right," she said, swirling her wine around in her glass. "I almost forgot about my surprise. What was it again? LMB?"

"LMP."

"And what does that stand for?" She blinked innocently.

"I'm not falling for your sly tricks," he warned.

"Can't fault a girl for trying." She flashed him a cheeky grin and sipped her wine. "I have a list of other things I was thinking about trying," she added, watching him over the rim of her glass, eyes hot as sin.

Theo gulped his wine. "I recall you mentioning a fondness for lists."

She set her glass on the table and scooted closer to him. His heart rate sped up, chest rising and falling rapidly as his breathing became shallow, the short quick intake of breath leaving him dizzy. And all she'd done was sit next to him.

Christ, he had it bad. His cock, already at half-mast

most of the day, reported for duty, springing to full attention. He shifted on the couch, setting his wineglass
down next to hers. When he leaned back, she moved closer
still, her arm brushing against his, their thighs touching. He stared at the hint of bare skin showing below
her skirt.

The freckle on her knee sent a rush of memories flooding through him: pressing her onto the hotel floor, her skirt
hiked up to her waist, kissing that freckle, licking the soft
smooth skin of her thigh, tasting her . . . He'd lived on
those memories for months, replaying those moments over
and over again. But no more.

It was time to make some new memories. Right now,
right here, in this moment. Theo reached out, letting his
hand slide across the top of her knee. Her muscles quivered. His fingertips flirted with the hem of her skirt. "I
want to touch you," he confessed, voice low and urgent. "I
need to touch you."

She nodded, spreading her knees, opening her legs for
him.

Theo groaned and slid a hand under her skirt, his other
hand reaching up, fingers threading through her hair as he
pulled her mouth to his. He kissed her, tongue going deep,
as his hand moved higher up her leg. He brushed against
her knickers, felt the wet heat of her on his palm before he
slipped one finger under the elastic band and stroked her.

"God, you feel good," he ground against her mouth, finger plunging inside her.

She gasped, body clenching around him. His balls
clenched in response. Gritting his teeth, he slipped another
finger inside. She was so tight, so wet. He ached to have
his cock inside her. He curved his fingers, moving them
in a slow circle, learning the intimate shape of her.

Mimicking the motion of his hand, her hips rotated,

bringing his fingers deeper. He picked up the pace, and so did she, body bucking against him, soft staccato moans tearing from her throat, building in intensity. His mouth kept moving over hers, devouring those sexy little sounds.

She kissed him back with fierce intensity, her hands gripping his shoulders, sliding down his back, over his hips, coming to rest on his belt. *Hell yes, oh please yes.* "Touch me," he whispered. "Please, put your hands on me."

"So polite," she said, a teasing lilt coloring her voice. "How can I refuse?" He held his breath as her fingers worked his belt, and then the buttons on his fly, until finally she was rubbing her hand along his length, through the fabric of his shorts, but still, it felt bloody fucking good. He jerked against her, pushing his cock deeper into her hand. She stroked him, over and over, traced the shape of him beneath the cotton with her fingers, played with him until he was ready to lose his damn mind.

He grabbed her knickers and yanked, ripping them off her. "Christ, sorry." He held up the torn garment.

She laughed. "Don't be, they're in the way." And then she was pulling his shorts over his hips, and he was helping her. Sliding his pants down, kicking them off, his shorts quickly following.

He stripped off his shirt, then made quick work of her skirt and top. Slowing down, his fingers traced the delicate lines of her bra, brushed against the clasp. "May I?"

She nodded. Theo undid her bra, and it slipped from her shoulders, falling to the floor. He reached for her, settling her on top of him, her gorgeous little tits bobbing right in his face. "Hello." He grinned, reaching up to cup her, squeezing her breasts together. He bent his head and ran his tongue over both hard, pink peaks.

"Oh," she moaned, "oh, I like that." She arched, head

tossed back, chest thrusting forward, filling his mouth with her.

He licked and sucked and nibbled until she was moaning nonstop, an incoherent incantation of need. She straddled him, rubbing against him, the curls between her thighs brushing the tip of his cock, making him wild. So close, so bloody close. He released her breasts and kissed her neck, licked the hollow of her throat, pressed his mouth to the rapid flutter of her pulse just under her ear.

His hands dropped to her waist and slid over the lush curves of her hips. He remembered the shape of her, had memorized each dip and swell the one time before he'd been lucky enough to have his hands on her like this. And now, luck was with him again. He hoped it never left him because he never wanted to stop touching her.

"Bonnie." Theo pulled back, gazing at her face, wanting to look in her eyes. "I need to be inside you."

She bit her lip, flushed cheeks growing rosier. Her sudden virginal shyness a sharp contrast to the vixen she'd been moments before. But if she was nervous, he'd wait. "Okay," she said, surprising him with an impish smile.

"Okay," he echoed, willing his heart to slow down before it pounded a hole through his chest. He nudged her, sliding her off his lap so he could bend over and retrieve the condom he'd stashed in his pocket. "No comments about being a perv. I wanted to be prepared," he said.

"I'm currently staring at your bare ass, so I'm probably not in a position to judge," she admitted, giggling.

He glanced over his shoulder, and sure enough, the saucy wench was ogling his naked bum. "Who's the perv now?" he teased, ripping the foil open. He sat back on the couch and began to roll the condom down over his cock.

Next to him, she watched intently, eyes following his every move.

It turned him on, knowing she was watching, his cock swelling in his hand, balls heavy and aching. *Bloody fucking hell,* he was going to explode soon. "Show's over, woman," he growled, pulling her back onto his lap. He was so close, he didn't want to risk coming before she did. This way she could control things better, determine how fast, how deep, and he could focus on controlling himself.

Straddling him once more, she stared down at their bodies as he held her hips and guided her into place. When the head of his cock was snug against her, he paused. Meeting her gaze, he told her, "When you're ready." *Christ, please be ready soon.*

She nodded, thighs trembling as she lowered herself and began to slide down his length.

Oh God, oh sweet Christ, she was tight, so fucking tight. Theo glanced down. He'd been wrong. The show was far from over. If he kept watching her sweet pussy take him slow like this, he'd lose it before he was fully inside her. He shut his eyes and ordered himself to breathe.

Five thousand years later, she'd almost worked her way all the way down his shaft when she suddenly stopped moving. His eyes snapped open. Her brow was furrowed, tongue pressed between her teeth. "All good?" he croaked.

She began to nod again, but then paused. "No," she said, shaking her head, "I can't."

His heart stopped, blood freezing in his veins. "What is it, love? What can't you do?"

"I don't think I can, um"—she shifted on his lap—"go any farther."

Relief flooded Theo's body, and he laughed.

"It's not funny!" She frowned. "I think I'm stuck."

With Herculean effort, Theo swallowed another chuckle. His cock throbbed where she gripped him, and more than anything, he wanted to thrust, to push up into her until he was buried to the hilt. But he kissed her instead, making love to her mouth, as much a distraction for himself as a way to help her loosen up.

It worked. She shifted, and he sank deeper. "That's it." He kissed her neck. "Almost there." He pressed his thighs against hers, forcing her to open more for him. Her shoulders relaxed, body melting around him, warm and wet. Electric heat curled at the base of his spine, and his control slipped.

"Fuck, you feel good," he growled, unable to stop from bucking his hips once, hard and fast.

"Theo!" she gasped.

"Damn. Sorry." Theo held still, searching her face. "Did I hurt you?"

"No, just surprised me." She wiggled her hips.

And now he was the one gasping. "Easy, love." His fingers dug into the soft skin of her hips, holding her still. He was balls-deep inside her now, as far as he could go, and every shift of her body was an erotic squeeze along his cock.

A smile lifted one corner of her mouth. "I like it when you call me that."

"What? Love?"

"Mm-hmm," she hummed, breaking free of his grip and wiggling some more.

Theo groaned, rough and guttural. "And I like it when you do that."

Encouraged, she rotated her hips again, and then again, her movements becoming more fluid as she found her rhythm. He fisted his hands at his sides, letting her work him the way she wanted. When her tempo increased with a sudden intensity that told him she was close, he pressed a hand between their bodies, flicking his thumb over her clit.

She cried out, gasping his name.

"That's it." He stroked her clit again. "Come on, love," he encouraged, kissing her jaw, her neck, her breasts, while her hips jerked back and forth, up and down. *Hold on. Let her have this. Give her this.* He continued to repeat the mantra to himself as she worked him harder, faster, little cries growing louder until a scream burst from her lips, shudders wracking her body. He held onto her, her forehead resting on his shoulder, face pressed into his neck.

When the storm of her orgasm passed, he twisted, gripping the base of his cock to keep the condom in place as he pulled out. He gently rolled her onto her stomach, bending her over the arm of the sofa. Getting on his knees behind her, he nudged her legs apart and pressed himself against the curve of her lushly rounded bum.

Before entering her, Theo bent over her body, chest to her back, and whispered in her ear, "I'm going to come inside you now, okay?"

"Okay," she breathed, bucking her hips backward, bringing him closer to exactly where he wanted to be.

It was all the invitation he needed. Bracing his palms on either side of her, he gripped the arm of the couch and thrust. Hard. He pumped into her. Once, twice, three times, his mind going blank as he gave himself over to his need, his hunger. Sensation crashed through him, and in a blink, he was shuddering against her, the rush of his orgasm sounding in his ears.

Before he collapsed, he leaned into her and kissed her flushed cheek. "Thank you," he groaned, and passed out to the sound of her laughter, too spent to wonder what she found so amusing.

The steady ping of raindrops against glass broke through Bonnie's languid stupor. She yawned and stretched, uncurling her limbs like a cat. The muscles in her thighs protested, body threatening mutiny if she didn't stop moving.

Go back to sleep, the soft hush of rain whispered. *Relax,* a distant roll of thunder suggested. Breathing growing soft and even once more, she was on the verge of nodding back off when cold wet droplets sprinkled her face.

She jerked, blinking madly through the tangle of her hair, wondering if a window had been left open.

"You're awake," Theo murmured, hovering over her. Water dripped from the ends of his dark hair, landing on her cheeks.

"And you're wet," she grumbled.

"It's raining outside."

"You were outside?" she asked, tucking the blanket she was wrapped in tighter around herself. "Why?"

"I had some things to take care of," he said, nuzzling her neck. "Come on, Sleeping Beauty, time to wake up."

"It's Saturday," Bonnie protested, giggling when his shadow-beard tickled her. "I sleep in on Saturdays."

"It's almost noon, love," Theo said, tugging on her blanket.

"Hey, I'm naked under here!" she yelped.

"Then it's a good thing I've brought you your clothes." He dropped her duffel bag next to the couch before tugging on the blanket again.

"Theo!" Bonnie snatched it back, clasping it to her chest.

"On second thought"—he licked his lips—"perhaps you don't need to get dressed quite yet."

He stared down at her, and her skin grew hot under his intense gaze. She pulled the blanket tighter, tucking it under her arms. He chuckled. The low male sound made her nipples tighten.

His fingers reached for the blanket again.

And this time, she let go.

Sometime later, they lay cocooned together under that same blanket. The rain had stopped, and bright afternoon sunshine spilled across the room.

"Christ, it's getting late," Theo groaned, chest rumbling beneath her cheek.

"Mmm," Bonnie mumbled, perfectly content to stay curled up right here on the couch with him all day.

"We really should get moving." Theo wriggled out from under her, evacuating their blanket nest. "I have one or two other matters needing my attention, and then we can be off."

"Off where?" She rolled to her side, enjoying the view as he pulled on his pants.

"Have you forgotten about your surprise?" Theo asked. "Now, there's a pot of tea on the counter, and a loaf of bread to make toast." He bent down, grabbing his shirt off the floor and kissing her cheek. "Be ready to leave within the hour."

"Yes, Your Grace," Bonnie mumbled at his retreating back. *Someone can be bossy.* She pressed her hand to her cheek where he'd kissed her, recalling last night, when he'd placed a soft kiss on the same spot. She smiled, laughter bubbling up again at the way he'd said "Thank you" in the epitome of British manners, right after pounding into her from behind, brutal and uncontrolled, like a beast let off its leash. Heat pooled in her belly, and she curled into herself, savoring the sweet sharp sting lingering between her legs.

But he was right, it was getting late, even for her Saturday morning sleeping habits, and she definitely wanted to find out what his surprise was. Gathering her things, blanket wrapped around her, Bonnie shuffled off to change.

By the time Theo returned, Bonnie had managed to locate an upstairs bathroom with a shower and was dressed and ready to go. She'd even had a little time to explore the cottage and was more smitten than ever. On the opposite end of the main floor was a large sunroom overlooking the undulating slopes of hillside meadows. Bonnie wanted to spend the evening in there and watch the sunset through the tall wall of windows, maybe write in her journal. She'd brought it along in case her muse decided to pay her a visit. After all, the Lake District was the source of inspiration for such literary greats as Coleridge and William Wordsworth.

They'd been on the road about twenty minutes, the last few clouds from the morning's storm drifting away, when Theo drove the car through a small village and parked alongside a churchyard.

"A cemetery? Is this my surprise?" Bonnie gave Theo some side-eye. "Wouldn't that be RIP, not LMP?"

"This is just a bonus stop *on the way* to your surprise." Theo chuckled, stepping around the car, and held her door open. "And it's not just any cemetery. This is St. Oswald's. One of my country's finest poets is buried here."

"I didn't know you liked poetry."

"I don't really," he confessed.

She snorted.

"But I do appreciate this man's poems." Theo led her through the graveyard, stone monuments still dripping with the remains of the morning storm. "Here we are," he said, coming to a stop.

Bonnie read the inscription. "Oh, Wordsworth. I was just thinking about him this morning."

"I believe it. His life and work are woven into the history of the Lakelands. What I liked best about him is how he strived to preserve the beauty of this land, to prevent his generation from destroying it for future generations. To provide for the future."

"I didn't know that," Bonnie admitted. "His work has never been a big part of my studies. I remember 'I Wandered Lonely as a Cloud' but that's about it."

"That's what most people remember." Theo grinned, raising an eyebrow in challenge. "Can you recall the last line of that poem?"

Bonnie scrunched up her face, thinking. "Something to do with daffodils."

"Not bad." Theo turned to face her. Clasping their hands together, he recited:

For oft, when on my couch I lie,
In vacant or in pensive mood,
They flash upon that inward eye
Which is the bliss of solitude;
And then my heart with pleasure fills,
And dances with the Daffodils.

His rich, crisp voice rolled over the words. Bonnie listened, transfixed. The man should be performing Shakespeare.

Still cradling her hands, he stared down at her palms, tracing a finger across the grooves in her skin. "It's about the power of memory," Theo explained, running his forefinger across her palm. "The happiness one experiences through reimagining an experience." His fingers trailed over the mound at the base of her thumb. "The pleasure it brings."

Bonnie shivered, her body infusing with heat, pulse throbbing in her wrists and at her throat. She could feel every heavy beat of her heart, the thick rush of blood in her veins—that's what this man did to her, made her aware of how alive she was. She shook herself.

"Considering our *experience* this morning," she observed, voice droll, "that poem is startlingly appropriate."

"How so?" Theo asked, guiding her across the slick grass toward the wrought-iron gate.

"Oh, you know, lying on a couch, being filled with pleasure . . ." She nudged him with her elbow.

"I'll never hear that poem in the same way again." Theo's eyes crinkled with laughter. "Are you ready for your surprise?"

In a way, this stop at Wordsworth's grave had been a surprise. It had revealed a side of Theo she hadn't expected. Not sure what else to expect, she nodded. "I'm ready. Surprise me."

They walked through the cemetery and then strolled down to the village square. At the doorway to a tea shop, he paused. "I admit to having an ulterior motive by taking you here."

"Am I finally going to discover the secret behind the mysterious LMP?"

"Actually, yes." He beamed and held the door open, following her inside.

"Lemon meringue pie? My big surprise is pie?" Bonnie sat next to Theo in a booth, staring at the dish of fluffiness he'd presented to her.

"This isn't just *any* pie. This is the most perfect slice of heaven you will find on Earth." Theo stuffed a bite into his mouth, the groan emanating from his throat nearly pornographic.

Residual shivers tickled Bonnie's spine as she recalled the way he'd groaned in much the same way last night when she'd wiggled on top of him, his cock deep inside her. "If you say so." She poked at the scoop of meringue crowning her slice.

"I can't help but notice you seem distracted," Theo said, regarding her over another forkful. "Tell me, if you had to pick one food that carried you off to a state of pure bliss, what would it be?"

That was an easy one. Without hesitating a beat, Bonnie replied, "Gingerbread."

"Really?" He cocked a brow at her. "Are you serious?"

"Oh yeah, I love it."

"Then, I may have *another* surprise for you today," Theo mused. "What's that old saying? The key to a man's heart is through his stomach?" He swallowed another bite. "Do you think the same can be said for a woman?"

"You pose an interesting question." Bonnie rested her chin in her hand, watching him devour her slice of pie as well, and forced herself to remain casual. Inside, her mind had begun to race. *What if he already has my heart?*

At first, she was worried she'd been using Theo to fill the hole Gabe left. But it wasn't that. It wasn't that at all. Theo wasn't Gabe—she didn't want him to be. And she was beginning to think she wasn't the same Bonnie.

"Shall we test my theory?" Theo asked, tongue darting out to lick a speck of lemon from the tip of his fork.

"Sure," she breathed, gaze locked on his lips.

He slid off the bench and held his arm out to her. Again, she took it without question, her body fitting against him easily. They crossed the village square, retracing their steps. "Where are we going?"

He pressed a kiss to the top of her head. "You'll see."

She didn't have to wait long to find out. On the other side of St. Oswald's Church, opposite from where he'd parked the car, stood the Grasmere Gingerbread Shop. Before they'd reached the green picket fence surrounding the shop, Bonnie could smell the rich aroma of baking gingerbread. She inhaled a lungful of molasses and spice, and now she was the one groaning in pornographic pleasure. And she hadn't even tasted it yet.

"An I had but one penny in the world, thou shouldst have it to buy gingerbread," Theo quoted.

She glanced up at him. "I know that's Shakespeare, but I'm drawing a blank on the play."

"*Love's Labour's Lost*," he said, following behind as she made a beeline for the counter where a woman dressed in an old-fashioned apron and kerchief was handing out samples.

"How is it you remember that?" she demanded, a tad embarrassed he'd outdone her.

"The Shakespeare quote about gingerbread?" the woman asked, offering Bonnie a bite-sized square.

Bonnie took it and nodded.

"It's on a sign out front," the woman said.

"You don't say." She eyed Theo over her shoulder, then popped the gingerbread into her mouth and forgot to be annoyed, forgot to be anything but a mouth and a tongue, tasting and chewing and, "Oh," she moaned, "oh, God, that's good."

"Best in the world." The woman nodded. "Says so on a sign out front too." She winked.

"You're right," she told Theo, accepting another sample from the woman. "I'm in love. Leave me here. I'm going to marry this gingerbread."

That evening Theo sorted through the pile of notes he'd taken while walking the property with the groundskeeper. Luckily, the cottage was in good repair. But still, there were several layers to the rental endeavor, from permits to insurance to marketing—and all of it was bloody expensive and time consuming.

As he feared, to have any hope of making the venture profitable, the cottage would have to be let out most of the year. It was selfish, he knew, to balk at giving this place up. Especially since he wasn't giving it up, exactly. But he wouldn't be able to pop in for a weekend holiday whenever the mood struck. Not that he'd been doing much of that.

But he also knew opening this place to the public would change it in ways that couldn't be measured in a ledger. Unlike the Abbey, which had always felt more like a museum than a house, the Lakeland Cottage was small, private, and felt more like a home than anywhere else in the world.

Setting the paperwork aside, Theo glanced over to where Bonnie sat on the other side of the cracked leather settee. The solar was perhaps his favorite spot in the cottage. The furniture was well-worn and comfortable, a collection of pieces relocated here once deemed unfit for other rooms. Appropriate, since anything placed in this room would soon start to fade after long days in the sun. The wall of windows overlooked the hills stretching up toward the Cumbrian sky, a breathtaking sight that never got old or faded, no matter how many years went by.

He eased back, pulling her legs onto his lap and rubbing his thumbs against her soles, gently massaging her feet. She glanced up at him, her pen pausing on the page. A smile passed between them, full of quiet contentment. Then she dropped her chin and resumed her scribbling. Leaving her to her thoughts, Theo enjoyed the simple pleasure of her nearness and the beauty of a summer twilight.

When the sky was full dark, he shifted his attention to her again. "How's the writing going?"

"Good." She arched her back, twisting her neck from side to side. "This place is working wonders for my muse."

"Your muse, hmm?"

"Yeah, she likes it here." Bonnie set her book and pen aside.

"What about you?" he asked. "Do you like it here?"

"I *love* it here." Her feet were still resting on his lap, and she stretched, pointing and flexing her toes.

Theo's heart swelled. It did something to him, to know she felt the same way about this place as he did. He wrapped his fingers around one of her ankles. "I'm glad you came up here with me." He moved his hand up, brushing the tender skin of her calf.

"I'm glad you asked." She smiled at him, closing her eyes as he massaged the soft curve of muscle. "Will it be hard for you?" she wondered, eyes still closed. "Having to rent the cottage out?"

"Yes," he admitted, again surprised by his honesty. "But I can't let my personal feelings get in the way of a sound business decision. It's not just about me. The Emberton holdings are sort of like a corporation. The Lindseys have worked here at the cottage since before I was born, it's all they know. And at the Abbey? Most of the town works for our family in some capacity. If we lose the Abbey, they'd likely lose their livelihoods."

"That's a big responsibility." Bonnie opened her eyes and watched him, brow furrowed in empathy.

"Enough about my duke stuff." Theo shifted, reaching for her other leg. "Tell me about your writing. What are you working on?" he asked, nodding toward her journal.

"I'm not sure yet," she said. "I have some story ideas, and I'm just kind of jotting them all down, seeing where they go."

"You enjoy writing, then?"

"Mostly. Sometimes it's incredibly frustrating. But I always come back to it." Her voice dropped, the tone almost shy as she continued, "It's been so long since I've spent any real time writing I'm still getting my bearings, figuring out what the story needs."

"How do you do that?" he wondered.

"Play around with the characters, throw different things at them until I find what works." She shifted her free leg, and her foot grazed his groin.

He stiffened—everywhere. "Why did you stop writing for so long?"

"Life." She went back to doodling on her paper. "I was too focused on all the things I thought I wanted, like a husband and a teaching career." The corner of her mouth turned up. "I was wrong about the husband . . . and lately, I've been wondering if I was wrong about the career too."

"You don't enjoy teaching?" Theo asked, running his fingers up and down her leg. She'd mentioned her breakup but didn't seem as bitter about it as before. If anything, she was more . . . resigned.

"Not as much as I thought I would." She shrugged. "I mean, it's not terrible, and the classes I've taught this summer have been really cool, but overall . . . yeah. No." Bonnie laughed and looked up at him. "Did that make any sense at all?"

Theo nodded. "Sure," he said, stroking the back of her knee. "You need to figure out what you need."

"I do, huh?" she asked, blue eyes flashing. "I think I know what I need right now," she purred, sliding the foot he wasn't holding back and forth. He bit his lip, his cock getting harder with each brush of her leg.

"I can't wait to hear more." His fingers crept up her thigh. "Why don't we go upstairs, and you can tell me."

"I thought you couldn't wait," she teased.

"Well, let's see how fast you can get ready for bed," he teased back.

"Like a race?" she asked.

"If you want it to be."

"Okay." She sat up, sliding her feet to the floor. "On your mark, get set, go!" She was off like a shot, racing out of the room before the last word was out of her mouth.

Theo stood, thundering up the stairs behind her. He didn't mind if she beat him. The way he saw it, anything that got her in bed faster was a win.

CHAPTER 24

THE FOLLOWING MORNING, Bonnie got out of bed early. Admittedly, she'd had some help from Theo, who'd woken her by pressing kisses all over her face and neck, coarse stubble tickling her cheeks before he abandoned her for the shower.

Bonnie tightened the little ribbon on the bodice of her nightgown and made her way down the stairs toward the kitchen. She loved the creek of the wooden floorboards beneath her, and imagined Theo as a child, racing across these floors, eager to get down to the creek to catch fish. She stood for a moment, still picturing that little boy as she stared out the window above the large farmhouse sink. Sunlight sparkled on the dewy grass, turning the meadow into a cache of diamonds.

What would it be like to live here? Wake up every day to this view, raise a family here? She could picture it almost too easily. An ache burned in the back of her throat. With effort, Bonnie swallowed. She needed to stop having those kinds of thoughts. She wasn't supposed to be thinking about the future. Besides, Theo had said his family was planning to rent this place out. Her heart twisted as she recalled his reluctance for the idea stamped plainly on his face.

Bonnie filled the kettle with fresh water and set it to boil. While it heated, she fussed about, setting out plates and teacups. She rummaged in the butler's pantry and was rewarded with a lovely tiered tray that would do perfectly. She set it on the table and pulled out some of the treats they'd brought back from yesterday's excursion.

As she arranged the gingerbread on the tray she began to hum, anticipating Theo's smile when he came downstairs and discovered breakfast was ready. The kettle whistled, interrupting her thoughts, and she filled a teapot with hot water, added the leaves, and set it on the table as well. She stood back, admiring her work.

"My word, this is all very domestic."

Bonnie turned, catching Theo's gaze as he entered the kitchen. His dark hair was slicked back, face freshly shaven. "Morning." She gestured at the table. "I hope you don't mind. I thought I'd—"

"It's perfect," he said, crossing the room and pulling her into his arms. "I can't imagine a better way to start the day."

She nuzzled into him, enjoying his clean, fresh scent.

"Well," he mused, voice rumbling in his chest, "there might be something better." His hands reached around, squeezing her bottom.

"Hey." She swatted at him. "Those buns aren't for breakfast."

"Oh no?" He dropped to his knees, nipping at her with his teeth.

"Theo!" She laughed, trying to wiggle out of his grip, but he held her tight, nibbling on her butt through the thin fabric of her nightgown.

The sound of a throat clearing, loudly, made Bonnie freeze. She glanced up to find the housekeeper hovering in the doorway. It was clear from the bright red hue of her apple cheeks she'd been there for some time. "Morning, Mrs. Lindsey," she managed, sure her cheeks were equally on fire.

From somewhere behind Bonnie came a muffled, "How are you today?"

"Fine, Your Grace, just fine." The housekeeper studied her toes. "I see you have breakfast handled."

"Ah, yes. Thank you." Theo got to his feet and helped himself to a square of gingerbread. He took a casual bite, as if nothing were amiss. As if he hadn't just been sinking his teeth into Bonnie's ass.

Bonnie busied herself with pouring the tea.

Mrs. Lindsey didn't move, but remained in the doorway, hands twisting in her apron. "Begging Your Grace's pardon, but her ladyship called. She'd like a word with you."

"My mother rang you at the cottage?" Theo frowned, brushing crumbs from his fingers. "Why didn't she try me on my bloody mobile?"

"She did, sir. Um, several times, I believe." The woman spared him a pitying glance. "She's in a right mood, sir. You best be returning her call."

"Right." Theo sighed. "Thank you."

Mrs. Lindsey nodded, offered Bonnie a shy smile, and then hurried out the way she'd come in.

"Is something wrong?" Bonnie asked.

"Don't know." Theo retrieved his phone from the sitting room, where he'd left it charging last night. He scrolled through his phone messages, brow furrowing. Three missed calls from his mother.

While he listened to his voice mail, Bonnie began packing up the breakfast things. The playful mood that had filled the kitchen with laughter only a few minutes ago evaporated.

Sure enough, after a moment he pocketed his phone, offering her an apologetic half smile. "I'm sorry, love, but we need to head back."

"Right now?" Bonnie couldn't help asking. "Are you sure?" She wasn't ready to go back to the real world. She wanted a few more hours here, alone, with him.

He nodded, but she could see how much he wanted to stay too. "I'm sure," he said, jaw tight, mouth a thin, grim line. "My presence has been commanded."

Theo stormed into the conservatory of the Abbey, where his mother sat enjoying the late afternoon sun. "All right, what's so bloody important?" he demanded.

His mother did not look up from her pile of "knitting." He couldn't believe, all these years later, she still indulged in this farce. Nobody cared if she wanted to read the gossip rags. Didn't she know that? She continued to ignore him, and he realized she was waiting for him to greet her properly. No matter if her meddling was going to ruin his life, the niceties must be observed.

Reining in his temper, he stepped to her side and bowed, taking her hand. "Good afternoon, Mama."

"Good afternoon, son. Did you have a pleasant trip?"

"No, I did not. It came to a rather abrupt end, but I believe you know that already," he seethed. *Patience.* "What was so important that my immediate presence was demanded? What's wrong?"

"I do apologize for the inconvenience to you, I'm sure you were *quite* busy up at the cottage." His mother set her knitting aside, taking care to make sure the magazine they both knew was beneath the pile of yarn was well-covered.

"I had an enlightening chat with Mrs. Lindsey on the telephone this morning."

Ah. Theo narrowed his eyes, the pieces coming together. His mother knew about Bonnie, then. Poor Mrs. Lindsey, she probably hadn't the slightest chance once his mother sunk her claws into her. And it's not like Theo had asked the housekeeper to keep the information about his overnight guest private.

"Really, Theo, what were you thinking, taking some girl, some *American*, to our summer home?"

I was thinking I wanted to spend time with someone who made me happy. To share a piece of myself that meant something, to show her a place that was important to me. But none of that mattered to his mother because you couldn't put a price on it.

"What I was thinking is not your concern." Theo wasn't going to let her guilt trip him with her absurd notions of propriety. She could give him a scowl worthy of winning the Snooty Dame of the Year award, but he was not budging. "Besides, what does it matter? You were ready to let the cottage to perfect strangers."

"About that, what's your opinion? Do you wish to move forward with the plan?" His mother raised an eyebrow, her tone belying her usual subtlety, "Or, now that you've apparently had some time to sow a few wild oats, are you ready to consider other options?"

Her look made Theo feel like he was the one on the market, not the cottage. Heat crept up his cheeks.

"But I didn't ask you to come home simply to call you to the carpet." She waved him toward her, and he helped her rise from her chair. "I have some important news to share with you. And I wanted to speak with you alone. Your sisters are out for the day. Come, take a turn in the garden with me."

Gritting his teeth, Theo took his mother's hand, and she leaned on him, her balance a bit unsteady. Theo held her arm, escorting her outside in silence. He didn't bother trying to engage in conversation again, knowing she wouldn't speak to him until they were well away from the house and out of earshot of the "tongue-wagging help."

Sure enough, it wasn't until they had passed under the arch of wisteria and retreated into the walled garden that his mother said, "You seem agitated, my boy. What's on your mind?"

"I'm trying to recall the maximum prison sentence for matricide," Theo muttered.

His mother made a scoffing noise of dry amusement in the back of her throat. "Have no fear, you won't need to concern yourself with the penalty for that crime." She stopped, settling herself carefully on a stone bench. "That's my news, you see. I won't be around to pester you much longer."

Theo's jaw fell open. He'd been joking. His mother, however, didn't jest. "You're serious, aren't you?"

"Oh, quite," she agreed. "Six months, according to the oncologist. A year, perhaps."

The stone-cold calm of her voice chilled the marrow in Theo's bones. He joined her on the bench. "Oncologist? What are you saying, Mama?" He stared at his mother. She'd seemed different lately, not herself, but he'd never thought . . .

"Cancer. Neuroendocrine tumor of the lungs. Which I'm told is quite rare. Always nice to hear one is special."

"Mama," Theo began, but stopped, at a complete loss. Floored by his mother's revelation. "How long have you known?"

"For some time."

Some time. Christ, that could be weeks, months, bloody years, even. "Why haven't you said anything?"

His mother coughed and suddenly Theo found himself listening closer. Should he have recognized symptoms? Were there signs he should have been aware of? A cold fist gripped his heart, squeezing, blood pumping icy rivers of fear and recrimination through his veins. Theo couldn't help asking. "Why tell me now?"

"Wipe that look off your face. I'm not dying today," his mother snapped, coughing again. "I had been waiting on a second opinion, can't trust those people to get it right. But it seems both specialists are in agreement. The diagnosis remains unchanged."

Theo schooled his features; he knew how much his mother detested pity.

"I've told you first," she continued. "I'll speak with your sisters when I'm ready, once I have a better idea what the treatment plan shall be."

"You can't expect me to keep this from them."

"I can, and I will." His mother eyed him, chin set, mouth pinched, *Snooty Dame Monthly* frown in place. "I want your word on this, Theodore."

His heart seized with a sudden swell of affection for his mother. She was so stiff, so stubborn, even now. Cancer didn't stand a bloody chance against her. "Of course, Mama."

"I want you to promise me something else."

Theo steeled himself. He sensed, deep in his gut, what was coming.

"When your father was born, outside of the royal family, twenty-eight peers of the realm held the title of duke. Now there are only twenty-four. You know how many centuries-old titles are on the verge of collapsing without an heir to perpetuate the line, let alone how many noble families can't afford to maintain their birthright."

"If the last few Embertons hadn't been such pathetic excuses for the role of head of household, we wouldn't be in this mess," he muttered.

"I quite agree with you," his mother said. "But for all his failings, your father did his duty. I myself was a wealthy young heiress once and counted myself lucky to snare a duke. I elevated the status of my family, and in return, the funds I brought to my marriage kept this estate alive, ensuring hundreds of people remained gainfully employed." She made to rise from the bench, and Theo moved closer, offering his arm for support.

They continued through the rose garden, moving on to the kitchen gardens closer to the house. Christ, the people employed to tend the grounds and gardens alone numbered in the dozens. His mother had a point. Who was he to take their livelihood away, to tell them they had to seek work somewhere else? Most of the people on the estate's payroll had been working for the Embertons for generations. And he was going to let that come to an end simply because he wanted to follow his heart?

Over the last few days, he'd allowed himself to imagine a different kind of life, a simpler one, quiet and cozy with Bonnie. They'd take up residence in the cottage. She'd work on her books, have the time she'd never had to write to her heart's content, and he'd set up an office and manage the Wharton holdings from there.

In the few quiet hours they'd spent together, he'd built an entire future with her. It was reckless and ridiculous, and he should have known better. It was a dream, a fantasy he indulged in for a weekend. But now, it was time to get back to reality. Deep down, he and his mother both knew he would never let all those people down, nor allow the Abbey to fall out of Emberton hands—not if he had the power to stop it.

As he escorted her up the steps to the house, his mother added, "Son, even if our plan to rent the Lakeland property pans out, it still won't be enough. It's a temporary solution. You know this. You have a head for numbers. I am sure you have seen the writing on the wall. It is only a matter of time."

Theo did know. And now that he'd reviewed the costs involved with renting the cottage, the solution was even more temporary than he'd originally thought. "You're right, Mama."

"There now." His mother smiled up at him. "I knew you would agree." For the first time in Theo's life, he'd almost say she was beaming. "By the way, you should know I've taken it upon myself to invite Lady Camille to tea."

Theo swallowed, his smile decidedly less bright while the doors of fate sealed shut as surely as the gate to the conservatory swung closed behind them.

Bonnie sat on the bed in her dorm room, staring at a blank page. As she had every night since her abrupt departure from Theo on Sunday, she'd tried to take her mind off things by writing a bit before going to sleep. But her ideas had abandoned her. She was pretty sure her muse was still hanging out in the Lake District, the traitor.

Not that Bonnie could blame her, she didn't want to leave the cottage either. If it was possible to fall in love with a place, she'd given her heart this weekend. It was as close to love at first sight as she'd ever come. Everything about the cottage felt right. As if it had been waiting for her to arrive, and now that she had, life could begin.

Not just her, but her and Theo together. The sense of

peace she'd felt when she'd sat stretched out on the cracked leather sofa, feet in his lap like they were an old married couple instead of two people still learning their way around each other. For a moment, she'd thought, she could stay in that house forever, live there with Theo until they were as old and gray as Mr. and Mrs. Lindsey. Bonnie imagined herself writing in the little sunroom, their children playing in the meadow, lit with the golden glow of the sunset.

This. She'd thought. *This is what I need.*

But it wasn't real. It was a fantasy.

Then why had it felt so right?

Clearly, Theo had not felt the same way. She shouldn't be surprised. They'd both agreed on friends with benefits. No strings attached. Once she'd started forming an attachment, he'd cut loose and bailed.

Bonnie had tried calling him several times after he'd dropped her off at the train station on Sunday evening, wondering what had happened that he needed to head home so quickly, hoping everything was okay. But he never answered his phone. Didn't return her phone calls or reply to her texts. Nothing but silence. He'd ghosted. Abandoned her as quickly as Willoughby had Marianne.

She got through the week one hour at a time, each piece of her day a stepping stone leading to the next. If she kept her attention on what she was doing, kept hopping from class to café to writing, kept moving forward, she'd get through to the next day. And she'd moved through the week in just that way—until Thursday—when her phone rang, lighting up with Theo's number.

Her thumb hovered over the answer key. Seeing his number on her phone now, after giving up hope, she was tempted to ignore it. But that was something the old Bonnie would do. Ignore the problem, worry about it tomorrow, deal it with another day. No. New Bonnie would deal with this now. "Hello?"

"Bonnie?"

Except, it wasn't Theo she was dealing with. "Tabitha?" she guessed at the identity of the female voice on the line.

"Got it in one!" Theo's sister laughed. "Look, he's probably going to kill me for nicking his phone, but I didn't have your number and was hoping we could talk."

"About what?" Maybe he had a good reason for avoiding her this week. Maybe it really wasn't his fault.

"Your friend's hen do, remember?"

"Of course." *Or maybe not.*

"Listen, I was thinking, I have loads of ideas and would love to go over them with you, but we should get together soon, seeing as the party is supposed to be end of next week."

Oh, God, that's right. Bonnie had been doing such a good job focusing on each day as it came, she'd completely blocked out what was next. "I appreciate the offer, I really do—"

"You're not getting rid of me that easy," Tabitha cut her off.

"I'm not?" *Why did Theo's sister care about this anyway?*

"Are you free tomorrow afternoon, around teatime?"

"Yes, actually." Tomorrow was Friday, and she was done chaperoning excursions.

"Take the train to the same station Theo picked you up at when he borrowed my car, the one near the Abbey. I'll come fetch you. You remember what my car looks like, right?"

"Sure . . ."

"Brilliant. See you then."

CHAPTER 25

STILL NOT COMPLETELY sure why she'd agreed to this, on Friday afternoon, Bonnie stood on the train station platform and watched for Tabitha. She recognized the car Theo had picked her up in exactly one week ago and stepped off the curb as it screeched to a halt in front of her.

"Hey!" Tabitha offered Bonnie a grin. "You in?" She peeled out of the parking lot before Bonnie had time to respond.

Bonnie buckled her seat belt and double-checked to make sure her door was securely locked. Of the two siblings, Theo was undoubtedly the more conservative driver.

In minutes, Tabitha was zooming past a gatehouse. "Here we are," she said, waving to the attendant as she flew by, twisting and turning along a neatly groomed gravel road through manicured gardens and parks. Bonnie spotted several deer as she stared out the window, keeping her eyes peeled for any sign of Theo's home.

Finally, after a mile or so, they rounded a bend, and Bonnie got her first glimpse of the Emberton family seat. If she'd had her doubts before, seeing Theo's house confirmed it. House was inadequate. Even mansion didn't begin to cover it. This was a palace. A residence fit for royalty . . . or the highest-ranking non-royal peer of the realm.

"Whoa," Bonnie breathed. It was the only sound she could manage.

"It's a lot to take in, I know," Tabitha agreed, her voice tinged with a good-natured note of self-consciousness. "One gets used to it."

Does one? This was not some fantasy; it was real life. And for Bonnie, it marked the beginning of the end to any dreams she may have still harbored in her heart for a future with Theo. What business did she have thinking she could be with a duke? Their lives were further apart than Lizzie and Darcy even.

Setting a brisk pace, Tabitha led Bonnie inside and through a maze of halls. Overwhelmed with the urge to dawdle and gawk at everything, Bonnie struggled to keep up. She could easily imagine how this place employed most of a town. It was the size of one.

Passing through another series of arches, Bonnie followed Tabitha as she rounded a corner into a small foyer. An older woman was exiting a room, tray in hand.

"Marjorie."

"Yes, Lady Tabitha?"

"Are they taking tea in the blue drawing room?"

"They are indeed."

"Brilliant. I believe we shall join them." Tabitha flashed a curiously wicked smile in Bonnie's direction. "This way."

It was odd to hear Theo's sister, the girl she'd met laughing and joking in Piccadilly Square, the girl who drove like she was qualifying for the Indy 500, referred to as "Lady." Tabitha walked like she was racing too. Bonnie quickened her steps, catching up to Tabitha just as she was opening a wide double door.

"Tabitha, you're late," a woman's cool clipped voice observed. Bonnie followed Theo's sister into the room and the voice added, "And I see you brought a guest."

The utter disapproval mixed with a strong dose of irritation made Bonnie pause, but Tabitha kept moving, briskly crossing the elegant room lined in pale blue wallpaper. In a moment, Tabitha had arranged two chairs near each other and was waving Bonnie over. Forcing her feet to move, Bonnie joined them.

Unfazed by the less than warm welcome, Tabitha offered the older woman seated next to a large tea tray a breezy smile. "Mama, I'd like you to meet my new friend, Miss Bonnie . . ." Tabitha trailed off, glancing back at Bonnie.

"Blythe," Bonnie supplied. *Should she curtsy or something?*

"Bonnie Blythe," Tabitha repeated.

Bonnie smiled weakly.

"Tabitha," Theo's mother sniffed, ignoring Bonnie completely, "if you're planning to remain, do sit down and get on with it before the tea grows cold."

Bonnie took the seat Tabitha offered her, thinking if the tea was cold, it was probably due to Theo's mother's frosty glare. Ice cubes clinked in Bonnie's stomach as she sat. Tabitha poured out a cup for each of them, nodding at the two girls seated together on a settee. "These are my sisters," she began.

"Thalia and Tessa, right?" Bonnie asked, recalling her conversation with Theo.

"Right. I'm Tessa," the younger-looking girl of the two replied, rolling her eyes. "Not 'baby Tessa.' And don't get me started on the *T* thing."

"You're talking to Bonnie Blythe, remember?" Bonnie grinned, relaxing the tiniest bit.

"Good point." The other girl laughed. "And I'm Thalia."

"Theo." Tabitha's grin turned sly as she glanced at her brother. "I believe you've already made Miss Blythe's acquaintance?"

"Yes," Theo grunted, hands fisted awkwardly at his sides, blue eyes icy as he returned his sister's smile. That he was pissed, was obvious. It was the why Bonnie wondered about. He'd been the one ignoring her calls. He turned toward Bonnie and nodded his head. "I've had the pleasure."

A rush of heat crept up Bonnie's neck at his choice of words while her brain provided a few reminders of exactly what kind of pleasures she and Theo had shared. Good God, this was awkward.

Theo's mother coughed loudly.

Unperturbed, Tabitha turned her attention to the woman seated next to Theo. "Lady Camille, how's it going?" Tabitha asked.

"Lady Tabitha, it's 'going' quite splendidly, thank you." The woman smiled at Tabitha before turning her attention to Bonnie. "I believe we've met as well, in Chicago."

"Oh?" Bonnie looked more closely at the woman and realized she did look familiar. She'd been having tea with Theo last time she saw her. "Right. At the Drake." She forced her lips into a smile. "Nice to see you again, uh . . . *Lady* Camille." Was this woman the reason Theo had been ignoring her? Why he hadn't called? Was she part of the big emergency that he'd raced home for, forgetting Bonnie even existed?

"Camille is fine," she said, giving Bonnie a sweet smile. Loose blond curls that reminded Bonnie of Sadie bobbed as she shook her head.

Despite herself, Bonnie returned the smile. The woman's sunny nature and kind face put her at ease. Unfortunately, that ease didn't last long.

Theo's mother tilted her chin, managing to stare haughtily down at her son despite being more than a head shorter. "Am I to understand you had tea with *both* ladies? How terribly rude of you, Theo, to be entertaining one guest and then invite another."

"That's not what happened," Theo said, voice so clipped it could trim hedges.

Bonnie followed the conversation, head bobbing like a ping-pong ball. Did "have tea" mean something else in England? Because really, what was the big deal?

"It was all quite civil, Your Grace," Camille assured Theo's mother. "Merely a happy accident. Your son was the perfect gentleman, and I was delighted with the opportunity to meet one of his friends."

"That is kind of you to say, my dear girl, but I would expect nothing less from a well-bred lady such as yourself."

If Bonnie wasn't mistaken, Theo's mother had just delivered one hell of a passive-aggressive insult. What had she done to earn such venom from someone she'd never met before?

Bonne felt her cheeks heat and wished she could fade right into the furniture.

"Camille," Tabitha said, stepping into the fray and boldly taking the reins of the conversation, "tell us what a well-bred lady such as yourself was doing in Chicago."

One of Theo's sisters sputtered into her teacup.

"Grad school for International Relations." Camille offered Tabitha a smile, not a bitchy-sweet smile, but a real smile, and Bonnie wondered if the girl was super nice or super oblivious.

"Admirable." Theo's mother nodded her head. "She'll make a fine partner for the right man. Don't you think so, Theodore?"

Taking his choked reply as an affirmative, she went on to say, "Lady Camille will soon be finished with her studies; you'd be wise not to let this one get away."

Heavy-handed there much, Lady Catherine? Bonnie had often wished to be in the middle of an Austen novel. Only now that she was, she couldn't wait to escape.

By the time the ordeal of tea was over, and Tabitha had led Bonnie through another maze of stairwells and halls, the ice cubes in her stomach had melted, leaving a luke-warm sense of dread sloshing in its place.

"I thought we could talk in my room," Tabitha said, opening a door and waving Bonnie inside.

Surprisingly, the bedroom of a twenty-something member of a ducal family was actually pretty normal.

"Have a seat." Tabitha gestured at the chair in front of a desk and flopped down on her bed, pulling a cell phone out of the back pocket of her jeans. "Let me show you what I was thinking for the hen do."

Bonnie sat. While Tabitha scrolled through her phone, Bonnie glanced around, taking in the photos littering the desk of Tabitha with her friends, smiling and goofing off. A soft smile lit inside her when she saw one of Tabitha posing with Theo and their two sisters. She thought of the tea party debacle downstairs. It was clear Tabitha had orchestrated their arrival on purpose.

"Why did you call me?" Bonnie suddenly asked, not caring if she sounded rude. "I mean, really."

"Totally because I want to help plan your friend's party," Tabitha said, blue eyes wide and guileless.

Bonnie gave Theo's sister her best teacher-done-taking-shit stare.

"Okay, fine," Tabitha admitted, taking a breath before she added, "because I also want to help my brother."

"What does he need help with?" Bonnie asked, tension lacing up the muscles along her spine.

"Pulling his head out of his arse."

"Is that all?" Bonnie laughed, relaxing a smidge. "Why do you think he needs help with that?"

"Because he has a hero complex." Tabitha reached for the picture of Theo and her sisters. "And our mum totally feeds into it. I'm sorry she was such a bloody dragon to you, by the way."

"Oh, um, it's okay." Bonnie waved a hand, flustered.

"No, it's not. She went full snooty dame on you." Tabitha screwed her face into a comically accurate copy of her mother's haughty frown. Then she heaved a sigh. "But I know, deep down in her poor, misguided, blue-blooded heart, she believes she's doing the right thing."

"How does Theo feel about it?" Bonnie asked. Though, really, she was dying to ask how he felt about Camille.

"My brother believes he must put the needs of the family above his own," Tabitha intoned in a deep solemn voice.

"Is that why he pulled a Willoughby on me?"

"Pardon?"

"Willoughby." Bonnie clasped her hands together. "He's a character in *Sense and Sensibility*."

"The Jane Austen novel?" Tabitha asked, brow furrowed. "Which one was he?"

"Very romantic. Handsome and dashing. Marianne, the heroine's sister, falls in love with him, and he with her."

"That doesn't sound so bad," Tabitha mused.

"Yes, well, it isn't. Until Willoughby drops Marianne like a hot coal and disappears without a word. No explanations. Later, when they run into each other at a party, he gives her the cut direct while making nice with a rich heiress." Bonnie glanced at Theo's sister, shaking her head. "Sound familiar yet?"

Tabitha let out a bark of apologetic laughter. "Look, my brother was wrong for treating you like that, and you have every right to ditch his ass. But I don't want him to make the most epic mistake of his life simply because he's convinced it's what the family needs. I want him to think about what *he* needs. He deserves to be happy." She set the photo back on the desk and reached for Bonnie's hand. "And you make him happy."

Bonnie squirmed on the chair. This conversation was sounding all too familiar. "How would you know? You barely know me."

"Sibling ESP."

A wry chuckle escaped her. "I don't have any siblings," Bonnie admitted.

"Too bad, I was hoping you had a brother." Tabitha grinned.

"No, just me. But I do have lots of cousins, and they are *all* boys."

"Tempting." Tabitha wiggled her eyebrows. "Trust me. I know my brother. And being with you makes him happy." She squeezed gently. "I know he's acting like an ass right now, but give him a chance to figure things out. Be patient with him. Don't walk away yet." She released her hold on Bonnie's hand.

Bonnie stared down at her hands, focusing, for the first time in months, on her bare left ring finger. She thought of her conversation with Theo in the cottage, about figuring out what she needed. She could give him time. At the very least, the time she had left here in England. She'd be heading home in a little over two weeks.

"Okay," she said, looking up at Theo's sister. "I can do that."

"Brilliant." Tabitha smiled wide, dimples winking merrily. "Now then"—she retrieved her phone—"it's time to get serious. We have a party to plan."

CHAPTER 26

SUMMER SEMINAR WRAPPED up and bags packed, Bonnie had one final cup of tea in the café next to the stationary shop. She had decided to declare this place the winner, though admittedly some favoritism may have affected her ruling. Afterward, she ducked inside the stationary shop one last time and treated herself to another journal with an Austen quote, this time from *Sense and Sensibility*. She was determined to keep writing when she got back home. Her muse had returned, and she wasn't losing her again.

Then she boarded her last train from Cambridge to London, this time to head to the Waldorf, where she and her friends would gather in the same suites they'd stayed in last summer. Together again in one room, sprawled across beds and chairs, it almost felt like they'd never left.

"This is kind of surreal you guys," Ana said as she fiddled with Cassie's hair. "Like multiplayer déjà vu."

"I know. I told Bonnie the same thing. Who'd have thought a year after our big trip, we'd end up back in the exact same place at almost the exact same time?" Delaney shook her head.

"It was so nice of your dad to give us the hook-up again," Cassie thanked Sadie.

"It was no biggie." Sadie yawned, covering her mouth and flopping onto the sofa. She'd been the last to arrive, hitching a red-eye.

Ana glanced up from pulling Cassie's light brown waves into an elegant side braid. "How did this round of auditions go?" she asked around a mouthful of bobby pins.

"I just finished the screen tests." Sadie sighed, digging through her purse to glance at her phone. "They start shooting in September, so I should have an answer soon. My agent is supposed to call me."

"Do you think you'll get it?" Delaney asked, pulling her long strawberry-blond hair into a smooth ponytail.

Sadie shrugged and took out her makeup bag. "The lead was down to me and one other actress." She made a pout, reapplying her lipstick. "Who was at least a decade younger."

"You're totally going to beat out some kid," Bonnie assured Sadie, joining her on the couch. "You have more experience."

"Ugh, experience just means old," Sadie grumbled, inspecting her reflection in her compact. "The character is supposed to be in her twenties."

"You *are* in your twenties!"

Sadie's mouth curled with exasperation. "I may technically be a twenty-something for another few months, but in Hollywood years, I'm ready for AARP."

"That's such bullshit." From her seat in front of Ana, Cassie snorted.

"Tell me about it." Sadie dabbed on some concealer. "In

the minds of most studio execs, when they hear I'm almost thirty, I swear they see a fifty-year-old."

"If you're fifty, I'm a hundred," Delaney said drily.

"Like I said, bullshit." Cassie shook her head.

"Stay still," Ana ordered, stabbing a few more bobby pins in place.

Cassie froze and let Ana finish pinning up her braid. "Ageism is a real problem, especially in the television and film industry. You know, once I wrap up the spotlight on women's sports coverage, I think that's what my next *Chi-Chat* feature could be."

"Fabulous." Ana patted Cassie on the head. "How about we finish your hair first?"

It was half past five, and per Tabitha's instructions, Bonnie had made sure the bride-to-be and her friends had gathered in the hotel's lounge, ready for a night of fun. They were, as Tabitha requested, dressed up, made-up, and ready to booze up.

"Okay, ladies, let's prepare for our adventure!" Tabitha clapped her hands. If there's one thing Bonnie had learned about Theo's sister over the last two weeks, it was that she took the art of partying very seriously. Tabitha circled the group, presenting each of them with a witch hat and a penis wand.

"We're not actually going out in public with these?" Delaney asked, eyes narrowing under the brim of her hat as she studied her wand up close. "Holy fudge bars, this is remarkably detailed for a party favor."

"Accio hottie!" Ana commanded, slashing her penis through the air.

Giggles erupted. "That's the spirit." Tabitha patted Ana on the back with her own wand. "And for our bride, we have . . ." She reached into the tote bag she carried and pulled out a large gold object hung on a chain-loop belt. "The Golden Snatch!"

"Oh my God," Sadie said, eyes wide with horror. "It's hideous."

"It's hilarious!" Ana chortled, handing the belt to Cassie. "Put it on, B2B!"

"B2B?" Cassie asked, wrapping the belt around her waist.

"Bride to be," Ana explained, helping Cassie adjust the snatch.

"You know what they say," Bonnie added, "first one to catch it, wins!"

Cassie glanced up, lips quirking with glee. "Did you just make a sex joke *and* a Harry Potter reference?"

"Um, yeah." Bonnie returned the grin. "I guess I did."

"Well done." Ana tapped the head of her wand against Bonnie's.

"Bitches! Or should I say, witches!" Done dispensing novelty items, Tabitha gathered their attention again. "Do you solemnly swear to be up to no good tonight?"

The girls whistled and cat-called, penis wands twirling.

"Then it's time to get this party started!" She turned, the cape she wore flaring out dramatically. Everyone gathered their things and hurried to catch up.

"That's really Theo's sister?" Cassie whispered, watching as Tabitha sashayed through the Charing Cross station ticket barrier.

"I know. Hard to believe, right?" Bonnie smiled. She knew Theo had a wild side too, he just preferred to keep it hidden. "And she's been great, helped me plan everything. To be honest, she did *all* of the planning, said she really loves this kind of thing."

"Hmm." Cassie grinned. "Too bad she wasn't available to plan my wedding."

"You're getting married in a castle," Bonnie reminded her, stepping on the escalator behind Cassie. "I'd say your wedding is going to be fine."

"Yeah, but remember all the 'fun wedding stuff' I talked about doing? I haven't had time for any of it."

"Champagne problem. You have a thriving career," Bonnie said, hopping over to the next escalator and continuing down to the underground station. "Look, you already have the location. You have the dress, right?"

"Picked it up this morning; it's packed and ready."

"And you have the cake."

"Logan's mam is making it."

"And you have the groom."

"He better be there." Cassie waved her penis wand menacingly as a train pulled up.

Bonnie laughed. "See? You're all set. Don't worry about the future, focus on the now."

"What's going on?' Cassie pretended to inspect Bonnie carefully as they settled into a train car. "Are you the real Bonnie, or did someone take a red curl from her head and make a Polyjuice Potion?"

"You realize most of these references are flying over my head, right?"

"I'd think that was impossible, considering how much you read, but then I remember you prefer books written before women were allowed to wear pants." Cassie gave Bonnie an affectionate poke with her wand. "Now you know how I feel when you're spouting Shakespeare all the time."

"Not all the time!"

"Fine," Cassie relented. "Sometimes you throw an Austen quote in too."

Bonnie laughed. "Is it wrong to admit I have a line from Jane Austen in my maid of honor speech?"

"Don't tell me!" Cassie held up a palm. "That's gotta be bad luck of some kind."

Following "Headmistress Tabitha's" orders once again, they exited the Tube and made their way up Clapham High Street to a nightclub. "Enter! Professor Gwen is waiting with your drink tickets!"

Inside the club, Bonnie spotted Tabitha's friend from that night in Piccadilly standing guard over an empty table. Gwen waved, and Bonnie led the way toward her through the crowd, Tabitha bringing up the rear.

"Nice to see you again." Gwen grinned at Bonnie, handing over the drink tickets.

"We'll take those, thank you." Sadie plucked the tickets from Bonnie's hand.

"Be right back," Ana added with a saucy wink from beneath the brim of her witch hat before following Sadie to the bar.

Bonnie shook her head. "That's Ana and Sadie," she told Gwen. "Otherwise known as double trouble."

"I believe it." Gwen chuckled.

"I'm Delaney, but you can call me Laney." Delaney shook Gwen's hand, her eyes tracking Ana and Sadie's progress at the bar. "If you excuse me a minute, I'm going to go referee those two."

"She can't help it," Bonnie explained. "Laney is a preschool teacher."

"Ah." Gwen nodded and turned to Cassie. "And you must be the bride."

"Thanks so much for helping out!" Cassie gushed.

"You're having fun, then?" Gwen asked.

"Best bachelorette party ever."

"Oh, just you wait, it's going to get even better," Tabitha promised. She exchanged a sly, secret smile with Gwen, but before Bonnie could ask what that was all about, Sadie and Ana returned, carrying trays of shots.

Delaney trailed behind, carrying a fishbowl-sized margarita glass.

"I thought you were going to 'referee' them, Ms. Mason," Bonnie teased.

"Ms. Mason knows a lost cause when she sees one."

Bonnie laughed, watching as Delaney tried to navigate the straw into her mouth while holding the giant glass with both hands.

"Here." Ana passed Bonnie a shot glass.

"What's in this?" Bonnie asked, sniffing the drink. She caught a whiff of cinnamon and high-octane alcohol.

"Liquid Luck," Sadie said, putting a shot glass in each of Cassie's hands before raising one of her own. "To the bride and groom!"

Everyone lifted their glass in the air, repeating the toast. People passing their table stopped to shout congratulations as well as offer bawdy suggestions. Cassie giggled, smiling radiantly as she slapped her two empty glasses on the table. "Mmm, Ffffelix Ffffelicis," she fizzed.

"They say third time's the charm," Tabitha insisted, and pushed another glass toward Cassie with the tip of her wand. "One more shot?"

"You're as bad as they are," Bonnie told Theo's sister, nodding her head at Ana and Sadie.

"Hey, a bride needs a little luck on her wedding night," Sadie said.

"'Cause you know she's getting lucky," Ana added, toasting her partner in crime. "Am I right?"

"Fine, one more," Bonnie agreed, eyeing her friend's pink cheeks and bright eyes. When it came to booze, Cassie was almost as much of a lightweight as she was.

Several more than one shot of Liquid Luck later, Headmistress Tabitha herded the group toward the stage. The club featured a male dance show, and for the next hour or so the bride-to-be and her band of merry mischief makers were entertained by Vikings, gladiators, and cowboys. Currently, several buff guys dressed as cops and firemen were onstage, gyrating to the pounding bass.

"This is doing absolutely zero for me," Delaney grumbled.

"The drink or the dance?" Tabitha wondered.

"The dance," Bonnie answered for Delaney, who was too busy still sucking down a gallon of tequila from her fishbowl. "Delaney has issues when it comes to men in uniform."

"Who doesn't love a hot firefighter?" Gwen asked.

"Me." Delaney pointed her penis wand at herself.

The number wrapped up, and the announcer returned to the stage. Bonnie turned to Tabitha. "We should probably get going soon; we have to catch the sleeper at nine."

"Just one more dance, okay?" Tabitha leaned closer to Bonnie and whispered, "And make sure the bride is watching."

"What trouble are you brewing?"

"Oh, trust me." Tabitha grinned, dimples just like her brother's making an appearance. "Something magical is about to happen."

Damn, why did they have to look so much alike? Now she was thinking about Theo. Bonnie stepped closer to Cassie, making sure to keep her friend penned in between herself, Delaney, Ana, and Sadie.

The announcer prowled the stage, mic in hand. "Week after week, our show brings you the hottest bachelors in London," he began, "but tonight, for one night only, we have something extra special for you."

The crowd whooped with anticipation, and the announcer waved his arms, revving them up some more. The lights on the stage dimmed as the beat of a drum began to pound through the speakers. Bonnie glanced at Cassie, wondering if she recognized the rhythmic thump of a bodhran.

Over the slowly rising beat, the announcer continued, "Direct from the Highlands of Scotland, joining us to celebrate his second-to-last night of FREEDOM . . ." He bellowed the word, *Braveheart* style, and the crowd roared.

"It's not . . ." Cassie turned to Bonnie, ". . . is it?"

Bonnie shrugged. "If it is, I didn't know about it." She thought there was a good chance it could be, but she hadn't been part of any such plan. She turned, seeking confirmation from their head witch, but Tabitha's attention was glued to the stage as the announcer wrapped up the introduction.

"Ladies, please give a warm, wet welcome to Chicago late-night host and former star of the UK internet sensation *Shenanigans* . . . sexy Scot, Loooooogan Reid!"

The crowd went wild as a spotlight cut through the smoky darkness onstage, shining over a pair of sturdy boots. The low whine of bagpipes joined the drums, and the spotlight crept higher, revealing the strong lines of a man's naked calves, a little higher, and the plaid pleats of a kilt were revealed. The room burst into hysterics, women screaming, whistling, and cat-calling.

As the drums and pipes increased in speed and volume, the audience began to clap, and the circle of light grew in size, until finally, every inch of Cassie's soon-to-be-husband, Mr. Sexy Scot himself, was revealed. As they watched, Logan turned to face the crowd, his gaze seeking Cassie's. He winked, and eyes on her, began to dance.

"He's got a nice ass, I'll give him that," Sadie observed.

"And he sure knows how to move it," Ana added.

Bonnie leaned toward Tabitha. "How'd you pull this off?"

"Theo." She smiled wickedly. "When your brother is the groom's best mate, you can manage these things."

Bonnie glanced around the club. "Is Theo here?"

Tabitha shook her head, smile fading. "He had to be somewhere else tonight—family obligation."

Bonnie was dying to know what that meant, to ask why Tabitha was looking at her with such apology in her blue eyes. But she refused to pry. She changed the subject, nodding her head toward the stage. "He's not going to get naked up there, is he?"

"He better not," Cassie growled. She was smiling right now, enjoying the show, but Bonnie had a feeling her best friend's mood might change if her fiancé's exhibitionist personality got the best of him. On cue, his T-shirt went sailing overhead.

"Six-pack, twelve o'clock," Ana said, sticking her index fingers in her mouth and emitting a loud, shrill whistle.

"Does he usually go commando under there?" Delaney asked Cassie, her gaze drifting up the Scot's kilt.

"Is that the same as regimental?" Gwen asked, gaze moving in the same direction.

"That's it," Cassie said, grabbing on to the edge of the stage, "help me up."

Laughing, Bonnie and the others hoisted Cassie onto the stage, so she could enjoy the show her hot Scot was putting on from a more up-close-and-personal angle. Bonnie thought Logan would end the number when he saw Cassie had joined him onstage, but instead, he gave his fiancée a devilish grin and pulled her body against his, dancing with her—for her. The crowd lost their damn minds.

All in all, it was a memorable performance.

* * *

In the wee hours of the night, in a dimly lit sleeper car on an overnight train headed to Inverness, Bonnie stared up at the ceiling of her compartment. The steady sway and rhythmic rumble of the train was soothing, and she should have fallen asleep ages ago. Especially after the shots of whiskey they did, toasting Logan and Cassie in the lounge car before turning in. But she couldn't settle down. Her cheeks ached from smiling too much, and her heart ached from wanting too much.

Watching Logan and Cassie together tonight, the two of them playfully teasing each other, their obvious attraction, not to mention the love they so clearly shared . . . Bonnie was ashamed to admit it, but she was jealous. She'd been doing fine, but tonight, the old green-eyed monster had reared its ugly head.

Tabitha had asked her to be patient with Theo, to give him time. And she had. But not once had he reached out. The last time she saw him had been at his house, the last time she spoke to him were those few awkward words muttered during tea.

By morning, she'd be in Scotland. The next few days would be a whirlwind of wedding activities. After that, she'd be going home. And his time—their time—would be up.

CHAPTER 27

BY THE TIME Theo's rental car reached the outskirts of Logan's hometown in the Highlands, he only wanted three things: a stiff drink, a hot meal, and a soft bed. In that order. If things had gone as planned, he'd have watched Logan give his bride-to-be the surprise of her life, enjoying an evening out with his best mate. He'd have been on that sleeper car with everyone else. Tossed back a few pints or maybe a shot or two in the lounge car, then slept in one of the train's new luxury cabins.

Instead, he'd kept his promise to his mother and accompanied Camille to another achingly dull event, where he spent the evening saying all the right things to all the right people, the whole time feeling like it was all wrong. Then he'd taken an early morning flight into Inverness and rented a car to make the drive to Lochalsh.

Finally, Theo pulled up to his friend's childhood home. He switched off the key and sat for a minute, eyes closed, head slumped against the steering wheel. He was bloody exhausted. Physically, mentally, and emotionally.

Something hard banged loudly on the bonnet of the car. He jerked upright. "What the—"

Logan was leaning across the front windshield, staring in at him. "Theo! You made it, lad."

"Barely," Theo groaned, rubbing a hand across his face. "I feel like hell."

"You look it." Logan reached through the open window and clapped Theo on the shoulder. "Come on, let's get you inside. Mam saved you some breakfast."

Thoughts of Logan's mother's cooking were just enough motivation to convince his tired body to get moving again. He slid out of the car and followed his friend up the steps and into the house.

"Theo, laddie!" Logan's mother, Fiona, wrapped him in a fierce hug, the faded red braid of her hair tickling his chin.

Both Logan and his sister, Janet, inherited their ginger locks from their mother. In her mid-fifties, plump and pretty, Logan's mam was nothing like his own mum. Where Theodora Wharton was sharp, Fiona Reid was soft. Where his mother was cold and calculating, Logan's mother was warm and tender. Theo knew his mother loved him, in her way. Deep down, though, he'd always longed for the sweet affection of a mother who cuddled and coddled. His mother was neither coddler nor cuddler.

A stab of guilt lanced him for the uncharitable thought as Theo returned the hug. "It's good to see you." He gave Fiona a peck on the cheek. "You look lovely as always."

"Och, off with ye now," Fiona cooed, running a hand over her hair. While still a vibrant shade of red, streaks of white threaded through the braid.

Theo wondered what Bonnie's hair might look like as she aged. To be the man to grow old by her side, years filled with memories like the ones they'd shared at the cottage . . . An ache, painful in its intensity, lanced his heart.

"What's troubling you?" Fiona asked.

"Sorry?" Theo shook himself.

"Woolgathering?" She clucked her tongue. "Ye must be tired after yer long drive. And famished. Let's get something in your stomach, aye? Then you can have the afternoon to rest before the festivities tonight." She patted his unshaven cheek. "Och, you're a wee furry beastie!"

"Leave the poor man alone, Mam," Logan said, handing Theo a finger of whiskey. "Here, to settle your nerves . . . and mine."

Theo accepted the glass gratefully and tossed it back. Swallowing, he savored the smoky sting as the alcohol singed a path to his belly, burning away some of the lingering frustration of the last few days . . . hell, the last few weeks. The edge off his mood, Theo joined his friend at the wooden bench lining the long farmhouse table. "You're just jealous I can grow a better beard than you."

"Och, aye?" Logan raised a brow as he sipped his whiskey. "Well, I can throw a harder punch than you," he teased; his brogue was always stronger when he came back home.

After meeting their first year at university, Theo and Logan had been best mates. Often trading stays at each other's homes while on holiday. He'd kept it to himself, but Theo had always preferred spending time in Lochalsh than at the Abbey. Like the Lakeland Cottage, he felt more at home here than in his own house, more relaxed.

"Here you are, eat up." Fiona set a plate in front of him, piled high with smoked kippers and fried potatoes.

"Could you fry me up some tatties too, Mam?" Logan asked as Theo dug into his meal.

"Ye already had two plates this morn with the lassies," Fiona chided, even as she began dropping slices of potato into the frying pan.

Yep, coddled. "Where are the girls now?" Theo asked.

"After breakfast I drove them back over to the flats we've rented across from the castle." Logan pulled the plate his mother set on the table closer. "Thanks, Mam." He wolfed down a few forkfuls before adding, "They're spending the day getting ready. I've no notion why, tonight's just a practice run, aye?" He shrugged and downed a few more bites.

Theo cleaned his plate, happily accepting a second helping. Hunger eased, he took his time, chewing thoughtfully. "Rehearsal dinner tonight, wedding on Saturday, and then home on Sunday?" he asked.

"That's the plan." Logan nodded. "We've put off the honeymoon for now. Cassie needs to get back for work, and my new season starts filming soon too."

"This will be your third?"

"I know, I can hardly reckon it myself." Logan shook his head. "I signed a contract for another two years. Good thing I'm getting hitched to an American, aye?"

"You've decided to live in the States, then?" Theo wasn't surprised, but he'd miss his friend. They didn't get together as often as either of them liked as it was, and it would be even less often if the Scot continued living halfway across the world.

"For now," Logan admitted. "But we're both open to where life takes us." He smiled. "And you?" he asked, mouth curling down in concern. "Are ye all right?"

"I'll be fine," Theo said, finishing the last of his food. "I just need some sleep."

"If you say so." Logan watched him carefully, and Theo knew he wasn't fooled.

He also knew Lo wouldn't pry. Which he was grateful for. Theo refused to burden his friend with his problems, especially not during one of the most important moments of his best mate's life.

"The spare room's all yours." Logan squeezed Theo's shoulder. "Go have a rest. I'll wake you in time to get ready." He paused, squeeze turning into a playful punch. "And I'll be sure to give you extra time to take care of the mess growing on your face."

Bonnie peeked around the curtain again, checking to see if they were ready to begin. At the front of the long hall, Logan's sister held up her hand, waving three fingers. Bonnie nodded and dropped the curtain back into place.

"Janet says three more minutes," she announced. "Everybody ready back here?" Bonnie looked over the group. Sadie, Ana, and Delaney were lined up by height, paired with two of Logan and Theo's rugby teammates from their university days, and one of Logan's former crewmembers from his internet show, *Shenanigans*. Beyond them, Theo stood waiting with Cassie and her parents. Bonnie swallowed. As best man, he'd be escorting her down the aisle.

"We're ready," Cassie called, voice a little shaky.

"It's only a rehearsal, honey," Cassie's mom was saying, rubbing her back, "you got this."

"Thanks, Mom." Cassie pushed the veil away from her face to look at her mother. She hadn't donned her wedding dress for the rehearsal but had decided to wear the veil so she could practice the whole kiss-the-bride thing. "I don't know why I'm so nervous. We applied for a marriage license in Cook County months ago."

"*What?*" Every female in hearing distance demanded at once.

"Yeah." Cassie shrugged. "At the courthouse down-town. To cover our bases, in case something went wrong overseas."

Before anyone could respond further to this revelation, the procession music started.

"Zip it and line up, people," Delaney ordered, going into full preschool teacher mode. "It's showtime."

The curtain parted, and the couples began to file out one by one. Bonnie took her place next to Theo. It was surreal, walking down the aisle with him, the soft strains of Pachelbel's *Canon* marking the rhythm of their stride.

Actually, it felt *too* real. How often had she imagined herself walking down the aisle? She'd spent years pictur-ing the music, the dress, the moment.

But this wasn't her moment, she reminded herself, it was Cassie's.

Bonnie and Theo reached the front of the aisle. Right before they split apart, for the briefest of seconds, Theo squeezed her hand, hard. Inside her chest, her heart con-tracted, as if that too, had been clenched inside his fist. Emotions all over the place, afraid to look directly at him, she nodded, keeping her gaze facing front. He re-leased her, and they separated, moving to their places on opposite sides of the bridal platform.

Then Cassie was coming down the aisle, her mom and dad at her side. Even though this was only a rehearsal, even though this was just a practice run, Bonnie's heart swelled with happiness for her friend. She sneaked a peek at the groom, waiting at the front of the aisle. The look on Lo-gan's face as he watched his bride approach was breath-taking in its raw intensity.

Tears stung at the corners of Bonnie's eyes, burned in the back of her throat. Not tears of sadness, but of joy. Joy for her friend, her best friend in the world, the sister of her heart.

Seeing how Cassie and Logan looked at each other now, Bonnie realized how petty she'd been to ever doubt their love could be as strong as hers had been. She'd arrogantly thought because Cassie and Logan had known each other for such a brief time, what they felt for each other couldn't compare to what she and Gabe had.

Ironically, she'd been right. It didn't compare. Except her relationship was the one to come up short. It wasn't how long you loved someone that mattered, but how well. Stepping forward to take the practice bouquet from Cassie's hand, Bonnie whispered in her friend's ear, "I love you, my bosom buddy, and I'm so very happy for you."

She couldn't see her face clearly through the filmy veil, but the smile Cassie gave Bonnie was so bright, it shined straight through to her soul. Heart lighter than it had been in months, Bonnie stepped back and let her friend have her moment.

After the rehearsal, everyone gathered in the common room for a celebratory dinner. It was a relaxed affair, a small group made up of the bridal party, Cassie's parents, Logan's mom and his mom's date, a man Logan introduced as Mr. Kinney, and his sister, Janet, and Janet's girlfriend, Clara, who it turns out was a drummer for an all-girl band called the Mermaids.

"You're going to play at the reception tomorrow?" Bonnie asked.

Clara nodded. "I promised Janet we'd even play some classical shit."

"That's nice of you." Bonnie sipped from one of the

champagne glasses she was two-fisting. She'd been avoiding Theo all evening, not wanting to deal with the messy emotions tangling inside her every time she caught his eye. She wanted to focus on the now, on the joy she felt for her friend, which was finally free of any taint of jealousy. "What kind of music do you usually play?"

"Och, all sorts." Clara waved a hand. "Whatever tickles our fancy."

"Ever play the Spice Girls?"

"Fuck, no." Her face scrunched in amused revulsion. "You're joking, right?"

"Nope." Bonnie took another sip of champagne, completely unashamed. "I love their music."

"Well, I suppose we could play one song," the drummer mused, "if you requested it." She winked.

"Leave off, you flirt." Logan's sister, Janet, nudged Clara. "Besides, you're spoken for."

Clara laughed and gave Janet a quick kiss before turning back to Bonnie. "How about you? Are you spoken for?"

"Nope," Bonnie said again. "Actually, I *was* engaged," she admitted, surprising herself, "but I ended it a few months ago when I found out he'd been cheating on me."

"What a wanker!" Clara seethed.

"He was," Bonnie agreed, lifting her second glass of champagne in acknowledgment. Downing the rest of the glass, she realized she didn't feel any twinges of guilt or shame. Before, even though she told herself it wasn't her fault, that she had nothing to feel bad about, Gabe's infidelity had made her feel bad about herself. But now, just like the jealousy she'd harbored for Cassie and Logan, those feelings were gone.

Her neck prickled, and she glanced over her shoulder. From across the room, Theo was watching her. Setting down her empty glasses, Bonnie got to her feet, a little wobbly. "If you'll excuse me, I need some air."

"Careful out there," Janet warned. "I think a storm is brewing."

"I will be, thanks." With a wave, Bonnie headed out of the common room. Focusing on putting one foot in front of the other, she made her way down the front steps. She didn't know if Theo followed her. Part of her was afraid he would, part of her was afraid he wouldn't.

They hadn't spoken to each other since that painfully awkward exchange over tea at his house. If that even counted, since he hadn't said a word to her directly. She should have seen it coming. There'd certainly been enough clues. But she'd chosen to ignore the warning signs. She was good at that. Look what happened with Gabe.

Bonnie walked for several minutes, hoping the cool night air and scent of grass and heather would calm her nerves. But she didn't feel calm. If anything, coming outside had heightened the restless energy building inside her.

Across the way, moonlight caressed the walls and parapets of the castle. As she watched, a flock of thick gray clouds swept across the surface of the moon, blanketing the landscape in inky shadows. The wind picked up, tossing Bonnie's curls into a swirling mass whipping across her face. She shivered, Janet's warning about the storm ringing in her ears. Glancing back, Bonnie debated returning to the party but stopped when she saw a tall figure standing on the steps.

Light ripped the night sky apart, throwing the lines of the man's body into stark relief. Even from this distance, she knew it was Theo. And she knew he was watching her. A roll of thunder echoed across the countryside, the ground trembling beneath her.

On impulse, she turned and ran, hurrying up the hill.

She hadn't gotten very far before she stumbled, heels of her shoes catching in the dirt and rocks. If she was thinking rationally, she would stand up, brush herself off, and go back. But she wasn't, so she got to her feet, kicked off her shoes, and kept running. More lightning flashed, and the rain began to fall, mocking her decision.

Thighs burning, Bonnie tore up the hill, raindrops pelting her cheeks and soaking through the thin fabric of her cocktail dress. Even though she was expecting it, the next clap of thunder startled her, and she tripped, her ankle twisting on the wet grass. Searing pain ripped through her as she fell, her hip slamming into the ground with bruising force.

For a moment, she didn't move as wave after wave of agony radiated from her ankle up her leg. She rolled onto her back and breathed slowly through her nose, choking on raindrops and fighting the bile rising in her throat. She was *not* going to puke. Through the matted tangle of hair plastered across her face, Bonnie turned and stared back the way she'd come.

But no one was there. The hillside was empty. He hadn't followed her. He must have decided she wasn't worth chasing. Even Willoughby had come to help Marianne.

Feeling a million different kinds of stupid, Bonnie knew she had to get out of the storm. Wiping her eyes, she rolled again, this time onto her stomach. She pressed her palms into the grass, fingers digging into the dirt and roots as she drew her knees up, favoring her injured leg, and moved to a semi-upright position. Near the top of the hill, tucked in a copse of bushes, stood a wooden shed. It would have to do. She half crawled, half shimmied up the rest of the hill. Her dress was completely ruined, and she would probably be hobbling down the aisle at her friend's wedding tomorrow.

Almost at the top, Bonnie stopped to catch her breath. On her hands and knees in the mud, she looked up and gauged how much farther she had to go to reach the shed. It was then she saw him, striding up the hill, wide shoulders slicing through the misting rain. In moments, he'd reached her and stood, staring down at her, blue eyes piercing the darkness.

She blinked up at him.

"You bloody little fool," Theo said in a hoarse whisper. He bent over her, leaning down until his face was mere inches from her own. Water sluiced off his nose and lashes and the bold slash of his cheekbones. And then his mouth was on hers, punishing in its intensity. The kiss of an avenging angel, stealing her breath, claiming her soul.

Before Bonnie's heart remembered to beat, before she could gather her wits and say something—anything—he lifted her, one arm around her shoulders, the other under her knees. Jaw clenched, he turned, stomping through the wind and rain. Theo marched toward the shed and kicked the door open, bracing her against his hip. "Can you walk?"

"I . . . I don't know." He set her down, and she took a tentative step. She winced but was able to support her weight. Taking another step, she nodded. "I'm okay."

"Well, I'm bloody not okay," he roared, slamming the shed door shut.

She whirled around, pivoting on her good ankle.

He stalked toward her. "What were you thinking? Tearing off like that in the middle of a bloody lightning storm?"

As if making his point, another bolt of lightning flashed, illuminating the interior of their shelter like the pop of a camera flash. Seconds later, an ear-splitting crack of thunder shook the thin walls. Bonnie wrapped her arms around herself, trembling.

With a curse, Theo turned away from her and began to ransack the small space, a shadow moving against the darker shadows. Bonnie heard the scritch of a match and a moment later, the wick of a kerosene lamp glowed to life. He hung the lamp on a hook screwed into the rafters and turned his attention back to her.

"Why did you run when you saw me?" he demanded, hair wild, eyes blazing in the flickering light. His shirt was soaked and plastered to his skin, chest heaving. A vein pulsed in his neck. "Answer me!"

His question was gasoline poured on the coals of her own pent-up anger, his demand the match. In a burst of white-hot rage, she exploded. "Why do you think?" she yelled, fury making her bold. "Because I was running away from you!" She took a step toward him and almost collapsed.

He lurched forward, grabbing onto her waist, stopping her fall.

"I was running away from my feelings for you." The admission tumbled out as she clung to him, arms sliding over his wet shirt. She wasn't sure if she wanted to push him away or pull him closer.

He ducked his chin. "What am I going to do with you?" he growled, the words barely audible over the rain pounding against the slate roof.

From some reckless place deep inside, Bonnie answered him. "Kiss me."

Clasping her hands behind his neck, she pulled his mouth down to hers. His skin was cold from the rain, but his lips were warm as she slid her tongue inside, seeking his heat. He groaned, and the sound rumbled between them like the thunder rolling overhead. Dropping her hands from his neck, she tried to remove his shirt, but the buttons were slick and kept sliding through her fingers. She gritted her teeth in frustration.

"Here," he said, grabbing the back of his shirt and lifting it over his head, buttons popping, little pings sounding as they sprinkled across the wood floor like hail. "Better?"

"Much." She placed her hands on his chest, eager for the feel of his bare skin beneath her palms. In the dim glow of the lamp, she watched as her hands, still muddy from her crawl up the hill, left streaks of dirt across his body. She ran her fingers over his torso, fascinated by the ropes of muscle rippling along his abdomen in the wake of her touch. She stroked her palms up and down his chest, marking him. *Mine,* those handprints said, a feral pleasure tearing through her at the sight.

She claimed his mouth again, marking that as hers too. His hands reached around her, tugging on the zipper of her dress, peeling the wet fabric away from her body. It pooled at her feet in a soggy heap. He stepped back, drinking her in. As he stared, she popped the clasp on her bra and slipped it off. Her nipples tightened instantly in the cool air, and she arched her back, offering herself to his hungry gaze.

Holding her steady with one hand, Theo reached out with the other, his forefinger slowly tracing a path over her collarbones, down between her breasts and around her belly button. She held her breath, wondering where his finger would move next. But instead of continuing down, he slid his hand back up, fingers following the curve of her breasts, up and around.

She exhaled, then quickly inhaled again, chest rising, and he tracked the movement, his own chest rising and falling rapidly with each shallow breath. Then he leaned into her, and she cried out as the tight peaks of her nipples made contact with his bare chest. She rubbed herself against him, back and forth, pleasure spiking through her with each touch.

His kiss grew hungrier, rougher, tongue plunging deep inside her mouth. He lifted her, kicking her dress out of the way as he stepped forward until her back pressed against the rough cool wood of the shed. Still supporting her, Theo shoved her panties down with one hand before working his fly loose. Then he leaned into her again, thrusting his hips forward, rubbing the tip of his cock back and forth across her clit, just as she'd rubbed her breasts against his chest.

The feel of him, hot and hard against her, made Bonnie achy with need. Heat radiated between her legs, and her knees wobbled. "You won't fall," he promised, gripping her hips, holding her flush between his body and the wall, supporting her weight on his thighs. "I've got you." He pressed his face into her neck and groaned, his breath an erotic tickle against her ear.

"Christ, Bonnie. I need to be inside you so bloody bad." He nipped her earlobe, a sweet, sharp sting making desire shoot down her spine. "But I didn't bring anything with me."

She glanced up at him. "You didn't come prepared?" she managed to tease, though she wanted to sob in frustration. She needed him inside her too.

"I wasn't expecting this."

She wasn't expecting this either, but now that they were here, in this moment, she knew what she was going to do. She squirmed free of his grip, gingerly setting her feet on the floor. Using his clothing as leverage, she worked his pants and boxers down his legs, sliding down the wall until her knees hit the floor.

"*Bonnie,*" he ground out, his voice like sandpaper. Rough and raw.

The sound sent off tremors inside her. She reached out with her forefinger, as he had done to her, and traced a line down his body, along the muscled *V* of his pelvis, up to his belly button and around, following the trail of dark hair dipping lower, until she reached the base of his thick erection.

She wet her lips, thinking of that day in the bridal shop, mouth curving at the memory of those popsicles. Reminding herself to go slow, she let her tongue dart out and taste him. His body jerked, and she pulled back warily.

"Sorry," he groaned. "It's just, *Christ,* what you do to me."

"I haven't even gotten started." She laughed, looking up at him.

The lamp he'd hung on a rafter lit Theo from behind, casting his face in shadows. She caught the curve of his cheek as he grinned and sensed more than saw those dimples. Dropping her gaze, she gripped his waist, thumbs pressing into the muscles stretched along his hip bones. She bent her head and placed her mouth on him again. This time, he held still for her, the sound of his ragged breaths sawing the air blending with the howling wind outside.

She licked him, the tip of her tongue circling the head of his cock before exploring his length. Teasing and tasting, she started with the lessons from her friends, but with each stroke she learned something new on her own—his groans of pleasure, the way his hands fisted in her hair—teaching her what he liked.

Ready for the next step, she opened her mouth and took him inside, sucking him slowly. In and out, little by little, she retreated and advanced, working her way down his shaft. His groans became guttural, his fingers digging into her shoulders.

The awareness of what she was doing to him, of how she could make him feel, filled Bonnie with a desperate need. Forgetting her fears, she sucked him harder, pulled him deeper into her mouth, wanting him deep, deeper, as deep as he could go. His hips jerked, but her hands held him tight, and she maintained control, dictating their pace.

"I can't wait, oh sweet bloody hell," Theo moaned. "Please, Bonnie, I can't hold on any longer." His hips surged forward, and she was ready. Not wanting to press her luck, she pulled back, releasing him from her mouth. She wrapped both hands around him, pumping him with hard fast strokes that took him right over the edge. He cried out, his body shuddering.

Theo collapsed, crumpling to his knees and pulling her close, the sharp rasp of his breath warm on her neck. "Thank you," he whispered.

She laughed.

"Again, with the laughing." He pulled back to study her, gaze narrowing in the dim light. "What's so bloody funny?"

"Your manners." She giggled.

His eyed widened. "What's wrong with my manners?"

"It's just"—she paused, holding back another giggle—"you always say 'thank you' after, well, you know."

"Would you rather I say something like, 'okay, babe, that was great, now please go make me a sammich'?"

She snorted with laughter.

"What did I say this time?"

He was so adorable, it was ridiculous, especially because he didn't even realize it. "Please," she answered him. "You said, 'please make me a sammich.'" She giggled again. "And was that your attempt at an American accent?"

"Maybe." He reached for her. "And yes, I have manners. Now," he began, hands stroking down her back, "may I please—"

"Touch my bum?" she asked. "You may."

"That's not what I was going to ask." Theo pressed her down to the floor, and she lay back, cushioned by the crumpled pile of their discarded clothes.

Her desire, banked while teasing him, roared back to life as he crawled on all fours, hovering over her.

"I was going to ask," he continued, crouching low, his breath tickling her belly, "may I please—"

"Yes," Bonnie said, "definitely, yes." And soon, she was the one thanking him.

CHAPTER 28

BONNIE DRIFTED IN and out of consciousness. After Theo had earned not one, but two very ecstatic thank-yous from her, he'd dug through the boxes in the shed and managed to scrounge up several picnic blankets. They'd laid them out, making a fort of sorts, and snuggled up together, warm and cozy as the storm continued to rage outside. Eyes fluttering open, she idly watched dust motes float in the swath of morning sunlight streaming through the little window. The storm had finally passed.

"Bonnie," Theo murmured, his voice the deep, low timbre of a man just waking up, "are you still asleep?"

"Yes." She sighed dreamily and closed her eyes, perfectly content to spend the rest of her life on this floor.

He chuckled, the sound rumbling in his chest, vibrating against her. He shifted, and the featherlight touch of his hand roved over her shoulder and back. "I love your freckles."

"Good, because I have a lot of them," she muttered, heart flip-flopping in her chest. He loved her freckles? What else might he love?

"You certainly do," he agreed, his fingers trailing spiral patterns on her skin. "I've never seen so many."

"Are you counting them?" Bonnie rolled over, turning to face him. "That's going to take you forever. I have them everywhere."

"Not *every*where." He gave her a sleepy sexy grin, propping himself up on an elbow to gaze down at her. "Not here." He ran a hand along the patch of creamy skin under her arm, then down to her breasts. "Or here." His hand drifted lower, over her belly. "No freckles here either." His long black lashes hid his eyes from her as he dropped his gaze, tracking the movement of his hand between her legs, brushing his fingers over the soft pale tops of her thighs. "It's like these are special places, hidden away." He looked up at her again. "Only for me."

"Like your eyes," she said, staring into the deep blue of his gaze, the burst of indigo vibrant in the morning sun. At his curious look, she explained, "There's a darker starburst of color around your pupils. The first time I noticed it, I felt like I'd learned something secret about you."

His grin turned tender, and he bent his head and pressed his lips to hers in a sweet, gentle kiss. "I've missed you," he whispered against her neck. Burrowing his face into her shoulder, he continued, "I'm sorry about these past few weeks. I should have come to see you . . . at least called."

"Why didn't you?"

He hesitated. "There were some things I needed to figure out."

"Have you figured them out yet?" she asked, sensing the tension lacing his body, not sure if she was ready for the answer.

"Honestly?" He lifted his head, meeting her gaze again. "I wasn't sure," he admitted. He swallowed hard, Adam's apple bobbing. "But I think maybe I am now."

Breath caught in her throat, she waited for him to say more.

Instead, he rolled over and reached for his clothes. "We should get back. Everyone will wonder what happened to us."

Bonnie nodded, heart slipping sideways. Tamping down her disappointment, she sat up. Outside the window, a rainbow spread across the endless Scottish sky. The breath she'd been holding escaped on a sigh. Unable to resist, she gave in to the soul-deep need and made a wish.

Theo saw Bonnie to her room and then headed for his own. He'd barely had time to kick off his boots and remove his shirt when a knock sounded on the door. "Yes?"

"It's Logan, open up."

Groaning, Theo moved to open the door. "What?" he barked.

"Is that any way to talk to a man on his wedding day?" Logan asked. The Scot's eyes widened as he took in Theo's disheveled appearance. "And what the hell happened to you?"

Theo followed his friend's gaze, noticing for the first time the streaks of mud running down his abdomen, dirty handprints marking his chest. He cleared his throat, the back of his neck on fire with embarrassment. "The storm. There was . . . an incident."

Logan arched a brow. "An incident, aye?" He pushed past Theo, inviting himself inside. "Well, that's what I've come to speak with you about."

Heart pounding, Theo stared at his friend. Did he know about what had happened with Bonnie? But why would Logan need to talk to him about it? "Sorry?"

"The storm, man. It's put us in a wee fankle." Logan

paced the small apartment. "We got a call from the wedding coordinator over at the castle, part of the bridge washed out."

"Bloody hell." On a small island, Eilean Donan was connected to the mainland by a long narrow stone bridge. "Boat?"

"I've thought about that already, aye." Logan ran a hand through his hair. "But have kindly been informed it's not an option."

"What *are* your options, then?

"I doona ken," Logan admitted, frustration thickening his brogue. "I thought we could move the wedding to town, but unless we want to have it at the fishery, it's a nonstarter. Everything is booked; Cassie checked."

"How is she doing with the news?" Theo could only imagine how one of his sisters would react if she'd been told her wedding was in danger of being canceled. Or taking place at a fish-processing warehouse.

"As well as to be expected." Logan rubbed his temples.

"Well, you two technically got married in the States, right?" Theo asked, taking the pragmatic approach. "Maybe you don't need a wedding."

"Doona need a wedding?" the Scot's voice rose in disbelief. "Will ye be the one to tell my bride that?"

"Uh, no," Theo admitted. "I'd rather not."

"She's a romantic, aye?" Logan raised his arms and waved them in a circle. "We need something *g-r-r-rand*," he insisted, panic thickening his brogue more than ever.

Oh yeah, his mate was on the brink of losing his shit.

"Let me think on it," Theo suggested. "Give me an hour to get cleaned up, and I'll meet you downstairs. We'll figure it out."

* * *

Precisely an hour later, Theo found Logan and most of the bridal party gathered in the rental unit's common room. The mood was more jovial than he'd expected.

"Theo!" Logan waved him over to where he was sitting with Cassie and her friends.

Including Bonnie.

As always, her red curls grabbed his attention, and for a moment, his gut tightened as he recalled tangling his fingers in those curls, gazing down upon her as she took him in her mouth and . . . *not now, you bugger.*

He joined them, taking the open seat, which was, of course, next to the source of his current state of arousal.

Oblivious to his distress, Bonnie beamed up at him. "I think I have a solution," she said, "but we're going to need your help."

"Anything," Theo offered.

"What if we moved the wedding to the Abbey?"

Anything but that. His mother would have a conniption. Besides, it was too far away. They'd no time to plan; it was a ludicrous idea.

"I know it sounds impossible," Bonnie said, giving voice to his opinion, "but I think we can pull it off. We'd have to move the wedding to tomorrow—"

"Which I'm perfectly happy to do," Cassie added.

"And arrange to get everyone on a train this evening," Bonnie continued.

"I've already confirmed with the night train; if we leave from the Fort William station, they've enough berths for the whole party," Sadie chimed in.

"And I'll help Logan's mom box up the cake for transport," Ana added.

"Nettie says Sunday is no problem for her; so my sister can still officiate." Logan wrapped an arm around Cassie's shoulders. "Clara said the band is happy to tag along too."

"And the location would be perfect. There's so much space at the Abbey. It won't be hard to set something up on short notice. I bet Tabitha could plan a wedding in her sleep." Bonnie finished stating her case, watching him intently. "What do you think?"

"I think . . ." Theo paused. He should say no, tell her it was bloody absurd, but he couldn't look away from Bonnie, couldn't break the contact of her gaze. Right now, when she was looking at him like that, with her heart in her eyes, Theo would give her anything she asked. Rearrange the bloody moon and stars if she so desired. Compared to that, moving a wedding to his home seemed easy. "Yes. Why not."

Everyone cheered.

"Oh, good." Bonnie breathed a sigh of relief. "Because I already called your sister."

"Sorry?" Theo blinked.

"That's my fault, mate." Logan clapped a hand on his shoulder. "I told her you wouldn't be able to resist the opportunity to play hero."

CHAPTER 29

TWENTY-FOUR HOURS HAD never flown by so fast. From the time they packed up in Scotland, checking and double-checking to make sure they had everything and everyone, until the moment Logan's sister told him he "may kiss the bride," Bonnie had been a bundle of nerves. But they'd done it. The whole thing had come off without a hitch, and now her best friend was hitched.

Bonnie stood next to Theo, watching as their two best friends moved to the center of the ballroom for their first official dance as husband and wife. She laid her head on Theo's shoulder, giddy with relief and so very grateful he'd said yes to helping them out. "Thank you."

"It was mostly Tabitha," Theo said.

True, Theo's sister had been a whirlwind of activity, taking charge and putting together a wedding worthy of a spread in a posh bridal magazine.

"And my mother." Theo shook his head, disbelief ringing in his voice. "I can't believe she agreed to all of this." He glanced around the ballroom. "More than half this crush are people she invited."

"Everybody likes a wedding." Bonnie smiled.

"I suppose."

The song ended, a few onlookers whooping and whistling as Logan dipped Cassie for a kiss.

"The Mermaids are actually pretty good," Bonnie said, waving at the drummer.

"They're not bad." Theo glanced at the band set up in one corner of the ballroom. "Give me a moment," he told Bonnie.

Curious, she watched him cross the room and speak to the band. A moment later, he returned, kilt swinging. "Have I told you how much I like you in a kilt?" Bonnie asked, mouth twitching.

"Too many times," Theo muttered. "Look your fill now because I'm never wearing one of these wretched things again."

She glanced back toward the band. "What were you up to, anyway?"

"It's a surprise." He winked.

She rolled her eyes and didn't bother asking for a hint; she knew better. Luckily, she didn't have to wait long to find out. A moment later, the lead singer got on the mic and announced, "This next song is a dedication from the best man to the maid of honor. Theo and Bonnie, the floor is yours!"

"Shall we?" Theo asked, offering her his hand.

Joy spread its wings inside her, fluttering through her middle. Taking Theo's hand, she allowed him to lead her to the dance floor. He wrapped his arms around her as the first strains of guitar began. Bonnie rested her hands on his shoulders, trying to place the familiar notes. "Wait. You requested 'Sweet Child O' Mine'?"

He smiled down at her, dimples winking. "You should know, Guns N' Roses is my favorite band."

Bonnie shook her head, grinning. "Not what I'd expect from a duke, or for a dance at a wedding."

"It's the perfect song," he argued. "Perfect for you." His hands warm on her waist, he swayed to the music with her.

Unlike the original, the Mermaid's version was sweeter, more tender, the female vocals of the lead singer adding an almost ethereal feel to the song. "You're right," she agreed. "I like it."

And when Theo began to sing along, quietly whispering the lyrics to her, lips brushing against her hair, her ear, her neck, Bonnie liked it even more. The entire world disappeared, drifting away as she and Theo swayed to the music together, dancing in their own private bubble. She rested her head against his chest, drawn to the rhythm of his heartbeat.

Tonight, her best friend had gotten married, had promised to share the rest of her life with a man she'd known for only a year. Again, Bonnie marveled at it. But this time, she didn't question it. There was no doubting the feelings Logan and Cassie shared.

Just as there was no doubting her own feelings for the man holding her in his arms.

She'd thought she hadn't known Theo long enough to fall in love with him. Had tried to convince herself that friends with benefits was all they could ever be in the short time they'd been together. Now, she realized how wrong she'd been. She loved the Brit, more than she ever thought possible.

The real problem was figuring out what the hell to do about it.

All too soon the song was over, and the bubble popped.

Theo began to lead her from the floor when a vaguely familiar voice floated over the speakers. "Hey, maid of honor! Don't go anywhere just yet."

Curious, Bonnie glanced back toward the band. Clara was on the mic. The drummer caught Bonnie's eye, tipping a drum stick cheekily in her direction. "This one's for you," she called out, right before the band launched into a Spice Girls song.

Bursting into laughter, Bonnie joined her friends in a circle on the dance floor and let loose. Even Cassie detached herself from her groom to get in on the action. After dancing to several fast-paced favorites, Bonnie was sweaty and winded and needed a break. She looked around for Theo but didn't see him, so she slipped out of the ballroom, heading for a pair of doors at the end of the hall.

Outside, the soft summer breeze lifted the heavy curls clinging to her neck and cooled her cheeks. Not ready to go back in yet, Bonnie strolled toward the nearby garden. The moon was high, lighting the white stone of the crushed gravel path, making it glow, and the air was heavy with the scent of honeysuckle and lilac.

Is there a felicity in the world superior to this?

Maybe it was okay to be like Marianne, at least sometimes. Bonnie paused at the flowered archway leading to the walled portion of the garden. Heart full, she made a decision. She would turn around, go back to the house, and tell Theo exactly how she felt.

As she spun on her heel to head back up the path, the sound of voices caught her ear.

Theo. He was speaking to someone on the other side of the wall, tone caustic, raised in a rare moment of anger. "I should have seen this coming. You always have a plan, don't you, Mama? At least now I know why you were so eager to help with the arrangements tonight."

"Really, Theodore, I thought we'd been through all this. You can't honestly say you're surprised. This is the perfect opportunity to ask for Camille's hand."

Bonnie bit down on her lip, holding back a gasp. Her legs locked. She stood in the shadow of the garden wall, the gravel path beneath her feet turning to quicksand, draining the evening's happiness from her body.

"I see. It's not enough for you to insist I marry someone I don't love. Now you wish to turn my best friend's wedding into my engagement party, is that it?" Theo's voice was a low growl.

"When did you become so melodramatic?" his mother chided.

"When did you become so Machiavellian?" Theo countered.

"It's not just the financial concerns." There was an edge to Theo's mother's voice now, a zealousness. "We must also think of our family's social capital."

"You can't be serious, Mama."

"I am *dead* serious. And you promised me, remember? This ring represents our family's future. *Your* future. Now, you are going to take this ring, a ring meant for a duchess, and you are going to offer it to the woman worthy of wearing it. Do I make myself clear?"

"Crystal." Theo's voice was resolute. "Give me the ring."

His words were cold and sharp, shattering the night air and Bonnie's heart. Forcing her legs to move, she ran up the path and back into the house. She needed a place to escape, to hide. Panic overloaded all her senses, and she stumbled blindly down the hall, hurrying past the entrance to the ballroom.

"There you are!" Tabitha called, spotting her from the doorway and grabbing her hand, dragging her back. "Come on, Cassie is about to toss the bouquet."

* * *

"Give me the ring, Mama," Theo repeated, straightening his jacket before adjusting the bloody kilt Cassie had insisted they all wear.

His mother handed him a velvet pouch.

Wordlessly, he turned it upside down, letting the ring slip out to land in his palm. Theo stared at the heirloom. Felt its weight. How many of his ancestors had proposed with this ring? How many, with all their wealth and power, had found happiness?

"Do I have your word?"

His jaw hardened, and he closed his fist around the ring. "I promise you, Mama, the woman I ask to wear this will be worthy of the Emberton title."

Her shrewd gaze locked on his face, eyes narrowing as if she suspected mutiny.

And she'd be right. Dancing with Bonnie this evening, Theo's soul had been under siege, his heart declaring war against his mind. *It was time for this bloody battle to be over.*

Before she could say more, Theo left the garden, stalking back toward the house. A small part of him, the part who wished for a mother like Logan's, had hoped his own mother would surprise him, but unfortunately, that was not to be the case.

Ah well. His mother would accept it, in time. And if not, to bloody hell with her. Theo was done playing games, done with the matchmaking and the drama. Life was too short. His mother, of all people, should understand that. But he couldn't force her. He could only hope she'd come around on her own. He'd wasted too much time already worrying about what other people wanted.

Bonnie *was* worthy. Smart and kind. Fiercely loyal. She was the duchess he wanted. The wife he needed.

But he was getting ahead of himself.

First, he had to propose. Theo stepped through the ball-room door just as Cassie raised her arm and tossed her bouquet high overhead. He watched the beribboned bundle of flowers sail through the air, end over end, landing at Bonnie's feet.

She bent down to retrieve it as all around her, guests clapped and cheered. *No time like the present, mate.* Holding up the ring, Theo made his way toward her. She looked up from the bouquet and watched him approach, her eyes unreadable from this distance.

Bonnie glanced at the ring in his hand, her face pale. An odd expression flickered across her features. Not surprised, not happy. But . . . stricken.

As he moved closer, she didn't return her gaze to his. Instead, she glanced to her left. It took Theo a moment to realize she was looking at Camille. Before he knew what was happening, Bonnie had shoved the bridal bouquet into Camille's hands, and spun around, racing from the room.

CHAPTER 30

THREE WEEKS AFTER his best friend married the woman of his dreams while he watched the woman of his own dreams run away, Theo sat at the breakfast table with his three sisters, staring into his teacup and ignoring their prattle. A crust of toast smacked him in the cheek and he glanced up. "What the hell, Tabby?"

Tessa clucked her tongue. "Better not let Mama hear you talking like that."

"How is she today?" Thalia asked.

"Full of as much spit and vinegar as always," Tabby said.

"I thought the expression was piss and vinegar," Theo remarked.

"Gross!" All three of his sisters frowned at him.

Theo shrugged, hiding a smile. The one bright spot had been when Mama had finally agreed to tell her daughters she had cancer. It had been a secret he'd not been happy to keep. The fact Theo viewed his mother telling his sisters about her illness as the high point in his life these past few weeks was not lost on him.

And honestly, if Mama hadn't said anything, Theo doubted any of them would have had a clue. So far treatment had been minimal, with the doctors focused on monitoring the size of her tumors. But Theo was glad his sisters knew. Preparing to help their mother fight her battle with cancer had brought them all closer. As had their latest venture to resuscitate the family fortune.

"Where is she, anyway?" he wondered.

"In the ballroom, Arguing about table linens with the vendor." Tabitha buttered another slice of toast.

Thalia glanced admirably at her older sister. "How did you ever convince Mama to begin renting the Abbey for weddings?"

"I showed her pictures from Prince Harry's nuptials. Told her if we played our cards right, by the time little Prince George is ready to get married, perhaps we could host the reception here."

"For a very pretty penny," Theo added.

"That's the point," Tabitha agreed. "And when Mama saw the profit margins I drew up, she pulled the stick out of her butt far enough to agree to it. And who was right?"

"You!" Thalia said.

"Whose plan will save the Emberton fortune?"

"Yours!" Tessa clapped.

"Damn straight. After a hundred years of Wharton men screwing things up, it will be a Wharton woman who finally fixes it."

"Huzzah!" Thalia and Tessa cheered.

"You can't take all the credit," Theo grumbled. "It was Bonnie's idea to move Logan's wedding here that inspired you. If I hadn't said yes—"

"If you hadn't said yes, then sure, I might never have thought of it. But you did and here we are." Tabitha narrowed her eyes at him. "I'm surprised you have the gall to mention *her* name at all." His sister paused, smirking. "Or should I say the balls."

"Tabby!" Thalia gasped.

"Oh, wait," Tabitha added, warming to her topic, "I forgot. Mama keeps your balls in her handbag."

Theo's face flushed as Thalia and Tessa snickered. "Sorry?"

"No, I'm sorry," Tabitha said, crossing her arms. "For a moment there, I'd thought you finally pulled your head out of your arse, but I was wrong."

"Care to explain yourself?" Theo stared at his sister.

"I saw your face that night, Theo. You were going to propose to her."

"Who? Camille?" Theo jerked his head. "I told Mama I won't marry her."

His mother hadn't outright forgiven him for going against her wishes, but with the new wedding business venture keeping her occupied, she'd dropped the matchmaking topic. For now. Theo knew the truce wouldn't last. Mama was too determined to let it go forever.

Theo was determined too. He would not marry someone he didn't love.

"We both know I'm not talking about Camille." Tabitha huffed. "How long are you going to mope around here?"

"I've been busy helping the solicitors draw up the Abbey's rental agreements as a wedding venue," Theo argued. "And I have *not* been moping."

"You've totally been moping," Thalia said.

"It's true," Tessa agreed.

"Besides, those agreements were finished ages ago. We're already taking bookings for the next season." His sister continued to berate him. "Got any other excuses?"

"She ran away."

"So? Chase her!"

Theo swallowed. His tea was cold and bitter. Rather like his heart.

"Spare me from men and their fragile egos," Tabitha groaned. "Is that it, then? Don't you want to know why she ran away?"

When he still didn't reply, another crust hit him in the face. He raised his head and gave his sister an icy stare.

"Answer me one thing," she demanded, matching his stare with one of her own. "Do you love her?"

Theo regarded his sister for a long moment. She knew him too well to bother lying. He'd spent the weeks since the night of Logan's wedding trying to lie to himself.

He closed his eyes and nodded.

"What's that?" she prodded.

His throat worked, tongue thick with regret. "Yes," he finally managed to force out. He opened his eyes.

Unperturbed by the storm brewing in his face, Tabby leaned forward, hand cupped to her ear in exaggeration. "I didn't hear you."

"Yes, I bloody love her!" Theo shouted, smashing his fists against the table, dishes clattering.

His sisters gaped, mouths hanging open.

Tabitha broke the silence. "Then suck up your wounded male pride, get off your stubborn bum, and go tell her." Grinning, she broke off another piece of toast.

"Don't you dare throw that at me," Theo warned. "But you're right." He stood. "I need to tell her."

"Finally." Tabitha told his retreating back.

As Theo marched out of the breakfast room, the scrap of toast winged him in the shoulder.

The summer storm blowing in off Lake Michigan had turned the late-afternoon sky above Chicago dark. Thick charcoal-colored clouds hung low, blotting out the sun. On the north side of the city, rain streaked down the glass windows of a coffee shop. A heavy roll of thunder set the teacups rattling in their saucers. Moments later, lightning flashed outside, briefly illuminating the few pedestrians daring enough to risk being out and about in this weather. It was a good day to stay indoors.

Brushing crumbs off the page she'd been reviewing, Bonnie licked a dab of sugared lemon peel icing from her finger. A few months ago, she'd sat in another tea shop halfway across the world and wrote in this journal for the very first time. Now, the leather cover was no longer stiff, the spine was cracked, the pages were almost full, and she loved it more than ever. She recalled the feeling she'd had that day, fingers stroking the cover, blank pages filled with fresh possibility. She'd been brimming with excitement to be out on her own, free to do as she liked.

She doodled in the corner of her page, staring at the swirling pattern of ink forming on the paper. It was the end of August, a new term would be starting soon, and for the first time in years, Bonnie wasn't caught up in the pre-back-to-school chaos. When she'd arrived home in Chicago, she'd been relieved Ana's offer to stay in her spare room still stood. It wasn't a permanent solution, but it allowed Bonnie the freedom to make some changes, spurring her next decision. She'd met with her department administrator at the college and applied for a sabbatical.

Bonnie wasn't sure if she wanted to quit teaching forever, but she knew she needed a break. She needed to give her writing a chance. She sighed, flipping through the pages she'd managed so far this afternoon and nibbling a corner of her scone. Just because she was giving it a chance didn't mean it was easy. Some days the words flowed, and other days, like today, she was just . . . stuck. Something was still missing. She needed a bolt of inspiration.

On cue, lightning flashed. Bonnie eyed the rain-swept street beyond the window warily. Her phone rang, and she jumped. But it was only Cassie. She shook her head, annoyed with herself. She was spending too much time in story mode. Not everything was a symbolic gesture. She slid her thumb over the answer button. "Hey, Cass."

"Hey, are you hanging out at the coffee shop on Sheridan right now?"

"Yep." Bonnie maneuvered around tables toward the front of the store, where her conversation wouldn't bother the other patrons. "It's late afternoon on a weekday, where else would I be?" She was a creature of habit, something a few exciting months living in another country had not managed to change. "Why?"

"Just checking," Cassie said with forced casualness.

Immediately, Bonnie was on alert. She knew that tone of voice all too well. "What's going on?" she asked, glancing outside. The rain had tapered off to a steady drizzle, and the sky, though still gray, had lightened considerably, the patch of emerging sunshine holding the promise of a rainbow.

Good. She could use a bit of luck.

"Don't freak out," Cassie warned.

"You realize when someone says, 'don't freak out,' the person being told not to freak out immediately starts freaking out, right?" Her friend's cryptic response did nothing to assuage Bonnie's nerves. "Cassie . . ." she began, then froze. Across the street, long legs dodging puddles and eating up the sidewalk, was Theo. "Why is the sixteenth Duke of Emberton heading toward me?"

"Maybe he wants to talk to you," Cassie suggested pertly.

"Maybe I don't want to talk to him," Bonnie replied, equally pert.

"Hey, you're the one who arranged for Logan to meet me for that supper cruise on the Thames, remember?" Cassie reminded her.

"That was different." Theo had almost reached the shop; he was close enough that she could see the raindrops glistening on his jacket.

"I hardly see how," Cassie argued. "Hear him out, okay? You need to give him a chance."

"I don't need to give him anything," Bonnie grumbled.

"Just do it. You can thank me later."

Before she could respond, Cassie ended the call. Bonnie clutched her phone, watching as Theo stopped at the corner. He stepped off the curb the instant the walk light flashed, confident stride daring the flow of traffic to deny him. *If you don't go, they won't stop.*

Seems he'd taken her advice to heart. In seconds, Theo was directly in front of the shop window, staring at her through the glass, dark hair curling in the damp. Seeing him this close made her heart flop sideways, erratic beats thumping painfully inside her chest.

Rather than move toward the entrance, he remained at the window. Watching. Waiting.

Fine. Be that way. She pocketed her phone and pushed through the door.

"Don't blame Cassie," Theo said by way of greeting. "I pestered Logan incessantly until he made her tell me where you—"

"What do you want?" Bonnie cut him off.

"To talk to you." A tentative smile curved his mouth.

She crossed her arms over her chest, pressing down on her traitorous heart, ordering it to behave. "So, talk."

"Why did you run away?"

"You came all the way here to ask me that?"

"For starters, yes." He shoved a hand through his hair, slicking back the wet strands.

"You were about to propose to your heiress." She shrugged. "I was just getting out of the way."

He stared down at her, blue eyes fierce. "I was about to propose to *you*."

"But . . ." Bonnie's mouth opened and closed. She must have looked like a fish. She felt like one—a foolish fish caught in a net, yanked from the water and gasping for air. "But I . . ." Brain deprived of oxygen, she struggled to form a coherent sentence. "I heard you and your mother talking in the garden. I heard about your promise."

Pulling herself together, she thrust her chin up. She knew what she heard. What she saw. This was *not* going to be like one of those big misunderstandings in Cassie's romance novels. "You promised your mother you would propose," she insisted.

"True," he agreed, pulling a ring from his pocket. "I promised to give this to the woman I believed worthy of wearing it."

Bonnie's heart stuttered to a halt. "But I'm not rich. What about saving the estate, your duty to your family and all that?"

Theo took a step toward her, his voice low and deep. "All my life I believed duty was more important than love— until I met you." Raindrops clung to Theo's eyelashes and dripped from the curling ends of his hair, trickling down his neck, soaking his collar. "You've bewitched me, Bonnie. Body and soul."

Towering over her, storm-tossed and intense, right now Theo looked very much like an Austen hero incarnate. He swallowed, Adam's apple bobbing. Bonnie concentrated on the movement, her own throat working convulsively. If she'd learned anything these past few months, it's that she didn't need Gilbert or Darcy or any made-up hero trapped between the pages of a book.

She needed real. She needed Theo.

"What are you saying?" she asked, refusing to hope.

"I'm saying"—he reached for her hand, placing her palm over his chest—"that I want you. I *need* you in my life. I'm not saying it's going to be easy. I'm not promising a life as perfect or pretty as one of your novels. But if you give me a chance, I will work to make you happy. Every. Single. Day."

Under her hand, beneath the wet cotton plastered to his skin, Theo's heart pounded, accompanying each word he spoke with a resounding thump. Bonnie remembered dancing with him at Cassie's wedding, listening to his heartbeat as she accepted the truth of her feelings. Head spinning, her own heart began to beat faster. What was happening right now?

Above them, the clouds shifted, the sky growing brighter as the drizzle slowed to a gentle patter. He held up his other hand, ring resting on his open palm. "I'm saying I want you to wear this. I'm asking you to wear it."

Bonnie stared at the ring, the gemstone glittering in the shifting light and shadow. "That's meant to be worn by someone worthy . . ." she paused, fingers flexing, tightening their hold on Theo's shirt as his mother's words rang in her ears, ". . . worthy of being a duchess."

"I said I want *you* to wear this, Bonnie. And I meant it. Anyone who has a problem with that can go to hell, my mother included." A muscle ticked in Theo's jaw. "I want you to be my wife, to be my duchess."

He wanted her to be his duchess? Bonnie shook her head, lost for words.

"If that's too much to ask right now, I understand. We'll figure something else out. We'll find a way." Theo cocked a smile at her. "I'm thinking of starting a writer-in-residence program up at the Lakeland property." His dimples flashed. "Do you know anyone who might be interested?"

The backs of her knees tingled, and she tightened her grip on his shirt still further. *Me!* She wanted to shout. *This girl right here!*

"Come home with me, Bonnie. We'll live in the cottage and take long walks and make love in the meadow and drink tea and eat too much gingerbread and you can write, and I can do, well, whatever duke stuff needs doing."

The corners of her eyes prickled. A soft August breeze tickled her cheeks, sending leaves from a nearby tree scattering. As she watched them take flight, she was transported to a night not so long ago. So much had happened since that April evening when she'd watched her last flower petal float away. So much had changed. *She'd* changed.

"Well?" Theo asked, eyes full of love and hope and a dash of fear. "What do you think?"

"I think this is the most awesome friends-with-benefits package I've ever heard of." Bonnie giggled nervously. She understood his fear. She was scared too. Like him, this wasn't what she'd planned, what she'd spent years telling herself she wanted. "Also"—she took a breath—"I think yes."

"Yes?" he asked, sunlight breaking across his face. He bent to kiss her, then hesitated, brow furrowing with a shadow of doubt. "Yes to which part?"

She released his shirt and plucked the ring from his palm. "All of it." She was about to slip the ring onto her finger, when he stopped her.

"Let me, love." Theo took the ring back, positioning it over her left hand. But before he put it on her finger, he paused, almost bashful. "I know you're smitten with the cottage but"—his blue eyes met hers—"you were joking about the friends-with-benefits thing, right?"

"Oh, Theo. You really think that's all I'm smitten by?" Bonnie raised her right hand, touching his cheek. "You were always more than just a Brit with benefits."

A tentative grin lifted one corner of his mouth. "Always?"

She brushed a thumb over his dimple. "Always."

Finally, he slipped the ring on her finger.

Bonnie sighed, relishing the feel of it sliding into place, the gold band still warm from his skin. She held up her hand. "How does it look?"

"You look good wearing my future." Theo brushed his lips over her knuckle, just above the ring. "How does it feel?"

"Honestly, I was worried it might feel weird," she admitted, staring down at the ring. "But it doesn't. It feels right." She lifted her face to his. "Good."

"Good." Theo's smile grew, dazzling in its intensity.

Immediately, Bonnie's knees buckled, and she reached out, clutching his shoulders.

He wrapped his arms around her, holding her upright as he bent his head and covered her mouth with his. The bold sweep of his tongue surprised her. Dizzy and breathless, she clung to him. This wasn't a sweet, chaste Austen-hero kiss. This was a raw, dirty, Theo-turned-hungry-beast kiss. If his dimples hadn't already knocked the ground out from beneath her, his kiss would.

"Christ, you taste like heaven," he growled.

"Lemon pie scone." She smiled against his mouth. "Want some?"

"Later." He moved to kiss her again.

She backed up, hand over his lips. "What would you have done if I said no?"

He shrugged. "Stood here on the sidewalk and waited for a bloody miracle, I suppose."

She laughed and then gasped, pointing overhead. "Like that?" Above them, the sun finally made good on its promise. Up and down the block, people stopped, gazing up at the vibrant rainbow streaking across the summer sky.

"Care to make a wish?" Theo asked, mouth quirking, knee-tickling dimples winking.

"Nope." Bonnie shook her head, heart full. "I have everything I need," she said, pulling her dashing duke closer, "right here."

ACKNOWLEDGMENTS

A love for literature runs deep in this book, and I would be remiss not to begin by noting my eternal gratitude for the works of Shakespeare and Jane Austen. Yes, I know neither of them will be reading this, but one must give credit where credit is due.

Next, to my Portland Midwest crew: Clara Kensie, Erica O'Rourke, Lynne Hartzer, and Melanie Bruce, thank you for the endless love and support. Shout-out to Clara and our long sock Sundays getting all the words.

Thanks to Shannyn Schroeder and Ricki Wovsaniker for their insightful, honest critiques. A big not-sweaty hug to Christine Palmer, my morning workout partner who understands what deadline stress is and was a constant cheerleader as I dragged myself across the finish line.

Much love to my Golden Heart sisters, the Mermaids and Rebelles, for their priceless words of wisdom and equally priceless sense of humor and generosity of spirit. Special thanks to Kari Cole and Alyson McLayne; I never would have reached "the end" without being able to sprint at all times of the day and night with you ladies.

My editor, Jennie Conway, who adores Jane Austen as much as I do. Thank you for gently pulling me back when I got carried away. Also, when you told me Bonnie and Theo are your OTP that was perhaps the best compliment ever, and I will never forget it. I'd also like to extend a note of thanks to my copy editor Christa Soule Desir, who makes me glow with happiness because she totally gets my sense of humor and catches all my references. I have been truly blessed with a phenomenal team helping bring this story, and this series, to the world, and I am grateful to everyone at St. Martin's Press for their time and talent.

To my mom, whose pride in me makes me feel like I can do anything, thanks for the unwavering love, and for telling every person you meet to buy your daughter's books.

To my daughters, both fierce and feisty redheads, clever and funny and beautiful, the heroines in their own stories. Thank you for filling my life with joy and understanding when mom needs her "writing time." Lots of love and thanks to my husband, whose affection for my freckles may have found its way into this book.

Finally, for my readers—most especially my fellow Shakespeare lovers and Austen-ites, and those who coo over stationary supplies and get goosebumps in bookstores—this one is for you.